About the author

The author is a senior scientist whose interests have always extended way beyond science. After he had reached certain milestones in his scientific career, he decided to take a challenge of writing fiction. His ideas come from the lives of everyday people, those that would never occupy headlines but are still depicting our world better than anything else could. Hence, his literary work is based on combining his experience and imagination with facts on historical and societal circumstances that influence the characters he writes about.

THE THREE GRANDFATHERS OF ARCHIBALD V JONES

Arthur Kay
_____

THE THREE GRANDFATHERS OF ARCHIBALD V JONES

Vanguard Press

VANGUARD PAPERBACK

© Copyright 2023
Arthur Kay

The right of Arthur Kay to be identified as author of
this work has been asserted by him in accordance with the
Copyright, Designs and Patents Act 1988.

All Rights Reserved

No reproduction, copy or transmission of this publication
may be made without written permission.
No paragraph of this publication may be reproduced,
copied or transmitted save with the written permission of the publisher, or in
accordance with the provisions
of the Copyright Act 1956 (as amended).

Any person who commits any unauthorised act in relation to
this publication may be liable to criminal
prosecution and civil claims for damages.

A CIP catalogue record for this title is
available from the British Library.

ISBN 978-1-80016-623-3

This is a work of fiction. Names, characters, businesses, places, events and incidents are
either the products of the author's imagination or used in a fictitious manner. Any
resemblance to actual persons, living or dead, or actual events is purely coincidental.

Vanguard Press is an imprint of
Pegasus Elliot Mackenzie Publishers Ltd.
www.pegasuspublishers.com

First Published in 2023

Vanguard Press
Sheraton House Castle Park
Cambridge England

Printed & Bound in Great Britain

2012, Basel, Canton of Basel-Stadt
Swiss Confederation

There were certain problems with the funeral of one Archibald V Jones, who died in Basel at the age of forty-seven.

First of all, no one really knew anything about his religion, since he had never discussed that with anyone. He had not been paying Swiss church tax in any case; so, judging by that, he had neither been Protestant nor Roman Catholic (the state religions in Switzerland, to which the church tax applied). On the other hand, there were many others in the Red Light District who were not paying the church tax, so his avoiding this obligation could have been understandable from a practical point of view even if he had had some Christian beliefs. Such behaviour was tolerated by both the Christian clerics and the city, and the reason was rather simple: everyone needed the District as a resort for the entertainment of hard-working and money-making citizens of Basel, those with perfect families at home—they were always paying the church tax and every other tax, hence money was always finding a way to reach every pocket. No clergyman ever complained, and the District lived in harmony with Christianity. This was an accepted misuse of otherwise strict Swiss laws—and it was considered to be a fact of life.

Secondly, it seemed that there was no person in the whole city of Basel—where Archibald had been living for quite a while—who truly loved him at the time of his death; though some certainly liked him, no one apparently had any feeling for him deeper than that. This implied that his funeral was most probably going to be attended poorly—which meant that making all of that too complicated would be actually silly. There was also a question of how many of his acquaintances who liked him even noted that he had passed away.

The death of Archibald V Jones was in a way annoying; everything about him had been easier when he had been alive.

The name of his wife—or just a girlfriend as many believed—was Sara, and she was of the Amhara people of Ethiopia. Being affiliated to the Ethiopian Orthodox Tewahedo Church, she said that Archie had not been openly religious and that this was the only thing she knew on the matter; she was quite determined in declining his possible Jewish or Muslim background—according to what she had seen in their bedroom. She said, eventually, that her late husband's religion was no one's business including hers.

Sara was a bronze-skinned lady of astonishing beauty—just as many other women from the Horn of Africa are—and roughly ten years younger than Archie. He had taken her to his home one Saturday night in the July of 2002 directly from a brothel in the Red Light District, situated in a part of the city called Kleinbasel (a small pocket of Switzerland on the right hand, actually the German bank of the Rhine); from that moment onwards, they lived a simple and compromising life together. He would not ask much, and she… even less.

'But how to bury him then?' asked Stefan, Archie's colleague from work. 'We'll definitely bury him at the Hörnli cemetery in Riehen—how to find another place in Basel anyway—but what about a priest? It's not common in Basel—and I'm a true Basler so I know—that a person is buried here without a priest.'

'I'm a true Basler as well, and I know a few things too,' replied Matthias, who knew Archie from the inns where they had been meeting over a number of years. 'It could go without a priest, but it always must be paid properly. And who'll pay for Archie? Not me, sorry. Well, that's it, apart from that we really don't know who he was. The main question is who is willing to pay for his funeral.'

'I know little about him too,' said Sara, 'but I'll pay. Enough has been left behind him. The least I can do for my man is to bury him properly. Maybe we weren't bound by madly romantic love, but he was still my man—perhaps too secretive—yet good and kind in his own way.'

'I still think we should bring a priest,' murmured Stefan.

This was followed by a few minutes of moderately sad silence at their table in a crowded, noisy inn, during which Stefan, Sara, and Matthias were drinking beer and thinking how to organise a funeral of this Archibald V Jones—who had always been around, neither in dispute with nor sincerely loved by anyone (perhaps not even by Sara).

Sara's feelings for Archibald were complicated. She had shared life and bed with him—often bragging how good he had been in sex—but did she ever love him? Not lately, she was sure of that, but maybe sometime in the past—when he was her knight and before his madness started to rule their days. Maybe… That evening, she somewhat hated him for leaving her just like that. This was the only thing she could feel at the time.

And his feelings for her? Difficult to say, as he would have never spoken with other people about his thoughts and feelings. He had been a cold person to some degree, or at least a very private one, which was in contrast to Sara's stories of his passion in bed. Every now and then, she would say that they managed to stay together for such a long time because the sex was great. She would never speak of any love.

Always polite and ready to compromise but never open and sincere to anyone—this was Archie. He tended to be introverted and reserved, but he would often become a master of theatre, charming his audience beyond belief. Since he was skilful in choosing words and putting them into the right context, he was capable of calming down any volatile situation by combining lively gestures and smile with intricate, catching phrases; the only limit was his incomplete knowledge of Swiss German, whereas he excelled in English and was also quite eloquent in High German. However, he did not speak a word of French, which would sometimes pose a problem when attempting to calm down a French-speaking, drunk Swiss. Most of the time, however, he would remain unnoticeable, in the shadow of the people and events in the Red Light District of the city of Basel.

No one could remember how and when he had come to Basel, and his whereabouts prior to that were not clear either. Moreover, many believed—which was just one of the rumours about his mysterious appearance—that he had a lucrative job elsewhere, but most of his acquaintances knew him from the District.

Being seemingly quite educated—also multilingual and well mannered—he was helping to manage the business of most of the brothels in Kleinbasel in a silent way. No one, actually, knew how he was keeping the annoying part of the administration of the Canton of Basel-Stadt away from the District. His methods possibly included special relations with the police, public health institutions, tax offices, and numerous other establishments which wanted to maintain the best possible relations with the lucrative business in the District, but this was only speculation discussed by the bartenders after he had died. One of his informal duties was also to keep the District free of troubles that drunk and horny people would occasionally cause instinctively—and he excelled in that as well, as outlined before.

During his 'reign', business in the District was going on as smoothly as any other in the rest of Basel (and the whole of Switzerland, in fact). A rumour that he did not charge the owners of the brothels much for his valuable services started gossip about his other significant income—possibly even as one of the proprietors of the colossal *Novartis* chemical company (with a huge installation in Kleinbasel, close to the German border). This was, of course, a silly assumption, but it was a fact that he did not depend on his revenue in Kleinbasel—he simply liked to hang about there on a daily basis.

As already pointed out, while everyone would always be happy to meet this nice man, Archie, no one in the whole of Basel really knew anything about him; and there was also not a single person who could say that she or he loved him. Sara maybe? Well, she was confused—and at the time just before his funeral, she definitely could not say that she loved him. And yet, these people still had to bury him somehow—so this whole mess was, naturally, a kind of irritation. If they had not been in Switzerland—in a country of high standards in both life and death—they would have probably to still show some respect just put his mortal remains gently into the Rhine, so that he could flow slowly towards the North Sea and eventually reach Britain—where he had, probably, been born and where he, according to this theory, actually belonged. Indeed, among only a few things he would have ever said about himself, they were remembering that he had liked to live in the UK—where the beer had been excellent and all the people but him were blessed with a unique, brilliant sense of humour.

'He came from England, right? Perhaps we should find an Anglican priest,' Stefan did not want to give up. 'Maybe there's one in Zurich? None in Basel as far as I can tell.'

'Well, this makes me think,' replied Matthias. 'You know that I worked for an English company. The surname of my boss was Jones, and he was Welsh. He would often say that the surname Jones is mainly Welsh. Catherine Zeta-Jones, Tom Jones... He was, in fact, talking about this quite a lot—that the surname Jones isn't English but Welsh—and then all of that British blah, blah, blah. Quite weird.'

'Blah, blah, blah—that's exactly how much I really care. An Anglican priest should do the job, I believe, English or Welsh. Why should we bother ourselves with such details? I'm not even sure that the Welsh have their own church. Hopefully Archie wasn't Scottish; they would never accept an Anglican priest, and I guess that this would be troublesome,' Stefan attempted to conclude the whole story.

'Would it?' said Matthias with a grin.

'I mean, I wouldn't want to see the ghost of Archie wearing Scottish tartan and haunting me through the night. However, this won't happen, and we should find an Anglican priest. I couldn't think of a better priest in this situation,' continued Stefan.

'The most important for us right now is that Archie wasn't Scottish, let us drink to that! The matter is closed,' exclaimed Matthias. 'The only thing we have to do now is to find an Anglican priest. This might not be easy though.'

However, this triumphal conclusion was spoiled by Sara, who remarked that Archie could have really been Scottish, because she had met some men called Archibald—at least four of them besides Archie—all of them being Scottish. And Archie had also been occasionally speaking a strange language that might have been Gaelic.

'Yeah, you met them in a brothel. Who says his true name in a brothel?' argued Stefan, unhappy with her raising this question.

'Well, many do, in fact. And at least two of them were pronouncing English badly although they obviously knew all the words. That's what the Scots usually do,' Sara replied.

'So do I, and am I Scottish?' laughed Matthias. 'But in case that Archie was Scottish, our trouble is much simpler than it seems. They're Presbyterians, which basically means Calvinists—and this is much like us. And Archie's English wasn't perfect. Right? The pronunciation, I mean. Could it really be that he was Scottish? He…'

'And you're now an expert in English?' interrupted Stefan, who was already tired of this conversation. 'One can't say anything about Archie on the basis of his English, he spoke it a zillion times better than any of us; as a matter of fact, probably better than anyone else in Basel.'

'But he spoke Gaelic too…' mumbled Matthias.

He then stopped talking, and Sara also did not want to say anything. As if she did not care, as if this whole issue was over for her: Archie was dead, her life was going to change, and she wanted to get on with it as soon as possible. Stefan drank down a bottle of beer rather quickly in order to gather enough strength for continuing and then possibly ending the whole affair. He realised that there was a tempting simplicity in bringing a local priest instead of searching for an Anglican one. All he wanted from the very start was to bring any priest to the funeral. Then he said, 'On the other hand, I agree that we can consider Archibald V Jones a Scottish person, possibly with some relatives in Wales, and to bury him in the presence of a local Swiss Reformed Church priest. Sara pays for the thing, and life goes on. Agreed?'

'Well, we should agree that he was maybe Scottish indeed, although we'll never know for sure,' concluded Sara. 'Does anyone object?'

'No, not me.'

'Me neither, I agree.'

And this was basically the end of this weighty, unpleasant, in a way sad conversation which had to lead to a decision on how to bury their friend. They eventually grabbed their freshly ordered beers and sank into the world of small talk.

That evening, it was concluded that Archibald V Jones was Scottish. Although this might have not been true, it was solving the problem of a priest at his funeral elegantly. At some point, it slipped through Stefan's mind that Archibald might have not been speaking Gaelic but the Welsh language instead, but this would complicate everything—because the Welsh probably had no connection with Calvinism.

When they were leaving the inn, Matthias asked, 'What shall we write on his tombstone apart from Archibald V Jones? Do we know when he was born, in the first place? We all know when he died, I mean.'

'He was born in 1965, I'm certain of that. When I was a young but clever prostitute, I checked his wallet. A girl must know things when a guy comes for the third time. On the other hand, I didn't pay attention to his nationality, he had Swiss papers for foreigners.'

'Good to know that,' continued Matthias. 'Then let us add something nice on the tombstone at a cost of a few hundred francs. Say, something like "a distinguished Scotsman". He would like that, I guess, even if it weren't true. His sense of humour was a bit weird'

'Whatever,' said Stefan. 'He obviously didn't care much about his death and funeral, so we can write whatever we want. It might be true, on the other hand, that he was Scottish…'

'Enough. Just make it so. I'll pay. Now I just want to go home and cry a little bit,' replied Sara and instinctively continued to walk southwards, towards the District, towards the Rhine, where she had met this decent man Archie for the first time. The two men walked with her for a while; it was about one after midnight when they split. Sara then had one more drink at the bar of a brothel; twenty-three days after having that drink, she visited the District for the last time, never to return.

Two days later, Archibald V Jones was buried after a short speech by a local Protestant priest who said many nice words on how everyone is home everywhere in the world as long as his faith in Jesus keeps his soul close to the Creator. Besides Stefan, Matthias, and Sara, only a handful of other people attended the ceremony, some of them from the District and some from the *Novartis* company.

On the tombstone, it was engraved:

Archibald V. Jones
a distinguished Scotsman
1965–2012

When they were leaving the cemetery, Stefan started a casual conversation to break the silence.

'Does anyone know what this V stands for? His middle name, I mean.'

'Yes, I know,' replied Sara. 'It stands for Vladimir.'

'Oh my goodness,' said Matthias astonished, 'how could this be Scottish?'

In the lands of everlasting war

I

1914, Krotko, Kingdom of Croatia-Slavonia Austria-Hungary

Matija Didić, who was the only blacksmith in Krotko—a highland village which numbered about one thousand five-hundred people—was lucky: he was, at the age of fifty-one, too old for going to a war declared on Serbia a few days ago. This was soothing, in particular because he had recently fathered a son again—probably for the last time for him. In any case, he had enough money for bribing someone, if necessary, or paying a poor man to go instead of him. This always worked, as the lands of everlasting war were pretty much the same as before.

'This new war isn't going to end soon, and it will not end well. Many will die for nothing,' said his father Anton, who was, at the age of ninety-two, barely able to walk but was still constantly asking for tobacco. 'One doesn't attack Russia! No one can win against the Russians! My grandfather Juraj had gone to Russia with Napoleon and never came back, my children. The strongest man in the county he was, never to return from that vast Russia!'

'Father, we've not attacked Russia, we've attacked Serbia.'

'Yes, yes, my boy, you've attacked Serbia and not Russia. Just as a cuckoo invades the nest of an eagle and thinks that the big bird isn't somewhere around. But this bird is called the eagle, it is formidable, and may God help those who are its target! And Russian eagles are not simple, my child. They are two-headed, these Russian eagles. I saw a picture in Dušan's house—he is Orthodox and he adores Russia, having all these Russian pictures on the wall.'

After an intense search through his pocket, the old man eventually found some tobacco and made a cigarette, which took him some time; then he lit it, tasted the thick smoke and spoke to his son again,

'His sons are hiding in the mountain now, trying to avoid fighting Serbia—probably because they are Serbs by nationality. More than that, they're afraid of what the two-headed Russian eagle might do to all of us. Dušan still remembers that my grandfather never returned. You should be afraid too. You should all be afraid!'

It must be explained here that Krotko was, during the time of Napoleon, in the so-called Illyrian Provinces—which comprised parts of present-day Austria, Italy, Slovenia, and Croatia—and this territory was an integral part of the contemporary France, being treated in the same way as any other French province. Generally, people in Croatia have always remembered that time with sympathy, because the enlightened French were building schools, hospitals, and roads while simultaneously supporting the use of the Croatian language—in contrast to the conservative Habsburg Empire, which was endorsing the use of Latin, German or Hungarian and was building little. Hence, it was not surprising that many Croatian men—including those from Krotko—would have joined the troops of Napoleon rather than to remain in the Austrian Army. They were welcomed by the French warmly, because it was known ever since the early seventeenth century that a light cavalry called the *Croats* (consisting of ethnic Croats mostly but not exclusively) was arguably among the best ones in the world. These swift horsemen were toughened in centuries-long everyday battles with the neighbouring Turkish forces from Bosnia and Herzegovina which was then part of the formidable Ottoman Empire—the dominant military power in Europe at least between 1400 and 1700. For instance, the word *cravat* (meaning essentially *Croat*) came to English from the French language, where it referred to a piece of the uniform of the Croatian mercenaries in the French Army during the Thirty Years' War of 1618–1648. In any case, this somewhat explains why the mighty Juraj ended his life somewhere in Russia as a follower of Napoleon.

Ivan Didić, the youngest son of Matija, was five-months-old when the Great War began a few hundred kilometres from the place where he had been born. He was lucky to be born in a family that was—according to the standards of that time—both well-off and influential.

His grandfather Anton was the first mild tempered head of a clan of indigenous and opportunistic semi-nomads of the Balkans, who had settled in Krotko probably sometime at the turn of the seventeenth to eighteenth centuries (there is a record which implies so).[*] Their true origin has remained vague until today, but it has been clear that they were for a long time distinguished from the local Slavic population by preserving freedom and managing to avoid the serfdom of the Middle Ages. There have been historians who have claimed that they were allowed to live like that because they were very valuable as mercenaries, by their fighting skills comparable to the indigenous people of North America.

It appears that the Didić clan was mentioned in historical books for the first time around 1490, when one Radunel Didić—called a Vlach duke—had a dispute with a powerful Croatian noble family with regard to the grazing of cattle on part of the nobles' land (this ownership was seemingly questioned by Radunel), which was happening about one hundred and fifty kms southeast of Krotko.[†] The other history of the clan was, apart from the mentioned record, shrouded in mystery until the mentioning of one Ivan Didić in 1749 in the birth records of the Roman Catholic Church in Krotko. He was apparently the last from the clan who could speak the Romance language of his forefathers, although he was always using Croatian in everyday communication. The oldest of his sons was Juraj, born in 1773 (that famous strong man who died in Russia

---

[*] *Clan* is here used as the most suitable English word for describing the relations within some of the peoples of Southeast Europe before the nineteenth century, who lived in moderately large groups of several families that were either related by blood or shared an interest. This term should not be confused with, e.g., *Scottish clan* or *tribe* in other societies.

[†] *Vlach* (in other forms, *Welsh, Waloon,* etc.) is a name that was originally used by Germanic and Slavic nations for the speakers of various Romance languages based on Latin. In consequence of the conquest and domination of the Romans, these languages developed all over Europe during their rule. Here, the term *Vlach* refers to the indigenous population of Southeast Europe, later in large part assimilated by the Slavs. Only the Vlachs of present-day Romania have preserved their language until today.

in 1812), who fathered another clan head named Ivan (born in 1796); and the next in the line of the heads was Anton, born in 1822.

Anton was the first gentle leader in the known history of the clan. Before Anton, every patriarch of the Didić clan had been vicious, and their physical strength had been quite useful in their bullying other people. Anton himself was about 205 cms tall, weighed roughly 115 kgs, and in his young age could have lifted a smaller ox; however, he never fought anyone—he was simply a mild person who liked tobacco, plum brandy, and having sex with his wife.

Anton's ancestors—these bad tempered giants—secured the clan wealth in an intimidating, sometimes even violent manner.

'I like this piece of land you have. If you let me have it, I'll let you live,' was their way of communicating with the other villagers.

Of course, a refusal to surrender so easily would in many cases be a reaction to their demands, but this resistance would always be short-lived and futile—and the clan's acquisition of a substantial area of arable land and forest in Krotko had been over before the Juraj and Napoleon's invasion of Russia. It would not be exaggerated to state that the heads of the Didić clan were for some two centuries the unofficial dukes of this highland valley—where some roaming Vlach herders of Roman Catholic faith had settled to gradually become the Slavs and eventually the Croats.

Anton was also the last true patriarch of the Didić clan. He was a hedonist who loved his wife deeply—having with her many daughters and six sons—and he cared little about other things. So he divided the estate into six equal parts, one for each son, after providing a decent dowry to each daughter. In this way, the medieval clan became six families of the modern time—of the late nineteenth century. Each of these six parts was big enough to ensure a comfortable life for a large family.

In time, differences in the characters and conduct of the six brothers—who were suddenly landowners—began to surface, and this decided on the bynames of their families. Namely, since the number of surnames and first names (mainly from the Bible) in Krotko was limited, it was usual for a family to have a byname in order that different people of exactly the same first name and surname could be distinguished from each other.

One of the brothers provided a byname 'the Idiot' to his family—because this suited him well—and all of his descendants have been until today known as the Idiots. For example, Nikola the Idiot would be a Nikola Didić from exactly this family of the former clan, whereas another Nikola Didić—from another family of the same clan—would be distinguished from him by a different byname. Of Anton's sons, three had, to some extent, neutral nicknames, and their traces anyway vanished from Krotko in time, while the remaining ones put roots down in Krotko together with their descendants

Hence, those who remained in Krotko were the Idiot and the Mad Bull (the name speaks for itself but will still be explained below) families together with the third one—the head of which was Matija. And he provided a more honourable byname to his family.

In fact, of all of his sons, Anton favoured Matija, who was not the oldest. Anton gave half of the original clan house—built sometime in the eighteenth century—to Matija and continued to live with him and his family until he died. The other half of the house went to the oldest son—which Anton regretted many times because the personality of this young Didić was dominated by the genes of the old clan heads: he was aggressive, rude, and disrespectful to his wife (in Anton's eyes, unforgivable!). This brought a byname 'the Mad Bull' to his family.

In contrast to his two mentioned brothers, Matija was very bright and serious-minded, having an enterprising nature that finally made him a blacksmith like his father had been before him—which added to the wellbeing of his family. No one in Krotko was his peer in anything, and this made him a respected man. His other trait was that he was his fully aware of his superiority—always being proud and sometimes even arrogant—but he was still an honest and decent man. To make a long story short, it suffices to say that Anton was even more pleased by his choosing Matija to be first among equals when Matija eventually deserved a byname for his family—which was a thing the village was deciding about. This byname was 'the Proud'.

In 1914, therefore, Ivan the Proud—who was later also going to be known as Ivan the Blacksmith—took his first glimpse of this world. It was the cunningness of his father that saved the family from disasters of the war, and thanks to him, Ivan had a happy and smooth childhood, during which he learned the secrets of the profession of a blacksmith and also numerous other things in the process of becoming a man.

Years later, Matija Didić died peacefully, watching his youngest son taking his position.

Ivan the Proud was both as intelligent and skilful as his father and as kind as his grandfather. He was the first grandfather of Archibald V Jones.

II

1918, Kletina & Zagreb

Kingdom of Croatia-Slavonia; Austria-Hungary (until 2 October)
Interregnum (3 October – 28 October)
State of Slovenes, Croats, and Serbs (29 October – 30 November)
Croatia and Slavonia; Kingdom of Serbs, Croats, and Slovenes (from 1 December onwards)

In the late September of 1918, Vladimir Količek was rather unhappy. Namely, he had hoped to join a splendid military school in the city of Varaždin, and then the owner of the school, that is, an empire called Austria-Hungary, was just about to collapse. At the age of eighteen, he was rather worried about his future, feeling that he no longer had any control over it.

He was from a respected but financially troubled family, a native of the town of Kletina (not far from Varaždin), and his choices for the future were quite limited due to the lack of money; on the other hand, he had been interested in military affairs for quite some time, thus his decision to enrol in a military academy—which meant that there would be no expenses for the family—was something that was making almost everyone happy.

Just as Vladimir had anticipated, it did not take long before the territory inhabited by the South Slavs—and these were the Slovenes, the Croats, the Serbs, and the Muslims of Bosnia and Herzegovina—seceded from Austria-Hungary to form a state called the State of Slovenes, Croats, and Serbs. However, this establishment remained unrecognised and it did not last long. On the first of December, it united with the

Kingdom of Serbia and the Kingdom of Montenegro to form the Kingdom of Serbs, Croats, and Slovenes. The new Kingdom was going to be ruled by Petar I, King of Serbia.

Vladimir cared little about the name of the state in which he was going to pursue a military career; he was neither influenced by any prejudice nor had any political preference—he was simply eager to leave Kletina, to go to a bigger and livelier place, to learn as much as possible and take any chance he might get.

The people of Kletina were generally not enthusiastic about the unification with Serbia. A number of them had fought in the Austro-Hungarian Army against the Kingdom of Serbia in 1914 and 1915, and some even until 1918 on the Macedonian front (where the Serbs had been helped by the French and, to a lesser extent, the UK, Russia, Greece, and Italy). The defeat against Serbia was humiliating for some, but these were not numerous, and concerns of the people of Kletina mostly had little to do with drunk monologues of the war losers in the local inns.

For most of the inhabitants of Kletina, Serbia was an unknown land somewhere in the east, where Turkish raids had been coming from for the past five centuries, always bringing death, destruction, and enslavement; this was a land where the people either worshipped Jesus in the Greek way or were followers of Allah, all of them wearing strange, oriental clothes and speaking a language which was understandable to some level but not completely. Serbia was, in any case, a source of uneasiness among the Roman Catholic population in Croatia (i.e., in the lands which were in Austria-Hungary called the Triune Kingdom of Croatia, Slavonia, and Dalmatia, consisting of the Kingdom of Croatia-Slavonia and the Kingdom of Dalmatia) and Bosnia and Herzegovina (where the Muslims were worried too), as well as in former South Hungary (with substantial Hungarian and German populations together with numerous other nationalities including the Croats).

In the eyes of many people in Kletina, this demonised Serbia was everything beyond the east Croatian borders, which included Bosnia, Herzegovina, Montenegro, Bulgaria, Macedonia, Romania, Albania, Greece, and Turkey, that is, the territory all the way to the distant eastern seas. A fear of the unknown assisted in spreading every sort of fantastic stories about the wild lands and peoples in the east; and the omnipresent lack of education and information was contributing to this anxiety additionally.

While the people who were the Serbs by nationality lived in certain parts of Croatia in considerable numbers, the area around Kletina was inhabited exclusively by the Croats—their first neighbours being the Slovenes of Styria behind the border which was about ten kilometres to the north—whereas the nearest settlement of the ethnic Serbs was more than a hundred kilometres to the south. Some traders, soldiers, and travellers of all kinds knew the Serbs of the Croatian lands quite well, and they were saying that these Serbs were not much different from the Croats in the same areas. The Serbs of Serbia, on the other hand, were a mystery.

Vladimir Količek was not afraid of the Serbs of Serbia, as it was not in his nature to be afraid of the unknown. This young man had already read vast volumes of books from the family library, and—though he had never seen any place or met any person from these books—he was painfully curious about peoples and places in general. Everything outside Kletina was for him unknown and yet recognisable. Hence, he had a burning desire to leave, to experience life beyond the boredom of his hometown, where even the disaster called the Great War would be noticed only when a coffin would arrive by train from a faraway battlefield. How could he, then, be afraid of anything—including the Serbs of Serbia?

Vladimir's father Filip knew that the only way his son could prosper was to leave Kletina, which was making him more melancholic than anxious or sad. This was going to break a centuries-long family tradition, and it was causing a feeling of helpless uneasiness in him. According to some sources, the first Količek had settled in Kletina in the fourteenth century, when Kletina had been just a tiny market town at the foot of a hill where there had been a castle built to resist every invader; Vladimir was going to be the first Količek to leave Kletina ever since, as the first soldier in the family history—and in an army which had no tradition in this small town. Filip simply did not like this whole situation, but he knew that there was no reasonable alternative.

He went to the garden of his house in the centre of Kletina and sat on a bench next to a carefully trimmed hedgerow. Taking care of the hedge had been calming him down during the long four years of the war, and this bench was the place where he would always find peace of mind. His two younger children were staying—but this was not making Vladimir's leaving any easier. Vlado was always the brightest youngster in the entire Kletina, and his father had been hoping that he was one day going to obtain a university degree and not only re-establish the old family glory but also bring it to a new, higher level.

'Nothing of that will ever happen,' mumbled the middle-aged man while tasting the last smoke from the last tobacco he still had for his pipe. 'He'll be lost and we'll be lost in this beastly time which is about to come.'

A new time was coming, and Filip was not certain about anything. The only thing he knew for sure was that it was not clear how he could live without his oldest, dearest, cleverest child. He did not want to think about the past, present, and future of his family—the past was known, the present was tense, the future was unknown—and the only image in front of his eyes was that of his Vlado. This image was fading away in a strange manner, dissolving in the smoke from the pipe and then becoming blurred before disappearing completely.

Regarding the family history, there have been stories saying that the first Količek who settled in Kletina was a former monk who learned how to read and write in one of those medieval schools for educating minor clerics—which were, at the time, institutions dedicated mainly to teaching the students only how to read and write. But when he met an astonishingly beautiful woman at a fair somewhere in the north—possibly in Czech, Slovak or Polish lands—he abandoned the priesthood and fled with the woman southwards, eventually to reach a growing market town called Kletina. Since he continued to read and learn everything he could, it did not take him long to take the position of a local notary—a person distinguished by his knowledge of the scripts and languages used in the trading at this crossroad of races and merchandises. After his business had already been established for about ten years, he was called to the castle on the hill to manage one of their smaller affairs;

he did that well—and on several later occasions too. Eventually, in 1405, he was summoned to the castle to write down everything about a marriage which took place there, and this was when Sigismund of Luxemburg (during his life, in various periods and sometimes simultaneously: Prince-elector of Brandenburg, King of Hungary and Croatia, King of Germany, King of Bohemia, King of Italy, and Holy Roman Emperor) married one Barbara of Cilli from a powerful noble family with estates all over Styria and nearby lands. Strangely, the first name of the first Količek in Kletina has neither been recorded nor remembered.

The family tradition revolved ever since about always raising well-read descendants—all of them having no formal degree but being educated to a high level within the walls of the family house. Every Količek—including females—would always be fluent in many languages and writing systems, as well as in medicine, natural and technical sciences, law, etc. Their erudition and literacy were an inherited occupation just as craftsmanship was in other families, and this was how the Količ̌eks were making their living.

This had been going well until 1914. The Great War brought a disaster to the family, as their services were seldom requested in the flaming world which excelled only in digging graves; in this world—where order relying on knowledge, intellectual services, and well written documents was no longer of importance—the family became lost.

'I suppose that my dear son has to leave,' murmured Filip after thinking, unwillingly, about the history of his family. 'There's nothing for him here anymore. There's no tobacco for my pipe any more. My son must go. I must go.'

Filip Količek—once a passionate smoker of the pipe—had stopped smoking sometime at the turn of 1918 to 1919; soon after that, he left—leaving his wife with two adolescent children—and no one has ever known anything about his later whereabouts. Many people in Kletina said that this was expected, because every bookworm must have become mad at some point; the reason was, as everyone knew, that reading books was not good for the liver—and bad liver would in most cases cause insanity.

It was, therefore, in late 1918 when Vladimir F Količek left his home in Kletina to pursue a career in the army of a country which did not start to exist properly yet. This army was based on the tradition of the army of the former Kingdom of Serbia—by the organisation, style of uniforms, names of ranks, etc.—but it relied heavily on personnel from other parts of the new state, since Serbia had suffered incredibly high losses during the war (by percentage, the highest of all the participating countries). Many ethnic Serbs from ex Austria-Hungary responded to the call to join the army that was forming—the other nationalities were not so enthusiastic—but this was insufficient and only added to the ethnic domination of the Serbs (especially among the officers), which was not prosperous: ninety percent of the commanding personnel coming from about thirty-five percent of the population in an ethnically diverse country can never be good for an army.

After stepping down from a train in Zagreb (the former capital of both the Kingdom of Croatia-Slavonia and the Triune Kingdom of Croatia, Slavonia, and Dalmatia), Vladimir walked towards certain army barracks where they would recruit every lost soul from this part of the country, irrespective of physical appearance, illnesses, criminal record… And despite that, there were few applicants so shortly after the bloodshed which was still causing tears in many households. In fact, Vlado was the only one that day.

Vladimir was eventually going to become a highly accomplished officer while remaining one of the gentlest persons one could think of. Over the later years, many unsuccessfully wanted to earn his sympathy, and they could only conclude that he was a polite but quite reserved person. He would always be rather careful with new people and situations, possibly because he had to be extremely calm and logical during certain periods of his rather turbulent life—as this was the main strategy for survival in situations where life could be trivially cheap.

Vladimir F Količek was the second grandfather of Archibald V Jones.

III

1929, Malo Selce, Primorsko-Krajina County Kingdom of Serbs, Croats, and Slovenes

In the Jarbašić family, Christmas Eve was always the most important event of the year.

It was—according to the Western (Gregorian) calendar—the sixth of January, but Christmas was in the Serbian Orthodox Church still reckoned according to the old Julian calendar.

This particular Christmas Eve was, on the other hand, tense, which most of the family members—the women in particular—wanted to put aside, mainly by speaking too much about painfully trivial things. That evening, namely, the family could not expect any visit from their Catholic neighbours living in nearby villages, which had been a long tradition of the past generations. Their Catholic, Croatian neighbours were quite disturbed, and every Serb was, at the time, in their eyes responsible for an obvious wrongdoing they were suffering from for months already—and in their own country, where their sovereign rights had been recognised by every conqueror for many centuries in the past but not by the present state.

On the Catholic Christmas Eve, two weeks earlier, a delegation of the Jarbašić family tried to pay a visit to their Catholic neighbours. They found closed doors everywhere and hence did not want to insist. For the first time since anyone could remember, politics became more important than the tradition; and being the Serbs, the emissaries of the Jarbašić family felt in a way responsible for this new situation although they had not done anything wrong.

All of that was related to an unfortunate event from a few months earlier, when some Croatian representatives in the Parliament in

Belgrade—the state capital and also the capital of Serbia—had been attacked by a rampaging Serbian representative who had started to shoot at them during a Parliamentary session, killing two on site and wounding three more. In August 1928, Stjepan Radić—the undisputed leader of the Croats in the Kingdom—died from his wounds.

As if this was not enough, the contemporary king, named Aleksandar, declared exactly on the sixth of January 1929 that he was dissolving the Parliament and taking unlimited control over the country (although the communications were slow at the time, the news spread rapidly and reached virtually every home the same day). For the Croats, this meant a dictatorship of a Serbian king in consequence of a murderous act of a Serbian chauvinist, and no Croat was willing to exchange visits related to Christmas Eve celebrations.

Thus, a custom which had lasted for many generations was lost for good.

Stevan Jarbašić was observing his numerous family that evening, and the joy of seeing all of them gathered under his roof again—albeit for this short time only—was helping him get over the sadness and restlessness about the unfortunate affair with his neighbours. He had a feeling that an important and strong bond was broken, and he wondered whether this ancient connection was ever going to be re-established. He was worried because he knew where they lived: in the lands of everlasting war.

They were warriors throughout the history, perhaps even by their nature, and so were their Catholic neighbours. Despite worshipping Jesus in unlike ways, both the Orthodox and the Catholic Christians at the border with Bosnia had been soldiers of Jesus, fighting infidel Muslims in the neighbourhood for many centuries. Sometime in the early eighteenth century, the border became finally stabilised after more than three hundred years of constant defeats and losses of the Christians; and it was then when Stevan's ancestors stopped living a nomadic life—becoming defenders of the border that was close to their new, first permanent settlement ever. A story says that they settled under the leadership of a Vlach soldier called Jarul—during the time when the common people of the Balkans seldom had surnames—who allegedly never learned to speak the language of the Slavs. Since he was the clan leader, or *baša* (in Turkish, *başi*—meaning *head*), the clan took a Slavic-Turkish surname Jarulbašić. The Turkish part of their family name, this *baša*, was a consequence of the Turkish cultural influence in the wider area. In time, the typical Vlach 'ul' in the surname was somehow lost, the Slavic 'ić' remained, and they also abandoned their ancient Romance language—to embrace that of the ruling Slavs. They became known as the Jarbašić family of the village of Malo Selce.

It seemed that these Vlachs were already Orthodox Christians when Jarul was leading them, and this was decisive in their accepting not only the Slavic language but also the Serbian national identity during the nineteenth century, mainly via the influence of the only Orthodox Church in the area—and this one was Serbian.

Stevan was watching the young members of his family—who were the future in his ageing eyes—and he felt a pleasant warmth around the heart. He was happy because of that, but something was still making him uneasy... His son Srdjan, who had decided to continue the military tradition of the family, was not there.

During the Great War, Stevan had managed to start a lucrative business as a merchant, and this was where he saw the future of his children. He liked this new capitalism, in which he did not depend on local priests, teachers, politicians, physicians, and other vain people who would offer help only in exchange for a bribe.

The family had paid a high price for this new comfort though, as two brothers of Stevan had never returned from the war—one from Italy, the other one from Ukraine (the local military administrators had been clever enough not to try to send the Serbs of Croatia against Serbia). As a Serb loyal to the state, and because of paying this price, he was treated well everywhere. During all of these war years, Stevan knew how to be shrewd and how to make things work for him; most importantly, he knew how, where, and when to use a bribe in the right proportions—never too little, never too much. His business success continued throughout the crises of capitalism after the Great War simply because he knew how to avoid greed and remain satisfied with what was ample already—and this was so because of his thoughtfulness and moderation in every situation.

And then, this troubling son Srdjan was standing in front of him, in the uniform of a cadet. He arrived only minutes earlier; it had taken him some time to travel from Zagreb to Malo Selce, first by changing several trains and then by walking for some fifteen kilometres through the snow.

'Dear father, I'm so happy to see you!' exclaimed Srdjan while approaching his old man who instinctively started to walk towards him. And their hug was long, so long.

'Where is mother? I'll be back to you, but I must see her first.'

'She's here somewhere, shouldn't be far.'

Srdjan's mother Mara was more supportive of his decision to pursue a military career. Her grandmother was still alive and she spoke only the Romance Vlach language—refusing ever to be called a Serb—but Mara had at some point in her life become a zealous Serbian nationalist and protector of Orthodox Christianity (so clearly endangered by the Latins, in her opinion). This was in stark contrast to Stevan, who was not troubling himself with any matter related to nationality or religion—and this was destroying their marriage from day to day.

Srdjan cared much about his mother, and their hug was at least as long and firm as the one with his father. She offered him a plethora of food and some wine 'from the damned Latins, who own all the vineyards'.

'Your father is too much into money, and I fear for his soul. He doesn't see what I see… Your father wants us to be friends with the Latins! Can you imagine that?'

'Look, mother, may we leave that for some other time? I just arrived… From Zagreb I arrived. And there, most of the people are, as you say, the Latins. May I eat in peace, please?'

'All right, all right. I see. But I said what I had to say. You'll all see that I've been right. I'll be going to bed soon, boy. You ought to stay in our Serbian Army, boy! I'll not say another word.'

'It's not Serbian only, I'm being trained to become an officer in the army of the Serbs, the Croats, and the Slovenes, you know…'

'Sober up, boy. You'll be a Serbian officer, both of us know that. Have a nice meal, and I'll see you tomorrow, my dear, I'm going to bed now. Give your mother a proper kiss now, boy.'

'What's wrong with mother?' Srdjan asked his father later.

'This has been like that for quite some time,' replied Stevan, 'especially after that shooting in Belgrade. She believes that the only future between us and the Croats is a mutual slaughter. She's paranoid now, because she thinks that they will this night come to slit our throats—since they believe that "we" killed their Radić. She thinks that this is the only reason why today they didn't come to greet us as they used to.'

'And her sisters?'

'More or less the same. All three of them are about to move to Belgrade, being afraid of the Latins, as they say. Their grandmother is cursing them in the old language from dawn to dusk. I'll let her go, she'll come to her senses, I hope. And if not, she can stay in Belgrade. We don't have much of a life together anyway.'

'Sad, so sad. Father, should we really be afraid? We are concentrated in these villages—a few thousands of us only—and they're everywhere. Should we be afraid, what do you think?'

'I believe not. This apparent feud with our neighbours will be over soon; we'll get drunk a couple of times together, and that will be it. We are village people, simple peasants. They'll see that we from our village didn't kill Radić, and all the hotheads from our side will see that the so-called Latins are not about to slaughter us all.'

'I hope so, father. The Croats in the army are not treated well, you know. They're calling them names frequently, and it's also clear that many of them are there for financial reasons only. I'm their friend but many are not—and this is my other concern, that the mother might be right. What if she is?'

'In this case, you'll become a merchant like me and not a stupid soldier! I pulled through the Great War and have made an even bigger business later—and you should follow me! For Christ's sake, I'm your father and I love you more than I love the world and the Universe combined, so I want only what is the best for you!'

'Or else?'

'There is no "or else", I'm not an "or else" person. But if you wish, follow your mother and be a new Serbian soldier who is going to protect us from the Latins only to die young in some trench eventually, like my poor brothers.'

There was a long period of silence after that. The two men sat quietly and smoked. The others had gone to sleep although it was not midnight yet; this was, in any case, a rather strange Christmas Eve in the house of Stevan Jarbašić.

'I'm so tired, I've got to go. Sorry, son. I've seen all of my children and their children too, and that's it. I am at peace with my maker now. Love, my child, and whatever you do—do it for love only,' said the old gentle man before going to bed.

Just after midnight, during the first hours of the Serbian Orthodox Christmas of 1929, the soul of one Stevan Jarbašić—who was known as a good man—went to the skies or to whatever god had created him.

The older of his two sons, called Jovan, continued his business and prospered until 1941. Their mother moved to Belgrade soon after her husband's departure (together with her two sisters), leaving her grandmother in Malo Selce with Jovan and his family. When Mara was leaving the house for a proper city for true Christians—one which was free of the Latins apart from some local Swabians—her grandmother was cursing the entire world in the old language and with a malicious expression on her face; another woman who still spoke the old language understood her, but this was not for a Christian soul to hear, she said.

Srdjan Jarbašić was the third grandfather of Archibald V Jones. Since Archie had no more grandfathers, he was obviously not Scottish, Welsh or English.

IV

1966, Kletina, Socialist Republic of Croatia
Socialist Federative Republic of Yugoslavia

If Vladimir had been a person prone to be agitated easily, the whole affair could have been more unpleasant.

'We'll find another priest,' he suggested to his daughter and son-in-law. 'There's one close to the place where you live now—he's a good man, a drunk but a good man. The boy should be baptised, and this priest will definitely do it. We'll bring him some wine although he would probably do it even without that.'

And that was it. Borna Didić was thus baptised in a village about twenty kilometres from Kletina, on the Croatian side of the Slovenian-Croatian border. The ceremony took place in a picturesque Roman Catholic church from the fourteenth century, on a hill from where one could enjoy a wonderful landscape of Slovenian Styria just behind a creek that marked the administrative line between the two Yugoslav republics. Only the closest family attended the ceremony.

The simple village priest—a true servant of God and shepherd of his flock—did not ask any question about the child, his parents, and grandparents: he was just welcoming a new soul into the realm of Jesus.

This was in contrast to the parish priest of Kletina, who did not want to bless a child from the family of a 'traitor to the Croatian state, that supporter of the Serbs'. He was referring to Vladimir, whose guilt was in the eyes of the parish priest unforgivable—with consequences for all of his descendants—as Količek took part in a plot against a quisling state called the Independent State of Croatia, a murderous creation of Mussolini, Hitler, and their criminal servants. In 1944, Vladimir had indeed been involved in an attempt to make Croatia a British and not

German ally; this coup eventually failed, and he survived the massacre of the conspirators by some lucky circumstances (as it was frequently happening in his life). The bald, tall priest could never forget the Vladimir's role in the plot, and as long as the priest was alive, Vladimir and his family were virtually excluded from the Holy Roman Catholic Church (which had been, by the way, an important supporter of the quisling state).

'Why have you named the boy Borna?' Vladimir asked his daughter Danka shortly after the baptism had concluded (the boy was given a Christian name Ivan—which was a kind of tradition in the family of his father). 'An archaic name, and also not common—at least not in this part of the country.'

'Father, I was reading a novel based on Croatian history while I was pregnant,' replied Danka, 'and the main hero was called Borna, like that duke from the tenth century. He was a romantic lover besides being a hero, and this is what my son is going to be too. My dear, wonderful son; women will love him.'

'All right, your choice, your decision. But since he's been given a medieval name that appears only among the Croats, will you ever tell him about his other ancestry? There were some others, not only the Croats, as you may know. And not all of them were Roman Catholics. I can explain to you in detail if you wish, he's got some Orthodox and Lutheran ancestors too. Lots of history behind that,' continued Vladimir, whose knowledge surpassed that of all the people of Kletina combined.

'I don't know, father. I know how much my mother suffered because of being related to different nationalities. This is not a simple country to live in. It's easier to have one nationality only, things still work this way.'

'I guess you're right,' responded the old cunning spy. 'This is how things work indeed.'

'Well, apparently no one has problems any more for being of this or that nationality, but I don't think that things have changed so much in people's hearts. You're a Croat, my husband is a Croat, my mother also feels this way, and I think we should make life simple for my boy.'

Vladimir then took a look through the window, observing snowflakes in their lazy descent towards the high street of Kletina and thinking how little things had changed. Then he remembered the painting of St John which Srdjan had painted. It was hanging on a wall in the house, and Borna might ask about it one day.

In time, it became clear that the boy had Srdjan's eyes, and it was just a matter of time when he was going to start asking questions. Borna was an unusually bright child—which was making Vladimir both happy and worried.

'It's never been easy for bright people to live in these lands of everlasting war,' he muttered one day before going to bed.

V

1933, Krotko, Sava Banovina ‡
Kingdom of Yugoslavia
&
1982, Krotko, Socialist Republic of Croatia
Socialist Federative Republic of Yugoslavia

'So what if she's older than him, you idiots! She'll be my daughter in law for many reasons and this is what I say and you'll obey because my word is the last in this family!' shouted Matija Didić at his family as they gathered by the fireplace.

'She's a tiny girl! Yes, she is, but she's stronger than two bloody Gypsy horses combined, she cooks well, respects and loves my son, pleases me by her good nature—and if Ivan wants her, she'll be his wife, bloody hell! And that's what I say and I'm not an easy man like my father and I'll break anyone's bones who wants to question me!' he continued angrily.

'Calm down, husband,' said his wife, 'no one questions you. Ivan is my son as well, and if he loves her, I'll bless them. But she's still three years older than him. What will the village say...'

'They can go to hell, these morons!' shouted the old man in a frantic way. 'If anyone in the village says one more word, I'll fetch that family iron rod from the cellar and remind them how we acquired that much land and why we're called the Proud! No one will mess with us—we're the still the dukes of this village and no bugger will question what we're

---

‡ The closest English word for *Banovina* is *Dukedom*. *Bayan* (in several Slavic languages, *Ban*) was the title of the leader of the Avars, a nomadic Asian warrior nation (now extinct) that led the Slavic-Avar invasion of the Pannonian Plain and the Balkans starting from the sixth century.

doing! Ivan will marry Roža—not because I'm telling him to do that but because this is what he wants. And you, woman, shut up! You haven't seen my ugly side yet but you might.'

Seeing how much Matija was irritated, no one dared to say another word. He was, after all, the patriarch of the family, esteemed blacksmith, bearer of the tradition of the Didić clan, and owner of the infamous family iron rod which had belonged to the famous strongman Juraj. The whole village was still quite afraid of the legendary iron rod which had shattered many bones.

Matija had chosen Ivan to be his successor, and for several years already, the young man was the blacksmith of the village of Krotko, only sometimes secretly receiving advice from his father on how to solve an unusual problem. As far as the village was concerned, he was the blacksmith and his father only a grumpy old man. At the age of nineteen, Ivan was less and less called Ivan the Proud and was becoming better known as Ivan the Blacksmith; until the end of his life, people were using both of these names equally.

Roža—who was not ugly but also not a beauty—saw young Ivan the Proud for the first time in 1931 when her father brought their only horse to the blacksmith and she accompanied him. She was unusually strong-minded, enterprising, and hardworking, which was giving her a special charm that better looking women would often lack. She knew well what she wanted to do with her life, and this quality was attracting many young men more than a pair of beautiful eyes could (as it frequently happens in highlands, where the quality of life is dictated by the harsh nature and the ability to cope with it).

Living on the other side of Krotko, she did not know the young man—who was only seventeen at the time—but his appearance made an immediate impression on her. He moved like a natural dominant male, speaking little but obviously knowing what he was doing. Neither tall nor bulky, he possessed the legendary strength of his forefathers, and she was seemingly not the only one to sense that: even the horse was unusually obedient, feeling Ivan's domination while he was working around the new horseshoes. However strange this may have seemed, Roža immediately wanted to make Ivan the father of her unconceived child (according to the contemporary standards, she was—at the age of twenty—more than ready for having her first child). Some would call this lust, love at first sight, foolishness, whatever—but the fact was that by the age of thirty Ivan the Blacksmith had fathered three daughters and two sons, the mother of all of them being Roža.

They had a good marriage from the very start. Although being older than her husband, Roža willingly assumed the role of an obedient wife, which was typical of the patriarchal society of Krotko and, in fact, of the whole country and the whole era. However, it happened many times—in World War II in particular—that Roža took a leading role and provided a crucial support to the family. Consequences of her struggle to overcome numerous dangers to the family were going to be manifested much later, in her old age—when her nerves often could not cope with even a tiniest disturbance. Ivan, from his side, was a good husband who always respected his wife and her efforts, never emphasising that he was, according to the tradition, the undisputed master of the family. They had a hard but happy life together until the very end, and many would envy them of that.

Despite belonging to the local gentry by some unwritten laws, both Roža and Ivan were illiterate when they married—just as most inhabitants of Krotko were at the time. There had been efforts by the French to establish a school in Krotko, but this was never realised; and the Habsburgs—who reclaimed the village later—never cared much about the education of their subjects in southern parts of the Empire. Unlike Roža—who died illiterate—Ivan learned how to read and write in his twenties, not long after his marriage. After that, he had another duty in the village—besides being the blacksmith and barber—and this was to read the news aloud to the villagers whenever something important would happen. A school in Krotko was finally opened in 1939, when the Banovina of Croatia was established as an autonomous part of the Kingdom of Yugoslavia.

In the summer of 1982, during his school holidays (when he was visiting Krotko) Borna heard the story of how Ivan learned to read and write. When Borna was a schoolboy, he would always spend at least two weeks with Ivan and Roža. He was very fond of them, liking their unpretentiousness and good spirit together with the tranquillity of Krotko; in time, his childish fascination with his grandparents turned into sincere love for these gentle old people.

Newspapers in the 1980s were available in Krotko only when someone would bring them from elsewhere—usually from the county centre—and Ivan the Blacksmith was already for years a passionate reader of any newspaper he could get. He would read a newspaper that was several years old as if it had been published the day before; and if a newspaper would be, say, in German or French, he would carefully inspect the photos, pictures, and maps. This was his window to the world, and he would never miss a chance to take a look through it.

In July 1982, a family from Belgrade was passing by, and they left a newspaper called *Politics* in a local inn.

'Take this newspaper to Ivan the Proud,' said the bartender to a boy, 'and he'll probably give you a coin. Only he reads every shit.'

The boy immediately ran with the newspaper to Ivan, shouting,

'Grandfather, grandfather, I've got a newspaper for you! It is written in strange letters, but it's a newspaper!'

Ivan—who was not the boy's grandfather but was simply called this way by almost every child in the village—took the newspaper and handed a coin to the boy.

'Here is your coin. And these strange letters are called Cyrillic letters. The newspaper is Serbian, this is how they write.'

'And you can read it? Are you a Serb?'

'Yes, I know how to read Cyrillic letters. And no, I'm not a Serb.'

Borna was rather surprised that his uneducated grandfather—a highly intelligent man but without a day of school—knew how to read Cyrillic letters. Considering his complete lack of formal education, it was amazing that Ivan could even read Latin script.

'So, grandfather, you read *Politics*? And in Cyrillic script, in Serbian?'

'Yes, of course. What's the difference between Croatian and Serbian anyway? We understand each other perfectly, and it's easier for me to read Cyrillic letters in any case.'

Borna was quite confused. He had ten years of school behind him and seven years of knowing how to read and write Cyrillic script—at the time, taught in Croatia as a second writing system—but he still had problems to deal with Cyrillic letters effortlessly (since he was not using them frequently).

'How come, grandfather, that it's easier for you?'

'Because this was the first alphabet I learned in the army, in 1937. I learned Latin script later, our priest taught me after he'd heard that I was reading and writing in the Serbian way. This was blasphemy for a Catholic, he said, so he taught me Latin letters although all of that is not very different.'

'I know it's similar. But in the army? How come?'

'Yes, the old Yugoslav Army was heavily dominated by the Serbs, and if someone was illiterate, he was taught the Serbian alphabet. This was obligatory—a soldier had to know how to read and write.'

'And the reaction of those who were not the Serbs?'

'Some were mad and thought that this was humiliating—Croats and Bosnian Muslims in particular—but I didn't object. I wanted to learn, I was illiterate, and this wasn't nice.'

'And in the Partisans?'

'It was mixed there, but mainly Latin letters, because my brigade was composed predominantly of the Croats. Enough chatting, Borna, I've got my newspaper now. Do something. Chase a girl or... Do something.'

When in 1937 Ivan went to do his obligatory service in the Royal Yugoslav Army, Roža was left with one daughter. In 1942, when he was conscripted into the Home Guard of the Independent State of Croatia, she was left with one daughter and two sons. In 1944, when he was picked up by the Partisans, she was left with three daughters and two sons. And during all of these years, she was keeping the family safe without a word of complaint.

She did not complain even when Ivan was, years after the war, stabbed eleven times by his second cousin (from the Mad Bull family) and barely survived. Josip the Mad Bull, who was a distinguished local communist, wanted to take a piece of Ivan's land by force and using his political influence, but the only thing he managed to do was the stabbing. Later on, an agreement was reached that the stabbing was going to be forgotten, the dispute over the land as well, and Ivan's sons were not going to take revenge against the Mad Bull family. Interestingly, a villager of Krotko once said that Josip the Mad Bull had backed off because of receiving an ultimatum from Ivan's Partisan brothers in arms (Josip was a communist but had not been a Partisan).

There were many situations like that in the marriage of Ivan and Roža, and their life was everything but easy. On almost every occasion when there was a true danger, it was Roža—this tiny, short woman—who would take the lead and settle the matter: she was simply that kind of a woman.

VI

1973, Kletina, Socialist Republic of Croatia Socialist Federative Republic of Yugoslavia & 1910–1918, places in the Kingdom of Croatia-Slavonia and the Kingdom of Hungary Austria-Hungary

Borna Didić was awakened by his father Luka. It was January, it was cold, there was some snow around, and the morning had an unpleasant greyish colour.

'It's early, but I have to go to work, Borna. Remain calm now. I'm afraid I must tell you that Babuška died last night. She was old and not quite healthy, and it's normal that old people die—so don't be afraid.'

'I'm not afraid, Papa. Mama told me already that Babuška was soon going to sleep forever. Is she sleeping now, Papa?'

'Of course she is, and she's dreaming about you.'

'I'm not sure she dreams about anyone. She didn't love anyone, Papa. People who don't love don't dream about other people.'

'Be ready for school now,' said Luka, disregarding his son's last remark.

Two days later, a horse-drawn carriage was slowly taking the body of Klara Zultner—who within the family was called Babuška—to the Kletina cemetery. This slowness was common at a funeral in the small town—where only the nearest family and neighbours would usually show up. A God-fearing passer-by would stop and remain silent for a few moments, and this was the only respect that the town of Kletina was paying to Klara Zultner on her way to eternity.

Klara's daughter, Ljerka, was crying while her husband Vladimir was holding her arm in the manner of a gentleman, which was typical of him; her daughters Danka and Barbara were walking behind them, showing little feeling for their bitter grandmother, who had, as far as they knew, never expressed any sentiment for them. However, Danka—the younger and more emotional of the two—would shed a tear every now and then. Borna was behind the two sisters and their husbands. He was walking in complete silence together with the other great grandchildren of Klara; none of them knew much about the old, aloof lady, and their lack of interest for the ongoing ceremony was understandable. All in all, this funeral was modest even by the standards of Kletina. A few tears, a dry sermon by the local Roman Catholic priest, grey sky, cold ground, not many flowers, not many attendants—and this was how Klara Zultner, née Gorinec, from an old Croatian artisan family, left the world of the living.

Once upon a time, Klara had loved passionately—and she became a grumpy lady (very fond of alcoholic beverages) much later, when the main troubles of her life were already behind her. In the evenings, she would often withdraw to the garden behind the house of her son-in-law, into the shade cast by that building where she, her daughter and granddaughters had lived since 1946; while sitting on a bench next to a carefully trimmed hedge (which was a legacy of Filip Količek), she would think melancholically about the misfortunes in her life, secretly drinking brandy from a small flask which had once belonged to her never forgotten husband. If she had been sure that no one had been coming, she would have even lit a cigarette.

Widowed at the age of twenty-five, in the last year of the Great War, and left with two small children (of whom the younger one, a boy, later died in a tragic accident with forgotten explosives from the war), she lived a bitter life for about half a century. The only comfort she had in the winter of her life were some happy memories from the time when a photo of His Imperial and Royal Apostolic Majesty Franz Joseph I—on the wall in every post office—had been reassuring the people that the age of peace and prosperity had been there to last forever.

When Klara met Ivo in 1910, he was already a promising young solicitor. And so handsome he was—thought Klara—with those green eyes and dark curly hair. It was her good knowledge of German that brought them together, because the true name of Ivo (as he was called among the Croats) was actually Johann, and he would often be in the company of the local Germans—who spoke German and not Croatian amongst themselves. When Klara and Ivo met for the first time, he could not realise that she was not German—this was how good her command of the German language was (in consequence of her private German lessons which she was taking since early childhood). They met in the town of Itonok on the Danube, at the border between the Kingdom of Croatia-Slavonia and the Kingdom of Hungary, where Klara's family was visiting certain noblemen who could have benefited from the knowledge of Klara's father on the breeding of some English racing horses.

Johann would never mind the occasional wrong accents in Klara's German, since he would sometimes have the same problem as well: German spoken in his house still contained parts of the dialect of Transylvanian Saxons. He was, actually, the only Saxon among his German friends—who were all Danube Swabians.

Klara and Ivo were married in 1912, when he was already a judge in Itonok and with a bright future before him. In 1913 they travelled to Transylvania—which, at the time, only well-off people could afford to do. They spent a lot of time in the area around a village called Keisd (near Brașov which has been until today called Kronstadt by the Saxons), the origin of his once Lutheran family. He was sad to learn that the surname Zultner had become extinct in Transylvania soon after his ancestors in 1601 had become refugees in one of the frequent local wars. Their whereabouts were vague for a century, and then they eventually settled in Croatia. Some speculated that there were no Lutheran priests in and around their new settlement—only Calvinist and more numerous Roman Catholic ones—so they chose to blend in by accepting the religion of the majority.

The happy marriage of Klara and Johann ended in 1918 with an official letter stating that he had died for King and the Triune Kingdom while fighting the Italian enemy in the Alps. In fact, no one has ever really known what was written in that letter, because Klara ran away shortly afterwards and destroyed it somewhere. She did not come home for eleven days, but she eventually survived—to become bitter beyond recognition. The only thing she said—shedding no tears whatsoever—when she returned was, 'He shouldn't have died in the Alps. He was German, but he wasn't for the Alps—he belonged to different Germans. And he belonged to me, and they took him from me.'

She survived the year of 1945, when her daughter's first husband was killed and her two granddaughters were orphaned. After all of them had found safety and peace with the good man Vladimir, she finally felt relief, lost her instinct for survival and discovered her own private refuge in the garden behind his house—where she would spend every moment she could. A flask containing brandy was frequently her companion, but who could blame her for that?

When the undertakers were lowering Klara's coffin into the ground, Ljerka was in tears and her legs could not support her; Vladimir was holding her firmly, and Barbara and Danka also came to help—both of them crying as well, being touched by the sight of their mother.

However, as soon as the coffin touched the bottom of the grave, Ljerka stopped crying and became unusually calm. It seemed somehow that she started to glow in an inexplicable way, and her daughters followed her instinctively—so the whole scene became in a way surreal. She looked at Vlado in a tranquil way, saying, 'Thank you, my dear, for being with me so much. You're always with me.'

No one knew the reason for her becoming serene so quickly.

And this mysterious reason was that her mother had a grave. She thought,

'In this grave, my Vladimir and me, this angel of my life and me, will rest too. Together. Every person deserves a proper grave.'

Before that day, she never had a grave to visit. Her father—a lieutenant in the Royal Croatian Home Guard of the Royal Hungarian Army—had been buried at an unknown place in the southern Alps, and for the grave of her only true love—Srdjan Jarbašić, who had been a major in the Home Guard of the Independent State of Croatia—it was dangerous to even ask.

VII

1937–1939, Tirana
Albanian Kingdom

Upon his arrival to Tirana, the first thought of Lieutenant Colonel Vladimir F Količek was that this place certainly did not look like Belgrade or Zagreb—not to speak of Paris—but there was still no reason for panicking; he was not there to have fun, in the first place, and the memory of the long preparations for this mission was helping him remain quite focused.

He was determined not to fail as his older colleague Dragoljub had done so humiliatingly in Bulgaria in 1935, when he had been identified by the Bulgarian authorities as a spy and asked to leave the country.

At the time of Dragoljub's failure, Količek was specialising at the *École spéciale militaire de Saint-Cyr* in Paris, and when this was about to be completed, he was urgently summoned back to Belgrade. Unlike Dragoljub Mihailović—who had been visiting the same institution in 1930 to study tactics—Količek was in Paris learning about military intelligence including history (which, in turn, had an important role in his later life). After more than a year of having a wonderful time in Paris, his studying started to interfere with the fact that the Kingdom of Yugoslavia simply could not afford to lose its strong position in Albania—a neighbouring country and vital for the Yugoslav war strategy—where the growing influence of Mussolini's Italy was not bearable any longer. Hence, after returning to Belgrade and studying everything about Albania, including the language, and going through an additional training in spying, Količek was in the spring of 1937 ready to join the intelligence battlefield called Tirana.

Since his assignment was quite delicate, it was a favourable circumstance that Količek, although aged thirty-seven, was not married and also not a womaniser. Then again, he never tried to hide from his superiors several short affairs he had in the past, and he also did not pretend that he was always going to be able to resist a woman's charm. His high level of concentration and the ability to separate private life from duty were an assurance that his possible occasional flirts would never endanger his primary mission.

As strange as this may seem, one of the reasons why he was sent to Tirana was his Croatian nationality. Sending Mihailović, a Serb, to Sofia was a terrible mistake, because the Bulgarians—in tense relations with the Serbs for centuries—were suspicious of him from the very start. It would have been even worse to send a Serb to Albania, because the relations between the Serbs and the Albanians were closer to mutual hatred than to rivalry. In particular, the issue of Kosovo—a historical Serbian land with an Albanian ethnic majority for the last several centuries—was the source of a constant dispute between the two nations. The Albanians considered the Yugoslav rule over Kosovo to be an act of occupation of their ethnic territory, and the Serbs were accusing the Albanians that they wanted to annex the nucleus of the medieval Serbian Empire. This feud was going to continue until modern times through a seemingly endless series of unfortunate and bloody events.

Appointing a Croat, who also spoke Albanian, as a military attaché at the Yugoslav Embassy in Tirana was a good move. The Croats were a nation that was quite mysterious to the Albanians, but the fact that the Croats were strong opponents to the Serbs within Yugoslavia was making them a kind of natural Albanian ally—according to the logic that 'the enemy of my enemy is my friend'. Moreover, the fact that a Croat, Količek, succeeded to occupy a distinguished position in Yugoslavia might have also been taken as a sign that choosing Yugoslavia—and not Fascist Italy with its imperial agenda—as the main Albanian ally and protector would not be utterly bad. The Albanians knew that they should buy some time before becoming strong enough to decide on their own destiny independently.

Količek was aware of the fact that simply staying at the embassy the whole day long could not be productive, and he was on the streets of Tirana in civilian clothes often, making acquaintances and organising his own network of trusted people. He never carried any weapon, and he relied solely on the protection of those locals who considered him to be their friend—which was in the strongly patriarchal Albanian society quite feasible provided that one knew how to play one's cards right. This was in stark contrast to the Italian and Greek agents, who—led by their supremacist disrespect for the Albanians—relied more on bribery, blackmail, and intimidation.

Since he had been in Belgrade learning Albanian from a person from Kosovo, Vladimir was speaking the Gheg (northern) variant of the language; this was helping him present himself as a person of partially Albanian roots from Kosovo. The sympathies he earned by speaking the Gheg dialect—and by being a pleasant, respectful man generally—were expanding his network from day to day, and the Albanians from his circles did not know that they were actually spying for him.

It took him only eight months to establish complete control over Tirana regarding international intelligence affairs, which was making the Italians extremely angry while the Greeks simply lost every influence and had to withdraw from the game. These activities soon (already in 1937) attracted the attention of Galeazzo Ciano—who was Mussolini's son-in-law and the Foreign Minister of Italy. His standpoint about Količek was changing on a daily basis, from intense hatred to deep admiration.

Since unsubstantiated rumours might represent the truth if being numerous and largely independent from one another, it was not impossible that, as many said, Ciano complained in late 1938 that he could have already taken Albania if this snake Količek, 'who makes everything so difficult and who is half-Albanian at least, if not more', had not been there.

From a story of an Albanian man in a refugee camp in Italy after World War II, which he told in 1947, one could conclude that Količek had been in love with a daughter of a local clan chief from the area northeast of Tirana, and that the chief had been not only approving but also strongly supporting this relationship. The refugee also said that some Italian agents shot the girl in January 1939, most likely in order to try to provoke Količek to avenge by doing something stupid instinctively, which would then give them a sort of formal reason to eliminate him, in whatever way, from the streets of Tirana or even from the whole of Albania. Količek apparently did not react at all, remaining perfectly calm and, as it seemed, unemotional about the whole matter. And did he react behind the curtain? One could only guess, but it was indicative that four Italian spies were not much later found impaled on stakes—in the same way as the Ottoman Turks had been doing—on a beach close to two Italian anchored ships. According to the refugee, it was Količek who informed some people of his choice who the Italian perpetrators were—since he was probably the only person in Tirana who could have known that—and the rest was done by the clan. They revenged the spilled blood because the ancient laws commanded so, said the refugee.

The above story has remained shrouded in mystery, just as many others from the life of Vladimir F Količek. Was the unfortunate Albanian girl the love of his life or not? How deeply was he devoted to her and what was the impact of this tragedy on him? No one will ever know. On the other hand, he had not been in any serious relationship for the entire time from his Albanian days until 1946, when he gave sanctuary to the widow and two small daughters of a good friend of his, of a friend who was a tragic victim of one mad time.

One could also be interested to know that Galeazzo Ciano started a special campaign on the ninth of April 1939 (two days after the Italian invasion of Albania had begun), dedicated solely to finding and apprehending Lieutenant Colonel Vladimir F Količek, the military attaché at the Yugoslav Embassy in Tirana. Ciano was in a total frenzy when he launched that operation, possibly because he could not forget the sarcasm and humiliating laughter of virtually the entire population of Tirana when in 1937 he had been named an Honorary Citizen of Tirana—and this humiliating reception had been, to Ciano's belief, organised and orchestrated by Količek.

Both historical records and every other possible analysis of the characters of the cunning Količek and the brute Ciano would set up the same picturesque scenery for the same play: early in the morning on the fourth of April 1939, sufficiently before the chase directed by Ciano started, Vladimir Količek had crossed the mountainous Albanian-Yugoslav border uneventfully, on a mule. After realising that his network of spies had become useless, that politics and rough force had become the main players on the stage, the virtuoso actor withdrew in order to study for his next role—which was going to be played before another audience.

VIII

1937, Savnik, Sava Banovina
Kingdom of Yugoslavia

Second Lieutenant Srdjan Jarbašić was conducting the training of the recruits under his routine command, mainly thinking about his wonderful bride at home and the child they were expecting. A highly ranked officer related to Srdjan, his second uncle, was a good spirited man who liked—in contrast to just about everyone in the family—the charming Croatian-German bride and the whole struggle of the young couple to start living a normal, boring life. This uncle had pulled some strings, and Srdjan eventually became stationed in Savnik—which was the hometown of his wife and the centre of the county his village of Malo Selce belonged to.

There, in Savnik, they had been feeling really well only before they got married; after that, people started saying behind their backs, 'She's our German girl and she married a Vlach—shameful! A child of God to marry a Croatian woman, a Latin—shameful! I'm a follower of the Pope, and I say that Croats and Serbs should never mix—shameful! Bloody Swabian whore, she took our nice Serbian soldier, she took him from us—shameful! What will this slut do when we finish with her Orthodox husband and the whole of his village? We should have dealt with these Croats in 1918 and filled the river with their corpses! Shameful, shameful, utterly shameful!'

And so on and so forth.

Their families were in most part hostile towards them. For Ljerka's family, town folks, he was a wild Vlach herder who just came out from a dirty forest and brought with him a terrible stink, mud on his bare feet, illiteracy, lack of manners, and shamanistic rituals from the East; he was stupid, malicious, aggressive, and dishonest by his unworthy birth if by nothing else; and his every move was orchestrated by Satan with only one purpose: to abduct an innocent girl from the righteous world led by His Holiness the Pope Pius XI, and to throw her into the abyss of the Great Schism. For his family, country folks, she was an evil witch, arrogant streetwalker who was using perfumes and makeup to bedazzle an innocent Orthodox young man and put wicked Western spells on him; she grew up by witnessing the animalistic fornication of the women of her kind with vampires and werewolves who lived on Catholic cemeteries, and this made her feebleminded, wretched, and of a dirty womb, which was typical of all Latin women—since every single one of them was conceived either by a travelling Gypsy thief or by a Turkish infidel.

Only two of their close relatives were supportive of the young couple unconditionally, although some of the others (for instance, Srdjan's brother) would also occasionally approach them in a friendly way. The first one was Ljerka's mother Klara, who cared little about daily matters and was content whenever her flask would be full of brandy. However, it would not be right to attribute her understanding solely to the dizziness she was so fond of; on one occasion, she was completely sober when she slapped and then chased with a broom her younger sister who said some terrible things about Srdjan. The second one was Srdjan's great grandmother, who once came to Savnik by foot from Malo Selce, in her only good dress, just to see Ljerka and ask her would she accompany her to a confectionery; there, Ljerka learned that the old lady actually knew how to speak Serbian but was reluctant to show that to the 'stupid people'. In Savnik, Ljerka and Srdjan basically had only their mutual love and no friends.

Since he was so much in love, Srdjan was trying to disregard all of that and revel in other things which were making the world a good place, and he was always keen to find a reason for life being enjoyable—not only at home but also at work. For instance, he liked—for some reason, quite instinctively—an illiterate conscript of the Catholic faith. This silent and disciplined peasant was unusually eager to learn how to read and write, in contrast to the other soldiers who would always search for a bottle or ask for a privilege of this or that kind. Moreover, once Srdjan spoke with the peasant he found out that his wife was pregnant too. Srdjan was also interested in discussing with the conscript the profession of a blacksmith, as his father esteemed this occupation—vital for the merchants who transported goods by using horses—as highly as that of a judge, a teacher, a doctor or a priest. And the conscript was a blacksmith.

'I must learn how to read and write, sir,' said the conscript to Srdjan, 'because I feel I'll get a son and I want him to have a father who can teach him how to read and write. There's no school in our village, sir. We own enough land, sir, and I'm a blacksmith too—so there's enough money—but my son will be as clever as my father was, and I must be able to teach him how to read and write.'

'And this is what you will learn,' promised Srdjan. 'Sergeant! This soldier must learn how to read and write in no more than three weeks! I make you personally responsible for that! We shall not wait for these slow official classes for just about every illiterate monkey, where no one can learn anything.'

'Yes, sir! Consider it done!'

'Very good!'

'I'm doing my best, sir!'

'May God bless you, sir, you and your family,' said the conscript to Srdjan before leaving with the sergeant to some other place.

'Look, soldier,' said Sergeant Ljubiša Petronijević, 'now go and find at least five others who want to learn how to read and write. I'll not give lectures only to you! Go now and we'll start tomorrow after supper.'

The soldier found eleven of his comrades and brought them to a classroom where Sergeant Petronijević was already waiting. The sergeant was a stocky, bald man in his mid-forties, from the town of Ub in central Serbia; being a son of a butcher, he was not particularly literate himself, and his reading could have been classified, at best, as slow. Of course, he could read and write only Cyrillic script, which he had learned in a hospital, recovering from exhaustion on the Greek island of Corfu in 1915. After participating in the Battle of Kolubara—which had taken place in 1914 not far from Ub and in which the Serbs had routed the Austro-Hungarian forces—he went through the later defeat and disastrous withdrawal of the Royal Serbian Army, being lucky to survive the escape march through Albania as well as receiving several wounds and nominally mortal diseases.

'Listen now, soldiers!' shouted the sergeant. 'You have your small blackboards here, and each of you will get a piece of chalk. Use the chalk to copy on your small blackboard what I write on the big blackboard! We'll start with the letter *A* because this is the first letter in the alphabet. You, soldier, you! Have you got anything to say? Speak or be silent when your sergeant is talking!'

'Yes, sergeant, excuse me, sir. It will not happen again.'

'Right, right. Now, the second letter in the alphabet is *B*. You see, this is how one writes the letter *B*. Now all of you write the letter *B* on your small blackboards.'

'But sir, I saw the letter *B* before and it looked different.'

'Shut up, boy! You'd seen the Catholic letter *B*, and here I wrote the Orthodox letter *B*, because in our army we use these letters. Is that clear?'

'Yes, sir!' all twelve of his students shouted simultaneously.

'All right now. If this is clear, we shall now go to the third letter of the alphabet, and this is the letter *V*...' the sergeant continued the first lecture Ivan the Blacksmith ever had about reading and writing. Many do not know, but the order of letters in the Serbian Cyrillic alphabet is not the same as in the Roman alphabet, and the Cyrillic letter which is pronounced as *V* is written as Roman *B*. No one cared: the twelve illiterate soldiers were following their literate leader with the same enthusiasm as the twelve Apostles had been following their Saint.

Doing things of that sort for his soldiers—and, as a matter of fact, for just about everyone and whenever he could—was making Srdjan happy. Ever since Ljerka had told him about her pregnancy, the world was a nice, colourful and pleasant place full of friendly people who would occasionally be bad only because of bad weather, etc. No one was really bad, thought Srdjan. Ljerka was less enthusiastic. She had grown up in the centre of the town of Savnik—unlike Srdjan, who had been raised in the countryside—and she knew well what gossips could bring to a young family. In such prejudicial surroundings, many things bar one would be forgiven eventually—and this thing was different religions of the spouses. In the case of Ljerka and Srdjan, it could not have been worse:

for ages, her mother's family was Roman Catholic, her paternal ancestors had converted from Lutheranism to Catholicism some two or three hundred years ago, and Srdjan's family was, as far as anyone could remember, Orthodox—which meant that the young couple inherited three historically confronted Christian denominations.

A great relief for Ljerka was—as mentioned before—the support of her mother, who lived with her and Srdjan. This was surprising to everyone, because Klara was, ever since the death of her beloved Johann, a woman known for bitterness and cynicism.

'This snake doesn't like anyone, just spitting venom all the time,' was often how people encountering Klara would speak of her.

'Love your husband and let him love you,' Klara would say to her daughter occasionally, 'and do it now, don't wait, do it all day long and as much as you can. Let your heart flow, my daughter, or you might regret later. Let your body tremble, don't restrain it. Who knows what could happen soon.'

On many such occasions, Klara would fall asleep soon after saying that, and Ljerka would then remove an empty glass smelling of cheap brandy. In time, she and Srdjan got used to Babuška having a glass of brandy, or two or even more, especially during those warm evenings which were obviously reminding her of certain notable events from her past. She continued to be unusually kind in these moments—giving advice about love—whereas she otherwise remained an unpleasant, grumpy woman who was spitting venom day and night.

If the marriage of Ljerka and Srdjan had been observed from the heavenly skies, without any bias, it would have been clear that there was a touch of perfection in it. They loved each other deeply, passionately, instinctively, and there was nothing conditional or negotiable in their sincere ardour for each other. She was extremely beautiful and could have been a competitor to every Hollywood star from the 1930s. Srdjan was about 185 cms tall, strong but not fat, moving slowly and never raising his voice. When Borna Didić found a photo of Ljerka and Srdjan together—he in a uniform and she a glowing wife—the only thing he could say was, 'Oh my goodness, how beautiful my grandparents were.'

IX

1980, Kletina & Krotko, Socialist Republic of Croatia
Socialist Federative Republic of Yugoslavia

The year of 1980 was to Borna Didić memorable for several reasons: in May, he witnessed the death of comrade Tito, who had ruled the socialist Yugoslavia for thirty-five years; in June, he became the champion of the whole County of Kletina in the sixty metre sprint for primary school pupils; in August, his beloved grandfather Vladimir died after a short and aggressive illness; in September, he enrolled in a middle school in Kletina and finally—as he thought at the time—he was no longer a child.§

Another notable event that year was the breakup of his first relationship (which had started around his fourteenth birthday, close to the Christmas of 1979, and lasted for roughly five months); being quite much in love, he was rather disturbed and could not find peace of mind for at least a year in spite of occasionally flirting with other girls. Much later, when recollecting this experience—which represented the first of his numerous love failures—he would be simply melancholic, not sad or angry. Eventually he learned to live with the fact that no woman, in his opinion, had ever loved him.

In those moments, he would occasionally remember the weeping of his grandmother Ljerka at the funeral of her husband. These sincere tears which were shed due to the departure of a wonderful friend and companion, her guardian angel, her protector, her guide. But this was not a cry for the loss of a lover: tears of that sort had been wetting her pillow

---

§ Josip Broz Tito, the leader of Yugoslav communists since 1939, of the Partisans during World War II, and of Yugoslavia after the war.

thirty-five years earlier, when she felt (in an autumn dawn, suddenly) that Srdjan was dying at a cursed, unknown, ugly place so far from her.

In his contemplations, Borna would always believe that Vladimir died at peace with the fact that he was not the love of Ljerka's life. Vladimir definitely knew that from the very first day of taking the young broken widow and her two fatherless daughters under his roof. Being a middle-aged man of a turbulent past, in which women had been playing episodic roles at best, he was quite pleased with finally bringing some family warmth into his big, empty house—and this was good enough for him. The house in 1946 was empty literally: his father had been gone for a long time, and no one knew anything about him, his mother had died before the war, his brother was continuing his travels overseas—which he had been doing since 1927—and his sister had emigrated to South America because she was, unlike Vladimir, a supporter of the Ustasha regime.**

As if he foresaw that no tear was going to be shed at his own funeral, Borna envied his grandfather, since many people had been crying at Vladimir's burial, especially Danka who had been very much attached to him and had not remembered her true father well. Then there had been neighbours and family friends, a peasant woman who had been a part time maidservant in Vladimir's house, some unknown old strangers with medals on their chests, and even one musician from a brass band that had been providing a musical background to the ceremony (among Croatian Catholics in the north of the country, folk songs would be usually played at funerals).

It seemed that Vladimir never experienced an instinctive passion together with a true, unconditional love of a woman (perhaps with the exception of the Albanian girl, but this has remained unclear). His life was filled with respect and silent admiration for the woman he was married to for more than thirty years, and he knew that Ljerka felt more or less the same.

** *Ustasha* means, roughly, *rebel*. This was the name used by certain fanatical Croats and Muslim Bosnians (those opting for Croatian national identity), quislings during World War II, who were in the Independent State of Croatia equivalent to SS troops in Nazi Germany.

The destiny of Borna—whose intimate relations were by far more numerous and intense than those of Vladimir—turned out to be similar in a certain sense. He eventually became a relatively handsome man, but a superficial and emotionless sexual desire (he would sometimes incite that in a woman) could never result in anything deeper than that. Then he came to Basel and met Sara, who definitely respected him—just as Ljerka had respected Vladimir—but was he her Srdjan too? And how deep were his feelings for her?

Perhaps there is a scientific explanation for the fact that many women wanted to have Borna in bed, but none of them, before Sara, would even think of him as a Prince Charming and life companion. Maybe it was something related to pheromones or evolutionary processes that shaped all of us? These disturbing thoughts started to haunt Borna even before he became Archibald. In any case, Sara never said anything publicly, and everyone could only guess what was behind their relationship—only mutual respect or maybe something more?

The impending death of Colonel Vladimir F Količek was rather slow, and it was going on in parallel with that of Josip Broz Tito—who was eight years older and hospitalised in Ljubljana, the capital of Slovenia, having the best possible medical care the country could provide. Broz—who had been a dandy, smoker, drinker, womaniser, and party animal (a bohemian in general, to be brief) for most of his life—had problems with his vascular system and they had to cut off one of his legs to try to save him.

Količek was leaving this world much less pompously, in the middle room of his house in Kletina, due to the multiple sclerosis he had become aware of less than a year earlier.

His recent book on military history was under review at the time, and he wrote a letter to the editor in which he stated that he was 'now home incapacitated, waiting for nirvana to come'. And he died before the review was completed; the whole thing was later forgotten, and his last work has never been published.

While everyone was very much concerned about the health of the great leader—who was the last living great commander of the anti-Hitler coalition from World War II—it was quiet in the family of Vladimir

Količek. Tito died first, in May, and his funeral was possibly the most memorable event worldwide in the entire 1980s, at least regarding political shows. Everybody came to pay their respects: The West, the East, the Non-Aligned, presidents, kings, prime ministers, emperors, democrats, dictators, friends, and enemies.

When the funeral of Josip Broz Tito was taking place, Colonel Količek was no longer able to walk, sit or speak. Day and night he lay helplessly in bed, assisted by his family and some nurses who would visit from time to time. Borna, in particular, was responsible for shaving him every third day. In June, the family had to organise night shifts next to his bed, because it was clear that the end was near. In early August, it was over.

Vladimir Količek had done a rather peculiar thing just a few weeks before he lost the ability to communicate. He wanted to see one of his grandchildren, namely Borna, to advise him for the very last time—and to give him something which was going to play a major role in his life years after. Borna came, entered the room and closed the door behind him, just as his grandfather requested. The old man did not look well.

'My Falcon's Eye, you are here,' said Vladimir in a feeble voice and using his favourite nickname for Borna. 'Come and sit next to me, my dear grandson.'

'Here I am, grandfather. Can you feel my hand?'

'Yes, dear. We haven't got much time, you know. I must tell you a few things while I'm still able to. You're the only one of my grandchildren who has inherited the intellectual capacity and natural curiosity of the Količek family. We're not related by blood, but you have that somehow.'

'Dear grandfather, I've learned everything from you, and you also know that relations by blood mean nothing to me.'

'This means little to everyone with common sense. Tarzan, for example, cared more about his ape family than for the humans who had given him life. But strangely, blood still counts somewhat. Silly things. Anyway, I'm putting all my hope in you, believing that you'll know how to use well what I'm about to give you. The others in the family wouldn't know how.'

'Hmm… I get it, grandfather, but they're still older than me and they might understand you better.'

'No, they wouldn't, what a silly thought. You know that Tito died, and this will bring changes, many of which will not be positive. In short: Yugoslavia will vanish.'

'But Yugoslavia is so strong and it can never…'

'Hush, Falcon's Eye, we haven't got much time—I'm getting tired so quickly. I know what I'm talking about. Yugoslavia will not survive for very long without Tito, because this Yugoslavia is Tito, and he's dead now. Yugoslavia will be dead in ten, maybe fifteen years, and it will die in flame and blood. There will be massive bloodshed. I saw it already and this will come again.'

'But grandfather, we all love our country and…'

'Be silent Falcon's Eye and let me speak. This disaster will probably occur sometime when you'll be a grown-up, perhaps with a wife and children. You must save yourself and them, don't be a fool and lose your life for stupid ideals which always eventually turn out to be rubbish, just one big lie!'

After expressing his last thought, he had to stop talking for a while because he felt exhausted; and then he continued.

'Now go to my room and bring me a piece of paper which you'll find on the piano. I asked your grandmother to put it there. She doesn't know what it is, though.'

Borna brought back a yellowy, rather old looking sheet of paper with some writing in blue ink from some other times.

An eclipse is upon us, but it will pass away, as it has never happened that a night is not followed by a day.

'Don't ask anything, just accept that this is a code for an old friend of mine who owes me something, and he'll return this favour to anyone who brings him this letter and says that his name is Falcon's Eye. Now you know why I've called you so. These words are a cipher.'

'But I'm sure I'll never need this.'

'Come, come, my boy, trust your old, dying grandfather. When the time for that comes, take this letter with you and find a way to reach

Aberdeen in Scotland. There, search for one Malcolm Forbes; he's from the Forbes Clan and this may narrow your search. Or find some of his relatives or descendants, they will also keep the promise. He was a captain in the British military intelligence in Belgrade in 1940 and 1941, keep this in mind while locating him. Obey me, please, take this letter with you and use it when the time comes.'

'You know, grandfather, that I will. I'll keep this letter and pass it to my child if I don't use it.'

'Do this, Falcon's Eye. The Scots remember, this is a bond for generations. Only a silly person might think that you'll not be the one to use it. Just hand them the letter, say that you're Falcon's Eye, and they'll know what to do. The Scots remember. And let me sleep now, I'm so tired. But return tomorrow, will you?'

After the funeral of Colonel Vladimir Filip Količek, his grandson Borna Didić—full of pain and tears that were refusing to flow—took a bus and went to see his grandparents in Krotko. There, he would sit under a pear tree in the evenings with Ivan the Blacksmith, who was a silent and compassionate man. Borna was feeling the tranquillity of the old man, and this was relieving his grief. About nine p.m., Ivan and Roža would go to sleep—just like every other proper peasant—and Borna would, like a true teenager, start to raid through the village full of girls, determined to get over his recent breakup.

In the morning, the sorrow for Vladimir would reappear shortly, but Borna would then take a look at Ivan the Proud and ease his soul by thinking, 'He's my only grandfather now. He's my grandfather, and I feel good. I'm too young to lose all of my grandfathers—I lost two of them already.'

X

1939–1940, Maribor, Drava Banovina Kingdom of Yugoslavia

The love of Ljerka and Srdjan flourished: it was, in every respect, a love that could fill a boring romantic novel for an afternoon reading in the shade of a tree.

She, a beautiful young mother full of ardour for her husband as well as for their born and unborn babies—since she was pregnant again—and he, a handsome lieutenant adored by his soldiers and completely devoted to his happy family. The young couple were also completely ignoring the feud between their relatives, acquaintances, and so-called friends back home—the Orthodox Serbs on one side and the Catholic Croats and Germans on the other. Hence, in spite of the instinctive malice of those who were supposed to be supportive—and who should have been, in a more normal world, pleased by the happiness of the young family—the life of Ljerka, Srdjan, little Barbara, and the baby in Ljerka was a fairy tale. It was good for the emotional stability of Ljerka and Srdjan that they were far enough from the intrigues which were taking place on a daily basis in Savnik and around it.

The newest Srdjan's assignment was, namely, from January 1939 onwards in Slovenia, in Maribor (the capital of Slovenian Styria and about two hundred kilometres from Savnik) at the Yugoslav-German border. Less than a year earlier, this had been a border between Austria and Yugoslavia, but then Hitler brought Germany thus close to Maribor by his annexation of the Republic of Austria. Since Srdjan and Ljerka lived a daydream, they were not noticing that the streets of Maribor were full of tense feelings.

Until 1918, the city itself was populated mainly by the ethnic Germans, whereas all the surrounding villages were one hundred percent Slovene. Since then, the German population was steadily decreasing, but the distinct German character of the city was still there; in particular, German was widely spoken, especially in the city centre where most of the influential people lived. Taking into account the recent political changes and the fact that the border was only ten kilometres to the north, the situation in Maribor was not simple. The Germans were split into two opposing factions: one supporting Hitler and Pan-Germanism, and one devoted to the self-identity of Austria, this foundation of former Austria-Hungary. The Slovenes were all endorsing Yugoslavia—this being supported legally by the 1919 *Treaty of Saint-Germain-en-Laye* about the drawing of the border between Austria and the state of the South Slavs after the Great War. A consequence of that was an informal coalition of the Slovenes with the latter Germans; this alliance was, however, not firm and not sincere either—just as it always happens with every love based on opportunism.

Srdjan and Ljerka were not discussing the bitter atmosphere in Maribor even if spotting something unusual or unpleasant—they lived in their faultless world detached from the dirt of daily events. This place was, in their opinion, much better than Savnik.

In the morning he would go to the barracks to carry out his duties for the day, and these would sometimes be interrupted by a meeting of the officers on the current political situation and related military affairs; Srdjan would seldom listen carefully at these meetings—he was in his mind always home with his girls. Ljerka would take Barbara out before cooking lunch, sit with her in a local confectionery and order a coffee for herself and something small for Barbara (in German, which was simply easier since she did not speak Slovene); afterwards, they would usually take a long walk along the Drava River or just find a bench in a park so that Barbara could play. And when Srdjan would return home around four or five p.m., the family would start to live its true life full of love. The day would continue playing with Barbara, and their dreams of the future would fill the evening; Srdjan would be touching Ljerka's big belly and they would always laugh and kiss. The next day would be even brighter than the one before, and life seemed to be no less than perfect.

Shortly after December—when Danka had been born—Ljerka and Srdjan would usually end their evenings by making love passionately.

The first disturbance in the wonderful life of Ljerka, Srdjan, Barbara, and Danka came in September 1940, when a certain colonel from Belgrade visited Maribor.

This colonel was rather different from the colonels Srdjan had encountered before—who had been mainly either bull-headed veterans from the Great War or nephews of important politicians. The colonel was moving slowly, he was never raising his voice and was treating even the simplest soldier with respect. His appearance was generally in contrast to the uneasiness, or even fear, that the other officers from the barracks would be showing in his company. Upon his arrival, he spoke only a few words with the other officers and insisted on meeting Lieutenant Jarbašić privately, 'for the reasons he is not obligated to explain to anyone'. When Srdjan arrived at the office established especially for the colonel in the main building, he addressed him in the way a lower-ranked officer was supposed to.

'Come, come, Lieutenant Jarbašić, let us make this less formal. I'm Colonel Vladimir Količek, you can call me Vlado if you wish—we're all brothers in arms.'

'Yes sir! Sir, Colonel Vlado!' reacted Srdjan instinctively, being somewhat confused.

'Sir, Colonel Vlado, because you wish so, orders you to sit down on this chair, lieutenant' replied Količek.

'Yes, sir!'

'Could you stop, please? Would you mind just sitting down and relaxing?'

'Okay, then,' said Srdjan, finally accepting that this colonel was really very different from the other colonels in his experience.

'There's a thing I'd like to discuss with you,' continued Vladimir. 'It has something to do with the state security, but it's not as serious as you may think—so relax please, nothing bad will happen. Where was I? Oh, yes. You know that France has gone as our main ally? And Czechoslovakia too—so the *Little Entente* of Yugoslavia, Czechoslovakia, and Romania exists no more. In short, our kingdom has no allies any more, only Greece perhaps. The British are too much into their own interests, the Soviets have compromised with Hitler, and the Americans have their own plans which are not clear. The others are of little importance.'

'Yes I know, sir. Vlado, I mean, sir.'

'Vlado, sir—that's good for the start, I guess. And our kingdom is all alone now, don't you think so, Srdjan? There's no one to help us in this violent world. Some suggest that we should find a way to turn to Russia, but this is—as you may guess—such a risky thing with the communists in charge there. And they've made a pact with the Devil, at least for now.'

'And with our communists here, everything is risky too,' remarked Srdjan. 'They seem to be a small group but quite fanatical, and I'm wondering what do they think about the situation now when Stalin and Hitler have become brothers.'

'They're not an issue now, although we should remain aware of them. If nothing else, their fanaticism makes them admirably brave, we should never forget that. But let me make a point now. Your wife frequently walks through Maribor with your daughters, and she speaks German perfectly. Right?'

'That's true.'

'Is she German?'

'By her father, her mother is Croatian.'

'And she's loyal to this country?'

'Of course she is, her German side is originally from Transylvania but for centuries already in Yugoslavia, not from Germany in any case.'

'Good, good. Look, Srdjan, your country might need your and her services.'

'In what sense, Colonel Vlado, sir?' replied Srdjan full of uneasiness. This was the last thing he was expecting to hear. Ljerka?

'In the sense of her being our ear in Maribor. She takes Barbara and Danka out every day, isn't that so? And she understands everything that is said in the cafés and streets—is that correct? We would like to know what she hears. This city borders Germany and is also full of Germans, many things are spoken here quite publicly. I can't predict our future relations with Germany, but we ought to be prepared.'

'I don't know…' hesitated Srdjan. 'Would that be safe?'

'Completely safe. The only thing she has to do is to memorise things she hears and write them down when she comes home; then she'll give the notes to you and you'll bring them here. No one will ever know. She'll not know either, we'll make up a story for her.'

'I'll speak with her, Vlado, sir, but I can't promise anything. I'll definitely not try to order her to do anything. I believe that it would be best before we start or if we'll ever start if she never saw you or anyone else related to you.'

'That's my opinion, too. She should indeed never become aware of my existence in any way, not just by seeing me. Just tell her that you need that for your own advancement in the army, and we'll spice this up a bit with some details.'

'All right, I'll try to persuade her, but I can't promise anything. She's got a mind of her own, and our marriage isn't based on the obedience of a small wife to her big husband. She's a lady.'

And this was how Ljerka Jarbašić became an apprentice spy for the Kingdom of Yugoslavia on the eve of World War II, in a city which was a hot spot in the contemporary German-Yugoslav relations. At this time, she did not meet the orchestrator of the whole operation, and only her husband knew where her notes were ending up. This whole affair had no immediate impact on the life of the Jarbašić family, and even less on the course of the forthcoming war: the family continued to live a perfect life for a few more months, and the war had its own, more trivial ways.

Colonel Količek was in Maribor, naturally, for more serious things than to only see Srdjan.

He would seldom be seen in his office in the barracks, having a car for himself and being almost always somewhere out of the reach of those who were hosting him. While most of his whereabouts in the Maribor area were going to remain unknown for good, it was certain that he was seen in Kletina—a bit more than fifty kilometres south of Maribor—at least twice during his sojourn in Slovenia. One could only speculate, but it was not impossible that he was preparing both himself and those dear to him for what was about to come.

He was, after all, a distinguished spy.

XI

1940, Krotko, Banovina of Croatia
Kingdom of Yugoslavia

It was quiet in Krotko at Christmas time.

The highland village was, as always at this time of the year, full of snow, and the people were—in the absence of hard work in the field—visiting each other, bringing presents or just dropping by to have a chat while plum brandy called slivovitz would be offered by the host. The women were preparing traditional Christmas food, whereas the men were taking care of the fires which were sending long columns of thick smoke through the chimneys high into the sky; the children were playing outside, coming home wet, with red cheeks and being hungry beyond belief. The harvest was good that year, the livestock were healthy, there were enough beech logs—and there was little to worry about.

It was not different in the home of Ivan the Proud. His tools were resting in the smithy, and he finally had some time for plain laziness; his visits to the smithy were restricted to really important interventions only, and he was spending most of the time with his older children and a newborn son, the third child in the family. Roža was very fond of that: she liked the demeanour of her silent, strong husband, as well as the view of her children around him in their humble but warm home. Nothing was too hard for her; the house was clean, decorated, and full of every possible delicacy; she even did not want to see Ivan close to the livestock, as she enjoyed immensely this wonderful picture of her husband with the children crawling all over him. Nothing should have interrupted that. The provider of the family could seldom afford to spend so much time with his children during the year—and she knew that.

Ivan the Blacksmith was enjoying that time as well, but he was not completely free of worries. Ever since he had learned to read, he was in touch with the outside world through the newspapers he would occasionally find abandoned in the inn. Although he was still slow in reading, he would mostly conclude that certain big players were playing some dangerous games. He was not, and he never wanted to be, one of them, but many things were clear even to an uneducated peasant like him: the world he knew was dying from a terrible, unknown disease, and it was not clear what to do under these circumstances. Being a God-fearing person, he would sometimes find comfort in thinking that all of that was part of a bigger plan which he did not understand completely. He would calm himself down by thinking that big plans for the world were not his business anyway: God was taking care of that, God was going to provide.

On the twenty-third of December, they received a visit. It was Josip the Mad Bull and a man who was called Mile the Angry (known for always carrying a pistol hidden somewhere). They were widely suspected of being communists, but there was no proof of that; and no one wanted to have anything to do with them because they always had much money in spite of not working on the land at all (or anything else, as a matter of fact, although being not much above the age of twenty). Since they were spending their days in the houses of the neighbours—where they would be offered a glass of slivovitz for free—or in the inn, the hardworking peasants were trying to avoid them intuitively.

Roža remained calm when they came into the house, although she did not like what she saw. She shared her maiden surname with Mile, but she was not related to him—which was so common in this village with only a few surnames and many family bynames—and she also remembered that her father had told her once, 'They are shameful, these the Angry people. Their byname speaks for itself.'

The men sat down, and then Josip asked, 'Is there a glass of slivovitz in this house for some humble servants of Christ in this holy time?'

'Of course there is, dear cousin,' replied Ivan and brought a bottle and some glasses. 'This brandy was blessed by our priest, may God bless his soul in the name of Jesus Christ, our Lord.'

'Just pour,' said Mile.

And Ivan poured three glasses full.

'And you, good woman, would you have a drink with us?' asked Mile in a quite provocative manner, raising his glass high.

Roža felt her rage: it was growing. One of the Angry people, such a scoundrel, to come into her house uninvited and to play games with her! She wanted to reply but...

'A wife should never drink—this is what men do. She can do it only if I don't see that. Am I right, wife?' intervened Ivan in a way that sounded aggressive towards Roža. 'Am I right, woman?'

'Of course you are, my husband and protector. I'd better take care of the children now,' she said and took the children into another room to take a deep breath and thank God for having such a wise husband.

'Good, good, Ivan,' remarked Josip. 'I see your wife knows her place. Let us drink now.'

Disrespect for women was in the very soul of the Mad Bull branch of the Didić clan, and Ivan immediately felt disgusted. They were smoking and drinking silently for maybe five minutes, and then Mile said, 'We've come here for a reason, Ivan. We must ask you something.'

'Hmm... So tell me.'

'You've probably heard about this new Banovina of Croatia and how this will solve everything. About the Croats and the Serbs, about the whole situation in the country—which seemingly revolves around their disputes. But it will not. A war is coming,' Mile continued.

'I'm not sure I understand.'

'Many do not,' added Josip, 'but the Banovina and the Kingdom will collapse once the Germans and the Italians attack. And they will.'

'But what could I possibly do about that? I'm just a blacksmith and peasant in a small village.'

'Yes, you can,' continued Mile. 'You can join us.'

'And who are you? And why should I join you?'

'Because we are those who will inherit this land after the big ones become weak. This will happen sooner or later.'

'But who are you?'

'You don't have to know for now. All we want from you is to hide some weapons for us. It will cost you nothing but will be greatly appreciated when the time comes. You've got the land, forests, and barns, the smithy and everything—no one has as much space as you have. And you're respected, no one will ever try to question what you have or don't have on your property. Do it for us, and it will be paid off.'

'When the time comes?' asked Ivan.

'When the time comes,' replied Josip.

'And if not?'

'Then you'll be considered an enemy to be dealt with.'

'When the time comes?'

'When the time comes,' said Mile and moved his arm in such a way that a pistol he was hiding under his coat became visible.

Ivan poured another round of the spirit, in his typically slow manner. This gave him some time to think about the whole matter without causing suspicion. He needed his wise and brave wife at this moment, but she had been sent away, and he had to make a decision alone.

'How much of that have you got?' he said finally.

'Two big boxes. We'll bring them tonight. Everyone is drunk and no one pays attention. You just have to find a place to hide them,' explained Josip. 'Don't be afraid, cousin, this will be just a game for you. No one will know.'

'And if I refuse?'

'Then—when the time comes…' concluded Mile who moved nonchalantly to show his pistol again.

Later that evening, Josip the Mad Bull and Mile the Angry brought two boxes of smuggled, obsolete Italian rifles to a remote spot which Ivan the Blacksmith had chosen as the hiding place for this Godless cargo, deep inside one of his forests. No one dared to enter a forest owned by the Proud people although they were for quite some time known to be peaceful. It was as if the memory of the old family iron rod of the Didić clan still existed as one of the legends of Krotko. Ironically, these rifles were later, during the war, not used at all; some said, because of the lack of Italian bullets and the abundance of better, German weapons—these would be everywhere next to the dead soldiers of Germany and their allies.

The boxes remained buried shallowly until 1951. Then a boy found them when the soil above was finally washed out by rain after all these years. Since this discovery came in the midst of the legendary dispute between the communist comrades Tito and Stalin, the boy's father was accused of being a Soviet spy and was sent to prison for six years.[††] Josip the Mad Bull and Mile the Angry pretended to be ignorant of the boxes, and Ivan the Blacksmith was too much afraid to say a word. The boy's father did not survive the prison—where the conditions were no more or less brutal than in other similar establishments of that time.

Roža knew about the whole affair, being on the alert but trying not to think about it. However, every October, she would light a candle and put some flowers on the grave of the unfortunate father of the boy who had found the weapons. Apart from the family of this man, she was the only one in the whole village who remembered that he had died in October.

Ivan would usually be silent when going past the boy's house, grieving in his own way but always remaining apparently unemotional. What Josip the Mad Bull and Mile the Angry thought about the whole matter was beyond the comprehension of a normal human being. They became, in any case, distinguished heroes of the communist world after World War II.

[††] Josip Broz Tito had started to rebel against Josif Visarionovich Stalin in 1948, keeping Yugoslavia independent of the USSR, and this was why Yugoslavia remained outside the Iron Curtain afterwards—to the great satisfaction of the West. This process was, however, painful in Yugoslavia, where Stalin had many supporters.

XII

1985, Split, Socialist Republic of Croatia
Socialist Federative Republic of Yugoslavia

Borna Didić sneaked out from a room where there was a bed for admirals. Then he went, as silently as he could, through the corridors to the place where plain seamen like him should have been spending the night shift awake.

A junior conscript had given him a timely warning that an admiral was coming, and Borna immediately woke up and brought the room to its normal, tidy condition, hoping that the admiral was not going to notice anything. And indeed, he did not. The elderly admiral had been very busy with dispatching water bombers that were saving the coast from the wildfires which were so numerous that hot summer—so he just collapsed on the bed and fell asleep in a split second, his shoes still on his feet.

In this facility, a senior conscript like Borna would occasionally, during the night shift, go to sleep in the most comfortable empty bed available, and the best ones were reserved for admirals of the Yugoslav Navy—who would be there only in case of a crisis. This would seldom occur, of course, so the seamen were using these beds regularly although they were forbidden to sleep during the shift. Captains and commanders—who would in normal circumstances be the commanding officers—had their own beds, and most of them would have not objected if a senior conscript had taken a nap somewhere, as long as this was out of their sight and provided that everything was running smoothly. Sergeants usually cared even less, apart from a few sadistic ones who would sometimes check every bed or other hideout hoping to find a conscript asleep. Their version of reaching a dirty climax was to shout at a young sleepy seaman and humiliate him in every other way—and in front of the other conscripts.

The facility under question was a six-storey building built inside a rocky but forested hill east of the city of Split—the largest Croatian/Yugoslav coastal city—which provided sheltered headquarters for the entire Yugoslav Navy. There, information from all the radars along the coast would be gathered and processed day and night, and every required action would start from this spot (e.g., sending armed ships to scare off or capture an intruding Italian fishing vessel or to follow, at some distance, an American or a Soviet warship that would be visiting the Adriatic Sea). In case of a war, this well-equipped, modern installation was supposed to be the central commanding centre for co-ordinating war activities along the Adriatic coast; and during peacetime, it was used for control and smaller affairs of no military importance.

As his days in the Navy were progressing, Borna found three friends among the seamen who were servicing this centre together with him. The first was Jura, a Croat from the northernmost and multi-ethnic part of Serbia (called Vojvodina), who would usually, by his good nature, prevent quarrels between other members of the platoon—saying that this or that was not worthy of a fight. The second was a tall guy from Rijeka, Croatia, who was calling himself Kit the Drunk although he got seriously drunk only once during the entire time he spent there; and the third was one Slobo from Pančevo in Serbia, who would always say that this or that thing was vicious. Borna, Jura, Kit the Drunk, and Slobo (also known as the Vicious) would have a good time together whenever possible, but all of that was relying mainly on benign stories from the days of their freedom and not on any true, deep friendship. Amongst the four, a special relationship existed only between Borna the Proud and Slobo the Vicious.

The incident which brought two of them closer together was an unexpected but intense drunkenness of Slobo the Vicious in the April of 1985, when he tried to break into a room with ammunition in order to load his *AK-47* and shoot himself—because he received a letter from his girlfriend, in which she wrote that she had been living with another guy for three months already. And when he was prevented from doing that, he tried to stab himself using an army knife. He was an extraordinarily strong man, and Borna (who was rather strong himself) had to ask for the help of three more men to restrain him. Then they forced Slobo to drink more than half a bottle of brandy in about twenty seconds, afterwards staying with him until he was completely drunk and helpless. Borna remained with him the whole night, taking care that nothing bad would happen.

'Where is Seaman Slobo?' a sergeant known as Pero the Cannon asked in the morning. He was an artillery specialist who, by some strange circumstances, ended up in a Navy unit stationed on the shore, probably because he was already old and useless in artillery troops but had considerable experience in disciplining the conscripts.

'He's sick, comrade Sergeant Cannon!'

'Is he? And don't you ever again call me Cannon, Seaman Didić. I am Sergeant Kovačić for all of you!'

'Yes, he is, comrade sergeant! And yes you are, comrade Sergeant Kovačić! Yesterday we had quite a few cans of old beans'

'And nothing happened to you, Seaman Borna?'

'No, comrade sergeant, I don't eat much.'

'Well, well. How much did he eat? A bottle or less?'

'Half a bottle but the slivovitz was strong, comrade sergeant! Maybe a bit more, but trust me that the slivovitz was very strong.'

'When he sobers up, the toilets are his for three days in a row. And I'll inspect them every morning.'

'Yes, comrade Sergeant Kovačić! And I'll take the first of his shifts! I'll do the first cleaning myself, comrade Sergeant Cannon!'

'Go to hell, Borna. Shut up, dear boy. I want to see all of you fit tomorrow and the toilets as clean as an operating table. Now get out of my sight and find yourself a place to sleep.'

Just as every father of a young son always is, Pero the Cannon was an understanding man. These guys were all between nineteen and twenty, he thought, how do you make an army with such children? Another thing that worried him was the influence of politics on the daily lives of his young seamen. After Tito had died, things were getting worse and worse:

everyone suddenly spoke of nationality and how Yugoslavia was bad because one was oppressed and humiliated by the others on the basis of one's ethnicity—and this was going on amongst all the nations of Yugoslavia, which were all providing the conscripts. One of the reasons why he reacted so mildly was that Seaman Borna, a Croat, had tried to protect his Serbian comrade, Seaman Slobo, which was an episode that was bringing him some hope. Originating from a Croatian-Serbian marriage, he was before all a Yugoslav. Scrubbing the toilet for a few days seemed to be enough. Unlike some of his colleagues, he felt no sadistic satisfaction in that.

After this incident, the Vicious would be mainly silent. His enforced drunkenness had not been recorded officially—since Pero the Cannon knew how to deal with the crazy age of his soldiers and possible consequences of their occasional madness—but Slobo was still avoiding alcoholic drinks and did not want to go to the doctor to get some tranquillisers either; then Borna somehow got a stash of weed from Kletina, and they would spend hours and hours together under a tree with a joint, laughing at the world and at each other. It was then when they became close friends, sharing more than it would be usual for two conscripts who had not known each other just a year ago. Kit the Drunk and Jura would join them occasionally, but it was clear that the shade of that tree belonged to Borna the Proud and Slobo the Vicious.

In August, their going home was just a month away.

Just a few days before they were finally going to be free again, they had a quarrel. Slobo was again in one of his moods about his girlfriend, and Borna was too much into his leaving to be willing to hear about that once more. Pero the Cannon was at the same time quite nervous, because an Albanian and a Montenegrin had had a fight that weekend, and this was dangerous: two mutually hostile ethnicities having a brawl during his weekend shift in the barracks! Then, to make things worse, the local Croats organised some motorbike races around the barracks, shouting against Yugoslavia and provoking the soldiers as if there was no Croatian conscript inside. Eventually Pero called his superiors: a colonel came and put the whole barracks on red alert—with ammunition distributed and the arms therefore ready for use. This alert lasted intermittently for the whole of the following week, and it looked like a war had started.

This was an early sign that Yugoslavia was going to disintegrate rather soon, just as Vladimir Količek had predicted.

Borna took an opportunity to leave when things temporarily settled down just for a day, whereas Slobo had to stay there not only for three more days—as it had been scheduled—but for a full month instead. One cannot rule out that Borna was released so easily because no Croat was fully trusted in the barracks any more. Slobo and Borna had never said a proper goodbye to each other, which Borna regretted for the rest of his life.

In Basel, in the tranquillity of his last days—when he was dying from an incurable sadness—he would often remember Slobo the Vicious. Did he survive the madness? Did he ever find another woman? Did he father a child? Did he ever remember their days under the tree? Did he remain the good man he had been? These days in Basel—when it was impossible for Sara to understand why her man was behaving so strangely—Archibald would never say a word about the Vicious, just as he would not say a word about anyone. In any case, Slobo was one of those people who appeared in front of Archie's tired eyes before he went to sleep for good.

XIII

1941, Belgrade, Danube Banovina & Sarajevo, Drina Banovina Kingdom of Yugoslavia

As it had been usual for half a year already, that Monday in March, Colonel Količek received a visit from Captain Malcolm Forbes—an intelligence officer at the British Embassy—who was an elegant, thin Scotsman from Aberdeen, with thick moustaches.

Over the past few months, they had been playing a game of cat and mouse: Forbes would always ask about the general military situation in the region—and he would invariably get detailed information on that—but when he would ask about the Royal Yugoslav Army viewpoint and activities, including strategic and tactical issues, Količek would start talking about Tarzan, never failing to emphasise that Johnny Weissmuller—who was portraying Tarzan in the films—had been born as Johann Peter Weißmüller on the Romanian side of the Yugoslav-Romanian border, being a Banat Swabian.[‡‡] Had the border been drawn just a bit differently after the Great War, he could have been listed as a Yugoslav citizen prior to obtaining an American passport in 1924, Vladimir would remark. Did the honourable Captain Forbes see the last Tarzan film? It was a very entertaining one, and also children could learn much from the moral standards evident in this motion picture.

It was quite clear, however, that Količek had no sympathies for the Axis Powers—in spite of his reluctance to share his knowledge of the current Yugoslav military affairs with the UK intelligence—and Forbes respected both this standpoint and the Tarzan stories as a way out from

---

[‡‡] Banat is a region on both sides of the present-day Serbian-Romanian border.

potentially long periods of tense silence. He was also aware of Količek's legendary episode in Tirana, where he had brought the Italian and Greek intelligences to their knees and possibly planted the seed of Albanian resistance to the Italians and any other possible invader. On a few occasions, he asked Količek about these events, and Vladimir would just grin and say that the only notable thing about Ciano was that he was Mussolini's son-in-law, so under these circumstances, his job had been everything but difficult.

Their meetings would always finish with a good lunch and the best wine one could find in Belgrade, and this demeanour of Količek added to Malcolm's admiration for his colleague—who was by all means a pleasant companion, widely educated and broadminded. Vladimir also liked his younger counterpart, considering him to be an excellent intelligence officer and a man of distinction. There was an intangible sympathy between them.

On the twenty-seventh of March, riots broke out in Belgrade, and the government was overthrown after it had been forced by intimidation to join the *Tripartite Pact* of Germany, Italy, and Japan. This episode received a cold reception among the non-Serbs in the country, who cared little about the Serb-dominated kingdom, why and who ruled it and with what agenda. By contrast, Malcolm Forbes was enthusiastic about the turn of events—which meant, as he thought, a definite change towards the UK becoming the main Yugoslav ally—but Colonel Količek sobered him up during their last regular meeting.

'Pack your things, dear friend. Soon it will not be safe here, neither for me nor from you,' Vladimir advised him. 'The Germans, the Italians, and the Hungarians are ready at the borders. We're doomed.'

'But…'

'But? If the Germans found you here, you wouldn't survive. They would definitely torture you, in any case, and their methods are extremely brutal. I know everything—so please trust me and pack your things.'

'Where shall we go?' asked Forbes, suddenly becoming aware of the seriousness of the situation.

'To Sarajevo, which is as far as anything can be from the borders, and I also know some people in the city. I could hopefully protect you there, because the Croats will take control over the city, and I'm a Croat. They'll not kill me; they'll negotiate with me. With some luck, you might even leave for Britain before they come.'

'The Croats? But they've got no army…'

'Mussolini trained and armed them, and they will come. Just trust me and pack your things as soon as you can.'

Hence, on the fourth of April—exactly two years after he had fled from Albania—Colonel Vladimir Filip Količek, the last Head of the Military Intelligence of the Kingdom of Yugoslavia, and Captain Malcolm Archibald Forbes, a British Intelligence officer at the embassy in Belgrade, took a car and headed towards Sarajevo. Their vehicle was stopped several times by irregular Serbian nationalist troops called the Chetniks—who were on the alert, foreseeing the Axis Powers attack and knowing the weakness of the regular Yugoslav Army—but since Količek wore his uniform, the royalist Chetniks did not cause any trouble. §§

Nonetheless, it took them quite some time to reach Sarajevo, sleeping in local inns for two nights. And by the time they were entering the city, Yugoslavia had already been attacked by the Axis Powers. Belgrade was savagely bombed by the Germans, and the Axis troops were advancing from all directions while the Yugoslav Army was inefficient in resisting; the troops in which the Serbs did not dominate would usually just surrender without a fight, and the Serbs had to confront modern tanks and aircrafts by using weapons that belonged in a museum.

The lack of any rule would be a good description of Sarajevo in the early April of 1941. Many politicians and influential people from all over

---

§§ *Četa* (*cheta*), meaning *troop*, is the origin of the name *Chetniks (troopers)*. They were originally armed men from the early twentieth century, recruited among the Orthodox Christian nations in the Balkans to fight the Turks. In World War I, they fought bravely as irregulars within the Royal Serbian Army but were always known for their aggressive Serbian nationalism. In World War II, their behaviour was complex, but they eventually sided with Fascist Italy and Nazi Germany.

Yugoslavia did the same as Količek did and came there, so the city was full of wealthy refugees from various parts of the country. They were of different nationalities, and soon a differentiation with regard to one's ethnicity began—as the Catholic Croats and the Muslims of Sarajevo (who suddenly started to express a Croatian national feeling) started to occupy vital positions in the city, expecting enforcements from elsewhere. They would frequently ask a passer-by about his or her nationality, which was a bad omen; they would, however, seldom react immediately. The Serbs realised the danger, and many of them fled to the nearby hills held by the Chetniks. The Jews were living in fear from just about everyone, and the people of other nationalities were mostly confused (those who had a protector would feel somewhat safe).

The protector of Malcolm Forbes was Vladimir Količek, who in the meantime, had changed into civilian clothes.

'Do you speak any German?' he asked Malcolm.

'Not a word.'

'But you still could say: *Ich bin Deutscher?*'

'I guess I could.'

'All right, just babble whatever you want in a Germanic way—but it shouldn't sound English. All of them can barely read and write, and this should suffice. As a matter a fact, don't speak at all unless you really have to. If you're asked something, just say *Ich bin Deutscher* using the strongest Scottish accent you know.'

'Is it so dangerous?'

'Just do what I tell you if you want to stay alive. You're a mortal enemy now, this is not Britain. Now practise: *Ich bin Deutscher.*'

'Yhh bean Douechaer. Correct? And later?'

'We must get you out of here, preferably before the fascists come. You'll be sent to the coast. We must find the communists.'

'The communists? Really? Do we really have to deal with these ratbags?'

'If you knew what I know, you'd understand what a silly question you've just asked. The communists, of course. They're the only ones who can help us, the only ones we can trust. So show some respect. They're fanatical and uncompromising, which is so useful to us at the moment.

And they might not even ask for any money, your pistol should be enough to pay for your trip.'

Captain Forbes was hiding in the cellar of the house of an acquaintance of Vladimir, where he was given a meal twice a day but would otherwise feel like a prisoner. The Scotsman, on the other hand, knew that this was necessary.

In the meantime, Colonel Količek started to move about, using his experience from Tirana. It took him some time and money to find 'friends' and connections—on the basis of mutual interest, bribe or manipulation—but he managed to complete this within three days. He found a trustworthy communist, Valter Perić, a Serb who detested the Chetniks (and, of course, the Croatian and Muslim nationalists as well), preparing himself and his comrades for the occupation of the city by the Germans and their local allies. A worldwide communist revolution was his long-term objective, but he was ready to go step by step: at the moment, rescuing a British officer seemed to be an opportune move which cost little but could bring some future benefits.

This was strange for a communist at the time, when Hitler and Stalin were still allies, but Valter had a mind of his own: he knew that the love between the Nazis and the Bolsheviks could not last long (which turned out to be so true some two months later, when Germany attacked the USSR).

In all of that chaos, the communists managed to transport Forbes to the Adriatic coast safely, where he was picked up by a British submarine after the Chetniks had conveyed the information on him for an ample amount of money (only the Chetniks had a few open channels for communicating with the UK, since the regular army was in confusion). The money for the Chetniks was provided by Količek, and the communists were paid by getting the Forbes' pistol.

Just before he left Sarajevo, Malcolm gave a piece of paper to Količek. He explained, 'I'm so grateful, you've saved my life. I don't know that I will ever see you again, but me and my family will always be indebted to you. And we're the Scots from Aberdeen, we never forget either bad or good done to us. If you or any of your descendants will ever need help, just come to Aberdeen, pronounce the verse written on this piece of paper and say that you're Falcon's Eye. And we'll help no less than you've helped me.'

They hugged each other as gentlemen should: showing little emotion but much affection. Then they shook hands and saluted to one another as officers should. After the car carrying Forbes to his rescue journey had left, Vladimir read the note:

An eclipse is upon us, but it will pass away, as it has never happened that a night is not followed by a day.

XIV

1941, Sarajevo
Independent State of Croatia

German-occupying forces entered Sarajevo on the fifteen of April without facing any resistance.

Vladimir was keeping a low profile as a quiet lodger in the house of a respected Muslim solicitor he had met some years ago, the same one who was hiding Forbes before his departure. To stay in the centre of Sarajevo was the most reasonable choice, because different militias and irregulars in nearby villages and smaller urban centres were taking advantage of the chaos and behaving like predatory beasts in search for any helpless prey, showing little respect for human life and being interested in plunder only. The Germans, on the other hand, were focused on securing the city and its infrastructure for their needs, showing little interest in local affairs; they were even paying no attention to the Jews—whose presence was more than obvious, as they owned many shops in the old part of Sarajevo. There were also two synagogues—one for the Sephardic community and one for the Ashkenazi Jews.

During the night from the twenty-third to the twenty-fourth of April, the first Ustashas arrived in Sarajevo, since the city had become part of the recently established Independent State of Croatia. In the weeks that followed, it became clear why the Germans were so uninterested in civilian matters: this business was the responsibility of the quisling Croatian state which not only copied the Nazi racial laws but also added some of its own. The main targets were the Serbs—the old Croatian rivals for supremacy in Bosnia and Herzegovina and beyond—while the Jews were, as everywhere else in Europe, guilty of everything. Until then, the Croats had seldom expressed any animosity towards the Jews (some of whom had been, in fact, convinced Croatian nationalists), but the new European order urged the Ustashas to start persecuting them immediately. In any case, it did not take long before the Ustashas started to round up the Serbs and the Jews, who would then be taken in an unknown direction never to return; this scenario was repeated for the next four years of the war.

Vladimir knew that he could not hide forever. It was, therefore, wiser to reveal his presence and start negotiating than to try to escape to Kletina which was almost five hundred kilometres away. His main asset was very simple: the young quisling state had to establish a regular army—it could not rely on a handful of twisted minds in black Ustasha uniforms—and there was a desperate need for qualified personnel capable of doing that. The number of Croatian and Muslim officers in the Royal Yugoslav Army had been rather small, so every trained soldier of a 'right nationality' was a valuable candidate for becoming an officer in the new army. Even the old ones from the time of Austria-Hungary were very much welcome. Količek hated the fact that he had to do it, but he simply had no choice; it was important to survive this initial bloody turmoil and wait for things to settle down at least partially—and then he could decide what to do, not before.

'Good day. I am Vladimir Količek from Kletina in North Croatia, a Croat and former colonel. Here are my papers,' said Vlado to an elderly man sitting behind a desk in the lobby of a house with a kind of Croatian flag hanging on the facade. The flag was clearly made from a Yugoslav one— turned upside down so that the order of the colours was red-white-blue and not the opposite, with a shabby patch representing vaguely the historical Croatian coat-of-arms (a red-white chessboard).

The man wore a uniform that was matching the flag: it was an old, stinky and dirty uniform of the Royal Croatian Home Guard of Austria-Hungary, with the insignia replaced with the ones of the new state. Vladimir turned around and saw that the people had all kinds of uniforms: Yugoslav, Italian, German, Turkish, French… And one even wore Cossack clothes from the Bolshevik revolution. The weapons they had were no different: from virtually all European countries and wars in the last half a century. At some point, a young man entered the building with a flintlock musket from the time of Napoleon!

'Well, well,' said the old man in a squeaky voice, in the local dialect. 'What have we got here... A traitor? A Chetnik? Human scum, I say!'

Količek remained silent. The old man was silent. They gazed at each other.

'A Croatian patriot and professional soldier, that's who I am! And I demand to speak with someone of my rank!' Vlado suddenly shouted so loud that the whole lobby went quiet. He knew that he had to attract attention. 'Or would you like to try to organise this mob into an army, you and not the people like me?'

The man behind the desk did not know what to say—he did not expect such a reaction, and suddenly he did not know what to do. He immediately regretted saying things he had said, and all of that became simply too much for his lazy brain. This brain could only process a proclamation that Bosnia and Hercegovina were always Croatian—which must have been true since he had heard that at a Sunday Mass from his almighty Catholic priest (hence, this was obviously what Jesus wanted!). For this reason, he had taken his old uniform from the wardrobe and again joined the forces of Jesus against the Serbian supporters of the Great Schism. But then everything became so complicated. The old man started to think that all of this was too much for him, and he started to sweat.

'Back off, Joso!' Količek heard a voice behind him. 'This is not your jurisdiction! I'll take care of that.'

Joso was relieved when he heard that, as he really did not know what to do.

Vladimir turned around and saw a short man in his thirties, wearing a considerably tidier uniform—probably of an Italian origin, since its colour was a kind of olive green.

'I'm Captain Banić, sir. Would you kindly follow me, please?'

They crossed the lobby and entered a luxuriously furnished big room in which the walls were full of pale rectangles at the positions where some pictures had once been. There were obviously no new pictures to replace them, not yet.

'Please take a seat, sir. Would you care for a glass of cognac? There's plenty of it.'

'No, thank you, dear captain. I prefer to get down to business right away.'

'All right, sir. May I ask you, then, for your name and rank again?'

Vlado recited his personal data in a very official manner; Banić wrote this down and continued,

'Now, tell me more about you…'

And Vladimir talked. Most of the things he said were true, but he was careful to hide tricky details—such as that he had been the main military spy in the collapsed kingdom. He knew that they were going to realise that sooner or later, but this was not the right time to be completely truthful; he just wanted to reach a safer place as soon as possible, in order to assume a position from which he could use his skills in playing the games of cat and mouse. What he insisted on was that he was a staff officer, with considerable expertise in organisation and strategy but with virtually none in training or combat—which was actually true.

The captain was very polite and a good listener. Now and then, he would write down a note or ask a short question, which Vlado took as a good sign. He, however, could not know that this young man was mainly silent not because he was shrewd or knowledgeable in military matters, it was quite the opposite: he was quiet because he was a carpenter by profession, knowing absolutely nothing about the functioning of an army. His notes were: knows how to organise… knows how to manage… understands complications… familiar with ranks… can read maps, etc. Nothing important, in short, and Vlado could have gone without all of that theatrical play in the first place—it would have been just the same.

'You're probably aware, Colonel Količek, that our young state needs a respectable military force in order to become stable and strong. We must mobilise men, train them, and organise the units ranging from platoons to corpses.'

'Of course I understand.'

'And what are your political views?'

'To be honest, I have none. I'm a soldier. But also a Croatian patriot ready to serve my homeland.'

'Good, good. However, you were serving the Serbs as well…'

'As I just said—I'm a soldier. Croatia had no army then.'

'Good, good. Please give me your address in Sarajevo, and don't leave the city. We'll contact you.'

Captain Banić then signed a permit for Vlado, so that he could move freely within the city.

'Carry this with you all the time, before the curfew of course—when you must be at home. I advise you to stay home as much as you can even during the day.'

Vladimir knew well what the reason was for the captain's advice. He had already witnessed intense violence in the streets—occurring even in broad daylight—since the Ustashas would relentlessly chase people, beat them savagely, tie them down and take them somewhere. During the night, he would sometimes hear loud, brutal voices and shots, followed by screams of the victims, whoever they might have been. And when he would leave his humble residence to find some bread and milk early in the morning, he would spot stains of blood on the ancient, paved streets of the old part of Sarajevo; he could also see ruined and plundered Jewish shops, as well as houses marked as 'Serbian house' on the facades.

'I'm Tarzan if this state can survive. To survive? What a silly thought,' Vlado would think in disgust, hating himself for having to sign a pact with the Devil. However, he knew that every contract could be broken.

In about four weeks, he was summoned to the newly established military command of the city, which was in another, bigger building. There, he saw that the carnival with uniforms was over: most of the people were wearing quite decent, greyish uniforms—similar to those of the Austro-Hungarian Royal Croatian Home Guard—and brand new cap badges comprising the Croatian chessboard.

Količek was met not by Captain Banić but by a man of his age. This disrespectful person explained in a few sentences that a train was going to leave for Zagreb in the morning and that Vladimir should be there, or else.... Vlado was going to become an officer in the Home Guard of the Independent State of Croatia, probably keeping his rank. In any case, this was not his business, added the man, since he would never let a servant of the Serbs, a Chetnik in his heart, become a Croatian officer.

Vladimir looked at this insignificant individual and remained calm. There was no reason to get excited: a new career ahead of him required a cool head.

XV

1941, Savnik & Malo Selce, Gora County Independent State of Croatia
&
Maribor
Interregnum; collapse of the Kingdom of Yugoslavia followed by Slovenian Styria becoming part of Nazi Germany

Ljerka was by her nature a defiant person, never afraid of anyone or anything and always ready to fight back—but she was really scared this time.

She was, together with her daughters and mother, virtually a prisoner in her own house. Two Ustashas would be in front of the house day and night, waiting for an order to kill 'the Serbian whore and her bastards' in case Lieutenant Jarbašić had fled from the Home Guard. An Ustasha officer—who was a barely literate shepherd from rocky Herzegovina mountains—instructed them not to waste bullets but to use knives and hammers instead, since 'the Serbian scum should die in pain'. However, the Ustasha guards were not at ease with their assignment, because they had been warned by a local to think twice before attempting to harm German people.

The local knew that the surname of Klara—and the maiden name of Ljerka, of course—was Zultner, therefore unmistakably German; there were no Jews with this surname, not only in Savnik but perhaps also worldwide, since it originated from a single village in Transylvania, where no Jew ever lived. Moreover, it was also well known that Klara was not an easy person to deal with. And only God could have helped these Ustashas if they had ever tried to provoke her, as she was capable of alarming Hitler himself, the local was thinking. He was aware of that, but he did not say a word about Klara's personality to the guards—he only explained to them that the surname Zultner was exclusively German and that this fact should be taken into account with caution. After leaving the Ustashas worried, he started to think what would have happened if they had harmed Ljerka or the girls.

'You've given weapons to these Balkan scoundrels so that they could kill the daughter and granddaughters of a German officer who had fallen in the Great War for the glory of the German nation? Is that what we can expect—to be slaughtered by the Balkan people while the Germans elsewhere prosper?' Klara would probably say, in perfect German and in every German office between Savnik and Berlin; and at least one of the offices would pay attention. This one office would have been quite enough to make life miserable for the entire Ustasha garrison in Savnik.

The local did not like this sudden coming of wild peasants from southern parts of the country into the urban area of Savnik. As much as he detested the Ustashas in front of the Zultner house, he was perversely hoping that they were eventually going to kill someone there and thus cause a brutal German revenge. A small price to be paid—only a few partly-German lives—for establishing peace and order in this town again. Only a few months ago, this ordinary man would have not even thought about something so horrible, but the savagery of that time planted all sorts of crooked ideas into people's minds.

It was December, six months after Ljerka and the girls had moved from Maribor back to Savnik—where Klara was living in the old family house—and the future of the family did not seem bright. They constantly had to do this or that just to emphasise their right to continue living—and almost no one was their friend. The only thing that was keeping them alive was this surname Zultner—and the reason was mainly, as already said, the fact that Klara was known as a nasty and uncompromising widow of a German solicitor. Only the fear of Klara's anger—and not any love or sympathy for the family—was helping them survive. It was then when a girl from the neighbourhood gave a Russian nickname Babuška to the mean woman across the fence—whose appearance and behaviour revealed, people thought so, some genuine Eastern wickedness. Klara Zultner went to the grave with this nickname although she never had anything to do with Russia (which was in Savnik before the war considered to be the source of every evil in the world).

This whole situation was so complicated and difficult, thought Klara. She and Ljerka would sometimes feel completely alone and helpless, because the natural protector of the house, namely Srdjan, was not with them.

The wonderful life of Ljerka and Srdjan in Maribor ended abruptly when German troops captured the city in a matter of hours, being resisted only weakly by a handful of fanatical officers and bewildered conscripts. Srdjan was not one of them; soon after the beginning of the invasion, he attempted to escape in order to take care of his family, but he was captured by the Germans and put in an improvised camp for prisoners of war. He spent a month and a half there while Ljerka and the children were fortunately left alone after changing the name on the door to Zultner.

Just a few days before a relocation of the prisoners of war to Austria—to work as slaves in the industry of the Reich with slim chances of survival—Srdjan was at the door of his flat, and no words could properly depict the excitement of the young couple: everything was wet from happy tears, kisses and warm hugs did not stop for hours, and so on. Srdjan then explained that this was most probably not the end of their suffering, since the reason for his release was a request of the Independent State of Croatia that every officer originating from there—regardless of nationality—should be returned to Croatia. Ljerka saw that as the end of their troubles but Srdjan was restless.

'May God have mercy on our souls,' was a thought which crossed his mind. There were rumours…

They had been transported directly to Savnik, where Srdjan again ended up in a camp for prisoners of war—this one held by the Ustashas. Just as every other Serb in the camp, he had to wear a piece of blue fabric around his arm; the Jews had to wear yellow ones, whereas the Gypsies were easily recognised and therefore excused from this bizarre fashion.

Ljerka took her daughters to the family house, where she found only Klara; her sister had got married and moved out in the meantime, whereas their brother had not yet returned from the war although they had heard that he was alive. When she saw her mother, Ljerka ran towards her like a small lost girl and wept,

'They took Srdjan, mother. The last time I'd seen him had been when we'd got off the train. I feel so helpless and I don't know what will become of us.'

'They probably took him to the camp. It's in the northern outskirts. They do that with every man in uniform and with many others.'

'But who are "they"? Those people in black? They seem so primitive and violent.'

'Yes, the Ustashas. Scum.'

'The Ustashas?'

'Yes, people like our neighbour Marko. Drunks and bums who have finally found their role under the sun.'

'Like Marko? Then it can't be good.'

'No, it's not, and this is why we must act immediately. They are rounding up the Serbs, the Gypsies, and the Jews, often taking them somewhere after a few days. No one knows where. None of them has returned so far. However, it seems that it's different with captured soldiers, and this is where I see a chance.'

'What chance, mother?'

'To make Srdjan an officer in the Home Guard, this might save him. But we must do it today, because a day is a long time.'

'But how... What should we do?'

'There are some of your nice dresses still here, I've saved them. And some of your makeup. Make yourself looking like a true lady, girl, and then I'll tell you what to do. I'll be looking after my sweet granddaughters in the meantime. Go now and do that.'

Ljerka rushed into the bathroom nervously, and nothing she wanted to do was going smoothly; then she sat for a while and told herself that this was not the time to be awkward or confused: she had to save the life of her beloved husband! In half an hour, she returned to the living room, looking like Greta Garbo.

'So, mother, here I am.'

'My dear, I've forgotten how beautiful you are!' exclaimed Klara. 'You'll bring them to their knees.'

'The Ustashas?'

'No, the Germans. We should avoid these Ustasha lowlifes. You will now go to the German command of the town. Immediately.'

'To the Germans? But Srdjan is held by the Ustashas…'

'Ustashas, Ustashas, blah, blah, blah. German puppies—they do what they're told to do. You'll speak only German and ask for *Hauptmann* Schmidt. He's a polite Austrian whose father knew your father. Both of them were solicitors by profession, and I think that Captain Schmidt met your father once when he was a boy. You'll say that you're Ljerka Zultner—don't mention the surname Jarbašić immediately—and explain that you are the daughter of the late judge, Dr Johann Zultner from Itonok. Once you're alone with him, you can speak freely and ask him for help.'

'Will he help?'

'I hope so. Just remember to repeat all over again that it would be tragic if two German girls were left fatherless because of some Balkan quarrels.'

Ljerka understood and then suddenly saw a light at the end of the tunnel; and she again became that defiant girl she had been for her whole life. She took a deep breath and started to walk towards the door, swaying her hips purposely—in order to practise for her role.

'Dear, just one more thing.'

'Yes, mother?'

'Do whatever you can to avoid Hans Otto from the neighbourhood, he wears an SS uniform now. He's always had a crush on you, and it wouldn't be wise to let him know about our problem.'

'Don't you worry, mother. And… About you…'

'Yes, dear?'

'Please don't drink while you're alone with the girls.'

'I'll drink whenever I want and whatever I want, even water at times. But not this time,' replied Klara with a comforting smile on her face.

Srdjan was home by sundown. He still had to wear the blue thing around his arm outside the house, but he was alive. Ljerka did not tell him that the whole affair was more serious than he thought, and that the only way to remove the threat at least temporarily was his converting to Catholicism; in fact, this was part of the deal she had made with *Hauptmann* Schmidt—who had to think about local matters as well.

Schmidt said that he was not almighty, and given the objective situation, that this was the only solution he could think of. Being a Zultner, Ljerka was German as far as he was concerned, he remarked, but Srdjan was a Serb—so he was able to protect, to some extent, her and the girls but not Srdjan. He also advised her to speak German in public as much as possible—to emphasise her German ancestry. He knew an important officer in the Home Guard, and he promised to contact him and ask for help—but Srdjan's conversion to Catholicism was the only guarantee that he could be safe regarding the murderous hostility of the new state towards the Serbs.

Srdjan Jarbašić was utterly surprised when he was summoned to the headquarters of the First Home Guard Corps of the Independent State of Croatia, stationed in Savnik, only a week after his release from the camp. He was in a brand new uniform of the Home Guard, and he kept the rank of a lieutenant—which was not surprising, actually, because the new army lacked qualified personnel so desperately—but he still had to wear a blue armband. He was commanding a platoon composed entirely of the Serbs who were more or less in the same situation: some wore a blue armband and some did not—as these had already converted to the Roman Catholic faith. In this absurd situation, the commanding officer was, in fact, less powerful than some of his subordinates—and such an army wanted to wage a war against the communists who were giving refuge to every persecuted soul regardless of anything! It was clear even at the beginning of the war that this army was doomed to be totally incapable.

'Lieutenant Jarbašić? Please wait here, sir, and the Head of Staff will see you soon' said a polite young man, obviously a conscript, who clearly knew who Srdjan was.

In less than ten minutes, the young man came again and directed Lieutenant Jarbašić towards a door ajar at the end of the corridor. Srdjan knocked, no one replied; and then he simply entered, saluted and said,

'Lieutenant Srdjan Jarbašić at your service, sir!'

The officer he had addressed was searching for something under the desk, so Srdjan could not see his face; and when he stood up, his smile became so familiar: it was Colonel Količek.

'My dear young man, dear colleague and comrade, it's so nice to see you again! I know that life has not treated you well lately, but you could hopefully forget about your worries from now on,' Vladimir greeted Srdjan warmly while shaking his hand. 'Please take a seat, dear lieutenant.'

'But how…'

'Calm down, dear comrade, everything always settles down by itself eventually. We just have to give it a proper push when the conditions are right especially if playing a game means to have stupid Ustashas as the opponents.'

'Well, they may be stupid, but this doesn't make them less dangerous. My wife trembles with fear because of them as we speak, in her own house.'

'Yes, they're nasty beasts, stupidly instinctive ones. Like lions in a pride. But if you isolate one of them, it's so easy to control him. Then you do the same with another one, like Tarzan used to. On the other hand, one can never be careful enough, because even a trained lion can bite you.'

'You've got a luxury to try that, not me,' replied Srdjan, gradually becoming more and more relaxed. 'See how marked I am? Lieutenant or not, I'm still a detested Serb.'

Then he showed his armband. It was just a dirty rag—the Ustashas were not stylish in marking their enemies.

'Well, this is one thing I can't help you with. In these matters, only the Ustashas decide. They don't trust any of us irrespective of our ranks. We are, I guess, not good enough Croats in their eyes. Such a silly standpoint—that I'm not a Croatian patriot simply because I'm not murderous! Anyway, let me get down to business immediately, we haven't got much time. Even the fact that your wife is half German won't help you any more. This has saved your life for a while, but that's as far as it could go. Some other things must be done.'

There were a few minutes of silence after Vladimir said that; he poured cognac into two glasses, handed one to Srdjan, sat down and took a sip. He was obviously waiting for Srdjan's reaction. And Srdjan, feeling that, was thinking intensely what his next question should be. Then he asked, 'So, will we have to live like that for the rest of my life? Me with a blue rag around my arm, and she facing two mindless black uniforms with sharp knives every time she wants to take the children out?'

'Not for the rest of your life, what a silly thought, I would be Tarzan if this happened. But something must be done to make your life long enough, and this is why I've called you to see me.'

'So you know the whole situation?'

'Guess.'

'All right, I remember you from Maribor—you obviously know.'

'Drink your cognac, Srdjan, and think about your situation in all of this madness,' said Vladimir after taking another sip. 'Once in a while, a man must sign a contract with the Devil at least temporarily. Later—when the madness has gone—this contract can be broken. The Devil is not such a clever creature as everyone thinks.'

'What do you want to say, sir?'

'It's about removing this rag from your arm.'

Srdjan immediately realised what Količek was talking about: he knew how the armbands had been removed from some of the soldiers from his platoon.

'Do you speak about my converting to Roman Catholic faith, sir? I'm not sure I could do that. We're talking about my abandoning the religion of my forefathers, the faith I grew up with, then there's the loyalty to my parents and my whole family in Malo Selce…'

Vladimir gave him some time, and Srdjan used it to talk about his childhood, his feelings and beliefs, the saint of his family (St John) and religious celebrations in his village, marriages in the local church and funerals at the local cemetery—all of that led by their good priest Manojlo.*** At the end of his monologue, he started to talk about Christmas—the last one he had had with his father in particular—and his eyes became wet. He stopped there.

*** In the tradition of the Serbian Orthodox Church, every family chooses a saint as a protector; there is no such tradition among the Croats.

Vlado poured more cognac into the glasses and took a deep breath, knowing that it was not going to be easy to fight against strong emotions.

'Believe me that I understand you fully. However, this is a dirty game—if you don't do it, they'll kill you and your children. The wife might survive because of her ancestry, but even that is not certain. In this mad world, things change on a daily basis, and just one lunatic is enough to end a story.'

'Would you do it? Would you change your religion just like that?'

'Young man, I've already signed a pact with the Devil, and changing religion would be just another signature on this unholy contract. I repeat—every contract can be broken. And yes, I would do it if this saved the lives of those I care about. Keep in mind that all of that can be reversed when the right times come. And I'm sorry that I must say this, you've got to decide now—since time is running out.'

'Running out?'

'Yes—running out. This is why I summoned you so urgently. You've already been scheduled for execution together with your daughters, even the executioners have been selected. They think you're too much of a threat now when the forests are full of the Partisans and the Chetniks. It is known that there are many Partisans of Croatian nationality, so what could they expect from a Serb who is not Catholic—this is their reasoning.'

'No choice?'

'None whatsoever. Sign this, it states that you agree to be baptised in a Roman Catholic church on the twenty-second of December, shortly before Catholic Christmas. I found a remote church where this will be barely noticed, and I bribed the priest. The days before that will give you some time to make peace with yourself, and your signature in the Catholic Church books will also cancel the order for the execution. Be also aware that I'm doing this behind the back of the Ustashas and that my intervention is completely illegal. Therefore, if we want this to succeed, you must sign it right now.'

Lieutenant Srdjan Jarbašić took a pen with a trembling hand, shook his head and signed the document by moving the pen over the paper slowly, in disbelief.

'Why are you doing that? Why are you helping me?' he asked when everything was over.

'Because you're a decent and honest family man guilty of nothing. And because I despise this despicable and twisted state and everything that it represents. I'm not done with it yet.'

Later on, their emptying the bottle of cognac helped the conversation become more relaxed. Eventually they made another deal: before Srdjan's conversion, he was going to be allowed to visit Malo Selce (as an Orthodox Christian, possibly for the last time), and Vladimir was also going to provide him with some paints and brushes so that he could paint St John in Orthodox style, in order to keep the memory of both the church in Malo Selce and his family tradition. This was very important to Srdjan, as he was about to become someone else; he simply had to leave a trace of who he had been for his whole life—and who he was going to remain secretly no matter what. The painting was going to be hidden by Vladimir until the dawn of a better time.

Srdjan managed to paint his protector St John in only two days, and the painting looked like it was from a shrine from the early times of Christianity; from somewhere in Greece or Asia Minor and from the epoch when the Byzantine Empire had been the main protector of the new religion. Two days later, Srdjan and Vladimir were in a car heading for Malo Selce.

They were accompanied by a number of soldiers on motorcycles with sidecars, because the forest was full of the Partisans and the Chetniks—who were attacking every uniform on the road. As a matter of fact, their behaviour towards civilian population was not much better than that of the Ustashas: they would occasionally burn down an entire village and kill the villagers, for political reasons or in revenge for an unresolved personal dispute from the past. There were some differences though: while the Ustashas targeted Serbian villages for no reason whatsoever, and the Chetniks were doing the same with Croatian villages, the Partisans were not obsessed with one's nationality. They would attack every individual or village suspected of collaboration with either the Ustashas, the Chetniks or the Germans; they would also—because of their communist animosity towards capitalism—sometimes execute a wealthy merchant or the owner of a lucrative business of any kind. No one was safe, in any case, in the lands of everlasting war.

Nevertheless, the journey of Količek and Jarbašić went smoothly. At the entrance to the village, they spotted some burnt houses; but when they reached the village centre, they saw that the church was, strangely, intact. The village was spooky, with only stray dogs on the streets and pathways, the human presence being barely noticeable—only here and there, a fast moving silhouette would appear and quickly disappear into an orchard or the ruin of a house.

'Oh my goodness, this… This can't be my village,' said Srdjan. Količek remained silent.

'We should go to my house; I must see what's there.'

They drove for a few more minutes until they reached the big house of the Jarbašić family, built by Stevan Jarbašić during the time of prosperity.

The house was not damaged seriously, but it was obviously empty, with the doors and windows broken. There were three signs on the facade, each in a different colour. One read 'capitalist swine', the other one 'Serbian bloodsuckers', and the third one 'Ustasha, don't return'.

'You see, colonel? You see this hatred?'

'Yes, I do. But calm down my friend, and remember that everything always settles down by itself eventually. Let us check if there is any living soul still here.'

While inspecting the house, they heard a noise in the cellar; and when they opened the door, she was there: Srdjan's great grandmother.

She immediately started to curse them in her own language, which made Vladimir confused.

'Is this Romanian? Portuguese, Galician? How come?' he asked.

'Our old language, some call it the Vlach language. She has never said a word in Serbian. Only once to Ljerka.'

The old woman then recognised Srdjan and started to cry; she rushed to hug him, and the kisses she was giving him almost made Vladimir cry. The situation was surreal: in the middle of an empty house without doors and windows, in a devastated village, there was an old, crying, pale woman overwhelmed by emotions, a young man in uniform, wet from his own tears, and a spectator who did not know what to do with his hands, putting them eventually into his pockets.

'It's you... You've always been a good boy... They're all gone now, but you are here,' said the great grandmother.

'But... Great grandmother, you speak the Slavic language!'

'Of course I do, I used to when I was a child. But I've been refusing to speak it ever since the people became stupid. Your mother, my granddaughter, first of all. I can't speak with you in the old language. And I want to speak with you. They're all gone, you know.'

'I see that, but why?'

'The Chetniks came first, and they took Jovan with them. He didn't want to go, but they took him. A Serb must fight for the king, they said. After five days, the Ustashas came with what was left of Jovan and some others, dead too, and they burnt their bodies here in the garden, behind the house. They set a big fire and were drinking the whole night long.'

'And his family?'

'Went into the woods on time but with some other ones—these wore a red star on their hats. Poorly dressed people, a number of them were the Latins I guess, the others were from our villages here.'

'And who ruined the house?'

'One of them, that no-good relative of ours, Živan of your father's cousin Milorad from the neighbouring village. Milorad left our village in 1932 when you were young. And Živan wrote that thing about you on the wall—that you're an Ustasha. A Latin with a red star wrote "swine". And the Ustashas the third thing, that we're Serbian scum.'

The colonel was sitting on a stone silently, with his hands in pockets. His logic was completely gone, since this was a situation he had never encountered before; in all of his games of cat and mouse, and even in truly perilous situations, like that in Sarajevo, he had never seen such a combination of confusion, emotions, brutality, and despair.

'I'm not done yet with the Ustashas, that's for sure,' he murmured, 'but are they the only bad guys here? Will I eventually have to fight against just about everyone?'

Then he returned to his philosophy that everything eventually settles down by itself: the logical life of Colonel Vladimir Količek was somewhat back.

This was a luxury however, which Lieutenant Jarbašić did not enjoy. He was holding his great grandmother in his arms, crying with her and thinking how small he actually was under this big sky: he had to wear a blue armband, some men in black uniforms wanted to slaughter his girls, his conversion to Catholicism was the only way to save his family and himself, and as if this was not enough, every memory of the happy days of his childhood was shattered.

The two men knew that taking the great grandmother with them would have most probably meant her death—a Serbian woman in Savnik, populated by the Ustashas, could not survive longer than a week, especially with a family that was under a strict surveillance. Količek saw no simple way of hiding her either. Then he proposed that he was going to try to establish channels for the delivery of food and clothes to this place, perhaps even a cow or a she-goat for milk. She could live with that, said the great grandmother.

'Great grandmother, please continue to be a mad old woman who speaks only the Vlach language. This is your passport to survival. This lunacy around us must end at some point, and then we'll meet again. Remember—you must be crazier than the craziest!'

And so it was. The great grandmother survived the war, to die in the ruins of the house in 1952, when she was possibly more than a hundred years old. She and Srdjan never met again.

Ljerka was exhausted from worry. Why did he not tell her what was going on? Klara was a bit dizzy from having drunk too much—nothing serious or unusual—and the girls were asleep. But it was getting dark already, and the curfew was close. Just before Ljerka was about to have a big drink too, Srdjan came home. He did not say a word. He simply started to kiss Ljerka passionately. His hands were all over her body, and when he undressed her, she felt tears on her skin while her wonderful lover was finding a woman inside her, awakening love and passion and making her the queen of the world. That night, their love was at its peak.

'I think that no woman has ever loved a man as much as I love my Srdjan,' was the first thought Ljerka had in the morning.

XVI

1941–1942, Krotko, Vinodol and Podgorje County Independent State of Croatia

In the August of 1941, the Chetniks slaughtered three villagers of Krotko in a nearby forest—where the unfortunate people went to prepare the wood for the winter—and there was much fear in the entire village. The massacre was reported to the Italians—who were the occupying force responsible for Krotko—but they said sarcastically that they had no available units to protect the village and that the Croats should organise their own defence just as they managed to carry out a massive carnage of the Serbs everywhere in the Independent State of Croatia. They had a state, after all, and it was their duty to establish law and order.

From a little more than one thousand four-hundred inhabitants of Krotko, three had joined the Ustashas and two the Partisans; some had been conscripted into the Home Guard, and the others were trying to avoid joining any army by hiding in the forests. The police station close to the post office did not exist any more, which was a new situation because both Austria-Hungary and Yugoslavia had always kept one or two policemen there. Even the French at the time of Napoleon had stationed a few constables in the village, but the new, dysfunctional state was obviously incapable of carrying out its primary duty—to protect and not persecute its citizens. In any case, there was no useful firearm in the whole of Krotko, because two-hundred-year-old muskets and some hunting rifles could not have been taken seriously. This, however, did not prevent Italian Fascists (also in black uniforms, not regular troops) from plundering the village and burning a few houses 'of the worthless Slavs' while searching for weapons, which had occurred before any other soldier was seen in Krotko. Until the capitulation of Fascist Italy in

September 1943, Italian troops of any kind would be seldom be seen in Krotko, and their occasional retaliations for the actions of the Partisans—even when no one from Krotko would be involved—were restricted to shelling from distance or bombing.

The people of Krotko were not only in fear but also completely confused. Having sympathies for the revival of Croatian independence after more than nine hundred years—since Yugoslavia had been generally suppressing Croatian identity by every legal and illegal method—they were eventually thrown into a whirlpool of violence and insecurity. They were peaceful, hardworking, undemanding folks, and—in spite of their enthusiasm for the resurrection of Croatia—they did not understand how harming their Serbian neighbours could bring them any good or why the Serbs would have to attack them. The massacre by the Chetniks was not just a warning that nothing was going to be easy in the near future, it was also the source of a polarisation among the villagers. And there were three factions.

The first one advocated a revenge against the Serbs living in a much smaller nearby village, although it was not certain that the Chetnik perpetrators had come from there.

'An eye for an eye, a tooth for a tooth,' they said, 'and we're stronger in number if not in weapons. We can use axes and scythes.'

The second faction called for a more moderate action, namely to ask for some weapons from the state and to organise guards at some critical points, remaining restrained and avoiding conflict as much as possible in order to prevent more bloodshed.

The third one, led by Josip the Mad Bull and Mile the Angry, proposed that they should blackmail the rich owner of the local sawmill and use this money to convince the Serbs that not only the Ustashas but also the Chetniks were their true, mortal enemies—together with the Italians.

As it could have been expected, the village was not unanimous. The first faction recruited more Ustashas, the third more Partisans, and the second—which had a majority support—was the one that Ivan the Blacksmith chose. Hence, he got an old Czech rifle and five bullets for it, being obligated to spend one day and one night during the week at different posts in and around Krotko. However, this did not prevent him from hiding whenever an army would be close to the village—because each of these armies would recruit young men against their will. In this way, and over the years, several men from Krotko ended up on different frontlines—from Eastern Front or North Africa to Finland, and so on—including those battlegrounds where the Partisans confronted the Germans, the Italians, the Ustashas, and the Chetniks.

Roža was the one who was meticulously organising the hiding of her husband—without even asking him whether she was supposed to do that. Every now and again, she would finish most of her duties around the house earlier than usual and would then simply disappear from everyone's sight, leaving the house to her seven-year-old daughter. Since she was a tough and determined woman, she would never ask the little girl how she felt when being left alone in the house with her two younger brothers, the stove, and the livestock. Among the highlanders, this was obviously not a question to be asked.

Roža set up seven locations, at some distance from one another, where Ivan the Proud would be hiding. At each of these spots, there was a well-concealed fireplace in the rocks, and also canned food and water for at least a few days. Other things, she thought, were not so vital. In addition, she had a rucksack for him at home, containing a small axe, a knife, a spoon, matches, a blanket, socks and underwear, a loaf of bread (replaced every third day), some bacon, and a breviary. She also put a comb, a razor, and a small mirror into a pocket of the rucksack—because her husband might have ended up in the forest for some time, but he should have not become wild. He was her man, and he was not going to become an animal!

Ivan the Blacksmith was, of course, using the hideouts, and he never asked how and when they had appeared in the middle of the wilderness; he knew his wife, and there was no sense in asking anything. She knew him, and she knew that he would never ask. During the winter—which would always be harsh in Krotko—the hideouts were useless, and he would then go higher into the mountain, where they had a small stone house close to the traditional pasture fields of the Didić clan (from the time when they had lived a semi-nomadic life). Fortunately, no army would ever go that far into the mountain through the snow—even the Partisans, forest dwellers, would stay below—and this special hiding place was therefore also quite safe.

After the slaughter by the Chetniks, in about six months, the number of the Ustashas from Krotko increased to seven and that of the Partisans to nine; simultaneously, fourteen villagers were mobilised into the Home Guard. Some of them were volunteers (in the cases of the Ustashas and the Partisans), and some responded to the letters of conscription (in the case of the Home Guard). Additionally, there were some others who were virtually abducted by the armies that were passing by: two by the Partisans, four by the Ustashas, two by the Home Guard, three by the Italians, and one by a German SS unit which appeared out of the blue. These abductions were spreading fear all over Krotko more than anything else, in part because it was very difficult for the abductees to contact their families later.

Roža was always on the alert. She knew that she could have done little if a conscription letter had come, but she was extremely well concentrated on spotting every truck or a column of soldiers on the road, as well as strange, unusual movements around the houses—and she would never get tired of that despite being pregnant again. Just as every other woman in the hamlet, she acquired a dog, and every unexpected motion would always be exposed on time by a barking concert of these hairy protectors of their mistresses. When an Ustasha asked why there were suddenly so many dogs in the village, a woman replied that recently there had been many wolves around; sensing that this might have been ironic, he got angry, but he could not do anything—because the villagers were not the Serbs, the Jews or the Gypsies.

However, troops were coming to Krotko infrequently, because this village was peaceful, and its inhabitants simply wanted to be left alone; a Partisan would occasionally come during the night to fetch some food or clothes from his home and reassure himself that the family was doing fine; or a Home Guard conscript would spend a few days of his leave there free of worries for tomorrow, living only for today. The Italians and the Ustashas moved their units to the areas of heavy fighting, mainly against the Partisans—because the Chetniks had recently become Italian allies, sharing with them an animosity towards any form of Croatian state (following their separate but compatible ideologies of expanding Italy and Serbia at the expense of the neighbours). In early 1942, the police station was re-established at the old place, and a few armed gendarmes would sometimes escort people when they went to work in the forests or on remote fields. The Chetniks almost disappeared from the area, because they did not have enough support for their units on this territory where settlements of the ethnic Serbs were not numerous and had also been largely destroyed in the raids of the Ustashas. The Partisans were also scarce, since the offensives of their enemies had pushed them eastwards, to Bosnia, Herzegovina, and Montenegro.

It seemed that life was back to normal. The only memorable incident was an intrusion of a group of Partisans in May, when they disarmed the gendarmes and went away with their weapons without harming anyone. Roža, then in an advanced stage of pregnancy, became extremely scared of the possible consequences and fled to one of Ivan's hideouts. The incident was considered insignificant by the Ustashas, and was disregarded since no life had been lost and no troops could be spared on such a minor affair. Ivan went for Roža as soon as he could, and she delivered a baby girl at home. Still, after a week, Italian airplanes bombed a Krotko hamlet (about two kilometres from the house of Ivan and Roža) with firebombs, setting four houses on fire; fortunately, no one died and the houses were later rebuilt. The villagers did not make a drama out of this incident, since they knew that they were in the middle of a war and because their ancestors had seen worse.

All in all, in the late summer of 1942, Krotko was an oasis of relative tranquillity in the world that was elsewhere full of grief, death, and destruction: work on the field was mainly over for the year, the cows, sheep, and pigs were still there (although some had been taken by different armies), and preparing the wood for the winter was nearly finished. Moreover, there was no news of any war casualty from Krotko—the Ustashas and the Home Guard conscripts were writing regularly, whereas the Partisans would visit their families occasionally, also bringing news about those who were further away.

However, the last quarter of the year was not happy for the family of Ivan the Blacksmith: a letter of conscription came in September. This was not surprising, because there were rumours that the Partisans were no longer just an annoying, marginal bunch of lightly armed men; several full scale offensives had already been launched against them in East Bosnia and Serbia, with partial success only. This new, more serious war required more soldiers, and altogether seven men from Krotko were consequently mobilised into the Home Guard. Ivan was one of them. Roža was comforting herself by thinking that simple peasants like Ivan would not be sent to the areas of intense fighting—where they would be largely useless even if somewhat trained before—and that they would mostly be used as auxiliary troops in towns, around industrial facilities, railways, and roads. She heard that from other women from the village, which was giving her some hope.

On the other hand, the recent heavy losses of the Partisans had almost eradicated their presence around the border between Bosnia and Serbia, and they started to move westwards, towards the western highlands of the Independent State of Croatia. The Chetniks—who were in good relations with the Italians but not with the Germans—were also moving in the same direction, trying to prevent the Partisans becoming the dominant guerrilla in this area.

This development was not good for Ivan, as Home Guard units were—due to the lack of better soldiers—more and more used in combat. Mainly because of that, he ended up in Herzegovina for a month, where he fought the Chetniks on several occasions, being lucky that the enemy consisted only of lightly armed, small, starved and scattered groups left behind their main troops. Later on, he would never say anything about that until 1993, when he was travelling through the area with Luka and his oldest daughter and started to talk about this part of his life.

Roža eventually found out that her Ivan had really been using his rifle, and she needed no other reason to react immediately. The illiterate, tiny woman found someone who knew the law and military regulations, and after hearing what she needed to hear—which cost her a bag of food and drinks—she went by foot to the county centre, to the local headquarters of the Home Guard, walking for about six hours along a road that was not safe for anyone. She had only a knife to protect herself, but no heavily armed warlord would be a match for her; and as if everyone knew that, the road was clear.

'I want to speak with your chief,' she said to a young guard at the entrance to the headquarters.

'But… You can't. You must have an appointment. No you can't, not even then! We're an army, woman, not a grocery store!'

'Look, you soldier of an army,' Roža stayed perfectly calm, 'I've got a bag here. And in this bag, I've got cigarettes, sausages, bacon, and plum brandy. I can wait until your shift is over and then ask another soldier or I can give this bag to you. Decide now, you soldier. The second bag is for your chief, and I think he might appreciate it. Maybe he'll later treat you better.'

'But… Then… Well… Maybe…' the guard became terribly confused. 'Right, put the bag there behind those planks and ask for sergeant Prpić, he's not the "chief," but he'll tell you what to do.'

It turned out that the sergeant was a distant relative of Ivan, and he listened carefully. Roža cited every (meticulously memorised) word of those paragraphs of the law which were stating that the only supporter of a family should be released from the army earlier in case his family had no means for living. Then she showed him a letter from the owner of the Krotko sawmill, in which it was written that the presence of a blacksmith was essential for the normal functioning of this facility, vital for the area in every respect including military issues. Sergeant Prpić took Roža to the 'chief'—who was a young, melancholic lieutenant from Zagreb—where she again recited her text perfectly and then opened the second, bigger bag that was full of cigarettes, food, and drinks.

On New Year's Eve, Ivan the Blacksmith was again with his family.

XVII

1985–1988, Zagreb & Kletina, Socialist Republic of Croatia
Socialist Federative Republic of Yugoslavia

Borna Didić was an excellent student of chemistry at the University of Zagreb, which had not been so at the beginning of his studies in 1985.

He had returned from the navy in September, and the semester started already in October—hence it was a shock for him to jump so abruptly from military primitivism into the sophistication of academic life. Another shock came from his moving from small Kletina to big Zagreb, where the lifestyle was much different from the one he was used to: he lived as a lodger in a large block of flats, had to use public transport, everyone was posh and frequently arrogant, every street was noisy and crowded, every inn expensive, every lecture room spacious, every professor aloof, every colleague (mainly coming from a better school) wordy, and so on. Because of that, he became quite insecure, and this was possibly the reason why he failed three and passed only two exams at the end of the first semester. However, in the next semester, his hard work and struggle with the developed fears eventually paid off: he passed all the exams, and as a matter of fact, never failed any for the rest of his studying. Maybe his personality lacked many traits that could help make life easier, but stubbornness and persistence were not among them.

Being a healthy young man, he had needs that were beyond his academic challenges—and these were about women.

During his previous years in Kletina, he was reasonably popular among the local girls and was enjoying sex with them from the age of sixteen, but all of his relationships were short-lived and without any significant emotion. At the time, he did not worry much about that and was always satisfied with being able to find a new girlfriend quickly—typically in no more than a few weeks—after the affair with the previous one had ended. However, as a student in Zagreb—meeting many people of his age—he was noticing that virtually all of his friends and acquaintances were finding steady girlfriends while he was always failing in that; when a relationship would apparently start to develop in this direction, the girl would say that there was not enough chemistry and that they should stay friends. After this had become a rule rather than an occasional misfortune, he started to wonder why but was still not panicking; there was a whole life ahead of him, and—as his grandfather Vlado would have always said—the nature of things was eventually to settle down by themselves.

He was visiting Kletina often, during weekends and holidays, and there, he continued to flirt with the local girls, occasionally managing to lure one—sometimes only once and sometimes several times—into the world of passion, which would on many occasions lead to wild sex at strange places such as park benches, bridges, orchards, meadows, backyards, different beds and sofas, bathrooms or pub toilets... As he was becoming more experienced, his skills as a lover were growing, and he became kind of renowned for always bringing something new and exciting into sex. A girl once mentioned that being with him was everything but boring. These rumours, of which he was aware, made him self-confident and somewhat proud, so he had no intention to stop exploring the realm of casual intimacy with young women of Kletina in spite of missing something—and this was to be loved and not just liked for an evening.

In Zagreb, on the other hand, he was much less a seducer and had a reputation as a hardworking student with little interest in girls or partying; an affair he had was barely noticed, probably because it did not last long. He liked more to get involved with the girls from Kletina who studied in Zagreb as well; he would frequently bring one into his Zagreb bed and spend a night or two with her before their relationship would, as always, end due to the lack of chemistry. Therefore, in 1987, Borna Didić was an experienced young lover who had already awakened the lust of about fifteen girls but had never been loved, not even once.

Then he met Suzana and Vesna.

Both of them were from Kletina and despised one another. The reason for that lay in their previous relationships with another young man. They had been competing for his love for a long time, in which the determination to win had been prevalent over romantic reasons. Eventually, the young man found another, less complicated girlfriend. Borna was not aware of this story when he met Suzana—who was three years younger than him and a fresh student at the Zagreb University—one November evening in front of a Kletina pub he frequented.

Suzana was a petite and astonishingly beautiful blonde with big blue eyes and perfect, fair skin; she was dressing casually, and her wonderful curves would be usually hidden by her clothes. She talked much and fast, always smiling and touching Borna with her hand while explaining something, and it was rather obvious that she enjoyed his company a lot. He liked her too—but in a way he had never experienced before: he just wanted to kiss her and hold her, not to simply take her to some place in the dark and take her panties off. Borna was truly in love for the first time in his life, and all of his previous adventures in the realm of sweaty, naked bodies seemed unimportant and superficial. They kissed already at the first date; Borna did not want to go any further than that, and he just walked her home.

They started to meet in Zagreb as well, but she did not want to come to his room for more than two months; and when she finally came, he learned that she was very easily turned on and ready for every lustful game (wet from body fluids and loud from passionate moans and screams) but one, and this was intercourse. For a long time, this did not bother Borna at all, because his strong feelings were making everything extremely delightful and worthier than any of his mechanical climaxes in the past—when his pleasure would last just for a moment and then disappear quickly. However, as it would always happen with steamy young men, his patience eventually started to weaken, and his discomfort began to grow.

Vesna was watching this relationship from a distance. She knew about Suzana's problem to accept a lover fully—since she was told that by the young man who had been the object of their past rivalry and the cause of their mutual hatred. Apparently, this problem of Suzana originated in her mother delivering her at the age of seventeen (shameful, in the eyes of the small town); hence, every danger of this happening again was in her strongly Catholic family fought by proclaiming that intercourse outside marriage was an act orchestrated by the Devil—and every young woman who would question this standpoint was called a whore. Vesna had no such problem, she always enjoyed intercourse intensely. In fact, the foreplay and games leading to the final act were for her just a necessary but not really so much important part of reaching an orgasmic satisfaction. Moreover, she had a years-long desire to find out whether the rumours on the love skills of Borna were true, and the only way to do that was to bring him into her bed. The fact that Suzana was also involved was also more than tempting—since there were some debts to be paid.

While being not so astonishingly beautiful as Suzana was, Vesna was quite attractive too. She was a tall brunette with piercing green eyes, full lips and a slim but curved body that her provocative clothes did not hide. Being also a student, she joined Borna on a train to Zagreb, one Sunday evening, after a weekend they spent in Kletina. A story depicting all the traps she there set for him would be rather long—so it suffices to say that she used his sexual frustration and her aggressive seductiveness to virtually abduct him and throw him under her lustful body the same night. Borna was again riding a big snake of passion, one that would in every such ritual devour the lovers in an instinctive ecstasy. This continued for weeks. He would every second day meet Suzana, playing with her orgasmic games with no intercourse; and the next day, he would go to Vesna, who was giving herself to him completely.

Borna became very confused.

While he did not stop to love Suzana—who was a dear person and to some extent satisfying in bed by her openness to every new thing but intercourse—he simultaneously also became very fond of Vesna, who was less dear but able to fill him with a feeling that he was for her a male in everything that this meant from the beginning of time (although sex with her was instinctive and somewhat mechanical, without fine shades).

He was, as strangely as this might seem, in love with two women at the same time. Their feelings for him were, on the other hand, complex and could not be described as true love—so Borna's failure to find a proper relationship continued. Suzana enjoyed the time with him very much, but she never considered him to be a man who stole her heart for good; Vesna was seeing him as a good lover who was, at the time, the only one she could think of, but it was obvious that a new lover was going to come sooner or later. The fact that these two affairs were going on simultaneously was largely irrelevant for what the feelings of his two girlfriends for him were—as they learned about his deception much later, when all of that had been long gone.

Suzana was the first to break up with Borna, when she realised that he had given her everything she needed: experience in a relationship, self-esteem, sexual versatility, and the feeling of being adored by a man; she was then ready to go on and find someone with that elusive something which Borna simply did not have. This was devastating for him, and he found comfort in turning to Vesna with his whole heart, which calmed him down for a while—since he could finally focus all of his emotions on her only, in bed and otherwise. However, Vesna soon got tired of Borna as well: it was obvious that the chemistry was not right.

Not much longer after this had been over—when it was clear that Suzana and Vesna were gone for good—Borna Didić sat down on a bench close to the chemistry department of the University of Zagreb.

He had just passed another difficult exam, but this was bringing him little joy. During the past months, he had been studying like a lunatic, soon to become the best student in his class, completing one exam after another with tremendous success. On that bench, he started to think that his life was maybe not real at all—that he was perhaps a character from a book or a film. How could one otherwise explain his failure in two very different relationships? Yes, he had made a mistake—being involved with both of them at the same time—but they had never known, and this could not explain a thing. Wait a minute, he thought, perhaps they had smelled one another on my skin and left me because of that? Then he smelled himself, which was silly but he still did it: and there was no odour at all. He did it again under his armpits: nothing, not even the smell of sweat. He started to smell different parts of his body and continued that at home, and he could still not sense anything; then he went to the kitchen and started to smell the food in order to check whether something was wrong with his nose, but the nose was fine.

'Oh my goodness, I think I don't emanate a single pheromone. I'm an odourless person. This was why they left!'

A few days later, he carried out a laboratory test for pheromones on samples taken from various parts of his body—and the result was completely negative. While he was still in doubt about his proficiency in analytical chemistry, the result was at least indicative: he was seemingly fit for charming a girl by his decent look and eloquence, he was apparently a good lover for a few nights, but his chances for finding a woman who was going to see the man of her life in him was… Virtually non-existent!

He had to cope with this new, alarming finding somehow, and the first changes in his behaviour were spotted by his friends who noted that he became somewhat more reserved not only in the presence of girls but also more generally. He also developed a kind of arrogant manners in communication with other people. Before, for instance, he would never use his intellectual superiority to look down on someone who was either uneducated or simply uninformed, but he was no longer pursuing this sort of politeness: the new Borna would often disregard such people completely and without any explanation. Though he would never insult anyone directly, his conduct was similar to our behaviour towards insects: he was no longer paying attention to them, and he did not care whether they lived or not.

He would still have an occasional one-night stand with a girl willing to put up with his new, stylish cynicism, but he was no longer the happy and worriless Borna from the past. In all of that, he was sure about one thing only: his every future relationship was going to be based on some sort of agreement and not on even a vague indication of an everlasting love. He simply did not give forth any pheromone—he was an odourless person.

It was 1988, and due to his obsession, he did not notice how much the world around had changed.

XVIII

1942, Marburg an der Drau, Territory of the Chief of Civil Administration of Lower Styria
Nazi Germany
&
1992, Kletina, Kletina County
Republic of Croatia

Maribor—now called Marburg and der Drau—had changed little since Ljerka had left; the main difference was that she was no longer a citizen of the state the city belonged to. Since there had been no serious military activities during the German capture of the city, the buildings were largely intact, so the only notable changes were the presence of Nazi flags just about everywhere and the new names of the streets, written in German and Gothic script.

She had been advised by some to apply for German citizenship for her and the children on the basis of her father's ethnicity, but she did not do that—because Colonel Količek, a man to be trusted, said that this might not be wise. He remarked that the world was still functioning according to a universal law that things would eventually always settle down by themselves. And this settling down could not bring any good to Germany, he implied. On the other hand, she knew that in Maribor she ought to speak only German and use the surname Zultner whenever she had to present herself. In her documents, however, she was Ljerka Jarbašić, since there was no intimidation, pitiful law or humiliating regulation that could persuade her to give up her devotion to Srdjan. She was his wife, and being a dedicated wife full of love and pride for her husband was the strongest pillar of morality in her life.

The reason why she was visiting Maribor was because she had to obtain a birth certificate for Danka so that the girl could be registered as a citizen of the Independent State of Croatia.

She entered a moderately large building full of Nazi flags on the facade and everywhere inside; this was the same building where she had gone to register Danka in the Citizen Register of the Kingdom of Yugoslavia two and a half years ago. Ever since the war had started, Danka was a stateless person: Yugoslavia did not exist any more, the Independent State of Croatia was still forming, and Nazi Germany was slow and suspicious in granting citizenship to those who had any connection with the Slavs.

'I am Mrs Zultner from Croatia, and I came for the birth certificate of my daughter, born in December 1939,' said Ljerka to a woman behind a desk. She was trying to remain perfectly calm and avoid showing any fear or discomfort; she had all the answers ready.

'Your papers, please,' replied the woman politely, and Ljerka gave her the documents she had from Croatia.

'Yarbassick? But you've said Zultner...' the woman said, pronouncing Jarbašić in the German style.

'My husband's surname. He's an officer in the Croatian Army, which is a German ally. Zultner is my maiden name, it's German and I'm still using it.'

'All right then. Wait here, please,' said the woman and went into a room behind the desk. She returned in about ten minutes, carrying a big book in brand new covers with Nazi symbols and inscriptions in German.

'Here we have your daughter's data, and I'll now write you a new birth certificate. Let me see... Danka-Mathilda Yarbassick, father Srdjan, Greek Orthodox faith, mother Ljerka, born Zultner, Roman Catholic faith...'

'Mathilda?' Ljerka was confused. 'But she is only Danka.'

'Dear lady, no more. Our Reich has added a proper German name to every child that was born in Marburg an der Drau and is still alive, and the name given to your daughter has been Mathilda. The original name is still there to avoid confusion with the church books. But you're German, right? This shouldn't bother you then.'

'No, it doesn't bother me. In fact, it's so nice to again have a proper German name in my family after such a long time,' replied Ljerka full of anger but being careful not to show it.

'Do you want to apply for German citizenship for yourself and your daughter? Both you and she are eligible, you know. And your other children too. You could benefit from being citizens of the Reich.'

'Many thanks, but no. Since Germany and Croatia are friendly states, and citizenship is hence not an issue, it would suffice if you gave me the certificate.'

'As you wish, dear lady. Heil Hitler!'

'Heil Hitler, and have a nice day,' said Ljerka as she left the building as quickly as she could.

Objectively, an extra name on a birth certificate was not something one should be nervous about, especially in this dangerous and mad time, but Ljerka was still very annoyed. Was there another state that was going to interfere with the humble and simple life of her peaceful family? Was this ever going to stop? Who were those people that were pulling the strings and playing with others as if these were just some names on future tombstones? And were there any laws for sanctioning these misdeeds, just as there were so many laws for playing with the very existence of those who never did anything wrong?

In 1992, when Danka went to an office in Kletina to obtain documents from the newly established Republic of Croatia, she was told that she did not exist. This was surreal: once being stateless, she ended up as a nonexistent person. She showed them her documents from Yugoslavia—which she had had for the past forty-seven years and from 1964 onwards as Danka Didić—but in the records, they had Danka-Mathilda Jarbašić-Količek, born on the same day of the same year in the same city as that alleged Danka Didić, as a daughter of Srdjan Jarbašić and Ljerka Jarbašić, née Zultner. There was a Danka Didić, married to Luka Didić, in some documents, but this was still not enough, because the mismatch was too serious and the new state had to insist on clear documentation.

'We can't help you right now,' they said. 'You must prove that you're the person you're claiming to be and then either apply for new documents as Danka-Mathilda or change your name officially to Danka.

Since Danka has been on your other papers from Yugoslavia, we would recommend the second option.'

Consequently, Danka-Mathilda again became Danka—being reborn in a way—and thought, 'Is there another state that would want to interfere with the humble and simple life of my peaceful family?'

But she did not get angry—she knew that she was living in the lands of everlasting war. She mumbled that everyone could go to hell: her boy was safe.

XIX

1942, Savnik, Gora County
Independent State of Croatia

After the blue rag had been removed from his arm, Srdjan was left alone for a while.

The Ustashas were no longer in front of the house; Ljerka was taking care of the household and the girls while he was at work—in the barracks or elsewhere for a few days—whereas Klara was behaving as usual (occasionally having a drink too much, not too often, and would usually be tame). Hence, this war was more and more looking like the previous one: distant frontlines, a corpse arriving sometimes, little food but no one was starving, little money but no one penniless, little freedom but no one was complaining, common people doing common things and uniformed people doing the rest, everything full of propaganda and no one daring to say a word; in the morning, the sun came up, and went down in the evening, and that was more or less it.

Something was making Srdjan uncomfortable though, and this was the leaving of Vladimir Količek a few weeks ago, when the cunning colonel had been assigned to a new, higher position in Zagreb. After he had structured the First Home Guard Corps properly, at least with organisational and administrative issues, Vlado was no longer needed in Savnik, where officers trained in combat were more useful—because the Partisans were growing stronger in the area, and only commanders experienced in battle could fight this dangerous guerrilla effectively by using smaller units. This was, however, working in theory only. In practice, they could not form any troops of well trained and motivated soldiers, because this army was composed of simple peasants who would surrender at the first shot of the frenzied Partisans—as these were merciless whenever someone would shoot back. Since the Home Guard units were pretty much useless, more and more Ustashas—who were no less fanatical than the Partisans—were coming to Savnik.

Srdjan was not involved in these activities, and he was still leading his platoon composed of the Serbs—now all of them without the armbands—to the places where they would usually take the role of guards kept away from any combat. They were useful but not trusted.

The recent appearance of strong Ustasha forces in Savnik was not an immediate threat in the eyes of the Jarbašić family, but they were still sleeping less well. They did not forget 1941 and the danger they had been facing then, and they were also missing Vladimir terribly—as he was the one who had helped them survive, in a somewhat intricate but still elegant way. At some point, Ljerka started to think that she should have accepted the offer to become a German citizen together with her daughters, but it was perhaps too late, and Srdjan was also telling her that Vlado was never wrong—so her decision had most probably been the right one.

These Ustashas were different from the primitive bullies in black uniforms from 1941. First of all, they had brown uniforms and also did not participate in mindless raids against the remaining Jews, Gypsies, and Serbs in the town, leaving this to the locals. Secondly, they would seldom be seen in the inns, appearing in public only when going somewhere for training, reconnaissance or another quiet activity. For a month, not a single action of these Ustashas was spotted or recorded in the area, and everyone started to wonder about the true nature of their assignment.

Ljerka was facing this unclear situation by becoming more and more devoted to Srdjan and the girls. With her husband's help, she built a magical world behind the walls of the house, in which Klara was a queen who remembered her king with love, she an enchanting lady, Srdjan a knight in shining armour, and Barbara and Danka beautiful princesses; thus, every humble supper would be a feast in a castle on a hill, provided by their grateful subjects who felt well under their noble protection. And the magic did not stop there. Srdjan would put his daughters on a small carpet and pull them through the house, because 'they were riding the good dragon Sveznadar', a servant of their house and dear friend. The girls would fly over distant, green lands and would feel protected by the mighty Sveznadar, knowing that nothing bad could happen as long as this good dragon was with them. This was the only memory Danka ever had of her true father. A vague memory—because she had been so small—but the only one she was going to carry with her into the future.

When it was the time for going to sleep, Klara would be the first to leave, then the girls, and Ljerka and Srdjan would do it slowly; they would be finishing chores in the kitchen by watching one another constantly and with lust, which would then explode in their bedroom. Their nights were intense and sweaty, and as if they lived for these hours only—in which their lips were soft and moist, their bodies strong, and their souls free. In the morning, they would again face the grey sky on the other side of the window, but this only meant that they had to survive another day and wait for the next evening to come—in which their kingdom was going to emerge from the world of dreams again. And every single one of these mornings, after Srdjan had left for work, Ljerka would mumble, 'I think that no woman has ever loved a man as much as I love my Srdjan.'

However, since nothing in the life of the Jarbašić family was destined to be simple, one day Srdjan was summoned to the headquarters of the Ustashas (not of the Home Guard!), located in a small building called 'the dark pit' by the conscripted peasants of all nationalities. Srdjan was trembling in fear at first; then he remembered his painting of St John, which was in the hands of Vladimir, and he could only hope that this good man was going to take care of his wife and daughters somehow. And of the memory of his family, represented by the painting of St John, and of his great grandmother in Malo Selce. He suspected that the Ustashas did not call him just to have a nice chat. After the initial minutes of panic had gone, he was at peace with his fate and ready to accept it.

After waiting in the lobby for maybe half an hour, he was escorted by a guard into a shabby looking room in this shabby looking building. There, he found two Ustasha officers in brand new brown uniforms, who were just finishing their supper. Their pistols were on the desk, one Italian-made submachine gun too, and the situation did not look good.

He was standing there for a few more minutes, and then the older Ustasha spoke,

'Lieutenant Jarbašić? At ease!'

'Yes sir!' Srdjan replied.

'Jarbašić, Jarbašić... Our new Catholic Vlach... Hmm... Hmm...' said the younger Ustasha. 'Our new Croat and brother in arms. Is that so, lieutenant?'

'Yes sir, it is so!'

'From Malo Selce? We were there recently. A small, empty village. And your father was?'

'Stevan Jarbašić, sir, he died a long time ago.'

'A merchant who was supporting our army in the last war?' asked the older Ustasha. 'We've heard that he was a decent man, a man of integrity. He had two brothers who died in that war as Croatian soldiers, is that correct?'

'Yes, that was him, sir,' replied Srdjan. He was afraid to add anything to his short responses and was concentrating on answering the questions as concisely as possible.

'Well, well... And you're a Croatian soldier too. How do you feel about that?'

'It's my duty, sir, to serve my homeland.'

'But you know Živan Jarbašić, I guess,' remarked the younger Ustasha in a provocative manner. 'He's not loyal to this country—he's a communist bandit now.'

'I know him, sir, he's my second cousin, but I haven't seen him for years, sir. I wouldn't know what he's doing now, sir.'

'But we know, lieutenant, we know, and we're here to deal with him and other outlaws. For that, we don't need your help. We need your assistance in another thing,' continued the older Ustasha who was obviously in charge although he was a captain just as his younger colleague was.

Srdjan got scared. This did not sound good.

'Calm down, Jarbašić, we understand how do you feel,' said the younger captain, 'but things have changed. We know that you think that we shall now burn another Orthodox village, but this is not so. You're alive, and your family too—isn't that so? We don't want to harm the

Serbs any more. All what we want is to give them an opportunity to be loyal to our new state just as you are, nothing more than that.'

'My colleague is right,' added the older Ustasha, 'we simply want to dissuade the peasants from supporting Živan and people like him. They're all in the forest now, but why? Because they're afraid of us, I suppose. But they shouldn't be. This is a state now, and it can grant safety to everyone who doesn't rebel against it.'

'But... Sir... What could I...' said Srdjan insecurely.

'Yes you can. You can help bring peace here. This war will end as soon as our German ally defeats the Bolsheviks in Russia—and you know that this is going to happen in no time—so we should continue with our lives already now,' the older Ustasha continued to speak. 'Once the rebels are gone, there'll be no reason for the peasants to remain in the forest. And this is where we could use your services.'

'My services?'

'Yes, you're one of them, in a way, don't feel insulted. You can try to persuade them to come home and stop fighting us. We're aware that you probably don't believe us at the moment, but just observe how we'll be from now dealing with the Partisans and the Chetniks while leaving the civilians alone—and then you'll learn to trust us. Many of the Partisans are Croats, for God's sake, and we'll not attack their families... Just watch what we do and draw your own conclusions. Next time we call you, you'll trust us—believe me. Use your own eyes and mind and then you'll trust us.'

'You are going to leave the civilians alone and deal only with the Partisans ad the Chetniks?' asked Srdjan after some hesitation.

'Yes, Lieutenant Jarbašić,' said the younger Ustasha, 'this is our main strategy for bringing stability to this country, and this is exactly what we're going to do.'

They offered him some wine and even shook hands with him. After that, Srdjan left.

He was completely confused and did not know what to think. Though they said that every conversion to Catholicism was going to be only voluntary in the future—because the state had been stabilised and there was no need for such drastic measures any more—he was very much in doubt. On the other hand, the two Ustasha officers were unusually polite and sounded reasonable. He decided to wait and see the outcome of their actions and then choose how to proceed. He did not reveal to Ljerka what he had been talking about with the Ustasha officers; he even did not tell her that he had met them. Just another unexpected duty at work (this was why he was late, he said), and this whole event remained, as he thought, unnoticed by her.

On the other hand, she knew by her woman's intuition that something unusual had occurred, and she felt uneasy; but their night passion made all of that irrelevant, just as it would happen with every other worry they had in that beastly time. They could think only about today, not about tomorrow.

During the next weeks, Srdjan was becoming more and more interested in what was going on around Savnik. The new Ustasha troops would often disappear for a couple of days and then return with Partisan prisoners—and with some Chetniks too—but there was no news of any atrocity in the nearby Serbian villages; in fact, the only ravaged villages were two Croatian ones, where the Partisans had been supported stubbornly ever since the autumn of 1941.

Soon, the area around Savnik became virtually free of the Partisans and the Chetniks, but the Serbian peasants were still fearful and were not coming home from their forest hideouts.

Ljerka knew only that their life was more peaceful than before, and Srdjan thought that the conversation he had had with the Ustashas was no longer important. However, the agenda of the Ustashas was different: for them, the peasants in the forest were the source of a new rebellion, and they had been ordered by the Germans to put an end to this because troops of the Independent state of Croatia were needed on the Eastern Front—where the Soviets started to fight back fiercely. Since the guerrilla was largely eliminated, there was a time to finish the job...

Srdjan was summoned to the Ustasha headquarters again in March, when the winter was about to end and the time for working on the field was getting close. For every peasant, to see fields overgrown by weed was worse than a death sentence, and this was what the Ustashas counted on. The Serbian peasants were still in the forest...

'Jarbašić? At ease, lieutenant.'

'Yes, sir!'

'Well, Srdjan,' said the older Ustasha officer while offering him a cigarette, 'a time has come for you to act. It's not a secret that we've largely destroyed the Partisans and the Chetniks in the area, and now your fellow peasants should come home and live peacefully with us, as they should. There's not a single reason why they shouldn't.'

'I know, sir, but what could I...'

'Calm down, lieutenant, we've organised everything,' added the younger Ustasha. 'We've been in touch with one of their leaders who has not been involved in the rebellion, and now he just wants to be sure that a Serb can live well in this country, without fear. When he'll see you, he'll know that this is true.'

'Yes, lieutenant,' said the older captain, 'you'll see him and persuade him to bring his folks home.'

'Sir, you think that this could be so simple? Namely, they are probably still very frightened and...'

'My dear comrade, it may not be so simple, but we must give it a try. You've got to give it a try. Frankly, you've got no choice whatsoever,' the younger Ustasha finally made things quite clear.

'I see,' Srdjan remarked and then turned to the older officer, looking directly into his eyes. 'Dear sir, with all due respect, can you give me your word that they'll be treated well? Otherwise I don't know how I could do it.'

'Of course, I understand your anxiety. And yes—you have my word.'

After this short conversation, Srdjan went to the countryside in a car, accompanied by two other Ustasha officers and a few lightly armed Home Guard soldiers on motorcycles. They did not say a word to each other during the whole journey, and soon they reached their destination—a small meadow where a forest road was ending. After the Ustasha officers exchanged certain ciphers with some people behind the trees, a man in his sixties approached the car alone and without fear (it was obvious that he was well protected by hidden marksmen).

It would take a long time to go into details of his negotiations with Srdjan—which lasted for almost an hour—but the outcome was that nearly two thousand peasants returned to their villages within a week or so. Finding their homes ruined, they started to rebuild them and also to work on the land; and no one was threatening them, no one was persecuting them—as if no war had ever started and as if no one had been killed in all of these mindless, bloody raids of the local armies against their own people. Srdjan was so much relieved, he felt so well—for the first time in more than a year.

The good situation continued well into the summer, and this new, unexpected peace had a deep impact on the life of the Jarbašić family.

The love of Ljerka and Srdjan continued to grow; their daughters were getting bigger and irresistibly frisky, and possibly because of that, Klara was less and less visiting the world of plum brandy. They had enough food, the women of the house were enthusiastic to make clothes for all of them, and the family even managed to store, on time, more than enough wood for the forthcoming winter. In early August, they also received a letter from Vladimir, in which he was informing them that he was doing fine in Zagreb but was missing them as well as his family and friends in Kletina; this letter was so warmly and nicely written that they would read it aloud almost every second day after supper.

As already said, nothing in the life of the Jarbašić family was meant to be easy—maybe because their Catholic, Orthodox, and Lutheran God simply did not like them in the same way as he, she or it liked those of a single denomination—and a new shock came in late September. While it would take many words to describe the natural beauty of September in Savnik and the surroundings, only a few were needed to account for the misery that the Jarbašić family was facing then. And these words were: disbelief, treason, pain, hopelessness.

When the peasants had finished their work on the field, every barn and pantry was full, the farm animals were big and fat, and vineyards and orchards had already awarded their owners with sweet smells and juices…

The Ustashas showed their true nature again.

Without any warning, they attacked the Serbian villagers (and some Croatian ones who had also returned from the forest), killed many and took the rest—including women and children—to a death camp (the only one ever ran by a state other than Nazi Germany) close to the village of Jasenovac. These servile and bloodthirsty servants of their fanatical Nazi counterparts, these shameful murderers who were criminalising the noble wish of their nation to be independent, got rid of the despised and unwanted subjects of their evil state and then stole the food and livestock to support their hungry troops in Croatia, Bosnia, Herzegovina, and the USSR. Everything was completed as it had been planned from the very start: no Serbs in the area, no rebelling Croats in the area, no Partisans or Chetniks, plenty of food and other goods plundered... And their victory seemed to be so close!

The only historical circumstance which saved the entire Croatian nation from a later horrific and possibly genocidal retaliation was the fact that many of them fought (or simply did not support) the Ustashas—like Tito, Vladimir F Količek, Ivan the Blacksmith, and numerous other intellectuals or ordinary people including also Franjo Tudjman.[†††] If all the Croats had been siding with the Ustashas, the history of Southeast Europe would have been much different, and Borna Didić would most probably have never been born.

The Ustashas never again summoned Srdjan to their headquarters, and he was back to leading his platoon to the places where they would be needed as guards; soon, however, his soldiers started to disappear in unknown directions, and the Partisans reappeared in the area—this time in numbers larger than before. It was obvious to his superiors, and to the Ustashas as well, that Srdjan was thinking about running away himself, and Ustasha guards were again in front of his house—not every day but, say, two or three times a week. One morning, when they were not there, he found a piece of paper nailed to his door; and on this paper were just

---

[†††] The first president of the Republic of Croatia, elected democratically in 1990, who was a Partisan during World War II and later a nationalist but with no sympathies for the Ustasha regime.

a Partisan red star and a Cyrillic letter Ž (Ж), both written in blood. Srdjan knew that Živan was telling him that he was still alive.

One morning, Srdjan realised that he was not going to survive this war regardless of who was going to win. He was hated by just about everyone. The only thing on his mind from that moment onwards was to secure at least some kind of future for Ljerka and his daughters; he was no longer protected by the good dragon Sveznadar, his castle was in ruins, his armour was rusty, and his sword was broken. Eventually he did the only thing he could do: he contacted Colonel Količek.

By Christmas, he moved with his family to Zagreb—since Savnik was no longer safe for them—where he got a minor position in one of the military offices. Vlado managed to conceal Srdjan's Serbian ancestry from the officials, and life was easier at least for a while.

XX

1943, Krotko, Vinodol and Podgorje County
Independent State of Croatia
&
1991, Krotko, Socialist Republic of Croatia
Socialist Federative Republic of Yugoslavia

Some people in Krotko thought that they were going to remain untouched by the war, but things were becoming worse as the year of 1943 was progressing and the fighting was becoming more intense.

In contrast to just about everyone's expectations, the Partisans had not been annihilated—they were becoming stronger, in fact. At first, this did not influence the life in Krotko much, since the main battlefields were again shifted to the faraway massive mountains of Bosnia, Herzegovina, and Montenegro, where it was much easier for (now substantial) Partisan guerrilla troops to thrive. In all of that, Krotko was affected only by not seeing its soldiers for months, and also the word came that a few of them had been killed in battle; the news referred to the unfortunate Home Guard conscripts and the Ustashas—as nothing was known about those of the Krotko Partisans that had left the area. All in all, four soldiers of the Independent State of Croatia from Krotko died during the bloody battles around the Neretva and Sutjeska Rivers, where the Germans, the Italians, the Ustashas, and the Chetniks—numbering more than a hundred thousand soldiers—tried to destroy a much weaker Partisan force, in which they obtained some tactical success but failed strategically. The core of the Partisan movement, led by Tito personally, was weakened but remained sizeable, and many smaller detachments continued to cause serious problems to the occupying troops and their local allies just about everywhere.

As far as Krotko was concerned, the most important outcome of these clashes was—apart from the four dead villagers—the appearance of the Chetniks in the region again.

The core of the Chetnik forces had been largely destroyed by the Partisans at the Neretva River—which resulted in a decline of the Chetniks at least outside Serbia proper. Those of them who survived the terrible defeat became scattered all over the territory whence they once had come from. They were travelling in small groups, hiding in forests or receiving pitiful help from the weakening Italians, being angry, hungry, poorly dressed, undisciplined, and irrational—as fighting units quite useless but more than fit to be thieves and perpetrators of different atrocities. Their ravaging of undefended Croatian or Muslim villages was no different from the actions of the Ustashas against the Serbs; they were not doing that for any logical reason from the military point of view but just to kill, settle some scores, and eventually, plunder. In August, such a Chetnik unit of about fifteen people established a post somewhere in the dense forests close to Krotko, waiting for an opportunity to come.

At the time, there were only three gendarmes in Krotko—in the old police station—and the village was otherwise unarmed, since the Italians had confiscated all of the rifles (even some muskets from Napoleon's time). There was no sign of any stronger Partisan unit in the area as well. The Chetniks did not know that at first, but it did not take them long to comprehend the situation: the big village of Krotko, consisting of eleven scattered hamlets (some of which were bordering the forest) was largely defenceless.

After Ivan the Proud had returned from the Home Guard, he, Roža, and their small children were enjoying a serene life. He would work in his smithy from early in the morning until afternoon—which was bringing them some money—and she would cook and look after the children and livestock; they would also always find enough time to work on the land or prepare the wood for the winter, which in August was not so demanding as it had been in July. For a reason they were refusing to think about, Ivan's hiding from the armies was not necessary. For months they had lived a life every peasant would want to live: everything was simple, straightforward, and in accord with the Bible.

One Tuesday, quite early, they heard several shots from the direction of the hamlet where the Chetnik casualties of 1941 had lived. This was a remote hamlet close to the forest and far from both the police station and the rest of Krotko. It was not unusual to hear a shot from the distance sometimes, so they did not take any notice at first. However, when the shots became unusually frequent, in about an hour, they saw a mass of people—entire families with their belongings and livestock—fleeing past their house in the direction opposite to the shooting; and they were shouting, 'Run! Run away! The Chetniks are coming, and they're killing everyone! They're back! Run for your life!'

As always, Roža was on the alert and therefore the first to react. She immediately gathered her children, all four of them, and frantically called Ivan, shouting that he should lock all the doors, bring the cows, the pigs, and the horse with him—setting the sheep and the dog free—and run away with her as far as possible from the shooting, together with the crowd that was heading in the direction of the coast. Ivan was a bit confused initially—as he was just about to complete a demanding procedure in his smithy—but when he saw that the gendarmes were fleeing too, he realised that his wife was right. He did as he was told, took the smallest child into his arms, put the older ones onto the horse, and led the family at an exhausting pace for some fifteen kilometres until they reached the house of his uncle in a village on the coast-facing slope of the mountain. There, they found a number of armed men at a barricade, who were somehow informed about the appearance of the Chetniks in the area and had also previously managed to hide a few rifles and some bullets from the Italians.

'Run, children, run—the Partiganee are coming!' shouted an old woman whose cow had been confiscated by the Partisans a year ago. 'They're going to take your cows!'

Valent the Grumpy—Ivan's uncle—yelled back,

'Mother, I wish they were coming, so would you now please go back to the house and take care of the fire! We've got our hungry relatives at supper!'

'The children are hungry? Then I should go now, but the thievish Partiganee will hear from me next time!'

Ivan the Blacksmith took a rifle and inspected it. He knew little about weapons, but he understood mechanical devices; and this rifle, as it turned out, could have killed only its owner. The other rifles were not in any better shape either, except one. As a proper blacksmith, he brought with him some tools and made necessary repairs in no time—it was mainly about cleaning them properly and fastening some screws.

Three hours after Ivan the Proud and his family had arrived, the village defenders spotted one Chetnik on the road. Ivan did not want to shoot at him, Valent neither. Then a boy aged about perhaps seventeen took a rifle and killed the Chetnik with a single shot when he was about fifty metres from the barricade. Fearful, the defenders did not approach the dead Chetnik before they became quite sure that no one else was coming, and this lasted for more than an hour. They didn't know that this Chetnik was not a threat—he was simply running for his life after Mile the Angry and his Partisans had found him and his comrades feasting in a house, next to the body of a raped and slaughtered woman. His death was actually a merciful one, because if the villagers of Krotko had known about the unfortunate woman...

This whole incident did not last long, and it had a rather simple resolution. The Chetniks had managed to occupy Krotko for a few hours—raping and then killing the woman and burning two houses before starting to eat and drink in a cellar—to be eventually spotted by a few hidden Partisans led by Mile the Angry. The Partisans surprised the drunk Chetniks and then overpowered them in a matter of minutes. Those who were captured alive by Mile the Angry died in terrible pain; after the war, he would say, 'I would always kill an Ustasha or a German with no mercy, would have some pity on poor Italian or Home Guard conscripts, but to kill a Chetnik was for me a matter of a different fight. These simply wanted to kill every Croat.'

Valent the Grumpy was a different kind of man. He was a mild tempered person who cherished his love for his wife more than anything else—similarly to Anton Didić—and who would always try to avoid every conflict.

To learn that there were some rifles hidden in his village was for him a nightmare, blasphemy against his Lord Jesus Christ; and when he heard that a wild bunch of the Chetniks had raided Krotko and were heading towards his house, he was completely desperate. He decided not to fight back, to die as a martyr, but he was still helping his neighbours make the barricade—which he was doing in his 'grumpy' way that had given him the byname. Seeing his nephew, namely Ivan the Proud, calmed him down for a while, because he always felt that the two of them were soulmates, of those people who would never hurt a fly, always trying to find an elegant way out from every trouble. But when Valent saw the eagerness of Ivan the Blacksmith in repairing the rifles, he knew that things were not so simple any more.

In 1946, he eventually slit the throat of a renegade Chetnik who attacked his wife while searching for food, at the time when the Partisans—now called the Yugoslav Army—were hunting the remaining Ustashas and Chetniks in remote areas. He regretted this for the rest of his life—and he thought that he was going to end up in Hell, because no one was supposed to give or take life but the Lord. He outlived his beloved wife—who died in 1956—and spent most of the remaining two years of his life at her grave (sometimes even sleeping there) in praying to the Lord and asking him the whole day long to let him see her at least once every two or three thousand years during his afterlife, because he was not entirely bad and because he loved her so much. Yes, he had done some wrong things during his life, this was so true, but the Lord might remember all the kind things he had done too—this was his hope.

Ivan the Blacksmith sympathised with his uncle and his grief. Until Valent died, they would meet roughly once a month. They would spend a few hours together at the grave of Valent's wife, discuss simple things such as the harvest of that year or the prospect of their children, and Ivan would then return to Krotko, leaving Valent at the cemetery and thinking that it was just about time for God to show some mercy to the lands of everlasting war, although a mortal should never ask about his mysterious ways.

In September 1991, Ivan the Proud was a widower for already four years. A month ago, this seventy-seven-year-old man had walked two kilometres to light a candle at the grave of his beloved Roža on the occasion of the anniversary of her death. She had never liked flowers, so he brought none. She had loved her husband and children—who were on that warm August day, one by one, coming to the cemetery with their own candles. After spending some time with Ivan, they left and he was alone again.

He was remembering that day a bit melancholically. The mild colours of September were everywhere around, and he enjoyed the scenery. He was sitting in front of the house with a glass of wine when he heard a frightening noise from not so far away—something like repeating thunders—and then he saw a fast airplane just above his head. Then another airplane came, and the thunders were in his neighbourhood—another cluster bomb was dropped, and the scent that soon reached him was that of the burning stables of his neighbour.[‡‡‡] He went to see whether the neighbour needed any help with the fire, but the only thing he heard was, 'Run! Run away! The Chetniks are coming! They're back! Run for your life!'

All alone, much slower and not so eager, he carefully locked the doors and then headed towards the coast. No livestock any more to take with him or set them free. He felt that the last thing in his life might be visiting the grave of Valent the Grumpy and his wife. Step by step—and it took him eight hours to get there—he came to the village where Valent had once lived. There was no barricade, because the Chetniks were not coming: it was just that airplanes of the Yugoslav People's Army—the crucial ally of the rebelling ethnic Serbs of Croatia in this new war—had bombed Krotko. And one might have called them the Chetniks or not, but this was a different war. Krotko was supporting the struggle for Croatian independence from Yugoslavia again, it was on a strategic road, it was bombed, but this war was local and not part of a worldwide conflict. After becoming confident that everything around him was quiet, Ivan went to the Valent's grave. He sat there for a while, and just before he left, he asked the man in the grave, 'What will become of us now,

---

[‡‡‡]A cluster bomb consists of many smaller bombs which scatter over an area upon the activation of the main bomb, with only one purpose—to kill people and leave the rest largely intact. This weapon is officially forbidden in modern warfare.

Valent? What will become of my children and grandchildren? And what will become of Borna? They all have this or that surname, but he's the only one who carries our name into the future, of us who are known as the Proud. I've got no other grandson whose surname is Didić.'

The older of the two sons of Ivan the Blacksmith, that is, Borna's father, knew where to look for his old man after he had not found him in Krotko the day after the bombing.

When they came back to Krotko, they saw that the estate was intact, unlike the neighbour's property: there, everything was burnt to the ground. They also found out that two boys from the village had been killed in their houses, whereas a local inn had been destroyed and seven people had been injured therein. No enemy troops were near, as the area was protected by the newly formed Croatian National Guard, this time not divided among the Ustashas, the Partisans, and the Home Guard of World War II. Well, this was a difference, but otherwise nothing changed much in the lands of everlasting war: everything was as usual.

XXI

1943, somewhere close to the Drina River Border between the Independent State of Croatia and the Territory of the Military Commander in Serbia

'Well, Vlado, long time no see,' said Dragoljub (better known as Draža) Mihailović—wearing a rather old and shabby uniform of the Royal Yugoslav Army—to his counterpart who just entered a small village house. This man was, unlike Draža, impeccably dressed, in a tidy uniform of the Croatian Home Guard. Mihailović was the host of this unexpected meeting, and both of them were unarmed. However, there were a number of soldiers of both sides, at some distance from the house and prepared to act in case of any trouble.

By most of his supporters, Mihailović was called Čiča (meaning *old man*), and he had been since 1941 the head of the troops entitled the Yugoslav Army in the Homeland, which had initially represented the remnants of the Royal Yugoslav Army after the Axis Powers occupation of Yugoslavia. In time, however, Draža and his followers became just another irregular army consisting almost entirely of Serbian nationalists—who were simply known as the Chetniks in spite of this name being borne by some other troops as well; they all shared the same Serbian chauvinist ideology, and the use of the same historical name was therefore not surprising.

The units of Mihailović were an opportunist force collaborating with just about everyone and awaiting a British invasion of Yugoslavia—which was never going to happen. For a few months at the beginning of the war, they had been negotiating with the Partisans about fighting together against the occupying armies and their local servants, but the unwillingness of the Partisans to behave opportunistically ended this, making the two guerrillas mortal enemies ever since. While having friendly relations with the Italians virtually from the very start of the war, the Chetniks occasionally fought the Germans but would sometimes also join them in attacking the Partisans.

Being weakened, they were ready to make a pact even with their primary enemy, and this was the Independent State of Croatia—the state which was the main obstacle to their efforts to establish a Greater Serbia by eliminating the Catholic and Muslim rivals on the same territory. In the perilous situation the Chetniks were facing at the time, even the quisling Croatian state could have been considered a valuable ally as long as the two nationalist armies could join forces in confronting the multiethnic Partisans.

Both the Croatian and the Serbian nationalists were seriously endangered by the Partisans—who did not care at all about the nationalities of their supporters and soldiers—and the idea that they could together try to get rid of the communist pest was not completely unattractive to the Croats either. Afterwards, according to this scenario, they were going to see what could be done to find a solution for their own interests—however conflicting these might have been—as it was easier to deal with an enemy who believed in tradition and conservative values than with the Godless communists who wanted to destroy the very foundations of civilisation.

The quisling Croatian state had a regular army, equipped with some heavy weapons, that should have been respected despite its obvious weaknesses; and since most of the Chetniks—including those in the Independent State of Croatia—were under Draža's command, he was also not a person to be disregarded. The Serbian position was, on the other hand, rather weak after they had lost the best troops at the Battle of the Neretva. The Croats were not doing much better either, because a substantial part of the territory of their state was out of their jurisdiction; most of these areas were controlled by the Partisans, with only some pockets under the influence of the Chetniks.

Colonel Vladimir Količek of the Home Guard was an ideal person for meeting Mihailović and negotiating with him, since they had known each other for years—from the time when they had been highly ranked officers in the Royal Yugoslav Army.

'I greet you, Dragoljub,' said Količek. 'Actually, I haven't seen you much since your Bulgarian episode, maybe just once or twice. This was a nasty game. The intelligence did not prepare the territory properly, in my opinion.'

'Don't remind me, Vlado, and I've heard that you were much more successful in Albania.'

'I had a better support, I guess. But these things are of little importance at the moment. Shall we now get down to business?' replied Količek without showing any wish to continue this small talk. He had once respected Mihailović for his fighting spirit and the initial resistance to the Germans, but the news of his collaboration with the Axis Powers and the atrocities of his troops against Croatian and Muslim civilians changed his view.

'By all means,' replied Čiča, needing no further reminder about his failure in Sofia; he also sensed that Količek was very official and not quite friendly. 'I used my channels to contact your staff and to ask what do you think about the communist threat. And what could be done about that. They're growing stronger from day to day, and this endangers both of us. It's not a secret that we can't beat them alone. We've got a same problem, you and us.'

'Yes, it's not a secret that we can't beat them alone either—even when locally defeated, they rise up again and again. They're a serious opponent in any case,' said Količek.

'I see. And you hence know that you and us have a problem they don't have?' Draža wanted to continue his last thought.

Vladimir looked at Dragoljub without saying a word; it was obvious that he did not want to reply before hearing what his opponent wanted to say exactly. Čiča continued, 'Our problem is that we're stupidly attacking and killing the Croats and the Muslims, and your problem is that you're doing the same with the Serbs. Civilians, I mean. Indiscriminately, whenever a local commander gets drunk. In the communist army, all nationalities are welcome and religious matters are not discussed. This is how they get soldiers all over again. Two are killed, three join. They are killing civilians too, but not because someone goes into a wrong church.'

'I know. It's not that they're not murderous, but their reasons are less scary for common people. And the problem is also that we don't do much to punish the local commanders—who are in large part just pre-war criminals and now heroes in the eyes of their illiterate followers. From our side, there's little chance that this could be solved. I'm sorry to say that, but I know the politicians. There are also rumours that the communists punish their commanders severely if they do something wrong.'

'Yes, this is well known,' said Draža without revealing his main standpoint yet. 'But I suppose that we must live with that for some time at least. Let us concentrate on military affairs now. That's the purpose of this meeting.'

'Military affairs? I haven't been aware of that.'

'Yes, military affairs, other things can wait. Every war is dirty, and the dirt of this war will surface at some point, but this isn't the time for that. Not yet. There are more urgent matters.'

Colonel Količek hesitated for a moment, trying to figure out what he could expect to hear; then he just said,

'All right, tell me what's on your mind.'

'As I said—military affairs. We must think as soldiers, which both of us are.'

'What do you mean? Be more precise, please.'

'I believe that we might think of taking some action against the Partisans together,' clarified Mihailović, 'with or without the help of the foreigners.'

Vladimir was not surprised to hear that, but he was also not ready to disregard the known unreliability of the Chetniks, especially at this time when they were so weak. So he asked directly,

'Why would I trust you? And what would my side gain from this supposed collaboration?'

'You would gain the territory now held by the Partisans and the pacification of your country.'

'And you would gain more, I think. I see only that you could infiltrate there where the Partisans are now, and this isn't a solution attractive to us. So silly, in fact.'

Draža realised that he was walking on thin ice and that Količek was not an easy negotiator. On the other hand, he did not expect anything else. Hence, he tried to divert the discussion towards more immediate goals, those which did not involve politics.

'We could talk about that later,' he replied, 'and this should, in fact, be the responsibility of our politicians. We are soldiers, you and me. For instance, I could notify King Petar about this initiative and ask him to issue a declaration that our differences should wait until a military resolution of our joint problem...[§§§] My troops will obey him. If you could try the same, then we might...'

'And I could notify Pavelić as well.[****] He'll obey me just as King Petar will obey you,' interrupted Vladimir sarcastically. 'Both of them want ethnically clean territories more than anything else—they simply don't understand the power of human instinct for survival. The people's love for their homes. And that's why there are more and more Partisans and less and less of us, my dear Draža.'

'I still think this could be done...' Mihailović tried to save the negotiations by using vague phrasing again.

'Let me be more direct, my colleague,' interrupted Količek again and started to speak in a less relaxed manner. 'What military affairs if we don't offer life? The Partisans offer life, or maybe death in battle, while we offer... What do we offer, Dragoljub? How do we recruit our soldiers—and who are they—and how do the communists find their warriors? Yes, they recruit angry and willing warriors who live for revenge only, while we're arming either frightened peasants or violent lunatics!'

Mihailović had no immediate answer to that. Količek made his point, and Čiča had to really present himself as a true soldier, one who

---

[§§§] Petar II was the last king of the Kingdom of Yugoslavia, who fled to London during the Axis Powers invasion of the country.

[****] Ante Pavelić was the head of the Independent State of Croatia.

was not behaving as a politician (which Draža, at least partly, had become in the course of time).

'I repeat, many of these things are purely political, and I still want to discuss only possible moves that we could do together as soldiers in order to get rid of the communist threat. The politicians could join us later, when things become clearer—and they can't unless we get some results in combat and make them negotiate with one another,' Draža continued.

Colonel Količek was willing to allow Draža to go on with his argument, but he was by no means ready to give up his position easily—because this whole situation looked like a cunning attempt of the Chetniks to find a way out from their difficult situation. He was also not very interested in helping the Independent State of Croatia solve its own obvious problems—because it was quite clear that this state was doomed and that every reasonable person should have thought only about surviving its unavoidable collapse.

'You really think that destroying a Partisan unit here and there,' continued Količek his reasoning, 'could stop their rebellion? What about the people who are making them. What they are? What could stop a new Partisan unit replacing an old one?'

'But we could still try... You said yourself that you can't control that alone...'

'Yes I did, and so did you. Tell me, Dragoljub, why would we want to do that with you as an ally in the first place? We have the Germans to help us, and your Italians are just about to collapse. What is there for us? We would just give you control over some territories which are now in the hands of the Partisans,' said Vladimir to make things completely clear.

'I believe it would be easier for you to work with us, the Germans are foreigners, and they don't understand us well...'

'So silly. Dragoljub, you know that you're now babbling, don't you?' replied Vlado stone-faced. 'We could also make a pact with the Partisans to destroy you. They are also not foreigners, and many of them are Croats, in fact. Some even say that their leader is a Croat. You're the weakest of us, and why would anyone want to have a weak ally?'

Mihailović suddenly became aware of his delicate position, but he still tried to find a way to continue these negotiations, so vital for the future of his movement. He stopped talking for a while and then said,

'I see, my friend. I understand your point of view, but could we just concentrate on our possible gains? Let us be reasonable. The control over a territory is not so much important right now, this is always solved by negotiations afterwards—remember the history of wars. You'll get the territory you want, we'll find a way.'

Količek did not answer immediately, and he deliberately kept the atmosphere tense for a while. He lit a cigarette, took a sip of plum brandy and inspected the Orthodox pictures of saints on the walls. Mihailović did the same, and the room soon became full of smoke and silence. Then Vladimir said,

'State what's on your mind. But be explicit this time, please, don't speak in ciphers any more. And remember that military history is my territory.'

'All right. I'm sincerely offering you a pact against the Partisans. A solid and honest pact,' specified Draža. 'We'll fight each other later if necessary. But I hope we could settle our differences as civilised people, without a fight, by finding a compromising solution when the time for that comes.'

'What pact would that be? Please explain again,' Količek provoked him.

'To destroy the Partisans first, as I just said. Our troops fighting together until we annihilate them. Then we'll see.'

'Dear Dragoljub,' Vladimir started to speak without hesitation. 'There are many problems with that. First, you can offer only about fifteen to twenty thousand soldiers with little heavy weapons—because your losses at the Neretva River were devastating. Secondly, you have been proven to be unreliable, which we know from the Partisan experience in 1941. Thirdly, we do not know that the territory inhabited by the Croats and the Muslims, now held by the Partisans, wouldn't be ravaged by your troops if you gained control there.'

'Are you certain, Colonel Količek? So negative?' replied Čiča, showing signs of losing nerves.

'Very certain. I've come here not as a friend or former colleague but to assess your offer as an officer, and I find nothing tempting in it. In my view, you're just trying to enforce your position now when Italy is in trouble, because you know that from now on you can only become weaker. You're still dreaming of a British invasion, and by eliminating the Partisans, you would suddenly become the only guerrilla ready to support the British. After a long period of your collaboration with the Axis Powers, this would eventually be forgotten. The alliance you propose could not be beneficial to us—and it will therefore never happen. This is my last word. These negotiations are over.'

After hearing that, Čiča became nervous—which was not typical of him. He stood up angrily, started to walk across the small room and tried to find the words of reply—since this game of cat and mouse, in which he did not succeed to be the cat, was so swiftly exposed. A thorough analyst might perhaps be inclined to conclude that Mihailović's failure in Sofia and the Količek's success in Tirana could be explained by something else than the differences in the logistic preparations for these two spying affairs. The ability to comprehend a situation as it is—without any romantic idea—is the most valuable quality of a spy, and this seemed to be the main difference between Količek and Mihailović.

'Then... Then, Vladimir, no deal! Colonel Količek! Let the communists do us all as they wish! See you in front of my pistol one day, damned you, or before a Partisan firing squad together with me!'

Vladimir did not add a word; he stood up, saluted and then left. In his frustration, Čiča started to think that he should perhaps order his troops to kill Količek immediately. Maybe he should have done that with Tito in 1941, when he had hosted him for similar negotiations; but then he remembered that he did not know how many troops Vladimir brought with him—and these were definitely hiding rather close—so he gave up.

While this short meeting has probably not been mentioned in any important historical record—perhaps because no one could have benefited from that, quite the opposite—the assessment of Colonel Vladimir Količek turned out to be justified by a number of later events.

Vladimir's prediction that the Chetniks were never again going to become a respectable force was fulfilled not much later. After the collapse of Mussolini's Italy in September 1943, there was a massive defection from the Chetniks to the Partisans all over the territory of the former Yugoslavia, and Mihailović became isolated with relatively small forces at the tripoint of Serbia, Bosnia, and Montenegro—which did not change much until the end of the war. In 1944, Petar II of Yugoslavia declared that the only Yugoslav fighting force supported by him and his government were the Partisans—who were from that time onwards considered to be the only British ally in the country, receiving substantial help. In 1945, the remaining strong Chetnik forces were withdrawing together with the Germans towards Austria, wanting to surrender to the Allies, but were intercepted by the last organised Ustasha forces and annihilated at the Battle of Lijevče Field in Bosnia—that much about any collaboration between the Chetniks and the Ustashas. Dragoljub Mihailović remained in Serbia after the Partisans' victory, hoping to organise an anti-communist resistance, but he was captured in 1946 and executed as a traitor and war criminal.

He faced a Partisan firing squad. Colonel Količek did not.

However predictable to some degree—taking into account both the local and global situations at the time—this development alone could not fully explain the conduct of Vladimir Količek at the meeting with Draža. He was from the very start quite unwilling to support this possible alliance (which was, in fact, not entirely unfavourable to the side he represented), because he had other things on his mind.

First of all, he was never loyal to the Independent State of Croatia, since he detested its racial laws, brutality, lack of democracy, and blind, irrational devotion to Hitler and his paranoia. He was just trying to stay alive within this system, acting against it whenever it would be safe enough (using contacts with either the Partisans or other, non-communist opposition). He was certainly endorsing the defection of Home Guard soldiers to the Partisans, which was happening from the very beginning of the war and not only after the collapse of Italy—as in the case of the Chetniks. Signing a pact with the Chetniks would have definitely endangered this process. Moreover, he did not want to help make the Chetniks possibly the only opposition to Nazi Germany at the time of the inevitable collapse of this empire of evil. Without the Partisans, many of whom were the Croats, the whole Croatian nation would have been doomed—and he knew that. Finally, there was also a non-communist Croatian movement against the Nazis; these people were acting slowly and secretly in the background of main events—and Colonel Vladimir Filip Količek eventually became one of them.

The attempts to find a 'final solution' for the historical Croatian-Serbian dispute over the lands of everlasting war did not end there, in that house close to the Drina River.

Some claim that an agreement was reached between Pavelić and Milan Stojadinović on a division of these lands between the Croats and the Serbs, which would take place after overthrowing the communist government of the post-war Yugoslavia through an imported revolution supported by the West.[††††] Their meeting allegedly took place in Buenos Aries in 1954, and a provisional border was apparently drawn on the map without caring much for the fact that real people with real lives occupied the territory. It seemed that the solution for this nuisance was found in a 'humane relocation' of unwanted nationalities, westwards and eastwards across the planned border. The implementation of this plan had to wait for a few more decades: in the 1990s, the same thing was called 'ethnic cleansing', it was condemned by everyone but was eventually accepted as a fact of life.

[††††] A Serbian politician and also dedicated nationalist, serving during 1935–1939 as the prime minister of the Kingdom of Yugoslavia.

XXII

1990–1991, Zagreb, Socialist Republic of Croatia
Socialist Federative Republic of Yugoslavia

During the turmoil in Yugoslavia in early 1990, Borna was largely unaware of what was going on around him.

He was concentrating on synthesising polyaniline—a new electrically conducting plastic—for his diploma thesis, which was not very complicated but was making him happy because this was the first time he encountered research chemistry in a real laboratory. Before that, everything was a mixture of lectures and exercises designed to demonstrate general principles of experimental chemistry to students, which was interesting but not challenging.

In July, he obtained a diploma as third in his class. He was not first only because he had injured his knee while playing basketball three months earlier, therefore not being able to walk for weeks. In consequence of his injury, he did not attend the first democratic elections in Croatia since before World War II, which was an event that brought major changes to his homeland. He watched this whole circus on television and did not like it: too much poison and hatred, as if the people were not going to vote but to fight someone instead. He thought that this country was perhaps not yet ready for that—for such a responsibility after more than three decades of a single-party system—but he was not concerned with that at all. He was eager to go to the lab as soon possible and could not think about anything else. There, he was home—and isolated from the political and ideological quarrels he disliked so much. After obtaining his degree, he cared even less about the stupid arguments of the stupid local politicians, and his main objective was to find a good job and start living an independent life.

He was lucky that his grandfather Vladimir had somehow managed to remain the owner of several small properties during the time of the socialist Yugoslavia, when expropriation had been part of the process of building a new world based on communist ideology—in which everyone had to, in theory, be in a position to share the entire wealth of the country. This theory, of course, never met reality, and all of that was just one big theft. On the other hand, Količek remained the owner but not user of a part of his property—in Zagreb, in particular—so his daughters and grandchildren had to live as tenants while studying. Eventually he left everything he had in Kletina to Ljerka, and all of his other property to Barbara and Danka. In 1990—when the socialist state was obviously collapsing in every way—his daughters succeeded to become both the owners and users of their inheritance. This was in reality not much—as Količek was not a wealthy man—but was still a good start for their children, who were entering the world of independent adults. Borna, specifically, got from his mother a small, quite modest but somewhat comfortable flat in Zagreb—where he decided to stay and pursue the career of a chemist (Kletina seemed too small and unexciting, and the available jobs were also rather plain and uninteresting).

After Borna had declined an offer to start an academic career as a PhD student—and some other job offers at minor companies—he hit a jackpot: he got a position in the research labs of a pharmaceutical company named *Pliva*, the largest in Southeast Europe and renowned worldwide for its role in developing and producing antibiotics.

He got a nice salary for a beginner and was assigned to a lab led by an Englishman who was living in Zagreb since the 1970s, being married to a Croatian woman. This man—whose name was Roger—had been one of the best students at Imperial College, London, and his subsequent career was full of successes and virtually without any failure; thus, the company was happy to pay for his services probably even more than he would get in the UK. With such an income, he lived in the socialist Yugoslavia much better than he ever could in capitalist England, where living costs were much higher. Because of that (and also due to his lovely personality), he was always happy, relaxed, and therefore able to concentrate on his work fully—always developing new solutions that would sooner or later result in a profit for the company. He would often sing while walking around the lab, and it seemed that working was for him just one big party. The good vibrations he was spreading built a unique atmosphere which was appreciated very much by most of his younger colleagues, and it was unthinkable that someone would try to disrespect or disobey him; he would never raise his voice, but it was quite clear that his decisions should never be questioned.

He was completely autonomous in running his laboratory, and no one in the entire company dared to even think of interfering with that. Thus, he set up some unusual rules. Firstly, there were no official working hours—something like from eight a.m. to four p.m.—and the only thing of importance was to get the work done well and on time. Working during weekends was usual, just as it was to stay home for a few days over the week—which applied to everyone including him. Secondly, he insisted on the English language (*lingua franca* of modern science and technology, as he would often say) being used in his lab exclusively—and Croatian was allowed during private hours only (when he would frequently amuse his co-workers by his Croatian, which he spoke quite well but only in the dialect of Zagreb). He was also insisting on British English in writing and pronunciation, because 'his young colleagues should never become misled by the twisted language of Her Majesty's colonial subjects'.

'Never come to this lab wearing pants only! Be decent and come here wearing trousers!' would be his usual reaction to someone using an American English word.

Or he would explain some phrases in English, which many native Croatian speakers would tend to construct by translating them from their language literally; for instance,

'A bloody computer can't get blocked—a valve might get blocked! A bloody computer is hung up—that's what you have to say!'

Some of the people in the lab found Roger's demands annoying—because these were not offering them any opportunity to be lazy intellectually—but Borna liked them and excelled from the very start, in both learning English and becoming a better chemist. While being skilful in standard procedures he had encountered during his study, he was not only hard working but also extremely eager to adopt new things and tricks that one could learn only directly from the masters of the profession. Very soon, he started to be innovative and proposed ideas for solving unusual problems—and Roger was more than pleased by that. His affection for Borna was brought to a higher level when the young apprentice once told him that he knew how to pronounce a sentence in perfect British English.

'And what would that be?' asked Roger sarcastically.

'My I have a pint of Guinness, please?' Borna replied without even the slightest accent that could distinguish him from an Englishman living next door to an English pub.

After they had finished their work for the day, Roger took Borna to an inn attended by the English speaking people of Zagreb, and there Borna had to repeat the same question to the bartender.

'Here you go, mate. I'd charge you two quid back home, but it's cheaper here,' said the bartender—not recognising that the young man was not from his homeland—and Borna was officially English for that evening.

To make a long story short, Borna spent fourteen months under Roger's supervision in *Pliva*. He learned numerous standard procedures and also certain valuable secrets in the chemistry of pharmaceutics, eventually becoming almost ready to lead his own team. It was equally important for his future that he became quite fluent in English—including British pronunciation—and the bartender thought that he was one Brian from the village of Grantchester, near Cambridge (Roger said that this was a nice and typically English village that he remembered from the time he had spent in Cambridge).

In December 1991, Roger was wondering what was going on—why Borna was not coming to the lab any more. But the cheerful Englishman had no time to ponder on that, as he was on his way back to England and quite busy with finding solutions for his family.

XXIII

1944, Zagreb
Independent State of Croatia

The condition of the Independent State of Croatia was in the August of 1944 everything but prosperous.

It was clear to everyone of common sense that Nazi Germany was losing the war; and without its help, the quisling Croatian state stood no chance. Furthermore, the Partisans had grown over the years to become a respected army that was no longer just a coalition of small fighting units scattered all over the country, and they were not only controlling a substantial part of the Independent State of Croatia but were also implementing their laws there—already integrating these territories into a new state they wanted to establish. And no independent Croatia was part of their plans.

In June, Tito signed an agreement with the Yugoslav Government in Exile (which was in London), according to which the Partisans were recognised as the only Yugoslav member of the anti-Hitler coalition—hence the Chetniks were abandoned by their King Petar II and were henceforth dedicated entirely to anticommunism even if this meant collaborating with the Germans fully (they anticipated the future confrontation between the capitalist West and the Soviets, but this did not help them).

Tito was a controversial person for his entire life, but he was definitely much more realistic and lucid than his main opponents—and these were the leaders of the nationalists, namely Pavelić among the Croats and Mihailović among the Serbs. First of all, he was aware that he could build a strong army and establish a political influence only by completely disregarding the feuds between the nations of Yugoslavia—where ethnically homogeneous areas were smaller than a country of the size of Switzerland (in Bosnia and Herzegovina being particularly small). In his strategy, religion and nationality were largely unimportant, and every tendency to introduce a national or religious character into the hierarchy of his movement would be crashed immediately and very brutally. Pavelić, on the other hand, insisted on a strict Croatian character of his state—in which the Muslims of Bosnia and Herzegovina were considered to be 'the flowers of the Croatian nation' while the Serbs were a foreign body destined to vanish by expulsion from the country, extermination or loss of identity. Mihailović dreamt of a new version of the pre-war Yugoslavia, in the form of a Greater Serbia in which the Croats, the Muslims, and the Albanians would be 'removed from the Serbian lands, which should have been done already after the Great War, when Yugoslavia was forming'. His problem was that these 'Serbian lands' comprised most of Yugoslavia—extending far beyond the Serbian ethnic territories in Bosnia, Herzegovina, Kosovo, and Croatia—and also encompassed the territory inhabited by the Macedonian Slavs, who never had any Serbian national feeling in spite of being Orthodox Christians.

No wonder that the common people—suffering so much from the attempts to implement the two opposing and murderous nationalist plans on the same territory—were joining Tito's forces massively, especially after it had become clear that both the Ustashas and the Chetniks were doomed. There was the Tito's coalition with the Western Allies—and their forces were advancing towards Germany from France—while the communist Soviets (the natural and main Tito's ally) were victorious in the east; thus, the only thing which should have mattered to a sane person was to find a way to be in a favourable position at the time of the unavoidable German downfall.

Borna once heard from an elderly drunk in a Kletina inn that the only reason why Tito had prevailed was that he had been far more intelligent than Pavelić and Mihailović combined; most of the people had not liked or hated Tito zealously, but his offer had been simply better, said the drunk.

'Cheers,' said Borna to the drunk and bought him another drink, knowing that he was right in many respects. After a while, the drunk asked for another drink—and Borna paid again, probably because he was not quite sober either.

Vladimir F Količek was no longer a colonel in the Home Guard: he had been retired in March.

For any army at war, it could never be wise to retire an experienced senior officer at the age of forty-four, but the whole situation, worldwide and locally, was making Pavelić nervous and even paranoid; at some point, he decided to get rid of every suspicious character in the army and state administration, and only the reputation of these potential enemies of the state prevented him from killing them instantly. In any case, the impotent Army of the Independent State of Croatia became even weaker by the loss of a considerable number of professionals in the Home Guard. An attempt to reinforce the Ustashas through a conscription of smooth faced children was disastrous and resulted only in a slaughter of these boys by the Partisans after the end of the war—when there was no mercy for anyone in a Ustasha uniform.

Pavelić was even more frustrated by his inability to deal with his main enemy within the local political circles—and this individual was Edmund Glaise von Horstenau, an Austrian in the German Army, who had served in the Great War on the General Staff of the Austro-Hungarian Army and had been the last Vice-Chancellor of Austria before the 1938 *Anschluss*.

As a distinguished member of the Nazi Party, he had been appointed as Plenipotentiary General in the Independent State of Croatia already in April 1941, and he was shortly afterwards shocked by the atrocities of the Ustashas—as he wrote in one of his reports. While being fanatical in his own way—mainly with regard to German nationalism—von Horstenau was still an Austro-Hungarian officer who would never accept that any suffering of civilian population could be justified by political reasons. As a realistic person, he warned Pavelić several times that Germany was a sinking ship and that Croatia could not do anything about that, which Pavelić—who was rather irrational by nature—never wanted to listen to. Instead, he eventually managed to remove Glaise from Croatia (with the help of the German ambassador) in late September. By then, a plot against Pavelić—which had been, in his strong opinion, organised by von Horstenau—was already crushed, and expelling the Austrian from his state made the reasonless nationalist leader feel completely victorious.

Vladimir and von Horstenau were not close friends, but they had known each other since 1943, when Količek on one occasion prevented an Ustasha raid against a Serbian highland village; in that, he asked the Germans to support him 'for military reasons, because this could only enforce the Partisans eventually'. And it was Edmund Glaise von Horstenau who provided that support.

From that time onwards, they would sometimes collaborate on similar matters, knowing (without saying a word to one another) that their compassion for simple, innocent people—and not any military issue—was the reason for their mutual understanding. They definitely respected each other, possibly because every war was for both of them a conflict of armed men and not a fight against civilian population for ideological reasons. In the summer of 1944, they would occasionally meet at some tea parties organised by Glaise, where he would gather retired and active senior officers of the Home Guard as well as certain pre-war democratic Croatian politicians, for relaxed but still serious discussions on the political situation. Količek would never stay long at these parties—and he would never speak, as a matter of fact—because it was obvious to the experienced spy that the parties were monitored by Pavelić via several of his informers. When the last party he attended was over, he warned von Horstenau on certain persons who were most probably Pavelić's spies. This may have been his only contribution to the plot that was under preparation—but the exact role of Vladimir Količek in all of that has remained unclear until today.

Since he understood his objective position, Vladimir was not surprised when—on the fourteenth of September, just after midnight—three police officers woke him up. Many of his friends, colleagues, and acquaintances had already been arrested—all of them suspected of participating in an act of high treason which was later going to be known as the Lorković-Vokić plot (named after the leaders who were highly ranked officials in the government). The goal of the plot was remotely similar to the unsuccessful plans of Mihailović for Serbia, namely to sever Croatian connections with Germany and redirect the country towards the Western Allies—in contrast to the Partisans, who were clearly more devoted to Stalin and the Soviet Union. This conspiracy involved present and past officers of the Home Guard as well as former politicians from the Croatian Peasant Party—the most influential Croatian democratic party before the war, founded by Stjepan Radić who had died from the wounds after being shot in the Belgrade Parliament in 1928 (which spoiled the subsequent Christmas in the Jarbašić family).

Thus Vladimir ended behind the bars for the first time in his life—after he had been in numerous situations that may have led to such an outcome.

He was first taken to an ordinary prison for just about everyone, where he was briefly interrogated—with no specific reference to why he was there—and then put in a cell full of regular people. Some were imprisoned for political reasons (e.g., supporting the Partisans), some because they were plain criminals, some because they had no valid documents, etc., which meant that the inmates were coming in and going out from the cell on a daily basis. More disturbing events in the prison were frequent screams from faraway parts of the large building (obviously due to torturing), the sights of hungry and abused women and small children from the territories retaken from the Partisans, and more than anything, deportations to the Jasenovac extermination camp—which was a place known to everyone after all of these years of the war.

On the third day of his detention, he was told that he had a visitor. He was surprised, because his fellow inmates were not receiving any visits, and he was also not sure whether visits were allowed at all. He was taken out from the cell and escorted by a silent Ustasha, walking awkwardly in shoes without shoelaces and holding trousers without a belt; and when he entered the visitors' room, he saw Srdjan Jarbašić waiting for him.

'But lieu... Captain Jarbašić! Well, this is a surprise! So nice to see you again, and tell me everything. How's your lovely wife? And the girls—are they growing fast? Has life treated you well after you moved to Zagreb? And...'

'Dear sir, everything is fine. My daughters drew and wrote something for you, here it is. We're all so grateful, and we always think about you.'

Then Srdjan handed him a piece of paper with some childish drawings of hearts, stars, trees, grass, animals, and things like that. At the bottom of the paper, it was written in capital letters 'unclo Vlado I love yee dnki an brbra'. Vlado was touched and was speechless for a while; after all, he was an old childless bachelor.

'Your sister called me to my office the other day, said that she couldn't speak, and then we met in the street. She told me about you. I've brought you some food and cigarettes, this is allowed here.'

'Is it? I wouldn't know,' Vladimir said ironically. 'So, what's going on outside? I know nothing.'

'Nothing about you in any case. This is kept secret. The newspapers are as always full of propaganda and of nothing else. I believe you know from your secret channels more than I do.'

'Not really, not this time. And you? You're a captain now?'

'Yes, not enough captains, so they made me one. Only a few senior officers know about my history, this probably helped. For everyone else, I'm just another Croatian officer.'

'Good, good,' said Vlado, 'but keep in mind that you have to know how to play this game. This whole thing will not last long, and you should think about your head. I've still got your painting of St John, don't forget to use it when it's opportune… with your people.'

Srdjan immediately became tense, but he tried not to show it. The image of the message nailed to his door in Savnik and containing only a red star and a Cyrillic letter Ž was making him restless.

'Yes, dear colonel, I'll not forget. But my head is at the moment less cheap than yours.'

'Is it? I wouldn't know,' Vladimir laughed ironically again. 'I guess I should try to keep it in one piece, but no one depends on my head, and my departure would be so smooth. Your head, on the other hand… Though things always settle down by themselves, one has to prepare for that. Tarzan would always do it. Oh, how I miss those films!'

'All right, I understand, but let us discuss more urgent things now,' Srdjan interrupted, becoming even more stressed by being reminded of his own situation. 'I've heard about a few things that could interest you. About your future whereabouts.'

'Shoot, dear captain—I'm ready to take every bullet.'

'You'll not remain here for long. They captured several other officers of your rank, and they are all in another, smaller and remote prison, where they are guarded by the worst sort of Ustashas, those in black uniforms and with a lot of experience from Jasenovac.'

'I see,' remarked Količek, suddenly becoming worried. He knew about these beasts and the place.

'But there's another group of prisoners, somewhere in this building, they are politicians from the Croatian Peasant Party and are in a better position because Pavelić is afraid of what could happen if he simply executed them. Ivan Pernar—who was shot together with Radić in 1928—is one of them, then Tomašić, Farolfi, Ipša, Pešelj, Torbar, Smoljan, and some others. Important political figures. Do whatever you can to avoid spending too much time in the small prison, try to end up with them here.'

'Enough talking!' interrupted a tall, ugly Ustasha with a strong southern dialect. 'You, sir,' he addressed Srdjan politely, 'please kindly leave. And you scum,' talking to Vladimir, 'take these trousers of yours into your hands and move your traitor ass back to your cell!'

And Vladimir Količek obeyed, secretly putting the piece of paper with the children's drawings into his pocket. Srdjan went where he had been going to for the last two years, and he knew that.

It was like Srdjan had said: in a couple of days, Vlado was transported to a house on a hill north of Zagreb, where he met several of his colleagues from the Home Guard. And the beasts in black uniforms were also there. He was aware that the black uniforms were reserved for the most fanatical Ustashas after the brown ones had been introduced. In order to remain sane, he was refusing to think about his future: he had lived a full life, and if his destiny was to die there as just another victim of that mad and evil time, what then? He had already witnessed so many meaningless deaths, and he was going to face the creator sooner or later anyway; he had nothing much to say to the creator—only that all of the divine plans had failed at some point terribly.

However, it turned out that his sojourn in the remote prison was much better than he had expected. First of all, they had a decent toilet. Secondly, they were treated as military prisoners and not as plain criminals, being somewhat respected by their guards—who just waited for a sign to slaughter the traitors but were still impressed by their ranks. Finally, as the time was passing, it was becoming clear that their fate was not to finish their lives on that hill, because letters started to arrive, and they were eventually allowed to write back.

About four weeks after Količek's arrival, all of the prisoners, including him, were moved to the big jail where he had started his new career of an inmate.

There, after spending a few days separated in different cells, all of them met again in a big cell where they found the politicians from the Croatian Peasant Party. It seemed that all of the conspirators were meant to be kept at a single place and isolated from the rest of the prison, probably because this was making it easier for the Ustashas to set up a precise schedule for interrogations. The plotters were happy to be together, but they did not know whether this was actually good or bad; they only knew that some of them would, after being taken out from the cell, return either exhausted or injured from torture. Even the elderly members of the group were not spared. Vlado was waiting for his turn and was trying to remain courageous.

But before that came, they received their sentences: he was, in particular, sentenced to three years' hard labour starting from the nineteenth of December 1944, because he had 'within the officer circles developed activities against the Independent State of Croatia and against the wellbeing of the Croatian people'. The surprises did not end there: on the eighteenth of December, Vladimir F Količek was escorted to Kletina, where he was about to stay in house arrest until further notice, as an enemy of the state. He remained in this position until the end of World War II.

The reason for this turn of events has remained unclear until today, especially if one takes into account that more than half of his fellow inmates from the big cell were executed by the Ustashas in April 1945, whereas most of the others had to flee to the West after the war, when the communists came to power. In any case, their elimination was the final nail in the coffin of non-fascist and non-communist Croatia, and many despicable individuals have benefited from that during the years that followed—as nothing could be simpler than having two colours only: black and white, without fine shades of grey.

After Vlado's death, his first neighbour in Kletina—who was only a few years younger—told Borna that his grandfather had been a big player throughout his life, having connections everywhere and also many documents which could have made life miserable to many people on all of the confronted sides of the war.

'Everyone has a secret or two that must remain hidden,' the neighbour said, 'so it was much easier for his enemies to let him live than to constantly think what he did with the information he had. I have no doubt that Vlado had a good deal with just about everyone. People both loved him and feared him, and he knew well how to use that.'

XXIV

1944–1945, Krotko, Vinodol and Podgorje County Independent State of Croatia

Ivan the Blacksmith would always try to avoid conflict, usually by just walking away from a person keen to solve a disagreement through a fight; he would just leave without saying anything, except for sometimes mumbling swear words (never involving God). It could be that Borna inherited this style from him, because both of his parents were fighting spirits, especially his mother. In Borna's case, such behaviour was on many occasions considered to be an acceptance of defeat, which would never happen with his grandfather—he would always only gain more respect. On the other hand, they lived in different times and surrounded by different people.

Ivan the Proud was not a coward; he only had a unique talent for turning the aggressiveness of an opponent into a weakness, eventually becoming able to manipulate the situation similarly to a small boxer who would use the momentum of his bigger rival to knock him out. Now and again, he would just wait for a proper opportunity—he could wait for months if necessary—but the victory was always his and without any physical confrontation. And it was the same with his survival during the war, as patience and thoroughness were behind his ability to do the right things at the right time. At the beginning of the war, when lawlessness had been prevailing, he had been hiding; when it was safer to be conscripted by the Home Guard than to hide, he stopped hiding. And when the end of the war was obviously near, he knew that a reign of anarchy was coming again and that he had to be there where one had a better chance to stay alive.

Thus, when the Partisans expelled the gendarmes from Krotko for two weeks in late 1944, he joined them—leaving Roža in tears but with enough money and food in the house, which had been his plan for quite some time. Although he had fathered a baby girl just a few months ago (which put Roža under more pressure), he assessed that their ten-year-old daughter was already fit to help Roža—and the six-year-old son too, at least partly—and that the future of the family would have been more secure if he had been a soldier in the victorious army. Speaking about his beliefs, he had no problems with joining the Partisans. He was only a peasant and had no political preference whatsoever—he just wanted to one day continue living with his wife and children as peacefully as possible.

After the collapse of the Kingdom of Yugoslavia and the establishment of the Independent State of Croatia, he at first had sympathies for the new state simply because it seemed to him that the Croats deserved to have a state of their own after so many centuries. However, when he realised that hardworking and undemanding people like him were persecuted only because of their religion or nationality, he lost every interest in that state. For him, every state had a right to set laws, collect taxes, recruit soldiers, etc., but it was not supposed to harass their citizens, as all of them were the children of God. The Partisans, on the other hand, had no state, at least not yet. They would execute a villain often—or even a suspected war profiteer—plunder, behave rudely or arrogantly, steal livestock, flour, dried meat or cheese, but there was no record of someone getting killed by them only because of having a picture of a wrong saint on the wall. For Ivan, in short, the Partisans were a bad army of lazy crooks—and led by Godless, despicable communists—but they were better than the others. And most importantly, they were winning the war…

The first days of Ivan the Blacksmith in the Partisans were relatively easy. Though he got a German carbine as a personal weapon, he was not meant to be sent into battle—he was much more useful as a mechanic. His talent and the understanding of the properties of metal, and so on, were compensating for his lack of experience with weapons. In particular, the Partisans had recently acquired some heavy weapons, but these were often breaking, mainly because of being mishandled. Some unfortunate people would even be killed or injured by malfunctioning cannons and mortars. It became clear to Ivan that most of what was happening was because no one was realising that these were fine machines which required regular maintenance, so he first asked for an ample supply of rags for cleaning and oil for lubrication. Consequently, he first made two howitzers work perfectly; and after that, he could ask for anything—so he eventually established a well-equipped mobile workshop.

His brigade was ethnically mixed—with about two thirds of the Croats and one third of the Serbs. It had been founded in 1941 as a unit composed entirely of the Serbs of Croatia, who were mistreated by the quisling Croatian state, but over the course of years, many Croats joined it—some by defecting from the Home Guard, some by force, and some voluntarily or opportunistically. In 1943, after the fall of Mussolini's Italy, a considerable number of the Serbs left the Chetniks and joined the brigade. In any case, those who would raise questions on someone's ethnicity or past would be court-martialled and in most cases simply shot. The same procedure applied to love affairs amongst the soldiers—many of whom were women—and every revealed romance would virtually always end before a firing squad. The Partisans were a determined, disciplined, brutal, and highly efficient fighting force. Expressing religious feelings was not welcome but was not sanctioned, for a simple reason: apart from a certain number of atheist communists, the Partisans were composed mainly of peasants, who believed that they were going to be rewarded one day for joining the forces of justice—and this reward was in the hands of their creator, whoever he was.

Ivan the Proud was not among the Partisans who brought an end to the war in Krotko (on the ninth of April 1945) by entering the village peacefully; the gendarmes—now in civilian clothes—showed no interest in resisting, and the whole process went smoothly. Some of the villagers thought that this was a liberation, some that it was a new Yugoslav-Serbian occupation, but most of them just said that the war had finally ended—as simple as that. Period. Highlands, simple and harsh life—period.

When the Partisans were coming, Roža was on the road with the children, hoping to see her husband, but he was not there.

He was on his way to the Istrian Peninsula, where the situation was confusing. *De jure*, the wider region was still part of Italy (since the Great War), although being inhabited (apart from the western coast) overwhelmingly by the Croats and the Slovenes—and these were taking revenge against the Italians and trying to advance towards Trieste, the largest city in the region. The local Partisan forces were still too weak to fight the retreating Germans and the Italian militia, and a strong reinforcement was sent to help them and resolve this matter once and for all.

The Partisans were approaching with some fifty thousand soldiers, heavy weaponry, and tanks, so the Axis Powers' defence was soon restricted to a small area in and around the city of Trieste.

It was not uncommon, as Ivan used to say later, to see Partisan and German/Italian troops walking just some hundred metres from each other without firing a bullet; they all knew that the war was over, and no one was willing to risk losing life. The brutality of the Partisans was, however, manifested in massive executions of the Italian civilians left behind their armed forces, but this did not concern Tito at all—he was determined to conquer Trieste and shift the Yugoslav-Italian border westwards as much as possible, even if this meant civilian deaths or a conflict with the British forces that were coming closer from the opposite side of the city.

XXV

1945, Trieste, Operational Zone of the Adriatic Littoral
Interregnum; formerly, part of Nazi Germany (State District of Carinthia)

The Partisans conquered Trieste swiftly during the first days of May.

Simultaneously, the British concentrated their forces north of the city, to show some muscle, and their units were composed mainly of New Zealanders—who were newcomers to this war and certainly no match for the experienced Tito warriors despite having an advantage in weapons. This situation was not without any danger. In fact, several hard-line communist agitators among the Partisans—advocating worldwide proletarian revolution and war against capitalism—were shot because they were 'acting against national interests' by trying to provoke a major conflict with the New Zealanders.

There were a number of ethnic Croats in the New Zealand troops, belonging to the first or second generation of immigrants to this country that was so attractive to European paupers. One of them was Nick (Niko) Velich (Velić), aged twenty-four, who had come to New Zealand just six years ago from a village in Dalmatia. In 1944, when he heard that an innocent woman from his Dalmatian village had been shot by the Germans in revenge for the death of one of their soldiers, he felt that it was his duty to join the war. So many Anglo-Saxons were doing that for Britain, he thought, so why would he be any worse?

Nick knew who was in Trieste and on the surrounding hills: the city had been captured primarily by the Ninth Slovenian Corps and the Eighth Dalmatian Corps of the Partisan Army, hence a confrontation with his Dalmatian neighbours or even relatives was not out of the question.

There were also some other Partisan units around, all of them heavily armed and angry. After more than twenty years of suffering and humiliation of the Istrian and Dalmatian Slavs—who were in Fascist Italy treated as a subhuman race—everyone without a red star on the hat was their enemy.

The two armies would indeed fight each other occasionally, in isolated skirmishes, and the New Zealanders would invariably lose—because they were still thinking in terms of a gallant war in which some rules were supposed to be obeyed. They did not know that there were no rules in this war. The British and the Partisans were allies officially, but the situation on the field was quite different, since the political agenda was changing on a daily basis. In all of that confusion, Nick Velich was only once in a perilous situation, and it would not be exaggerated to state that he survived it only because he was at the mercy of a man who cherished every life. Nick was going to remember this event for the rest of his life, always wondering about the identity of his saviour.

Ivan the Blacksmith was spending his time far from the hot spots of Trieste, by maintaining cannons, mortars, machine guns, and tanks. All of these were for him just machines which had to be clean, well lubricated, and without broken or deformed parts; although he did not understand in detail how they were functioning, he was very successful in keeping them working well. He was also taking good care of his German carbine, but he had never used it and he hoped that he was never going to.

And then the New Zealanders tried to do something really stupid.

Only gods from all known religions might have known what came into the minds of these naive white Pacific children when they tried to steal a flag from the Partisans. This was, presumably, just a game for them, something characteristic of a rivalry between two colleges, and they were definitely not aware of what they were really attempting to do. They could not understand that their counterparts were not some cheerful guys from the neighbourhood—who would gladly acknowledge the skills of their rivals later in a local pub—but the people whose lives had been ruined in their very foundations, who were storming through this war by seeking revenge and leaving pools of blood behind them, who were killing without remorse and asking for more, until their pain would disappear just for a moment in such an act of frenzy. After a killing, they would take a deep breath, calm down for a while and then go for another one.

Nick, who had been challenged to lead the whole operation because of his Croatian ancestry, was crawling away from the site of the doom of his expedition, hearing screams of his comrades who were having a hard time before dying in whatever way. This incident has definitely never been recorded, for political reasons, and officially all of them died in combat against the Nazis. And just when Nick was about to reach some bushes, he saw a pair of boots in front of his eyes—and a carbine above. He tried to grab his pistol (he found it earlier next to the dead body of an officer who had joined the mission) but a boot stopped him, almost breaking his arm. Then he started to cry and to pray in Croatian, expecting the worst to come.

'You pray in Croatian? How come?' he heard a voice from above the boots. 'Anyway, remain still and let us pray together for these poor children there. Our Father in heaven, hallowed be your name...'

'But, but... You'll not kill me?'

'No, why would I?'

'You're a Partisan.'

'Yes, and a blacksmith. I maintain and repair things, I don't destroy them. Those who made them may destroy them. And only the Lord can give and take life.'

Still trembling in fear, Nick raised his head and saw a slim but strong man in his early thirties or late twenties, concentrated on the prayer and not holding the rifle any more. His big and strong hands—much bigger than one could expect for a man of his size—were entwined, giving a certain dignity to this surreal ceremony.

'You really have no intention to kill me, sir?' asked Nick in disbelief.

'I've told you, it's not me who has the power of giving or taking life, only our Lord can to do it,' replied the man between two sentences of his prayer. Nick stopped asking and then joined him: Hail Mary, full of grace, the Lord is with thee... And after they had finished, Nick asked again,

'And you're not a communist?'

'No, just a blacksmith.'

'Will you let me go? They'd kill me if they caught me.'

'Without your pistol, go. You can't have it. There's been enough death for one night, and we're not even enemies—so the bosses say.'

After Ivan explained to him where he should go, they heard someone shouting,

'Ivo! Hey, Ivan! Who's there with you? Are you speaking with someone?'

'No!' Ivan shouted back, 'I'm just cursing this damned mule here! Any trouble?'

'Not really, we're only having a handful of redheaded English idiots at supper. They're even stupider than the Germans and the Italians combined!'

'I see!'

'Good night, Ivo, and catch a redheaded fiend if you can!'

Ivan the Proud did not respond, and he turned his head to the young man who was still in disbelief.

'I'll not ask what you're doing here,' said Ivan in a calm, fatherly tone of voice. 'I know that I've got to be here, but you... War is a shitty place to be, think about that and crawl to these bushes and later proceed as I told you.'

When Nick returned to his unit, there was no sympathy for him, but no one was blaming him for anything either.

'These things happen,' said a lieutenant, 'in this bloody war. Your friends are not the only ones we lost. The Partisans are maybe animals but they're on their own ground—and we must keep a low profile until ordered otherwise. You're going to a hospital now, corporal, and there you'll forget.'

The Trieste crisis was solved politically and without a major clash between the Partisans and the New Zealanders: the city remained Italian, whereas Yugoslavia acquired most of the surrounding territory.

Nick Velich survived the war and lived long enough to witness the birth of the new Croatia in the 1990s. He even visited the country of his origin several times before and after that. The identity of his God-fearing saviour remained a mystery for the rest of his life. In any case, neither he nor Ivan the Blacksmith could have known that the blood of their families were going to be mixed one peculiar night—during an odd encounter of two troubled souls.

XXVI

1945, Kletina
Interregnum; under the command of the Provisional Government of Democratic Federal Yugoslavia

Kletina was full of the Partisans who awaited something. They did not look like jolly people.

It was late May, and only a few weeks ago Kletina had been full of defeated soldiers of the Independent State of Croatia—both the Ustashas and the Home Guard conscripts—who had been fleeing in the direction of north, towards Austria and the British Army there; they were accompanied by many civilians, some of whom were their relatives, some supporters of the fallen quisling state, and some just ordinary people frightened of what would have happened if they had been left at the mercy of the Partisans. There was a lot of fear and anxiety in the air. This was, altogether, a chaotic mass of desperate individuals without any command. Their only goal was to turn themselves in to the British and thus avoid surrender to the Partisans—who had a terrible reputation. The leaders of the collapsed state, however, did not have this problem: they had fled some time ago with stolen Jewish gold and were already heading to South America, using the ratlines organised by the Catholic Church.

Amongst the evacuees, there were also many people who had nothing to do with the Independent State of Croatia. First of all, a number of the Chetniks were fleeing in the same direction; they and the Ustashas—mortal enemies during the war—were mixing together as if they were just two branches of a same army. Then the infamous Circassian irregulars, Albanian *Balli Kombëtar* troops, Ukrainian Cossacks, Crimea Tatars, German civilians from Romania, Serbia, East

Croatia, and parts of the Soviet Union; one could also spot convinced anti-communists from the quisling armies of Hungary, Bulgaria, and Romania, and even some Italian fascists who continued to fight even after the fall of their silly empire. This was a colourful crowd, with all these uniforms, which somewhat reminded Vladimir F Količek—who was not under house arrest any more—of the situation in Sarajevo four years ago, at the beginning of the war. He was watching this circus from a wide open window of his family house in Kletina, in civilian clothes. The circumstances were, on the other hand, completely different: in Sarajevo, something had been forming, and the same thing was, at the end of the war, dissipating right before his eyes.

After the circus had left northwards in a slow, seemingly endless line of distressed and frightened souls, the high street of Kletina was at first unpleasantly silent, but Vladimir was still watching it in anticipation. He felt that the street was not going to remain empty for long. Indeed, in a matter of days, the Partisans were there. Some proceeded to the north without stopping, and some remained, capturing the town without a fight.

They stood silently in the street and waited. Not a single one of them looked like a merry person. Some of the local Partisans—hidden so far in nearby forests—joined them with the same expression. The next day, they waited too. And again the day after; and so on for about a week. Vlado continued to observe them from the window of his house.

One afternoon, an unusual commotion among the Partisans first started abruptly and then resulted in their forming lines on both sides of the street. Suddenly, a mass of slow moving and shabby looking, ghostlike creatures emerged from around the corner: they were walking in rows of four, being guarded by the Partisans on both sides of the procession. Vladimir recognised the captives: they were of the same people who had been fleeing northwards a few weeks ago. He could not know that the British had refused their surrender on Austrian soil, leaving them to face the Partisans and their wrath. After some sporadic and futile resistance (the last fighting in Europe in World War II, lasting until the fifteenth of May), the quislings had to lay down their arms and face their doom as captives of the Partisans.

Those walking in front of Vlado's window were just part of the forces which had surrendered at the Austrian village of Bleiburg. Many had already been executed in Slovenian forests before they could reach Croatia—their numbers later being estimated to be as much as several tens of thousands—and the others were continuing their journey into the unknown, to face their bitter repatriation. It was a tragedy that the victims were not only the Ustasha fanatics—who really could not have expected any mercy—but also many of the boys conscripted into Ustasha troops hastily at the end of the war. There was also a considerable number of Home Guard soldiers who were targeted due to personal revenges, rumours about their roles in the war or, even worse, simply because of the deep hatred planted by the murderous ideology of Pavelić and his comrades into the hearts of their victims.

Vladimir could not know of the summary executions, but he understood the character of the past war and the human instinct of revenge—so he recognised the danger every prisoner was facing by simply belonging to this crowd. He also suspected that Srdjan had tried to avoid meeting people like his cousin Živan by joining the refugees in the hope that he could disappear in this mass like a drop of water in a lake. Many tried to do the same, but the zeal of the Partisans did not leave them much chance: those who had not been singled out for immediate execution were forced to join the repatriation and wait for another check of their right to continue living.

Količek was by his window all the time, observing patiently and trying to spot a familiar face. He was looking for his fellow inmates, who were hated by both the Ustashas (for committing treason against Croatia) and the Partisans (for committing treason against Yugoslavia); then for his casual acquaintances or occasional helpers in the humanitarian actions organised by him and von Glaise Horstenau, and also for other good and innocent people he had met during this long war. But more than anything, he was focused on that dear man Srdjan—whose tragic life had attracted his attention quite some time ago.

Srdjan's suffering without any guilt, his desperation and sadness without any complaint, his wish to simply live a decent life of a small man—with a humble family where the change of generations would be determined by nothing but nature—were in Vladimir's eyes a living portrait of the madness and bestiality of the past four years. And every message of hope that this bloodshed was never going to happen again, thought Vlado, should be told to future generations by Srdjan. He should get his painting of St John back, celebrate Christmas in his family on both the twenty-fifth of December and the seventh of January, visit Lutheran churches in Transylvania together with his wife and say a prayer there; and then, as an old man, gather children around him to tell them stories about the human kindness and compassion that made him pull through some rough times.

'Every reason for our ruling this planet will die together with Srdjan if they kill him,' Vladimir mumbled.

And then he spotted him: he was in a row together with an Ustasha, a man in civilian clothes, and a person looking like a Circassian horseman or a Cossack.

Vlado rushed down the stairs to see if anything could be done…

'I'm Vlado Količek, until recently a prisoner of the Ustashas confined to this house,' Vladimir addressed a Partisan guard.

'And?' replied the Partisan in the local dialect. 'I don't know you, and I'm from here.'

'I haven't been here for a while, young man, because I was doing some things for our cause elsewhere, just as some people you've captured had. You've made a mistake in some cases, and they should be released. I see one of them here.'

'Do you? And I see only a bunch of criminals here.'

'Come, come, young man, I know what I'm talking about. These are not silly things. May I speak with some of the officers? I'll explain everything in detail to them,' Vladimir tried to confuse the guard, but the young Partisan could not be swayed.

'Would you? Then go to Zagreb and explain. I'm here doing my duty and you'll not pass.'

Realising that this would not work, Vladimir went to another Partisan guard. And to another, and to another… All of them were ignoring him, obviously having strict orders not to let anyone interfere with the fate of the captives. Then he looked around and saw numerous women and men trying to do the same, all of them with a story and a reason of their own; and the guards were invariably remaining perfectly calm, disciplined, and merciless. No one could penetrate their line, not even to give water or food to the prisoners—who were continuing to march without any expression on their faces: they looked like people who were already dead.

After concluding that there was nothing he could do Vlado rushed to let Srdjan know that he was there.

'Srdjan, I'm here, endure!' he shouted. 'Here I am, Količek! Vlado! Endure! We'll find a way!'

Srdjan raised his weary eyes and looked to where the voice was coming from. At first, he could not recognise the face; and when he finally did, he was utterly surprised. He knew that Vladimir was from somewhere in this part of Croatia, but this still looked surreal: colonel Količek again—this could not be true! So many times he had been there for me and my family, Srdjan thought, but this time, only some magic could give him the power to perform one of his tricks that would lead to things settling down by themselves.

He looked at Vlado briefly, nodded his head and continued to walk with his head down; the only hope he had was that Količek was going to take care of his women—this was the only magic he wanted from that dear colonel. Živan was waiting somewhere at the end of the road, he knew that.

Vladimir F Količek, once a distinguished officer, spy, and skilful intriguer—now just another civilian of a suspicious past—tried to leave Kletina and follow Srdjan to Zagreb or to wherever his destination was, but he was stopped. They told him that he was still in a kind of house arrest—which meant that he was not permitted to leave Kletina in any direction, because his activities during the war were not clarified yet; if he had disobeyed, he would have been shot immediately, they said.

He had outwitted Ciano and Mihailović, survived the Chetnik fanatics on the way to Sarajevo and the Ustasha butchers therein, negotiated with the communists and saved Captain Forbes, conspired with von Horstenau, manipulated just about every local quisling or Partisan commander within his reach, and eventually survived a prison from whence almost everyone was taken to an execution site… And this time, he was finally helpless.

He was defeated for the first time in his life, by this new reality, and he felt that not even the mighty Tarzan could change that.

XXVII

1945, Savnik, People's Republic of Croatia Federative People's Republic of Yugoslavia

There were three officers behind a desk, all of them in freshly designed, Soviet-like uniforms of the new Yugoslav Army.

The uniforms bore no resemblance whatsoever to those of the pre-war Royal Yugoslav Army, a feeble force that had been only at the beginning of the war represented by the troops of Mihailović—and which faded away from the history of the Balkans smoothly during the war. The new army emerged from the Partisan movement—which had been a guerrilla force with no official uniforms—and standardising the uniforms was important in emphasising the fact that the new Yugoslavia, dominated by the communists, became internationally recognised as a state. The three officers—one of whom was a woman—represented one of the many martial law courts that were all over the country deciding on the destinies of survivors of the repatriation.

Srdjan entered the room accompanied by a guard, which brought back some memories: he had been in the same room in 1941 as a lieutenant of the defeated Royal Yugoslav Army, at the mercy of the Ustashas; this time, he was a major of the defeated Home Guard of the Independent State of Croatia, at the mercy of the Partisans. In 1941, he had been simply identified as a Serb and enemy of the Croatian people and their new state, told that he should wear a blue armband all the time and then left to live in fear; this time, he was about to face a trial as a Croatian chauvinist and possibly war criminal. He knew that there were only two outcomes of the trial: they were either going to accept his explanation of the events from 1942 or not, and he was either going to be executed or walk away as a free man. Sending someone in a quisling uniform to prison would seldom occur, and the results of these trials were usually very simple: die or go home.

In any case, Srdjan was at peace with God.

Being back in Savnik for a month already, Ljerka knew what was going on—and she was crying day and night. Klara was drinking, day and night—there was no one she could ask for help, and she felt useless. Barbara and Danka were playing with the only doll they had and did not know a thing; they were anyway by far too young to understand the crooked world of grown-up people. No one from the family was allowed to be present during the trial, because this was—as they had been informed—a strictly military affair since Srdjan was an officer.

'Jarbašić, Srdjan, father's name Stevan, born in Malo Selce in 1910, lieutenant in the Royal Yugoslav Army, major in the Home Guard of the Independent State of Croatia. Of Serbian nationality, Roman Catholic. Married to Ljerka, née Zultner, of German nationality, Roman Catholic. Father of two underage daughters. Captured near Bleiburg on the seventeenth of May 1945,' read the uniformed woman from a piece of paper. 'Is that correct?'

'Yes it is,' replied Srdjan.

'You are here because of a war crime in September 1942 in the Savnik area, when you participated in the murder of more than two hundred civilians on site and in taking another thousand peasants into the Jasenovac death camp, of whom only a small number survived. What have you got to say in your defence?'

'I didn't do any of that. I wasn't even there.'

'But you did negotiate with the peasants to come home from the forest?' asked the younger of the two male officers. They obviously knew everything, and this gave Srdjan hope that the whole affair might be finally clarified—his innocence first of all. Many had lost their lives simply because of misinformation and negligence. He knew that.

'Yes I did, I had to. The Ustashas were threatening my family, and they also assured me that no one was going to be harmed. I had no choice. As a Serb in their army, I had no luxury of making choices.'

'Why wouldn't you tell us the whole story in more detail, major?' asked the third, older officer, who had been silent until then. 'This incident has been remembered for its really tragic consequences, but little is known of what exactly happened.'

It was not clear whether the older officer was concerned with details due to his own curiosity or because knowing more was of some importance to the Partisans for other reasons. In any case, his interest did not seem to be a bad sign.

And then Srdjan talked. He was standing completely still and was speaking slowly—he was at peace with God, and only his lips were moving.

He explained everything from the very beginning: about his capture in Maribor and how he had been in this camp already, with a blue piece of cloth wrapped around his arm; how the Ustashas had wanted to slaughter his family and why he had converted to Catholicism; how he had been blackmailed all the time and about his troops mistrusted by the Ustashas; how he had spent the rest of the war in Zagreb in military administration, never firing a bullet, and then about his fleeing to Austria because of an instinctive fear and the lack of any other option...

The court members listened silently. It looked like the young officer was disapproving of his excuses, but the woman and the older officer seemed to be more understanding. It appeared for a while that acquitting Srdjan was perhaps not impossible—and then another officer entered the room: Živan.

'Comrade Colonel Jarbašić!' exclaimed the older officer, and then all the members of the court stood up.

'At ease, comrades, at ease. Well, well, what have we got here? My dear cousin Srdjan! I see you at last. A major now, right? Pity you've got no army any more. I have one, see my uniform? Cousin... Dear cousin.'

'Comrade colonel, we have just been about to complete...' spoke the older officer only to be interrupted.

'Shut up, you... idiot, you!' shouted Živan and started to walk across the room nervously. Then he continued.

'To complete what? There's no trial in this case! Take this miserable scum out of my sight... For good! And don't mark his grave! Where should I sign? You're dismissed, I'll sign. Where?'

And then he left as quickly as he had come in. Srdjan was, strangely, not disturbed much, he was completely numb—he somehow knew that this was about to come sooner or later. He felt that there was no place for him in this world. Being at peace with God, he had known that for a long time.

Klara was the first one in the family who learned about Srdjan's trial and its conclusion. Such sentences would seldom be conveyed to the family, because in the communist world, traitors did not deserve any eulogy and were meant to disappear without a trace. It was just that Klara knew some cleaning women in Savnik, who would always hear every news, and she had invested some money into making them pay attention to this particular case.

One of the cleaning women said that this was very dangerous, and Klara then told her,

'Don't you know who I am? I am Babuška, the evil woman of Savnik! So take this money and do what I ask or face my wrath!'

The woman went to a church to ask for advice, but no one was there; she therefore decided that she should simply obey the witch.

Klara again stopped drinking.

'Look, child,' she said to her daughter after a day or two, 'this must not end like that. You should rescue your husband, and you should do it fast. This is not impossible, and I've already arranged transport for your whole family to the coast, from whence you'll go to Argentina. This has been arranged too.'

'Mother...' replied Ljerka full of tears.

'Start talking now. Here is a loaf of bread, and inside is a rasp. Now be a proper wife and take that to Srdjan. Once he's out, I'll know what to do—everything has been organised. I'll eat grass after that, but he'll survive. And later you'll join him together with the children. There's a place for you to hide in Dalmatia, and then you'll go to Argentina! Your family must survive—I owe this to my Ivo!'

'My father Johann... Ivo. Yes, he. And you mother... How...'

'Stop talking, girl, and go now!'

Ljerka ended up in jail and did not save Srdjan. The whole plan was like from a novel, too romantic and naive—it simply could not work. In the meantime, Vladimir Količek was doing his best to solve his problems in

Kletina and then join the rescuing of Srdjan. However, this was going rather slowly, and the only thing he managed to do was to reach Klara and ask her about the status of the affair. Due to the lack of proper channels for communication, they were running out of time.

Eventually Vlado found a way to contact an old friend of his, who was influential enough to interfere with the whole situation. The first thing this man managed to do was to free Ljerka from jail, and then he arranged the safe travel of Vlado to Savnik.

XXVIII

1946–1948, Savnik & Kletina, People's Republic of Croatia
Federative People's Republic of Yugoslavia

'At ease, comrade colonel,' said General Tomić to Živan Jarbašić—who was sweating. 'But be very, very careful from now on, I'm warning you. I'm leaving the two of you alone now, and my good friend Vlado will later inform me on how you've been getting along.'

Then he menacingly slammed the door shut and left. Behind his tiny stature was obviously a formidable personality.

To be visited by General Pavao Tomić was the worst nightmare of every officer, since this man was extremely dangerous and merciless. Rumours on his sending to jail, or even before a firing squad, those who misused their power in the post-war time—especially with regard to unnecessary executions—preceded him. There had been enough deaths, and the country had to be rebuilt; the revenge, therefore, had to stop. Since things had to settle down, he had the full support of the government in Belgrade to participate in resolving this problem once and for all, in order to help bring prosperity and peace of mind to the injured land. Many suspicious characters were skilled and knowledgeable in different professions, and useful people did not come out of the blue. Yugoslavia was in large part a state of barely literate peasants, who could not do much more than produce food, and there was a desperate need for those who knew more.

Tomić had been a Home Guard colonel before he defected to the Partisans in 1944, bringing them the information that—according to some historians—undermined the Independent State of Croatia more than two full Partisan corpses could have; and in the Partisans, he advanced to the rank of general in no time, taking part in military intelligence affairs. His assignment was not random: before the war, his superior officer in Belgrade had been Colonel Vladimir F Količek, the most competent spy in the region. Two of them were also bound by passion for military history, which was later going to be the basis of their decades-long scientific collaboration.

On the other hand, Živan Jarbašić was just another expendable colonel—a person who had got this rank because of his bravery in the war—being quite useless in the army that wanted to become a modern military force. He knew that, he felt that, and this was why he was sweating.

'Jarbašić, comrade colonel,' said Vlado from his chair after a few moments of silence. He was aware of his advantage in this situation. 'You are then this comrade Colonel Jarbašić.'

'Yes. Comrade?'

'Količek, comrade Colonel Količek for you,' replied Vlado. 'Address me this way, if you please. Comrade General Tomić may explain to you why if you wish, but don't be misled by my civilian clothes.'

'That wouldn't be necessary, comrade colonel. I've always respected the rank.'

'Good, good. So have I, comrade colonel. And do you know why I'm here?'

'No, not really.'

'I'm looking for an old friend of mine. His surname is also Jarbašić. A nice, dear, innocent family man. And also an officer.'

Živan's mouth went dry. He started to realise what this was all about.

'I don't know anyone with this name within military circles, comrade Colonel Količek,' he said after hesitating for a while. 'Perhaps he's a Jarbašić from somewhere else? Would that be possible?'

Vladimir was becoming angry but did not want to show it. Of course Živan knew—but this was not a time for showing emotions. He stood up and then walked across the room silently for a while. Then he continued,

'No, it wouldn't. You know very well what I'm talking about—stop pretending. And be very careful with your answers from now on unless you want to see the comrade general again.'

There was a long period of silence after that, during which Vladimir poured some brandy into two glasses and handed one to his sweating opponent; then Količek sat down again, opposite to Živan, and said in a rather threatening voice,

'Yes, you wouldn't know. Stop playing games with me. Tell me where he is. And choose your words well, comrade colonel.'

Živan realised that this situation was everything but easy for him, especially when he remembered the determination of General Tomić and his reputation. It was also quite clear that no lie could bring him any good.

'Not with us any more. Gone.'

Vladimir knew that he was going to hear that, but he managed to restrain himself from reacting. Instead, he started to gaze into Živan's eyes—which this man could not stand.

'When did this happen?' asked Vlado.

'A few months ago, in a forest. Together with some others.'

'Grave?'

'With the others... Somewhere, I don't know.'

'You don't know... And he was your cousin, right?'

'Yes he was.'

'Then—why?'

'You wouldn't understand. Količek? This isn't a Serbian surname, you're probably not a Serb. Or?'

'No, I'm not a Serb.'

'He betrayed us, our Serbian honour and tradition, by marrying a Croatian woman and renouncing Orthodoxy; he simply had to die according to our ancient laws.'

'But comrade colonel, he never did anything wrong. Marrying a Croatian woman was a matter of love, and renouncing Orthodoxy a way to survive. Or should I depict you how it was during that time? Are you that stupid or ignorant?'

'This is your argument, whereas our old laws have a logic of their own. You can't understand, you're not a Serb.'

'So you killed a good man because of some prehistoric, stupid logic?' asked Količek in an agitated way, which was everything but typical of him. Živan felt that he was walking on thin ice, and he decided to choose his words more carefully.

'Look,' he said, 'many others from my family would have done the same if they'd had a chance. I just did what was expected from me.'

Vladimir was outraged. He did not know how to react—which was also not typical of him. In fact, he had no power to punish this despicable man, he was just playing a game he had arranged together with Tomić, with one goal only: to save Srdjan's family. They knew that Srdjan was dead, but his women were still alive, and only this mattered. He continued the game carefully, trying not to lessen the fear in Jarbašić and also not to irritate him.'

'And his family? Tell me, Jarbašić, and don't pretend that you don't know.'

'Living in Savnik, still unharmed. But our unwritten laws might reach them sooner or later. Not by me—by someone else.'

Vladimir F Količek stopped speaking for a while. The idiot before him was right—another moron might have been waiting somewhere in order to finish the job. Vlado suddenly became the one who had to be careful with words.

'Look, Jarbašić, I'll now offer you a chance to survive,' Vladimir gambled, 'and you should know that you're so close to a firing squad—which has been the intention of my friend Pavao ever since he heard what you had done. This is a one-time opportunity. You'll never get it again.'

Živan hesitated for a moment, trying to comprehend other possible scenarios—in most of which he was eventually dead. To kill Količek on site, for instance? And then? He would not stay alive for more than a few minutes. To try to run away? Where? He would become just another renegade, and everything he had done during the war would be disregarded.

'Say what have you got to say, comrade colonel,' he finally replied.

'After I leave this room, I'll forget that I ever met you, and I shall take Ljerka and her girls with me. We'll never even visit Savnik, and we'll cease to exist in your mind. And in the minds of those who could care one way or another. You'll spread word that they have gone never to return, that the whole matter is over, and none of your people will ever again ask about them... Never! You have the power to do that, and if you don't… I'll be back with the comrade general. Sooner or later—don't underestimate us. We're bigger than you, trust me.'

'And may God have mercy on our souls…'

'Exactly. And now get out of my sight.'

Živan Jarbašić stood up from his chair and headed towards the door; he was very angry, his vanity was hurt, but he was too scared to react—only God knew who or what was behind this cold and ominous Količek. General Tomić—that was for sure—but who else? The whole matter was not worth continuing: Srdjan was dead, and the rest was largely irrelevant. Their honour was saved, after all, and he was the one who did it; this thought made him feel good.

Vlado found the house in complete disorder, although Klara's sister and brother were back. Ljerka's aunt was minding her own business, whereas the uncle was constantly visiting his old friends from the neighbourhood to exchange stories on how all of them managed to stay alive. The house was, all in all, divided between two worlds: one of happiness for the coming of peace, and one of sadness for the death of good old days. And these two worlds did not touch each other.

A new situation was that Klara was sober—looking after Barbara and Danka—and Ljerka constantly drunk, in her marital bedroom where she had locked herself in (refusing to come out). She would eat something occasionally but would mainly leave the bedroom only to go to the toilet, paying no attention to either of her children or anything else outside her asylum. During the night, she would cry, so loudly that the whole neighbourhood would hear,

'Srdjo, Srdjo, Srdjo! I betrayed you! I didn't save you! I betrayed you, Srdjo! Why am I still alive? Why?'

And this was went on for weeks.

The girls would ask Klara what was happening with their mother, and the bitter middle-aged woman would reply, as gently as she could but still showing little empathy,

'Life isn't fair, girls. Don't you ever forget that!'

Vladimir came to the house with flowers for the women and a doll for the girls, but there was no one to open the door; in fact, the door was ajar, and the girls were playing alone on a carpet in the corridor. They were sitting there and were pleased to see anyone who could, in their minds, possibly help get their mother back.

'Hi, mister. Our mummy isn't well. Will you help us? We miss our mummy,' said Barbara. 'And our father isn't here either.'

'And we don't like our grandma,' continued Danka, who was always more direct than Barbara. 'She's an evil woman who doesn't love us. Our mummy is much better than her.'

Vlado was deeply touched by the sight of the lonely girls playing with some rags and wooden sticks. He gave them the doll and was glad to see their joy; then he put the bouquet onto a chair and observed the corridor to see if anyone else was there: the place was empty.

'Yes, girls, I've come to help your mummy. She's very sad now, and all of us must help her, especially the two of you,' Vlado approached them carefully—because this was a new situation for a bachelor like him, someone who had no experience with children. On the other hand, he was always very fond of the girls, and this made the whole thing easier.

'Vlado! Colonel Količek!' shouted Klara when she spotted him, and then she ran towards him instinctively before hugging him firmly. After a moment, she became embarrassed by that and suddenly moved away.

'Dear Mrs Zultner, I know everything, no need for any explanation. Where is Ljerka?'

'There in this bloody room, for weeks already. She neither eats nor speaks with anyone, just cries and shouts day and night, curses and swears. And drinks more than I ever had—there's not a drop of liquor in this house outside that room any more. She took it all. And she's buying more through the window from a woman who passes by now and then.'

'Show me!' said Vlado.

And then he sat down on the floor in front of the door of the marital bedroom of Ljerka and Srdjan Jarbašić, this shrine of one big love. And he felt small there, realising that he was about to put an end to the greatest love story he had ever encountered. But in this merciless time, all of them had so little choice. He thought that life was not fair, as if he had heard that somewhere already.

He knocked on the door.

'Ljerka, it's me, Vladimir Količek, how are you?'

'Who?'

'Količek. The colonel. The one always on your side.'

Ljerka was silent at first. Then she started to weep. And to scratch the door with her fingernails.

'Colonel Količek?' she eventually asked in a distant voice.

'Yes, it's me. How are you, Ljerka? Would you like to tell me?'

'No.'

'Why not?'

'Because you're not Srdjo. I need Srdjo. I love him, I don't love you.'

'But you still like me?'

She obviously needed some time to think; Vladimir knew that and waited patiently. Then she replied,

'Yes.'

'How about opening this door and seeing me? You say you like me, right? We haven't seen each other for a while, why not now?'

'I don't know, you're not Srdjo.'

'No, I'm Vlado. Remember when the three of us were together?'

'Yes,' said Ljerka in a calmer way.

'Would you open this door for me now, please? I've always been your friend—can you remember?'

'Yes.'

Being in a somewhat long but narrow valley, Kletina was a small town the expansion of which was limited by the steep surrounding hills. When Borna Didić was growing up there, it had no more than five thousand inhabitants—and when Vladimir had been getting off the train in 1946 together with Ljerka, Barbara, Danka, and Klara, the number of people living in Kletina had been maybe half of that or a bit more.

There, everyone knew everyone, and this event did not remain unnoticed. People are by their nature like birds of prey: even if they are not hungry, they observe the ground below and mark their future targets due to either an anticipated hunger or just an instinct of playing games with the weaker ones. Hence, the comments of the people of Kletina were: 'the horny bachelor has finally found a woman who would want him'; or 'the old goat has found a tart at last—*O tempora o mores*!'; or 'what a shame to bring completely unknown people into our neighbourhood, and none of them are men! We need men after this war!'

Vladimir's big old house was not empty, but no Količek was inside. Only the ground floor was occupied, by renters: there, a solicitor had an office, and a poor old woman lived in a small one-room flat. Upstairs, there were three big rooms with roofs almost four metres high, a big kitchen, and a bathroom. This was the new home of the four refugees from Savnik. Klara spotted a nice garden first—noticing a small hut there—whereas Ljerka did not care. The girls were thrilled by plenty of space for playing.

Vladimir took Ljerka—who was still feeble from her sorrow—into his arms and carried her like a princess into the house. Klara was looking after the girls, liking the place quite much.

While Vladimir was carrying her in his arms, Ljerka looked into his caring blue eyes and thought,

'He's actually quite an attractive mature man, this Količek.'

Immediately after that had come into her mind, she became ashamed and started to cry, thinking about Srdjan—and she wanted to be dead, together with him in some distant grave.

Vlado spotted her sudden sadness and respected her grief. He took her to the biggest bed in the house and laid her down as gently as he could. She rested there for days, and no one bothered her. In time, she left the room and started to show some interest in the world.

In the meantime, Klara was taking care of the unmaintained house; she asked Vladimir whether he had any objection—and he had none. He was, after all, an old bachelor who knew nothing about these things. His newly found joy was spending time with the girls, and he liked them more and more from day to day; he would also often see Ljerka—who was gradually recuperating and becoming stronger.

In a matter of months, they started to live a proper family life; it was just that the 'father' and the mother were not really a couple. However, the gentle personality of Vladimir enchanted Ljerka within a year; they got married, and he adopted the girls officially—which many disapproved at the time but eventually forgot the reasons for their complaints. The girls, since recently surnamed Jarbašić-Količek, were within a year or so fully accepted by the inhabitants of Kletina, which was not surprising—because this was at the core of these openhearted, decent, and good people who would sometimes be grumpy, conservative, harsh, and complaining just to make their lives less boring.

On Christmas Day, 1947, Vladimir came into the living room, holding a framed photo,

'It's Christmas, and we should now remember the people who have been ours and who should never be forgotten.'

And he defiantly (considering the contemporary situation in Yugoslavia) put the photo on a wall in the living room: it was a photo of Srdjan.

On the seventh of January 1948, Vladimir gathered the family again, holding a framed painting this time. He said,

'It's Christmas, and we should now remember the people who have been ours and who should never be forgotten.'

And he gave the painting of St John to Danka and Barbara.

XXIX

1946, Krotko, People's Republic of Croatia Federative People's Republic of Yugoslavia

Ivan the Blacksmith stopped for a while to observe Krotko in its full glory.

Being some five hundred metres from his house—on a hill above the village, from where he could see the whole valley and the big mountain behind—he sat down on a fallen tree. He took a deep breath and just watched, making no move or sound. As much as he wanted to see his family after such a long time, he could not resist spending some time alone, to enjoy the sight he had dreamed about for a year and a half.

He had not had to kill anyone in order to survive, and the merciful Lord had also decided that his destiny was to live. Ivan was very grateful for that—so he eventually mumbled a prayer: Our Father in heaven, hallowed be your name. Your kingdom come...

He was finally home.

There were some specks of snow (barely distinguishable from whitish rocks) all over the valley, whereas the mountain above was still wearing a dense white coat; wild hazelnut trees between dormant meadows and ploughed fields waited for the warmth of spring to wake them up; houses with their fuming chimneys looked like steamboats grouped into small fleets on a lake; and a silhouette moving fast between the buildings and orchards would occasionally show that this sleepy place was not deserted.

Ivan thought how strange it was that he had never before noticed the beauty of the place where he had lived for his entire life. He stayed there for more than half an hour, absorbing smells from the valley and noticing every sound—such as the barking of a dog or the dull noise of a busy axe. Overwhelmed with emotions, he then started to descend towards the picturesque scenery. As he was approaching the village, he could see that the houses were mainly intact, but there was no one outside—only a fast moving silhouette here and there, disappearing very quickly behind a door. He could sense fear in the air.

And he knew why. A lone person on the empty road was a sight that was making the villagers uncomfortable. It was April, and the war had been over for almost a year, but the forests had been throughout the winter echoing with occasional shooting, keeping the people of Krotko on the alert; there were rumours about some Chetniks and Ustashas still hiding in the mountain, probably more because they had nowhere to go than their wish to continue fighting for their causes. On the other hand, the shooting stopped about a month ago, and it seemed that peace was returning to the remote village, slowly and without a big parade—in the same way it had left five years ago.

'Did we dream? Did it ever happen?' asked Roža while resting her head on the chest of her husband. 'Was it all just a bad dream?'

Ivan the Proud did not answer: he had already fallen into a deep, dreamless sleep.

XXX

1991, Savnik area & Zagreb

Interregnum; *de jure*, the Socialist Republic of Croatia of the Socialist Federative Republic of Yugoslavia; *de facto*, the unrecognised Republic of Croatia, containing the secessionist, self-proclaimed and also unrecognised Republic of Serbian Krajina, a part of the questionable border between the two unrecognised states being south of Savnik

J Skoko had a dream: he wanted to be a war hero. Although he had no military experience whatsoever, he managed to become an officer in the Croatian National Guard which was more a militia than an army—but this was the only viable armed force the young Republic of Croatia had in the beginning of its struggle for independence from the Socialist Federative Republic of Yugoslavia.

He became a major through political channels, as a fanatical member of the Croatian Democratic Union led by Franjo Tudjman—which was officially a Christian democratic party but in reality a right-wing movement based on the most conservative parts of the ideology of the Catholic Church as well as on a xenophobic version of Croatian nationalism.

Major Skoko had a problem that could have been solved only by him becoming a war hero: he was a son of a Croatian couple from Herzegovina, who had been opportunistic atheist communists for years before becoming reborn Catholics and zealous supporters of the Croatian national revival in the late 1980s and early 1990s, and this hypocrisy was a burden that was pressing his small and undeveloped brain on a daily basis. He simply had to be a war hero in order to remove this shame from his family name!

Another thing which was bothering him was that the Croats of Herzegovina were in Zagreb—the place of his birth, childhood, and adolescence—in strained relations with the majority consisting of Zagreb natives and immigrants to the city from northern parts of Croatia. Not only did they speak different dialects, they also had incompatible cultural heritages: while the Herzegovinians belonged to previous *subjects* of Ottoman Turkey, the northerners belonged to previous *citizens* of Austria-Hungary. The former culture pursued conservatism intertwined with religious zeal and nationalism, whereas the latter was liberal and open to concepts that did not follow any strict ideology; one could, for instance, say that the Herzegovinians were devoted to medieval traditions and collectivism while the northerners were functioning mostly as individuals of a modern European type.

For example, during World War II, the Herzegovinians were predominantly supporting the Ustashas, whereas the northerners were primarily at least anti-fascist if not dedicated to the Partisan movement (as many of them detested communist ideas). This difference—originating in long past centuries—had not been overcome during the decades of peace after the end of the World War II, possibly because the Herzegovinians were not showing any wish to be integrated into the culture of their hosts, keeping their values stubbornly and despising everything else.

And Major J Skoko—having a really tiny brain besides his other problems—was a product of this situation. Having in mind only that he had to be a war hero to somehow settle down the confusion in his head, he led three hundred inexperienced Zagreb boys into a fight that was meant to liberate the Savnik area all the way to the Bosnian border. In that, he was shot by a sniper only a few hours after he had crossed a river which was a border between the National Guard and the rebelling local Serbs, and this is where the story about him—who was nothing more than a contemptible careerist thinking only about becoming big one day—must end.

The story should continue by addressing the fate of three hundred young men who lost their childhoods that night—and one of them was Borna Didić.

The advantage of consuming alcoholic beverages excessively—only for an evening perhaps—became clear to Borna immediately after he had been virtually abducted from his flat because of being able to open the door in consequence of not drinking enough the night before. Had he drunk more, he would not have been fit to do that.

It was Sunday, five a.m., and Borna's Saturday evening had not been wild enough; thus, he responded to the doorbell and saw three men in uniforms, who grabbed him and left him only a few minutes to check that he was leaving everything in order.

Borna, whose only military training was in the navy and poor in infantry drill, was given ten bullets for his rifle. The rifle was semi-automatic, a slightly improved Yugoslav version of the Soviet *Samozaryadnyj Karabin sistemy Simonova*, designed in the 1940s and chambering exactly ten bullets—so Borna had no extra ammunition to reload. After hearing a confusing and politically motivated speech of Major Skoko, Borna had to join his three hundred comrades in a bold adventure aiming to liberate a substantial portion of the Republic of Croatia, then held by the Republic of Serbian Krajina (and the Yugoslav People's Army of the Socialist Federal Republic of Yugoslavia as its crucial supporter).

The operation was ill-prepared. Borna's unit and some other ones—altogether about a thousand men—crossed the river in inflatable boats successfully around midnight, soon managing to establish a bridgehead and also to capture a few small villages (these were empty villages of the Croats who had fled when the area had come under Serbian control). However, the other troops were late and eventually did not cross the river at all—because some three hours after the operation had started, the Serbs began to fight back using their superior artillery and armour. The National Guard had only a few heavy artillery pieces in support (obsolete American *M115* eight-inch howitzers from World War II) and little armour—three or four old tanks that managed to cross a captured bridge—so the planned conquest became a chaotic withdrawal by morning. Borna had to run for his life.

Nikola Jarbašić had no problems to eliminate a Croatian officer with his sniper rifle. He was shooting extremely well ever since he could remember, and this officer was an easy target—he looked like a peacock while commanding his troops to go left or right, obviously being overconfident and having no experience in moving on a battlefield.

Nikola made another kill and was proud of that. He was defending the right of the Serbs to continue living in Yugoslavia and not in some new Croatia—this was what he thought—and he also had a feeling that he had a special obligation to do that because of a betrayal which was burdening his family name so heavily. Namely, his grandfather Živan, a former war hero, took sides with the Croats in their efforts to establish an independent state, cherishing his easy life in a once Jewish, luxurious villa in Zagreb more than the honour of his Serbian family. He was even pretending to represent all the Serbs in Croatia, this bastard, being on Croatian television so often!

After the two kills, he scanned the river for more targets. The Croats were fleeing in panic, leaving their rifles and other equipment behind and entering the cold river (it was December) hastily in order to swim back to the safety of their territory; he saw some of them disappearing beneath the surface due to the cold, the weight of their soaked uniforms or lack of swimming skills. He targeted one of those who managed to reach the opposite bank.

At the same moment when he pulled the trigger, a shell from one of the obsolete Croatian howitzers exploded some five metres from him, creating an enormous pressure that lifted him up and almost torn his body to pieces; thus Nikola Jarbašić met his creator, whoever or whatever this being or force was.

The news of the death of Nikola came to Malo Selce within hours, and this was considered to be the end of the bloodline of a Vlach named Jarul. This family had been devastated during World War II, both in Croatia and in Serbia; only a mad old lady and Živan survived—and he had just one grandson and no living children. The fact that another Jarbašić, a person once known as Srdjan, had two daughters was not even mentioned, since he was a Catholic traitor, and his name was not to be spoken. Živan was also a traitor—and the clan of Jarul was in the eyes of the villagers gone for good.

Two days later, the Orthodox priest of Malo Selce dedicated his sermon to the extinction of the Jarbašić family, and the whole story was over and forgotten as soon as his flock left the church. No one showed any emotion—this was just another war, and they were soldiers in the lands of everlasting war for so many centuries. All wars were alike.

Borna Didić was holding in his hand a bullet that had missed him by only a few centimetres while he had been struggling to get out from the cold river. He had dug it out from the river bank clay. No doubt, this was a 7.92 mm *Mauser* bullet from a Yugoslav sniper rifle (if it had been from an *AK-47* or another, larger weapon, it would have been either smaller or bigger). It was easy for him to recognise that—as he had once been in this army.

He was in a Zagreb hospital, waiting to be treated for serious cold burns—which was a consequence of his swimming in the almost frozen river. Maybe twenty of his brothers in arms—in basically the same condition—were in the same corridor, on auxiliary beds as well, since the rooms were crowded with badly injured soldiers. In 1991, the Republic of Croatia was losing the war, and many young men were in the hospitals, waiting to meet their creator, whoever or whatever this being or force was.

The hospital was in chaos—because it had not been built to deal with war casualties—and Borna was, knowing that, very patient, not trying to exert any pressure on the doctors and nurses. They were doing their job the best they could, being completely unprepared and astounded by the number and nature of the injuries they had to cope with.

Borna then received a visit from his parents.

Danka—who was always a dedicated mother and completely enchanted by her son—showed little emotion, as strange this may have seemed. Luka, on the other hand, started to cry immediately when he saw Borna so helpless, and he was cursing his lack of initiative—since he had done nothing to save his son from becoming just another nameless victim of this idiotic war. Most of all, he was blaming himself for not sending his only child straightaway to his relatives abroad when the madness had started.

While Luka was crying, Danka thought without saying a word,

'No man from my family will take part in this or any other war. No more. Only over my dead body.'

Then she looked at her son, caressed his head and told him gently,

'You're now going with us, dear, you're going home to Kletina.'

'But mother, they'll not let me, they took all of my papers,' replied Borna, knowing well what he was talking about. Although injured, soldiers in the hospital were still a property of the state and were not allowed to go anywhere without permission.

'Don't you worry, son, let your mother handle that.'

The confusion in the newly formed army then helped the Didić family, since what followed could have certainly never taken place within any better organised military force.

Danka went to search for a doctor, and though it was not easy to find any who would want to chat with the visitors, she eventually managed to have a word with one of them. The busy doctor could only say that Borna was relatively fine, that his feet were not to be amputated, and that he was going to recuperate in about a month; he also remarked that he could not say what was going to happen with Borna later—he was just treating the wounds and not deciding on what the army was going to do with their men. She could ask a lieutenant who was in a room at the end of the corridor, he said, a person that was supervising military affairs in the hospital. Thus, Danka went there right away, without showing any emotion or nervousness.

Luka followed her. She told him that his crying could be of no help, that she was more concentrated and that he should therefore just wait for her outside. So, she entered the room and Luka waited at a bench.

At first, he heard a conversation behind the closed door; then the voices became louder; a sound of chairs tumbling; and finally he heard his wife shouting... He opened the door.

'Close the door!' yelled Danka. And Luka did that instinctively.

The scene he saw looked like one from adventure novels and films: Danka (a tiny woman of about sixty kgs) was behind the lieutenant (who was not a small man), gripping his hair and holding a pocket knife under his throat, being wild-eyed and in some other world.

'Sign it! Sign it or I'll spill your blood all over this table right now! And then I'll go to your home and butcher your wife and your children and your dog!'

The lieutenant was shaking in terror, and then he signed something.

'Take this paper with you, Luka, and leave the room! I've got something more to discuss with this officer!'

Luka went out as quickly as he could and looked at the signed sheet of paper: it was a form in which it was explained that Borna Didić was allowed to go to Kletina to recuperate in his parents' home. Suddenly, the commotion in the room stopped; Luka could only hear Danka's voice which sounded flat and unemotional. In about five minutes, she left the room and said through her teeth,

'We'll not hear from this gentleman any more. Let us go home now. Let us go home with our son.'

Her husband looked at her. Her eyes suddenly reminded him of Ljerka when the late old lady would have been angry, which was rather strange and somewhat frightening: Danka's eyes had always been very gentle—because she had, and Borna too, Srdjan's eyes.

Luka was looking into the narrowed eyes of a Saxon she-warrior—who inherited her blood from fierce Teutonic knights.

Despite all the clamour, no one even noticed that this incident had occurred: everyone was too busy with the blood, pain, and death in the corridor and the rooms. And even if one had noted anything, one would have probably not taken a risk to face the wrath of a defending mother.

The whereabouts of Borna Didić, Helmut Meindl, and James Trevor Smith

I

1992, Kletina, Kletina County
Republic of Croatia

Borna Didić was enjoying the view from a window of his family home in Kletina.

It was like in a long forgotten fairy tale: the street was smooth and shiny under the early morning sunlight, covered with fresh, virginal white snow and looking quite unreal—as if it belonged to another, heavenly world that existed in the mind of a magical creature who had created everything we know and feel. White roofs, white trees, white meadows, white dogs, white cars, white people—a soothing symphony of the colour white whispered through the scenery of Borna's childhood, making him feel calm and safe.

    The neighbours were busy with cleaning the street, front yards, and walkways, occasionally taking a break to drink some mulled wine; their wives were refilling a jug faster than it could get empty, to be rewarded with lascivious games of words and touches in this theatre that foreshadowed moments of lust after the surrender of the light of that day to the night—when the body was going to long for the warmth of another body. This brought back some memories of the time when he would have joined them, always trying to be seen by girls (in particular, by Vesna, who lived close by). Then he heard how his neighbours—who were for this or that reason not eligible for conscription—started to discuss the war zealously, shouting and quarrelling on what should or could have been done in this or that situation. Listening to them was making him sad, not angry or disturbed—because he was a melancholic soul who would always back off rather than fight for a cause. So, he limped back to the couch where his daily position before a TV set was. His feet still hurt, but not nearly as much as his other memories.

For the rest of his life, he hated rivers, cold, and perhaps people, although he would always be careful enough not to show any of that.

During these moments in the living room of the house of his parents, next to the window, he would feel only a strong dislike for his neighbours—who had been very dear to him throughout the past years. Somehow, he was not any more the same person he had been: he was often silent, would seldom smile, and would obviously enjoy solitude more than anything else. His parents hoped that this was going to change in time, but their hope was in vain. Much later, Borna became fond of a river, whereas everything else stayed pretty much the same.

Though remaining well-mannered, he became a person who would seldom open his heart to anyone. The fact that the visits of his childhood friends and ex-girlfriends during his recuperation could not cheer him up was the first sign of that.

It would be wrong to conclude that his battle experience was the only cause of his transformation; many had suffered more and were still able to go on with their lives, at least after the passing of some time. The reason why Borna decided to remove himself from the dirty reality of this world was that he was sensing evil in people—and the war was just spicing up this feeling a bit.

The war was important to some extent, since it was bringing the worst in people to light so clearly, but Borna was sensing the iniquity of humans more profoundly and was not willing to accept it only because it was obviously there. Hence, he decided, at some point, that he was going to learn how to live differently, to manipulate and not to be manipulated (using his thoughtfulness, growing erudition, and concentration as ample weapons), because no one was ever again going to make plans for his future without his consent! He was a grandson of Vladimir F Količek, after all! The only criterion was that he would never intentionally hurt anyone in order to prosper—which was a principle he was sticking to, as much as he could, for the rest of his life. In some future episodes, there were slight departures from these rules, for practical reasons, but this was of little importance: his viewpoint on the world was completely reshaped during his recuperation in Kletina—when he had enough time to think about the roles and rights of every living being on Earth.

His ethical standards were set during the years of his growing up under the roof of his parents—who were provincial and conservative but honest and unassuming—and influenced by those who had brought them up. By his unfortunate grandfather Srdjan, whom he had never met and whose eyes he inherited; by his second grandfather Vladimir, who had lived in the neighbourhood and played a decisive role in his quest for knowledge, courage, and decency; and by his third grandfather Ivan the Proud, who gave him not only the surname but also an introverted personality. And by his brave grandmothers: by Roža (died in 1987), who had been protecting her family for a long time without a single complaint, and by Ljerka (died in 1990), who had endured more than a mortal should ever have. The standards which Borna inherited from these people included love, compassion, honesty, dedication, moderateness, kindness, understanding, and—more than anything—the ability to comprehend his own mistakes and correct them.

The world around Borna was offering only the opposite as a recipe for success—and he simply did not want to put up with such a decline of the basic laws of humanity; his defiance to accept the everyday triviality of the sheep in a flock was the only fight for a cause he was ever going to have. While looking through the window, he murmured,

'This is not for me. I adore this place but this really isn't for me any more. Things have changed.'

No, it was not the war that caused the birth of a new Borna, it just triggered it, and this would have probably occurred with or without the bloodshed he had unwillingly taken part in.

The development of his misanthropy began three or four years ago, when the crisis in Yugoslavia started on the basis of ethnic disputes. In this turmoil, objective human qualities were completely disregarded and defeated by a madness relying on the most backward tribal traditions; this brought success to the worst lowlife within every nation of Yugoslavia—to a caste of trivial and vulgar chauvinists who were ready to soak the country in blood for their private interests. The existence of the caste did not bother Borna intensely—his disappointment arose from the willingness of the masses of people to follow these crooks blindly and without thinking. While observing the events around him silently and analytically, Borna concluded that he was always going to belong to a minority in every confrontation of thoughtfulness and primitive instincts, as the latter ones were always more attractive to the sheep in a flock. Therefore, he decided to refuse taking part in any activity relying on the number of participants.

Thus, Borna had been gradually becoming a kind of misanthrope much before his traumatic battle experience. The fact that he was an odourless man, who could not incite any emotion in a woman, was certainly making him even more reclusive. For instance, his sexual escapades—in which he had previously been such a virtuoso—were already for quite some time restricted to situations in which he would not have to try hard, mainly to drunken parties where every inhibition would be removed by nature and instinct.

Moreover, it should not be disregarded that he was born in morally the most questionable era of humankind—in the twentieth century—and there were certainly many stories on characters similar to him, in and out of the regions which suffered from tragic events such as war, hunger or any such disaster. No, it was not the war that caused the change in Borna, it just accelerated it; in some happier parts of the world, the same thing was happening to some other people of the late twentieth century but perhaps only slower.

On the other hand, there were some occasions when Borna would still show a kind of affection for certain people. This, for example, occurred when he again met Roger in England, and also in Switzerland when he became enchanted by a young and astonishingly beautiful lady of bronze complexion.

'Borna, this is a good time to discuss your future,' said Danka after kissing her boy. 'There is a war here, people are dying, and believe me I know how to tackle this. In my family, we had such things. Too many such things. Not in your father's family, so you'll listen to what I've got to say. First of all, in how many wars we should shed our blood? Not in a single one, not any more, if anyone wants to ask me.'

'Father?' Borna turned to Luka, because he was sensing some aggression in his mother, something he had not experienced before.

'Listen to your mother, Borna.'

'Your grandpa Vlado gave you a certain piece of paper, right? Don't you try to lie to me, I know—he told me everything! Look at me! He gave you a piece of paper, a note—didn't he?' continued Danka.

'Yes, that's true,' replied Borna before he could think properly about the whole situation, 'but I can't leave anywhere—the army will come and get me sooner or later.'

'Over my dead body! Over my dead body!' shouted Danka without hesitation. 'You'll use this note and go to Scotland, damned be Croatia and Yugoslavia and Serbia and their fights, I have only you and I don't care about anything else! You'll go to Scotland!'

'Father?'

'I agree with your mother,' replied the middle-aged man. 'Visit us one day with our grandchildren but now listen to what she's got to say.'

And then Danka talked, slowly and without showing any emotion or insecurity, as if going to Scotland was the easiest thing in the world. A problem was that Borna could not enter the UK without a visa, but Danka had a plan. She revealed only some parts of it and said that she was going to explain the whole thing in more detail later. This was not something that Borna would expect from his mother—who was in his eyes just another Kletina woman from the neighbourhood, definitely not an intriguer or adventurist.

The next day, Luka returned with quite a bit of money, all in Deutschmarks: he had just sold the car, which was part of the plan.

'What's the status of your German, Borna?' he asked after stacking the pile of cash onto a desk. 'I'm wondering because you'll need it. This is a critical point, because it's a long way to Scotland.'

'My German?' Borna was surprised. 'Not bad, I guess. I still remember a lot from school, although I didn't use the language much during my study. My grammar is probably still all right. I remember most of it. And I've been told that I haven't got a strong accent, possibly because I encountered the language at an early age in both school and the family.'

Then Danka came, carrying with her a number of books including some dictionaries.

'See these books? This is what you're going to concentrate on from now on instead of watching TV the whole day long,' she said. 'You'll read these books in German and have intense conversation lessons with me. Did you know that your grandma Ljerka was in fact German? You've been given a task now, my dear son. Your way to Scotland is paved in Austria and Germany.'

'What your mother wants to say is that you should become fluent in German as much as possible, before springtime. Nothing can be done now during this snow and cold. The rest has been arranged,' added Luka a bit mysteriously. 'At the moment, think only about one thing, son: improve your German.'

'But... I'm not sure I understand.'

'And you don't have to,' remarked Danka, 'just start reading the bloody books. The conversation lessons will start tomorrow.'

Danka was a harsh teacher. Always being a kind and understanding mother, fully dedicated to this role, she now cared even more, turning into a devilish character when it came to teaching her son proper German—and the recuperation days of Borna became everything but easy. Consequently, Borna's fluency in German was in the April of 1992 (when the USA finally recognised the independence of Croatia, three months after most of Europe had already done so) more than satisfactory. After learning how to control his usage of this intricate language, and having no strong accent, he was ready to leave for the world of German speaking people. He also regained the fitness of his body, and he was capable of crossing high mountains by foot if necessary.

To do so was more than required in the plan of Borna's parents, but his physical fitness was still important. At that time—when the Republic of Croatia was still losing the war and was desperately needing soldiers—it was not easy for a young man to leave the country, especially if he had any connection with the army. Luckily for the Didić family, Kletina was only about ten kilometres from the border with Slovenia, and this north-western Croatian border was—due to the troubles in the east and south of the country—not guarded well. The Slovenes cared little about who was crossing the border (they were making a significant income from the smuggling of weapons, for example) as long as this was not endangering them, and the main worry of every illegal border crosser was to avoid the Croatian police, which would occasionally patrol there. One had to be fit to do that, which Borna was.

He slept for a few hours in the house of some trusted people who lived roughly two kilometres from the border. At about two a.m., he started his lifesaving journey to the West.

When he was passing by the church where he had been baptised in 1966, he could not resist coming closer and observing the small, old temple perhaps for the last time. He could not know whether he was ever again going to be allowed to return to Croatia after his cowardly act—which was a probable characterisation of his leaving. Was his destiny to look at the church from the Slovenian side of the valley just below the hill, if overwhelmed with nostalgia one day? To come back to Kletina or Krotko or Zagreb, was this ever going to happen? Then he remembered how much he detested the mindless nationalist hysteria he was running away from, the darkness he was leaving behind, and everything became so easy.

He crossed the border without being spotted—the only trouble was that he had to wet his feet in a creek—and this occurred before any inn was open to welcome the local proletarians on their way to work early in the morning.

The border had not changed at all—it only had become, a few years ago, a line that separated two independent states and not two federal republics of Yugoslavia. There was a large factory on the Croatian side, and every morning the workers from both countries would go there just before six a.m., usually first taking a sip of plum brandy in one of the inns that would open on time to host these heroes of everyday life. No new border could change that, because life had its own agenda.

Borna was in Slovenia already at three thirty. He looked back only once, and then he left in tears, by foot, towards German speaking lands. He did not miss the people—he missed the landscapes of his childhood.

II

1992, Slovenian-Austrian border north of Maribor & Vienna
Republic of Slovenia & Republic of Austria

While waiting at the Slovenian-Austrian border—sitting in a bus he boarded in the town of Ptuj after five hours of walking from the Croatian-Slovenian border—Borna the Proud was looking through a dirty window and thinking how well he knew the place: the houses, trees, bushes, and meadows were looking much the same as before, when he had been crossing this border checkpoint free of any trouble; it was just that the police uniforms on the southern side were Slovenian and not Yugoslav.

In some happier times, a long time ago, he would occasionally go with his family to the small town of Leibnitz on the Austrian side for shopping, and sometimes they would even go a bit further to Graz—the largest city in Austrian Styria. In contrast to the rest of the communist world, the socialist Yugoslavia had been allowing their citizens to travel abroad from the 1960s onwards, so Borna's first travel out of Yugoslavia was in 1975, when he visited Trieste, Monfalcone, and Grado in Italy. But Leibnitz always had a special place in his heart, with its large square full of wonders that belonged to the capitalist world of consumerism, shops where one could buy the wonderful Austrian sweets called *Mozartkugeln*, numerous sales that were calling people to leave their money there, kiosks which were offering Austrian fast food—mainly sausages in warm pastry—and foamy beer… Every visit to Leibnitz—especially during Christmas time—would be a celebration of good life for his folks and him, when they could make use of the money they had saved over the year for this special occasion. It was a tradition of the Didić family of Kletina.

Even then, on the bus, Borna was wearing a cap he had bought at a sale in Leibnitz in 1979, although it was perhaps already too warm for that. He just liked the cap, and it had remained on his head ever since early in the morning, because the nights of this April were rather cold, and he had to walk for a long time before catching the bus in Ptuj. In his anxiety, he forgot to take it off.

His waiting for a bus in Ptuj also brought back some other memories. In fact, his short journey northwards through Slovenia was bringing back many memories, which was probably due to the fact that all of these places were quite important in his life. From time to time, he would feel like being partly Slovene, as the traditions and mentality of the Slovenes across the border were pretty much the same as those of the Croats of Kletina; even his northern Croatian dialect contained so many elements of Slovene that he could understand this language perfectly although he was not able to speak it fluently.

While in Ptuj, he remembered how he had bought his first fancy bicycle—one with five gears—and his first guitar there in the late 1970s (being closer to Kletina, Ptuj was considered better for shopping than Zagreb). And that Ljerka had been hospitalised in the renowned Ptuj hospital before she died in Barbara's flat two years ago. He knew the town quite well, but he had no time to explore it once again, which he regretted.

When he was passing through Maribor, he remembered that his mother had been born in this city, and also that his father studied mechanical engineering there for some time, just before they got married. He knew little of all of that—and virtually nothing of the touching love story of Ljerka and Srdjan in Maribor—but he felt somewhat connected to the place. When he was crossing the Drava River, he suddenly became sad: was he ever going to see it again?

Was he ever again going to see any place of importance to him? And why did he have to leave in the first place? This was on his mind, and he had no answer to these disturbing, intimate questions.

'So, Mister Didić, where are you heading to?' asked a Slovenian policeman at the border checkpoint.

'To Vienna.'

'For what purpose?'

'Visiting my girlfriend, she's there.'

All of that was spoken in Slovene. The officer looked at Borna's passport, which did not contain any proof that Borna had entered Slovenia recently.

'Hmmm,' he mumbled, and then again, 'Hmmm.'

Then he looked at Borna—they were of about the same age. Only some deity may have known what was on the policeman's mind, but he eventually said,

'Have a nice journey.'

Roughly the same thing happened with an Austrian policeman who was checking the passports.

'Have a nice journey,' he said. Borna's conversation with him was in completely fluent German.

Thus Borna crossed the border and left the lands of everlasting war behind him as the first of his family to make such an escape.

It was not a secret that both Slovenia and Austria were siding with Croatia during the war, possibly because of sentiments related to the long joint history within Austria-Hungary, the same Roman Catholic religion, similar cultural values… Or perhaps simply due to lucrative businesses relying on the softness of the borders. In any case, Borna entered Austria smoothly; he did not want to think about the reasons—he was running for his life.

After crossing the border, soon he saw (vaguely from the motorway) the humble lights of Leibnitz and then the much more intense lights of Graz.

'I'm now like Nikola Tesla,' Borna started to amuse himself. 'He left the lands of everlasting war to study in Graz, possibly by the same route as I did. And he ended up somewhere else and prospered there, just as I hopefully will.'

However, this could not occupy his mind for a long time, as he was about to face something completely unknown. For instance, he did not know who his supposed girlfriend was—he only knew that he should somehow reach a street close to the opera house and that her name was Suzanne Ritter. He was loaded with cash—most of it in Deutschmarks but some also in Austrian schillings—and he had been instructed not to try to save some money by walking but to simply take a taxi, because this was what the Austrian money was for.

Danka was the one who had made the plan and instructed him. No one should ever underestimate a mother even if she may look like a humble wife from the neighbourhood. If necessary, mothers turn impossible into possible, settle disagreements and wars, make peace with the Devil, do surprising things... And there was a surprise waiting for Borna at this mysterious place close to the Vienna Opera. The surprise was, as Borna was soon going to find out, the result of a secret conspiracy of the women of the world, so incomprehensible to men, in which nothing could win against the primordial instinct and solidarity of the deliverers of life.

Hence, he took a taxi. The first thing he noticed was that Vienna was much bigger than Zagreb: big streets and avenues, big buildings, big bridges, big trees, big river, big shops, big inns and restaurants... Everything was so big for a Kletina boy who was comparing the bigness of things with what he had seen in Zagreb (after coming from his small, provincial hometown full of quite small things). This place was bigger in everything, this Vienna.

He went out from the taxi in front of a building which was objectively not very big but it still seemed so.

'This is the capital of a former empire,' he thought, 'and things must be big here, I guess.'

Borna then remembered that he had to pay for his fare, and he eventually paid too much; the cabby thought it was a generous tip, but it was just a mistake of an inexperienced young man from a country at war. Apart from being educated and speaking some languages, Borna the Proud was still a bewildered provincial boy.

He found the name Ritter on the door phone, pressed the button and said in German,

'I'm looking for Mrs Suzanne Ritter.'

'Miss Ritter. May I ask who are you?' replied a woman.

'Borna from Kletina, if this means anything to you.'

'Come up, my dear Borna. Oh my God, how much I want to see you,' replied the woman in Croatian.

III

1992, Vienna
Republic of Austria

The woman who opened the door was someone Borna knew so well: it was Suzana.

She did not seem surprised, and she immediately hugged him strongly, pressing her firm petite body against him (despite his wet jacket) as if he was still her lover, her Prince Charming or knight in shining armour, who just come to defeat a dragon and bring back the old days of romantic love. Then she kissed him on the cheek, dangerously close to his lips; he kissed her back, on the cheek as well but closer to the nose than to the lips.
Their hug lasted for some time—it was quite a long one in fact—and then they stepped back to observe one another. Definitely, this was the same old Borna (though an untidy version of him), and this was the same old Suzana—but looking better than she ever had. Her blonde hair was shorter than before but amazingly stylish, suiting her perfectly, her hands were smooth and with classy fingernails, her eyebrows were shaped impeccably, and she smelled like a hundred roses from an oriental garden; and no, this was not the adolescent, somewhat childish Suzana from their days in Kletina—she was the object of the lust of every man in the world, an elegant lady with perfectly tanned skin and big blue eyes capable of conquering every conqueror.
'Come in, please come in, dear Borna,' she said after the long hug had stopped. 'I knew you were coming.'
Borna came in and took a look at the place: it was a small but very comfortable flat, looking rather girly. She has always been so girly, so many bright colours, thought Borna.

'You're limping?' she asked, worrying a bit. He sat down on a sofa.

'Yes, my left leg. I had a long walk today. It's mostly a problem with the ankle—but that's a long story. Forget it, I'm altogether fine.'

'The war?'

'Well... Could have been worse. Forget it.'

'Your mother told me... That you'll possibly have problems with your legs,' she said after sitting down next to him. 'My dear, dear Borna—what has become of you? What the hell has happened since the last time we met?'

'My mother?' he was surprised. But then he remembered that he actually did not know every detail of Danka's plan.

'Yes, she somehow found me here. I don't know how, but on the other hand, Kletina isn't a big place. She simply found me.'

'After not liking you when we were together?'

'Women. We do things for each other when it's important, that's our way. You men don't understand that. You're here now, and this is what counts, let us forget your mother from now on.'

'That dear, fighting witch. But let us forget her, yes,' he replied after looking at Suzana again: she was gorgeous. During the conversation, he was observing the flat and avoiding eye contact. 'And what has become of me? Not much, apart from that I'm now a deserter and refugee.'

'My dear Borna, you're neither of that any more, not here. Now you should eat something—you're still very handsome but too skinny for my taste.'

He ate little, only some bacon and a piece of bread.

'It seems that I'll remain skinny for a while,' he laughed. 'But I'd really enjoy a glass of wine. Have you got any?'

'White? I have red as well, but I remember that you always preferred white.'

They went back to the sofa and sat down at some distance from each other—possibly because they had not seen one another for such a long time and were therefore somewhat confused. What to do after all these years? How to start a conversation? What to ask? What to say? Borna was still avoiding eye contact and observing the flat even when speaking; it was a girly flat indeed—as he had noted upon his arrival—but it was more than that: everything was placed orderly, and this was not the signature of a teenage girl but of a grownup woman, revealing sophistication and style. This was so new to him, but it was clear: though being only twenty-four, Suzana was everything but an innocent and inexperienced Kletina girl.

The wine was helping make the atmosphere comfortable, and they soon became rather relaxed. At some point, Suzana went to change the music on the stereo and then sat down closer to him. It did not take long before she started to touch him while laughing or gesturing (like she would have often done when they had been together in Kletina), at first in the manner of a friend and then by making the contact longer and more sensual. They did not speak about any recent, heavy stuff, only about the bright days of the past. Thus, Borna did not find out why, when and how Suzana came to Vienna, what she was doing for a living, why her name was Suzanne Ritter, what her plans were for the future, was she involved with someone, and so on and so forth.

The pain in Borna's ankle disappeared.

Suzana lit three candles: one on the table before them, one at the window to the left, and one on a small cabinet to the right. They formed a triangle. And then she lit the fourth candle behind the sofa, on another small cabinet—hence they were suddenly in the centre of a tetragon set by the four candle lights. She did not say a word while doing that. Then she returned to the sofa and started to gaze into his eyes. He touched her hand and took a sip of the wine. She took his hand and intertwined their fingers.

Borna could not move—he wanted this moment to last forever.

'Maybe you'd like to take a shower,' she said. 'Don't worry, I'll not run away. There's a bathrobe for you after you've finished, and leave your clothes and underwear there, I'll wash them later.'

Borna was enjoying the hot water, steam, and smells in the bathroom immensely. As his tiredness was gradually diminishing, his mind started to work, and he was growing at the special place, which was making him uncomfortable—what if she did not mean to spend the night with him, what if all of that was just part of her being gentle and kind but without any lust? How to come before her? As much as he was trying, he was not getting any smaller, and then he decided: he was going to try to hide it under the bathrobe, although this was maybe not going to be necessary...

He came out from the bathroom shyly and tried to hide his erection by entering the room really awkwardly. When he finally managed to look at the centre of the tetragon set by the candles, she was there, on the sofa: in black lingerie, wearing a perfect, strong but seductive and carefully done makeup (some might even call it whorish), whereas her hair was slicked back. She was a goddess of lust, and she obviously wanted him.

They first did it on the sofa as two instinctive beasts. Then he took her to the bedroom in his arms, where they became less animalistic and more sophisticated in exploring their desires, bringing the night to a kinkier level. The bed was soon completely soaked with their body fluids. Then they moved to the dining table where they did it again, and then again in front of the sofa, on the carpet, seeing the lights of the candles extinguishing as they were approaching the climax.

'I've always known you are good,' Suzana screamed while grabbing his buttocks, 'they told me in Kletina, they told me! Why didn't I have you before? Why... Why?'

She stayed home the next day—and they continued to make love until again falling asleep exhausted. After they woke up, she made dinner.

'What are you thinking about, Borna?' she asked while putting the plates on the table, because he had been mostly silent when she was preparing the food.

'Not sure. I didn't expect this would happen... With us. I had some other plans, but I'm not sure any more.'

'Let us eat first, and then we'll talk,' replied Suzana with little joy in her voice. She knew what she had to explain and say, since the magic of that wonderful day was about to disappear. The atmosphere during the dinner was not tense but was not cheerful either.

They were still managing to have small talk and laugh occasionally, but this was far from the joy of the previous night—when everything had been purely instinctive, emotional, and worriless. When the world around them had not been real, when the only living beings on the entire planet had been they—Suzana and Borna from a small Croatian town, stranded somewhere far from home but blessed by a passion that could shake the Universe.

They ate little. Then Borna asked,

'Do you regret what happened?'

'No. And I never will. I wanted this to happen… No, no regrets. But things are complicated, you see.'

'I guess they are, you haven't told me anything about your life here,' said Borna without any bitterness in his voice but with a mixture of disappointment and resignation. 'Tell me then, what's going on? How come that it's complicated?'

Without saying a word, she left the table, went to the kitchen and returned with a glass full of some reddish liqueur.

'I'll need this. Want some? Or something else? I've got a nice selection of tranquillisers.'

'No, not really. Maybe later but not now.'

'I've got a good job in Vienna, you know,' she began her story. 'After my study had been completed, the war was starting, and I simply didn't want to remain there. I detest rudeness and hatred—I'm a woman, for heaven's sake—and you know what it was like. And I also couldn't get any job there, neither in Zagreb nor in Kletina. Hence, I simply wanted to go somewhere where life was normal. And Vienna was close. I applied for a job in a consulting company, they hired me—and this was how my new life started a year ago.'

'Okay, no complication so far—but please continue.'

'I met someone.'

'Oh, I see,' things became clearer to Borna. She was a very desirable woman, after all, so this did not surprise him much. 'Are you in love?'

'I'll not tell you that, that's my business,' she replied without hesitation, making it clear that her feelings belonged to her only. On the other hand, she was a gentle soul, and she said this in a gentle way, trying not to hurt Borna. It also seemed that she was about to shed some tears.

'All right, sorry, this really isn't my business.'

'He's forty-six but good looking, a good man and my boss at work. This flat belongs to him. And I'm not cheating on him—the night with you was the first and last time, believe me. By the way, I'm now Suzanne

Ritter, an Austrian citizen, because he organised this. It's easier to live like that, and his surname isn't Ritter, by the way.'

'Well, it has started to be complicated,' said Borna and then asked, 'May I now have some whiskey if you have any?'

'I have. He likes it too,' said Suzana and went to the kitchen to fetch a bottle. 'And please don't ask about our sex life—the passion with you was a matter of our old days and not of my present sex life with Hans.'

Borna did not say anything. It was clear that the wonderful night and half of the next day were everything he could have counted on, and that he could not expect anything more from his jumping into other people's lives out of the blue. He immediately made peace with the vagueness of his future, once again, and decided to simply remain grateful to Suzana for her kindness and hospitality at a time when no one but his parents had any emotion for him. And this was how he behaved for the rest of the evening.

Once everything was clarified, their cheerfulness was back, and the two stranded people became relaxed again. Around midnight, they became wild again; for the last time, Suzana said, because Hans was going to come tomorrow in the afternoon and Borna therefore had to leave earlier.

When he was departing early in the morning—much before Hans was going to arrive—there were some tears in Suzana's eyes, but Borna the Proud did not see that because he left hastily. He was rather depressed but also in a way happy for seeing that Suzana had become a distinguished lady in full control of her life, in that mad time when everything was seemingly going to hell.

After his departure, Suzana called Danka to tell her that everything had gone well.

He decided to find a cheap room and stay for a few more days in Vienna—which was not part of Danka's plan—but not to see Suzana again. In fact, he decided never again to interfere with her new and seemingly fragile fate; he felt that she was afraid of unnecessary complications in her life more than she wished her hidden desires to come true. Things had been going too fast during the last days; he simply needed some time to calm down and put his mind in order—as he was going to need strong nerves for a journey ahead of him.

After finishing breakfast, he walked through the city centre for a few hours, being again astonished by the splendour of the place: by the magnificence of the buildings and their facades, numerous monuments, carefully maintained and perfectly clean streets—in short, by the subtle interplay of an imperial architecture and the modern time. However, he was most of all impressed by the happiness of the people. Everywhere he looked—there was a joy on their faces be it walking, chatting in cafés, eating in restaurants, listening to street musicians and performers, and so on.

Everything was so different from the scenery in the lands of everlasting war—this frontier of the Empire for centuries, its defence wall against every intruder or conqueror—where blood was flowing like rivers, poverty and hunger were part of the tradition, and religious fanaticism the only way to search for peace in some other life, beyond physical existence in this world of sadness, suffering, and pain. Borna the Proud then woke up from these strange thoughts and remembered that he had to keep a cool head. He decided to find a bench and just sit there for a while to suppress his sentiments as much as he could.

There was a perfect bench in a park close to the Danube, relatively far from the rush and still close enough to the magnificent sights of this world that was so strange and unknown to Borna but the only future he had—and a part of which he therefore had to become as soon as possible in order to survive. He had no choice, his only chance was to become accustomed to this world, and he knew that. There was no option of going back: he was a deserter from an army at war, and back home, he could find only contempt, imprisonment or even a bullet in the head.

So he sat down on that bench and decided to think about absolutely nothing, to empty his mind of any thought and find some strength for facing the future unemotionally. After a few minutes, he heard someone crying on a bench nearby. A young brunette—probably in her early twenties—was sitting there and obviously going through a private hell; she would weep occasionally for a minute or so, and then, when this stopped, motionlessly gaze into the horizon.

He approached her, instinctively and without thinking much, offered her a handkerchief and sat down next to her.

'Thank you very much,' she said in English but with a relatively strong accent that was not typical of native German speakers. Being fluent in both German and English, Borna could recognise that.

'You thanked me in English? You're not Austrian?' asked Borna in English as well.

'No, and I don't speak German at all. I'm an exchange student here, and the only foreign language I speak is English.'

'I hope it's not too much to ask, but what is your mother tongue?'

'Croatian. I'm from Croatia and will be staying here for the next three months.'

At first, Borna wanted to run away immediately. This was not something he could welcome at this time—to meet someone from Croatia—but his mind was already purged enough to realise that nothing bad could happen, because he was out of the reach of Croatian law. Then he decided not to hide his origin and name, because he had certainly already been qualified as a traitor in Croatia, and the good looking Croatian girl in Vienna could not add anything to that.

'What a coincidence,' he said with a comforting smile, 'I'm also from Croatia. We can speak Croatian now, I guess.'

'Oh, yes! Yes, please! My English is so bad and I'm always missing words. And the grammar! Awful! And your English seems so perfect, I've thought you're British,' she replied in Croatian.

'Your English is just fine, but let us forget any English now and try to make you stop crying,' said Borna quite charmingly. 'What has happened? What has been so bad and irreparable?'

There were tears in the girl's eyes again. And then some silence. She tried to start speaking but then began to cry again.

'The war?' asked Borna as gently as he could.

'The war. And my fiancé. In this war.'

'How bad?'

'Very bad. He's dead.'

After saying that, she started to weep again, and this time she could not stop. Borna realised that the best way was to remain silent and give her another kind of support—whatever that could be—and this support soon turned into a hug. And then into a kiss.

She told him that her fiancé was from North Dalmatia, and that his village had been attacked by the Yugoslav Army and Serb rebels; then he had to flee together with his family. Afterwards, he joined Croatian troops and fought everywhere for six months, but his death... According to some rumours, he was killed by certain drug traffickers when he was on leave, because he had apparently discovered that some barracks and posts of the National Guard had been used for distributing heroin and cocaine among the troops and further into the urban centres both in Croatia and the rest of Europe. The trial was a despicable one, a farce, and the perpetrator was *de facto* set free (*de jure*, he was sentenced to a year in jail and soon released under parole).

Borna listened to this story wordlessly, as he really could not say anything that would not aggravate the situation. He understood well the character of the newest war in the lands of everlasting war. This war had nothing to do with noble things such as the liberation of a nation from oppression by another nation or with the establishment of democracy after almost half a century of a single-party political system; this war was a clash of criminal clans that were fighting for control over the wealth of a country burdened by religious and nationalist tensions and feuds. And the common people—those who were so much and so irrationally believing in the power of religion and nationalism—were used in this war as expendable pawns on a chessboard.

Her name was Marta Velić. She was a student of geology and a native of Zagreb. The family of her mother was from Zagreb since everyone could remember, and from her father's side (he was from Dalmatia), she had many relatives in New Zealand, who would occasionally visit the country of their origin. She was obviously a zealous Croatian nationalist—like most of the Croats were at the time—and Borna therefore did not want to share his views on the war with her. He revealed his name and the place of origin—because he started to care little about his past—but he still did not say anything about the nature of his sojourn in Austria. She was sad and good looking; he was depressed and simply wanted to have more fun before leaving for the unknown, frightening world. And that was it, no more, no less.

The evening lights of the ancient city of Vienna—together with their lust intensified by the wine they had in different inns—led to the kisses becoming more intense and sensual as the midnight was approaching. They ended up in her room.

The sex they had was everything but making love—it was an instinctive copulation of two troubled souls who were seeking comfort and oblivion. At some point, Borna started to think that this should have never happened, but his state of mind was such that he could not think about anything clearly. His first thought in the morning was to run away as quickly as possible, but he still wanted to do it as a gentleman, a fake one but still a gentleman. However, Marta did not allow this to happen: she shouted as soon as she woke up,

'Please leave. Leave! This was such a big mistake, so wrong! Don't misunderstand me, you're probably not bad, but I could never end up with someone like you. Please go!'

Under normal circumstances, Borna would be disturbed by being virtually thrown out from a girl's room just like that—but this time, he did not care. He went out without even saying goodbye. And then, while heading towards his hostel and further into the world, he decided to forget the whole affair. This was, after all, just another insignificant, meaningless sexual encounter with another worthless girl, whose sorrow for her dead fiancé was just as ugly as the whole memory he had of his homeland.

No, there was nothing worth remembering about this one-night stand. It should have never happened, as Marta had said. Of all of his past experiences with girls, this was by far the worst one.

However, shortly before boarding a train, Borna could not restrain himself from smelling his body at certain places, and he again became amazed by the lack of any smell.

'I could make love to a myriad of girls in this world, do it well, but this would never lead anywhere. I'm simply an odourless man—not a trace of any pheromone,' he muttered.

In any case, this was a moment when he finally put up with that. The world ahead of him was maybe terrifying but also big and challenging—and he suddenly felt that he could make use of that, one way or another, with or without the odour.

IV

1992, Regensburg, Free State of Bavaria
Federal Republic of Germany

The next stop for Borna the Proud was Germany. There, he had to do something very important—as Danka had instructed him.

He had no problems at the Austrian-German border, because he had Austrian and Slovenian passport stamps, which reminded him that the lands of everlasting war were far behind indeed—and he suddenly felt a touch of freedom for the first time after a long time. However, he was not free yet, and he was aware of that but still full of hope that freedom was going to embrace him one day, sooner or later, some way. Of all possible levels of freedom, he was, at the time, longing for just a very basic one—to stop being an object in a sick game of history—but this was not a kind of freedom that could make a person fully satisfied, as he was going to learn later.

    He was all alone again, but this was nothing new. While travelling from Munich to Regensburg—which lasted for an hour and a half—he could not stop thinking about women. Strangely, he did not reflect on any of his past love failures; he was contemplating on the unusual, inexplicable strength of women in general, a phenomenon so elusive to him.

    First of all, his mother. The merry, funny lady (though always ready to fight, because of being a skilled chemical engineer in the world of men) never seemed to be such a bold person who could plot his getaway so skilfully, over such a short period of time and with this kind of determination. On the other hand, on one occasion, when Borna was barely able to walk after his battle episode, she said to him,

'I'll face the Devil himself if this is a price to be paid for keeping you well. You are part of me and I'll never let you down, no matter what. This is what mothers do.'

And the memory of that day explained so much about the heart of a woman.

Then Borna remembered how Danka and Suzana came to an agreement after disliking one another intensely during the time when he and Suzana had been a couple in Kletina. In Vienna, Suzana did not say much about the whole thing, and he started to understand this better while watching the Bavarian landscape through the train window. Her unleashed lust—which was still confusing him—was another matter, something very private and outside the realm of the primordial instincts of a woman.

And Roža, then. Ivan the Blacksmith was an easy-going man who would simply let things happen and react only when something would become really critical. He sincerely believed in his Catholic God and the existence of a reason for every single thing, which was not to be sought in worldly trivialities and the will of humans. Roža would take a different standpoint, like a true fighter, like a wife and mother whose instinct was pushing her to respond to every threat without thinking much, by following only her nature—given to her by a decision of a deity or by any other force of the Universe.

Klara was a bitter drunk, lost soul, nasty and rude woman—some would say. But when things got rough, she would sober up and do everything she could to take care of the family, fighting like a lioness by legal and illegal means—and she would never stop, not until exhausting all of her powers. And even then she could always give good advice.

Finally, Ljerka. Her tragedy could fill many pages in a book on deep but unfortunate love stories that might teach us all how to love unconditionally; she loved Srdjan in a way that only some could understand, and this was then destroyed in a hurricane of malice. She wanted to die, but she survived for the sake of her daughters; and then, she found another strength: she was able, while never forgetting her first and only true love, to embrace a new future with a kind-hearted man—her second husband Vladimir—which eventually brought tranquillity into the life of her family.

Yes, women are those who keep us alive, our whole species, thought Borna on a train from Munich to Regensburg.

Regensburg: the northernmost point of the Danube. This lovely, old city—once the most populous in the Holy Roman Empire of the German Nation—was a dreamy, peaceful place. There, the Danube was mighty and slow, dominated by an ancient stone bridge that was surrounded by houses containing elements of antique, medieval, and more recent architecture; the city centre was around an impressively big medieval cathedral (at a walking distance from the Danube), and it was full of narrow streets paved in stone and connecting small squares seemingly ever since the time of the Roman settlement called Castra Regina.

Borna was not used to such tranquillity; the things he had gone through over the last two years had made him oblivious to a worry-free life which to many others seemed as natural as the reason for birds singing, trees growing, and people smiling. He then noticed that many women and men wore small, typically Bavarian hats with a feather while heading to traditional inns to drink beer and eat local food. And the food appeared to be not much different from that in Kletina: simple but well spiced and sometimes fatty meals based on pork, beef, poultry, potatoes, sausages, carrots, cabbage, and so on. Nothing very healthy but keeping people happy. Later on, in Switzerland, Borna learned that the cuisine everywhere around the Alps—and Kletina belonged to this area as well—was more or less the same, for hundreds of years and with no sign of changing sometime soon only because a modern nutritionist would advise so.

After finding a modest hotel—where dinner was still as expensive as expected for any hotel restaurant—Borna went to explore the city. He eventually ended up in one of the traditional inns, ordered a beer and a proper meal at an affordable price. The place was crowded, because these Bavarians were really enjoying life: enough money, enough joy, little stress, rich country... It was so different from Croatia, where the mild Yugoslav socialism had been replaced by a greedy, corrupt capitalism void beyond belief of any human compassion and justice (and this phenomenon had little to do with the ongoing war).

Then, three Bavarians came and asked whether the seats at his table were free—since the inn was full. Hungry Borna was too much into his food to even notice this properly, so they simply sat down after his casual approval. Then they ordered beers—and they ordered one for him as well.

'Cheers!' they exclaimed and raised their glasses high—and Borna joined them. They were very happy and joyful people, and he suddenly felt so well—thus the next round was on him. This was such a pleasant experience, reminding him of the days of his adolescence in Kletina, when the same thing would have happened quite often. While being unable to speak the local dialect, Borna used his decent knowledge of the German language to hide where he was coming from—saying that he was a Hungarian German on his way to visiting his relatives in Augsburg—because being a refugee and deserter from a country at war would not be a good reference. He simply did not want to open any discussion on the country of his origin, which could definitely attract too much attention.

In any case, with these three Bavarians—and, my goodness, they could drink a lot—Borna tasted the flavour of another world, one beyond the Croatian gloomy reality. And when they finally separated, his views on life were not the same as before. If nothing else, he knew that he never again wanted to go south, to the lands of everlasting war. This was the reason why he later started to understand Suzana better. However, he did not forget that he had to reach Scotland eventually—and that he had some important things to do the next day. On that day, at roughly ten a.m., Borna the Proud was going to become one Helmut Meindl, a native of the Bavarian city of Landshut (situated between Munich and Regensburg), thus acquiring the first of his false identities.

Borna had been instructed by his parents to wait for a man—who should present himself as Andreas—in a certain café in the centre of Regensburg, close to the cathedral, and to have two thousand Deutschemarks, already counted, in his pocket. He had also been told that this person was neither German nor Croatian.

'The Proud?' asked a young man of a Mediterranean or even Arab appearance. 'I'm Andreas. And I drink coffee.'

Borna understood the message and ordered another coffee. The man looked like someone from American mafia films, with his shiny clothes and gold all over his fingers and hairy chest. His German was much worse than Borna's, in fact, hence his name was definitely not Andreas. In his mind, Borna gave him the name Hassan.

'I must hear your German! Well, speak now,' said Hassan rudely.

Borna the Proud demonstrated his German by saying a few sentences without any noticeable foreign accent, and Hassan seemed to be pleased.

Hassan later explained that he would never give a German passport to someone who could not speak the German language well enough, as this could compromise his business ('What could happen at some border?' he remarked). It also turned out that Hassan was actually a Kosovo Albanian (name—Enver) and a cousin of a confectionery owner from Kletina, who lived there for some three decades and who knew Borna's father rather well.

Enver also admired the Croats because of their resistance to the Serbs, he said, and since two thousand Deutschemarks had already been paid in Kletina, he was willing to take only another two thousand—which was a discount price for the quality he was offering and the market for the people from the former Yugoslavia generally. The usual price was five thousand—for every desperate refugee—but he was willing to lower it in order to honour the contribution of a Croat who had been brave enough to fight the common enemy, namely the Serbs.

'Kosovo will be Albanian one day,' he said in his bad German, 'you Croats have just started what must be done. Much of this money is for our cause, and we'll do what should be done.'

Uninterested in this comment, Borna took a look at the passport rather carefully—and it was really a superb piece of work: a true German passport, with a high-quality photo of him and all the details taken care of perfectly. Enver also instructed Borna on what he should remember about the personal details of the fictional character called Helmut Meindl. All of that appeared highly professional, and Borna gave Enver the money under the table when they were sure that no one was watching. Enver counted it using his fingers only, under the table and without watching, checking the size of the banknotes, their consistency when touched, and their number. This took him some time.

'Good money. And the right sum. If you want to live—we've never met,' said Enver and left without even saying goodbye.

Using his new identity, Borna the Proud—or should we say Helmut Meindl from Landshut—entered the UK at Heathrow airport without any trouble.

V

1992, Aberdeen, Scotland
United Kingdom of Great Britain and Northern Ireland

Helmut the Proud had no problem in finding a room, in a modest hotel not far from the centre of Aberdeen, but his pile of money had become rather thin by then: he could count on about two weeks, at most, with his Deutschemarks which had become British pounds in a local exchange office. This meant that he had to make a lot of phone calls in order to locate the descendants of Captain Malcolm Forbes as soon as possible.

He first had to figure out what to say over the phone. And his first attempts were silly; he would call and ask,

'Is this the Forbes' residence? I'm looking for someone who could give me information on one Captain Malcolm Forbes who was an intelligence officer at the beginning of World War II in Yugoslavia, in 1941. My name is Falcon's Eye.'

And this was leading nowhere, as he would in all of these cases receive pointless or rude replies, such as: my son is Malcolm Forbes but he's only seven, who are you and why are you calling—I'll call the police; you bloody English provoker (Borna had an English accent he had acquired from Roger), I'll find you and you can't hide; no, there's no Malcolm in our family, and as a matter of fact, there are none in the whole of Aberdeen; I really don't care about any Malcolm, you idiot; you're obviously working for my late husband, that lowlife Forbes, and tell this bastard that I'll find him and sort out my alimony; I'm a Forbes but not Malcolm, and we could meet if you're as sexy as you sound over the phone; what a bloody name is that—Falcon's Eye? And so on and so forth.

Six days had passed, and he was really getting nowhere after possibly more than fifty calls. Then he decided to change the strategy and be more direct; he dialled the next number on the list and said,

'Falcon's Eye from Yugoslavia calls. And I say: *An eclipse is upon us, but it will pass away, as it has never happened that a night is not followed by a day.* If I've got to explain this, then I've dialled a wrong number.'

There were some seconds of silence, but the person he called did not hang up; Helmut could hear breathing on the other end of the phone line, and this was the most promising sound he heard ever since he had started to use the phonebook of Aberdeen. He was about to hang up when he heard a female voice,

'Where are you? Mary Forbes is speaking. We've been expecting to hear this sentence for about fifty years.'

'In Aberdeen,' replied Helmut, 'and I need your help.'

'And you'll get it.'

They met in a pub not far from the Marischal College. The pub was a relatively small but picturesque and quiet place, perfect for having a private conversation while enjoying the most delicious local ale—and it was obvious that Mary Forbes knew how to choose a good place.

The pub looked quite old and very Scottish, which Helmut liked; this was a new experience for him, and every small pleasure of that kind was helping him accept that he had to forget his entire past and find another life so far from home.

Mary was a slender and fair-skinned redheaded woman, possibly in her early forties, not astonishingly beautiful but still good looking, having a nice figure and wearing an impeccable green dress; her makeup was moderate and suited her well, whereas her fingers were thin and long, ending with perfectly manicured fingernails painted in violet. Though she lacked natural beauty, she was looking classy, and one could not say that she was not attractive—especially because she had the manners of a true lady, swaying slowly and seductively while walking and being so elegant when moving her head and arms in a truly feminine way. She also wore very decent jewellery: a wonderful gold necklace, a few thin bracelets on her left wrist (several rings but not too many), and relatively large but quite stylish earrings.

When Helmut spotted her entering the pub—and he knew it was she because she had explained over the phone what she was going to wear—he thought instinctively that she looked better than he could have hoped for.

On the other hand, the look of a woman was the last thing on his mind, and this was so, at least partly, because of the recent events in Austria. He raised his hand to let her know he was there, and she approached him with a big smile.

'Mr Količek, I presume. I'm Mary Bridget Forbes.'

'Yes. In a way. In fact, a grandson of Vladimir Količek.'

'Colonel Vladimir Količek… A man of honour who saved my father. And who liked films about Tarzan.'

She sat down and recommended a local ale—which was, she remarked, dangerously strong but appropriate at this moment.

'Let me look at you,' she said. 'I thought this would never happen, but I guess life takes many different paths.'

'It surely does. Is my story of any interest to you?'

'Well, you may want to tell it—but no, I'm not really interested. I'm a Forbes of Aberdeen, my father gave his word, and I know what I ought to do. As far as I'm concerned, you can be a murderer, and I don't care.'

Helmut the Proud liked this honesty, as well as her obvious cherishing of traditional values despite the ever-changing standards of the modern era; it was as if some ancient rules of Celtic and Vlach clans were brought alive by what she said, defying the habits of the twisted contemporary world. His anxiety was lessened, and he was becoming relaxed—feeling that his life might take a positive turn soon.

'No, not a murderer, just running away from a war. No blood on my hands. But I simply need to get rid of my past and start a new life as someone else. You've said that you're not interested in the story, so I'll not bother you with that.'

'Good enough for me, no story is necessary indeed. And I believe I can help you with your problem,' replied Mary Forbes and emptied the pint. 'One more, young man? And by the way, your accent sounds very

English, though you still have to work on it. Did you ever live in England? You speak a kind of proper RP English.'

Helmut smiled, remembering how Roger was teaching him English.

'No, I just hung about with a man who helped me with my pronunciation. He was an Englishman and quite educated. RP English?'

'It means "received pronunciation", which is usually the easiest for non-native speakers to learn. It's very neutral and many native speakers use it too—so your friend taught you well. And this should help you here indeed, because we could place your roots basically anywhere in, say, southern England without arousing much suspicion,' Mary continued. 'England is much bigger than Scotland—and this is where we should find a place from whence you allegedly came. Have you got any profession we could work with?'

'In fact, I have. I've got a university diploma in chemistry and some experience with pharmaceuticals. But—for the reasons which are quite obvious—I have no papers to prove that. Just skills.'

'That's good and should lead us somewhere,' Mary smiled and emptied the second pint, though as slowly as a lady should. 'One more, young man? What's your first name by the way?'

'Well, my first name is at the moment Helmut, the surname is Meindl, and I'm, at the moment, a German citizen—with fake documents of course. And I speak German rather well, in fact. This helped, don't ask how and why. I could remain German in any case. And my true first name is actually Borna. Not Količek though, Vladimir was from my mother's side.'

Mary laughed out loud, but this looked charming and not disrespectful, especially because she touched his arm casually; then she said,

'A German in Britain? No way. We'll make you British. And your new fake documents will be British. Your hometown? I don't know, Brighton would do I guess, considering your RP English and that the place is big enough. But we'll deal with that tomorrow, there's been enough for today. And Borna? I've heard of many Slavic names—such as Vladimir—but never Borna. Tell me about it.'

And Borna then started to explain the origin of his true name, which soon turned into telling her about his roots and the peculiarity that he had three grandfathers, of whom only Ivan the Blacksmith was still alive. He also said that Vladimir was most probably the only Slav amongst them, and that the widespread belief that the people of the Balkans were mostly Slavs was oversimplified. Mary was quite amazed by the story, especially by the tragic love of Ljerka and Srdjan. She was surprised to hear that the history of Borna's family included Catholic, Orthodox, and Protestant traditions, which seemed to be something rather unique: three main Christian denominations in the ancestry of one person! Then she told Borna everything she knew about the Forbes Clan and her father Malcolm—who had died seven years ago—and also some practical issues about life in Britain.

But she was not a naive woman, and Borna was also not stupid. It was obvious to him that she would intentionally ask some unusual questions, clearly intended to check whether he was really a grandson of Colonel Količek or just a crook who had somehow got the information on him and then wanted to make use of this. Of course, Borna answered everything correctly, and this thing was resolved once and for all. The situation then became completely relaxed.

However, Borna was still a bit confused. He knew that his grandfather had been a highly ranked officer in the Royal Yugoslav Army, but he had no idea what had happened between Colonel Vladimir Količek and Captain Malcolm Forbes—and why was he, therefore, sitting there with Mary. The only thing he knew was that he had received a yellowy piece of paper and some instructions from his dying grandfather back in 1980. After being sure that he passed the exam, he explained how little he knew of the whole matter—as Vladimir Količek had never spoken much about his past.

She was not surprised, because her father had explained to her the fragile and sometimes dangerous political situation in post-war socialist Yugoslavia, how Količek had to be careful and cunning. It was obvious that she knew much about Vladimir, from the Albanian episode to his conduct during the war and the quiet post-war living. Borna was actually learning from Mary about an important part of his family history, and he was astonished by how little he had in fact known before that evening.

It also turned out that Mary Bridget was rather fond of beer, and as a matter of fact, of other alcoholic beverages too (in the meantime, she had a few shots); hence, they spent the rest of the evening in small talk, enjoying it tremendously and ordering round after round. They were laughing a lot, as if they were good old friends who had not seen each other for years—and this was the first truly comfortable time Borna had enjoyed since leaving Kletina. Until then, he always had to think about the next day—but it was not like that with Mary in the pub: with her, things simply looked good and easy.

Mary Forbes was a peculiar kind of drunk. She was, namely, becoming more and more charming as her drinking was progressing; with every new pint, her moves were becoming more catlike and enchanting while her eyes would to a greater extent glow in a special way. However strange this may have seemed, her drunkenness was making her more charismatic and classier, but it also must be said that she knew when to stop—she could recognise the moment when a fascinating woman could be in danger of becoming a slut.

Hence, it was not strange that Borna was tempted to make a move on her—because he was not so disciplined when drunk, and she was simply gorgeous in displaying her radiant personality—but there were simple, barely noticeable but firm signs that she was not into that; this was supposed to remain a friendship based on obligation and honour, nothing more than that.

'We should go home now,' she said just before the last call.

'All right, my hotel is not far from here.'

'And we'll go there only to pick up your things. You'll be staying at my place.'

'Really? But…' Borna was confused.

'Of course, young man. I've got a nice, big flat and a spare room in it. We can't work on your future if you're in a hotel, this requires some concentration and planning. And you should also save some money—although we'll soon take care of your income too. You've got good skills, and we should use that to find you a nice job once we get your papers sorted.'

Mary lived alone. She had never married. This was why her surname was still Forbes. Her flat was close to the pub; it was big and on the first floor of an old house. Borna did not ask, but it was obvious that she was a well-off woman.

'This is my sanctuary, I simply love it,' she said after opening the door. 'Please come in and make yourself at home.'

Borna did not have any serious luggage—just a rucksack with underwear and other basic stuff. He had had to travel by foot, bus, and train from Croatia to Slovenia, Austria, and Germany, avoiding any suspicion at the borders, where he had to look like a travelling student. Seeing his rucksack, Mary laughed merrily and said,

'I guess we'll have to buy you some clothes quite soon.'

She showed him his room. He expected her to recite some general rules for sharing the bathroom, the kitchen, and so on, but she did not do that. Mary was an easy-going person and apparently rather happy to have company in her solitary life at least for a while; on the other hand, she showed him where the drinks were, and said that he was allowed to drink whatever he wanted to and in whatever quantity.

They soon went to sleep without any big words or romantic escapades—which were left hanging in mid-air—by simply saying 'good night' to each other.

In the morning, Mary reminded Borna that he should let his parents know that he was well—if he had not done already. Borna called Suzana in Vienna, and in a rather short conversation asked her to call Danka and tell her that he had safely reached the UK and that everything was going as planned. The falcon had landed, he said—this was the cipher to be used.

Just as details of the moves of Vladimir F Količek in critical situations have been destined to remain a mystery, the way of how Mary eventually handled the unfavourable situation of Helmut Meindl will probably never meet any clearer explanation either. It was possible that everything had been prepared by Malcolm Forbes a long time ago, and that his daughter was just about to execute this plan, but it could also be that she was acting on her own—perhaps being as shrewd and capable as the enigmatic Colonel Količek. Mary Forbes was, in any case, a formidable woman who was able to do what was expected from her in no longer than a month (as it turned out later).

In the meantime, they lived together in perfect harmony. Now and then, they would watch videos of *Tarzan* films, drink excessively, sing, dance, laugh for no reason or just talk until well after midnight; they would then simply go to sleep after a simple 'good night', being ready to face any dream that would prowl around their solitudes which were separated just by the doors of their bedrooms.

Borna would occasionally hear—through the thin walls of the old house—her restless walking deep into the night.

Then, one day, she said that she had everything ready for him: fake personal papers and a fake diploma in chemistry, a fake *curriculum vitae* matching his expertise, a fake childhood with fake parents. All in all, he was about to become a new, fake Englishman from Brighton. His name was going to be James Trevor Smith.

He packed, and she drove him to the train station.

She found him a job in Cambridge—where there were many small high-tech companies that were hiring well educated people without asking many questions as long as these could help bring profit. He was going to stay, she said, in a village called Grantchester, where she had a friend who needed a lodger.

'Be careful with your English, as it's still not quite proper, and avoid people from Brighton at least for a while.'

'I shall, my dear Mary. How could I ever thank you for all of that? I can't remember anyone who has ever done so much for me without asking anything in return.'

She started to gaze into his eyes, and then she took his head into her hands very gently, caressing him with her perfect fingers. After a few moments of looking at him, she said,

'Kiss me, young man, kiss me as if I'm the love of your life.'

His lips found hers in a soft kiss that lasted longer than his entire previous life, and he suddenly did not want to leave; he wanted to stay in Aberdeen and become Scottish with this woman, and not some James Trevor Smith from Brighton, a fake person with a fake past and a fake future. He did not want to seek another home or another woman once again, since everything he wanted to have was there, with this amazing woman and in this nice, remote city.

And when the kiss ended, he asked,

'Will I ever see you again? Can I visit you sometime? Would there be any chance for us? I don't care about the age, you know.'

Mary did not know what to say at first.

After waking up from her heartbreaking thoughts, she gathered some strength, and Borna heard the same old story.

'It's not the age. It's not the kiss. I've wanted to kiss you from the very first moment I saw you. And I dreamt many times of having you in my bed. I needed this kiss, I really did, but something is missing... I'm attracted to you, and I would always have you as a lover... But visiting me? Being in a relationship? I don't know why, something is missing here. Sorry, dear, good, handsome Borna, but I can't do it.'

'I see,' replied Borna resignedly. 'On the other hand, don't you forget me, dear lady, at least not at the very moment I leave.'

'Rest assured, I shan't... Never. I'll never forget you.'

On the train, James the Proud smelled himself at certain critical places, when no one was looking. Nothing, odourless.

VI

1994, Cambridge & Grantchester, Cambridgeshire, England
United Kingdom of Great Britain and Northern Ireland

James the Proud was doing fine in Cambridgeshire despite being a fake. He could only guess whether he was really the only one there who was pretending to be someone else (which would occasionally come to his mind), considering the number of different nationalities and races attracted by the famous University of Cambridge. But no one was asking any questions, and he really did not care who the people around him were.

Since he had arrived, his command of the English language gradually became so good that he no longer had to be careful with every word; he was considered by just about everyone to be another educated English young man pursuing his career far from home, and his skills were appreciated in a company located in the science park in Milton—just north of Cambridge—where he was working from the first day of his arrival from Aberdeen. He was still living in Grantchester—a village south of Cambridge—because he simply loved the place, and it was easy to commute to work in a small car he had acquired in the meantime.

In the evening, he would sit in front of *The Blue Ball Inn*—a nice pub in the neighbourhood—having a pint of beer and watching the meadows just across a small road. These meadows were famous, he was told, because a *Pink Floyd* song had been named after them, and he ended up living so close to such a legendary spot. He knew the song. Most of all, he enjoyed the serenity of his days, free of any irrationality characteristic of the nationalist frenzy in the lands of everlasting war.

From day to day, he was truly becoming James Trevor Smith—who had been, for a while, a mysterious Helmut Meindl from Landshut in Bavaria, and before that a person once known as Borna Didić.

The only connection to his previous life were phone calls to his parents and three photos on a wall in his room: one of Ljerka and Srdjan from their happy Maribor days (looking like Hollywood stars from the 1930s), one of Ivan the Blacksmith and Roža (posing on a meadow), and one of Vladimir and him together (in colour, taken by a local photographer in Kletina in the early 1970s).

James was very fond of Cambridge, its unique architecture and spirit, and sometimes he would go there to simply enjoy the scenery or have a beer in one of the traditional pubs close to King's Parade. He visited Oxford once, and then he understood why people used to say that Oxford was a city comprising a university whereas Cambridge was a university comprising a city. Or he would just walk along the River Cam and observe the people of his age having fun punting and preparing themselves for a wild night in their student rooms. He would often envy them, as he had once been one of the best students of his generation at a university that was still quite competitive—and he was simply missing the opportunity to be one of them instead of making profits for the unknown owners of a high-tech company. He could have become a graduate student in Cambridge—this would be on his mind occasionally—and this doctorate could make all of his trouble worthwhile. However, the frustration would never last long, because he was actually happy to be one James Trevor Smith who was allowed to live a simple life without being asked anything.

He did not have any high hopes for his life any more.

His emotional life was rather uneventful. At some point, he became involved with a girl from India, who studied chemistry and was affiliated to the prestigious St John's College, but this was just a short affair based entirely on sex. While being very passionate and sometimes pleasantly kinky in bed, she belonged to an upper Indian caste and was looking down on James, who did not take any part in the university life—and this ended their relationship as soon as a more appropriate young man showed interest in her. James the Proud did not take this hard. When thinking about that, he would just smell himself at certain critical places and go to meet the sunset with a beer in *The Blue Ball Inn*. Later on, he was showing little interest in women, apart from occasionally flirting with a secretary at work—but this was never serious.

From time to time, he would call Mary. He was still thinking a lot about her—who was in his mind the only true lady he ever met and incredibly attractive too, not only because he was finding her beautiful but also because of her great charm and personality. She would always be sincerely happy to hear from him, but the line she had drawn between them was still there; in time, when he realised that this line was never going to be removed, their goodbye kiss became just a pleasant memory of a good time that was never going to come back. James did not regret anything.

He never again called Suzana but was calling home often. His mother told him that a woman named Marta had called several times from Zagreb, speaking vaguely about their encounter in Vienna and that there were some consequences of that. Danka would always tell her that she knew nothing of her son's whereabouts—saying this because she was afraid that all of that might have been just a provocation—and the woman called Marta would then say a few inconclusive sentences before hanging up. The woman had been calling roughly once a month during the last half a year, said Danka, without explaining anything clearly on any of these occasions. James clarified briefly that he had had met the woman in Vienna but that this had been something he was eager to forget. This was good enough for Danka.

In comparison with what James had been working on with Roger in Zagreb, his duties at the company were rather simple. He was just a small gear among other similar gears, and he was aware only of bits and bobs, never of a whole project behind his work. He would carry out a synthesis of this or that kind, analyse results which meant nothing by themselves, write a report on seemingly meaningless steps he had taken… And that was it. But James did not complain; the salary was decent, no one was bothering him, he excelled in everything, and all of that was just fine with him. Although he would sometimes be frustrated by the lack of any intellectual challenge, he was gradually becoming numb, losing enthusiasm and starting to believe that every job in the whole wide world had only one purpose: to ensure as much money as possible for as little work as possible. He soon stopped envying the students at the Cam.

He would occasionally hang about with people from the lab for drinks after work and at weekend meetings in pubs, which were held quite frequently and were meant to bring them closer together (sometimes the company would even cover the expenses). Although he was already accustomed to the English style of life, he would never feel comfortable with these people, who had their own things of importance and habits which were still somewhat strange to him. For instance, he never learned either the rules or the terminology of cricket—wicket, cow shot, waft, swish, and so on—and he would have simply left politely if a chat had started about a recent match against Pakistan or Australia.

He established a friendship—as much as this was possible within the scheme of his growing misanthropy—only with his landlady. She was a schoolteacher, and her name was Hazel. Divorced and a mother of a son and three girls, all of them grown up, she was in her fifties but very fit. In contrast to the situation with Mary, there was never any romantic or lustful thought between them—although there were several occasions which by all means called for that—and both of them were remaining satisfied with supporting one another in their solitudes as soulmates only. Soon after he had arrived in Grantchester, the fact that he was a Hazel's new lodger immediately became a source of rumours in the relatively small village, where everyone knew everyone. Once James went to a small grocery store nearby—where the local housewives would often come not so much to buy something but more to have a chat with their neighbours—and as soon as he entered the store, everyone went silent: three ladies were looking at him as if he came from Mars.

'Hello, dear. You're new here?' asked an old, fat woman.

'Yes, in fact I am.'

'And where are you staying, dear? Do you feel comfortable here?' asked the woman next to her.

'Yes, most comfortable. I'm a new lodger of Hazel Ashton.'

'Oh, you're a new *lodger* of Hazel Ashton? Well, you must feel comfortable then.'

The women started to giggle. He ordered his things, got them, and then simply wanted to leave as soon as possible; but then the third lady, who was silent until then, asked,

'And where are you from, dear?'

'Brighton. I'm from Brighton.'

'Brighton!' exclaimed the fat lady. 'My husband is from Brighton; you could perhaps meet sometime.'

'Of course, of course, when we find some time.'

And then he went away as fast as he could, remembering what Mary had said about meeting people from Brighton.

Hazel Ashton and James Smith lived in harmony with each other, under the same roof.

They would cook together sometimes, and James would then say that the strange meals he was preparing were from a book on the cuisine of Central Europe, which he had become fond of during a visit to South Germany. Otherwise, he explained, he could not cook anything. For quite a while after his arrival, he disliked English meals and wanted to bring back some spicy tastes and smells of his lost home at least during these hours. Kletina would then materialise in Grantchester—and every meadow, forest, hill or orchard of his childhood would become real at least on the table. Strangely, James would never become truly homesick; the smells were, like a drug, just enough for making him serene—and he would then fall into a state of losing his identity, becoming more and more James Trevor Smith and forgetting his true name. Hazel was cooking typical English meals, and James began to like them eventually. And she adored everything he would prepare.

When the weather was right, they would sit in a small garden behind the house and talk for hours, having some tea, coffee or wine. Or they would watch TV together until ten or so, before going. to sleep in their solitary beds. In the morning, they would have breakfast together, sometimes coffee as well, afterwards departing to work without saying much to one another but obviously being happy that the house was not going to be empty in the evening.

VII

1995, Krotko, Lika-Senj County
Republic of Croatia
&
a journey there from England through Italy, Slovenia, and back

Upon his arrival to Italy by airplane, James the Proud rented a car and headed towards Croatia which was still at war.

When crossing the border between Italy and Slovenia close to Trieste, he was sweating—not because of the August heat but because of the sight of Slovenian police uniforms and the sound of a language which was reminding him that he was back in the lands of everlasting war. Slovenia, Croatia, Bosnia, Serbia, and beyond—all of these countries were for him just the provinces of one big territory where the states and borders had been changing so fast that a person would have got a new citizenship, sometimes several times in life, without moving anywhere. And this would have always produced a big pool of blood. The Romans, the Franks, the Normans, the Byzantine Greeks, the Venetians and other Italians, the Hungarians, the Slavs, the Bulgarians, the Germans, the Arabs, the Turks, the Russians, the French, the English, and some others too—all of them had been fighting for centuries to gain control over this objectively insignificant, small, and poor piece of land. What for? If all of that brought only misery and no one eventually gained full control—what for?

Ivan the Blacksmith died in a hospital in Rijeka two days ago. Quietly, just as he had lived. The property in Krotko remained empty: without sounds, livestock, and pets, without fire and smoke from the chimney; without a new generation that would continue living under the roof of the old house. No warmth, no coldness, no joy, no sadness; everything was still, as if time had stopped. The era of the true patriarchs of a branch of the Didić clan, the one known as the Proud, was over. The dearest son of Matija Didić died at the age of eighty-one, and there was no one to replace him on his humble but respected throne. Ivan the Proud had only one grandson that bore the Didić surname—his name was Borna, and no one knew anything about him for quite a while. He was supposed to become the heir one day, but he was gone, and the family iron rod was destined to decay into rust in the cellar.

The lonely old man had not been showing any wish to live without Roža any more; his last remembered words were that joining Roža without his gangrenous leg (possibly a consequence of an old injury) was out of the question—and the poisons in his body ended his life gently and sometime during the night. No one knew when exactly; in the morning, he did not breathe. Borna the Proud was comforted by knowing that the last of his grandfathers had been fairly well until a month before departing, that everything was quick and that he did not suffer. It seemed somehow that Ivan the Blacksmith went to another world when he wanted to, not sooner, not later, and Borna, faced with that, decided that one day he was going to do the same, with or without an illness to assist him.

It was dangerous for Borna to be in Krotko, although he had another name, a passport of another country, and a car with Italian registration plates. Though he had not been visiting Krotko too often as a boy or teenager, his face was still familiar to many of the villagers, and some also heard the rumours that he was a deserter from the army. He could not join the family at the funeral and was hence standing far from everyone's sight, with a hat on his head and wearing sunglasses. He was hoping that his Italian car would be somehow considered to belong to someone Ivan the Blacksmith had met in Trieste as a Partisan—and it seemed that it was indeed so.

The funeral was a big one for Krotko, which had been by then reduced to some seven hundred souls. Virtually everyone from the village was there. However, there was no eulogy, not many tears were shed (apart from those of three Ivan's grieving daughters), and everything was done in dignified silence. This was common among the highlanders, who truly believed in their Catholic God and thought that births and deaths were just part of a big plan which was governing their lives in a simple way from the very beginning of time. The priest said what he had to say, a few prayers, the casket was lowered swiftly, people paid their respects by throwing some earth or flowers into the grave, and the whole thing was over in about twenty minutes.

Borna saw many young men in uniforms at the funeral, and they appeared more serious than he had been during his short battle experience—they looked like soldiers of a real army.

Later on, the family and friends met at the house of Ivan and Roža for a funeral feast. But Borna could not be there—he was crying elsewhere, as lonely as always.

He met his mother and father on the road to the coast, well outside Krotko, because he had to leave the village before his presence could have been be spotted. Both Danka and Luka were crying all the time, but they did not speak much—as they had been talking over the phone with Borna regularly for the entire time he had been away. This burst of emotions was more due to all of them being again together in person after such a long time; no photo, voice or memory could ever bring so much joy as seeing someone in the flesh, and on such occasions every parent would become weak and fragile. But they had little time: Borna had to leave soon and reach Italy before dark, since the situation—as Danka and Luka explained—was becoming volatile again. Borna did not ask why, and he did not want to know why—he was simply glad to see his parents again. After hearing what they said, he wanted to leave and never to return. He told them that they could in the future meet only in another country, say, in Austria—maybe in Leibnitz for the sake of good old times.

While driving towards Rijeka, and later towards Trieste, Borna the Proud saw many uniformed men and military vehicles. As in Krotko, he noticed that the new uniforms and vehicles were much different from those he remembered from the time of his unfortunate combat adventure, when the Croatian Army had just been forming. Although all of these soldiers were unarmed, Borna was sure that plenty of weapons were around, just waiting to be displayed, distributed, and used. There were also many police units checking cars more thoroughly than one would expect, and the streets in the small towns and villages along his route were too empty for a Mediterranean summer. Something unusual was happening, obviously.

He entered Italy at about nine p.m. on the third of August, without having any difficulty at the Croatian-Slovenian and Slovenian-Italian borders. It seemed that every uniform was largely uninterested in a car with Italian registration plates and driven by a British person.

After all the negotiations had failed, around five a.m. on the fourth of August, the Republic of Croatia—now a United Nations member state—attacked the rebellious and self-proclaimed Republic of Serbian Krajina, located within the internationally recognised Croatian borders. James the Proud heard the news in a hotel in Venice.

This was a short campaign. Croatia was secretly supported by the Americans, and (besides a mass of mobilised civilians) had well trained and amply equipped professional troops, whereas the Croatian Serbs had only an army of conscripted, aged peasants with obsolete Yugoslav weapons, being—in contrast to the situation in 1991 and due to a shift in political interests—abandoned by both the Bosnian Serbs and Serbia proper. In four days, everything was over.

James was completely unemotional regarding the glorious Croatian victory, and this lack of any interest became even stronger when he heard from his parents that the whole situation did not affect anyone of importance to him. He never had any romantic nationalist ideas, not even during his life in Croatia—when he had been exposed to this ideology on a daily basis. He simply detested, from the day of his birth, this way of thinking, especially after learning about the history of his family and his complex ancestry. Being utterly disgusted by every news from the lands of everlasting war, he concluded that Borna Didić had died at nine p.m. on the third of August 1995. He was one James Trevor Smith from Brighton, and no offspring of this man was ever going to suffer as a pawn on the chessboard of politics and war. This decision brought a special kind of relief into his life, as he was determined to care only about those things which were making life simple, easy, worthwhile, and pleasurable.

Back in Grantchester, Hazel cooked lunch for him.
 'Was your journey fine, James? Venice is still nice?' she asked.
 'A boring trip, didn't see much of Venice. Just meetings and things like that. But it wasn't too bad,' he replied, trying to hide the last remnants of his emotions.
 In the evening, they drank some white wine in the garden; he played guitar, and she sang *Scarborough Fair*, a traditional melancholic English ballad.

VIII

1997, Cambridge, Cambridgeshire, England United Kingdom of Great Britain and Northern Ireland

Of all the pubs in Cambridge, James the Proud liked *The Bath House* in Bene't Street the most; there, he would regularly, and always alone, have a pint or two of *Guinness*. It was no different on that Saturday afternoon: he came in, a waitress called Alicia (who already knew him well) brought him a pint of his favourite beer without asking anything beforehand and said,

'Cheers, James. What's new? Have you got five pence on top of two quid or just two quid as usual?'

'Just two quid,' he replied with a grin.

'Five pence after five pence... You'll have to pay for that eventually. I'm gonna get you one day,' she winked seductively.

'Dream on, girl.'

'You'll see, handsome.'

They would always speak with one another like that, and it was not clear whether Alicia was serious or not. James was not, although Alicia—a woman of about thirty-five or a bit more—was not unattractive, quite the contrary. In *The Bath House*—and in some other pubs as well—James was a well-known guest, liked for his pleasant nature and the fact that he would never get awfully drunk in spite of sometimes having five pints or so. Just like Mary Forbes, he knew when to stop.

He was also known for never wanting to say anything about his origins. Many tried to trick him into that, but no one ever succeeded, so all of them finally gave up—accepting him as a pleasant companion who simply chose to remain somewhat mysterious, just as numerous other people in multicultural Cambridge did. He was partly forgiven for being so secretive, because he was, in contrast to many other shadowy characters, at least English.

That afternoon in *The Bath House*, however, a man entered the pub, suddenly recognised James and then shouted,

'Borna!'

Luckily for James, the word was quite strange and sounded like gibberish. Also, there was much noise in the pub, and no one took any notice although Roger repeated the name several times quite loudly.

'Borna, is that really you? What the...' said Roger when he finally reached the table. James swiftly put a finger on his mouth and whispered,

'Shush! I'll explain everything, just sit here and be quiet! Alicia! Bring us...Roger, what would you like?'

'Anything...'

'Bring us two pints of *Guinness* please, Alicia!' said James, whereas Roger remained speechless.

'Borna, what are you...'

'James, if you don't mind, I'm James now. James Trevor Smith. Please get used to it and help me remain that.'

'All right, James Trevor Smith,' and this was everything Roger could say before grabbing the pint and almost drinking it in one. Then he just sat there obviously waiting for an explanation.

'You see,' James started his confession, 'I've been running away from the war for quite a while. You could perhaps remember how I disappeared from *Pliva* without a word. But I was not running away then—I was sent into battle. And this experience changed my life, it was so ugly.'

'And then you decided that this was not for you?'

'Exactly.'

'But... England? How come? Did you have anyone here?'

'In a way, that's a long story, I might tell you sometime later but not now. The command of the English language you gave me helped me blend in here, and now I'm an Englishman called James. Borna Didić is dead for everyone but my parents back home.'

Roger emptied his pint and ordered the next round. While being obviously happy to see James, he still seemed melancholic for some reason. There were some minutes of silence after James' explanation had ended and before he started to tell what was disturbing him.

'You know, Bor... I mean, James, I'm glad that you did that. My children are half-English, but they've never wanted to leave Croatia. At least Nigel was young enough to stay out of the war, but life is really shitty there. My daughters have eventually even become Croatian nationalists, for God's sake.'

'Don't be surprised, this often happens when a nation is forming a state after a long time. I've been thinking about this phenomenon for quite a while. They grew up there, this is their world, and just as I want to blend in here, they're eager to blend in there. Just as I want to be more English, they want to be less English,' commented James, 'but at least they've got a choice I didn't have. I was destined to become just another casualty in a struggle for something I didn't believe in. And I'm not talking about the idea of an independent Croatia but about the whole bloodshed and war profiteering. I had to leave simply because I didn't want to die for someone else to prosper.'

'And have you got a job here? I could help you with that, you know, I've got a lot of connections,' offered Roger in his typical manner of a caring senior and fatherly figure. He was, after all, only a few years younger than Luka.

'Many thanks, my dear friend, but I've got a good job already, at a company in Milton. As a chemist, in fact. Nothing as exciting as it was in *Pliva*, but it keeps my wallet full and my nerves strong.'

'This seems good, but if you ever decide that you want to become a member of my team at the university, there'll always be a place for you. You were excellent in *Pliva*, such a brilliant brain!'

James was a bit surprised, because he never knew that Roger was interested in an academic career.

'At the university? Not at a company? I remember you as a skilled producer of commercial drugs, not as a person of formulae.'

'Things are different here, Bor... I mean, James. Academia and real economy here are not so much apart from each other as they are in Zagreb. And did I ever tell you that I've had a doctorate since 1968?

Probably not. And I was in Zagreb publishing my research results intensely, it was just that I didn't talk about that. People at *Pliva* did not object, in fact they were encouraging me to do so. For them, this was free advertising, a reference they could use.'

'And why academia?'

'Because I've got less stamina than before; it's easier to work with students, and write a paper occasionally, than to struggle with hectic demands of greedy capitalists. I've chosen a quieter life, in short.'

James understood him well, as he was also very fond of living without stress. Nothing could be as valuable as a quiet life, he thought. The whole history of his family taught him that. Still, he could not avoid noticing that Roger did not appear happy or fully relaxed, and then he asked him,

'And your wife? Is she with you?'

'No, she's with the children. She has never wanted to leave Croatia. Well… This bothers me in a way. And what about your love life, young man?'

James could not answer immediately. For some reason, he again started to think that he was really a despicable traitor to his country, one who had run away when things had been rough. This was unlike Roger's children, who had real connections with the outside world but had chosen to stay. However, James was always a logical, analytical person, and his journey into the realm of guilt did not last long. Just when he was about to answer the question, Alicia came with two pints; she was giggling, and then she exclaimed,

'Two more pints for the two distinguished gentlemen, on the house! And who's this charming friend of yours, James? Dear sir, whatever your name may be, I hope that you will—as a man of experience and wisdom—explain to this senseless bloke that he could never find a woman like me. I'm trying to seduce him for a year, and—nothing!'

Then she continued to laugh, and it was again not obvious whether she was serious or not. She gave James a kiss on the cheek; he hugged her and kissed her back, saying,

'Dream on, woman.'

'You'll see, stud.'

This was a thrilling moment for Roger—reminding him of his younger days in pubs—which brought back a smile on his face.

'An attractive woman, and cheery too. Is she your girlfriend?'

'No, no, I've got no girlfriend. She's just a good friend.'

'And as a man of experience and wisdom, I say—make a move on her, bloke! Life is short, you know.'

'Drink your beer, Roger,' replied James and laughed. 'There's been enough chatting about women for this evening.'

They drank many beers by the end of the evening, but the next day was fortunately Sunday. Afterwards, they would meet every Saturday at five p.m. in *The Old Bath*; and they would speak about Britain only, never about Croatia or any piece of ground in the lands of everlasting war: memories from there were hurting both of them. James eventually learned everything about cricket.

IX

1998, Aberdeen, Scotland
United Kingdom of Great Britain and Northern Ireland

James Trevor Smith went from the railway station directly to Mary's flat. She had been very brief over the phone, and he had no idea what was so urgent, why she needed to see him so badly—after six years of being in touch but never seeing each other in person.

'My dear James, my lovely young man—let me see you first,' she said happily after opening the door. 'What a proper Englishman have you become! I see you've got some money now—no trace of that ragged fugitive once known as Borna.'

'And you're as charming as always, my dear,' James complimented her back.

She looked great. Though she was approaching fifty, her charm and elegance astounded James again. Apart from a few new wrinkles around the eyes, she was pretty much the same as before: she had not gained any weight, her skin was still quite smooth, her makeup was impeccable, and she still possessed those catlike moves that interplayed with her natural classiness of a distinguished and desirable lady. There was a lot of pride in her appearance, and she was still a true Forbes.

He entered the flat and made himself at home, feeling as if he had never left. Mary did not behave any differently; her young friend was home again as far as she was concerned—and there was a meal for him on the table, just as it would have happened many times before.

'Let us have an aperitif first and then eat. I've prepared something I know you like.'

The table was set beautifully, which he had not seen during their previous life together—when meeting at supper would have been just part of the daily routine. There were some candles lit too. And she wore a very stylish dress that accentuated her curves of a much younger woman. The meal was her version of mince and tatties—the food that James had always enjoyed tremendously, she remembered (probably because this Scottish delicacy reminded him of the cuisine of the Pannonian Plain and the whole region bordering the Alps). He took a look at the food and then at Mary—and he liked what he saw, wondering why it had taken them so long to meet again.

The evening was developing pleasantly, with a lot of small talk about their experiences from the past six years, which led to an even more relaxed atmosphere even before some wine came onto the table. No, Mary did not drink less; and yes, she was still more charming after having a few glasses.

James knew all of that so well, and he was really enjoying the return of a rather good part of his life. After the supper, they sat down on the sofa with full glasses and continued their joyful reunion. For some reason, they were sitting at some distance from each other. Were they afraid of what would have happened if they had been closer? Did they ever forget their only kiss? Or had their mutual affection been lost over the course of the past years? Neither of them seemed to be sure.

'Borna, I must tell you some bad news,' said Mary suddenly interrupting a quite relaxed discussion. James was somehow expecting this—because she had been quite serious and sounded disturbed during their conversation over the phone.

'James, please, I'm now used to be called James, you know. And what's so bad?' he said.

Mary poured more wine into her glass and emptied it almost immediately. She then poured some into James' glass and started to explain,

'The point is, James, that you can't be James any longer. Because of all this talking about some other countries being considered to join the European Community, they've been checking out the papers of some people—maybe by random choice, maybe due to some suspicion, I don't know—and they checked out your papers.'

'Meaning?'

'Meaning that my connections did something that was appropriate in 1992 but not in 1998. We'll have to do this better now.'

James' mouth went dry. What did all of that mean? What about his life in Cambridge—his comfortable, nice, decent life? He emptied the glass in one sip and topped it up immediately after that. Then he took a deep breath and asked,

'Tell me, Mary Bridget Forbes, what now? Who should I become now? Not a James, not a Trevor, not a Smith, obviously, and I was already Borna Didić, or Količek or the Proud, not to mention that I was also Helmut Meindl for a while. What would my next name be—and where could I go? What diploma I'm going to have, if any, and where might I find another life? And life means job, salary, accommodation, peace of mind...'

Realising that it was not Mary to be blamed for the misfortunes in his life, Borna then stopped talking and clearly sank into despair. He could not even drink any more.

Mary's eyes became wet, and she sat closer to him; then she took his head into her gentle hands, looked deeply into his eyes and smiled in an attempt to cheer him up.

'Everything will be fine, Borna. Trust me—it will be just fine,' she said using the most comforting tone of voice she could.

'How could anything be fine, after these bloody six years...?'

'It will be fine. You're forgetting something.'

'Forgetting what, my dear lady? I'm almost thirty-three now, and there's not even a stray dog who could look at me and think that this man could offer him a home. Because there's no home! Bloody hell, what have I ever done to deserve this?'

He started to cry at first, but then he stopped abruptly, as if some black curtain fell over his face. Mary, a clever woman, waited for this to start and then to end—as she knew that it was supposed to happen—and then she again took his head into her hands, continuing to speak softly,

'You're forgetting one thing. And this is that I'm Mary Bridget of the Forbes Clan of Aberdeen, the only child of the honourable General

Malcolm Archibald Forbes of the British Army, and that you're Borna the Proud, the dearest grandchild of the great Colonel Vladimir Filip Količek of the Royal Yugoslav Army, and that some promises had been made before two of us were even born. A Forbes will never abandon a Količek—and I shall not say this again. Just believe it or not.'

Borna looked at her. She was obviously dead serious—and astonishingly beautiful. But he could not feel any lust; he just took her left hand and kissed it—this was the only thing he could do. When he did that, her whole body shook. She took a deep breath and bit her lip.

'Falcon's Eye, just listen. An eclipse is upon us, but it will pass away...' she said.

'...as it has never happened that a night...' Borna continued.

'...is not followed by a day,' Mary finished.

Their fingers remained intertwined for quite some time, and Borna was gradually accepting the fact that he could not remain one James Trevor Smith from Brighton, living in the village of Grantchester in Cambridgeshire, and that he had to instead become the embryo of another person who had never existed and who was going to give him a chance to build some new, different life. A life in which it was possible to exist as a small man whose only ambition would be to share, with the rest of humanity, his natural right to live in his own way and die of old age.

'Your surname will be Jones—this has been our choice which we don't need to explain—and you'll be from Cardiff, a Welshman. You'll have a diploma from the Cardiff University School of Chemistry and *curriculum vitae* with a reference to your time spent in a company from Aberdeen. I own it, don't worry. No Cambridge in your *curriculum vitae*, don't you forget that. This is 1998, and my connections now know how to arrange all of that better than in 1992. But we've decided to let you choose your first name and middle name.'

There were a number of scenarios for the future in Borna's mind, but all of that was leading only to a big confusion, so he concentrated on what Mary just said—on the choice he was given.

'Your father's middle name was Archibald, right? Then my first name will be Archibald.'

'I'm so honoured!' exclaimed Mary. 'And your middle name?'

'Must I have one?'

'Yes, you must.'

'Let me see... Vladimir! My middle name should be Vladimir, and I insist on that despite the risk. Everything in my life has so far been risky anyway.'

'That's no risk,' replied Mary soothingly. 'People in the UK give all sorts of middle names to their children. Henceforth, my dear friend, you'll be one Archibald Vladimir Jones. Get used to it. You'll receive an envelope with all the documents and instructions in due time. Until then, remain James and become Archibald only at the airport when finally leaving. The state is sluggish, but you'll have to leave the UK in not much more than a month. We'll leave the rest for tomorrow—let us now make a toast to your new and hopefully happy life! My good man Archie!'

The next bottle of wine was filling their glasses like a waterfall after the unpleasant discussion had ended, and this time the wine was red—as Mary would always choose. Borna, or should we say Archibald, did not complain—since Mary Bridget definitely deserved her choice to be respected. They eventually separated their hands and moved back to the opposite sides of the sofa, opened a new bottle and became again engaged in small talk. At about two a.m., they finally got terribly sleepy. It would take a long time to explain every detail of how they ended up sleeping together on the sofa, but when Borna woke up in the morning, he was behind her, and their bodies were touching from head to toe. She was holding his hand on her breast firmly and with a half-smile on her face. He managed to free himself from this awkward position in spite of her unconscious reluctance to let him do that (which turned her smile into a frown), and then he went to prepare breakfast—just as he would have done it on many occasions six years ago if he had been the first one who had come out from their separate rooms.

She was still asleep, frowning in another position, when he took another look at her: her makeup was messed up, and her age was more discernible, but she still looked like a true goddess—at least to him. His feelings from the event of leaving Aberdeen years ago were coming back. However, he realised, once again, that there was no room for him in her life—as she was a distinguished lady deeply rooted in Aberdeen and he just a Borna, Helmut, James, Archibald, an escapee, with no past and with a vague future ahead.

'Good morning, dear,' she whispered while stretching on the sofa and with a smug smile on her face. 'Did you sleep well? Are you well now? Oh, you made us breakfast!'

Then she stood up and said,

'Oh, what a mess! I'm a mess, too. Would you mind excusing me for a while, please? I'll come back in no time.'

She came back in some ten minutes—wearing another dress, with fresh makeup and her hair done—and she again looked at least ten years younger. Borna could not stop gazing at her.

'Thank you, Mary, for everything you've been doing for me.'

'I said yesterday what I had to say, no need for any thanks.'

'I know, I know, but still…'

'You'll go to Switzerland,' she interrupted him suddenly. 'To Basel. It is Basel where you'll end up if you want to prosper, and this is what I can offer. This is the best offer you'll ever get.'

'But why Switzerland? Why Basel?' he replied, surprised by this swift change from trivial to important matters.

She took a seat, stretched her arms wide, and being obviously relaxed and happy, said,

'Because Switzerland will never join the European Community and because I've got some really strong connections in the *Novartis* company in Basel. My company works with them.'

'Meaning?'

'Meaning that you'll blend in there without any problem. You'll be out of the reach of any European Community administrator, they'll accept your diploma without asking much, and you'll earn at least fifty percent more than here. Life there is more expensive though, but I think you can manage.'

'But aren't the Swiss very strict in everything? The strictest in the world, I've heard. Their immigration office, and so on?'

Mary started to laugh out loud, almost choking herself with the bacon and eggs that Born had prepared.

'No, no, this is just a silly prejudice. They are only the most logical people in the world, and that's why they're doing so fine.'

'Meaning?'

'Meaning that they would make a deal with the Devil as long as this is logical—efficiency, profit, no questions asked, and so on. This is on their minds. As long as you're paying taxes and making no trouble, it is the safest place in the world. And this is where one Archibald V Jones, this mysterious character, should live from now on.'

His train was leaving in the afternoon, and the situation was quite similar to the one six years ago.

'Borna, find a good woman. This heals everything,' whispered Mary in a trembling voice, and Borna did not reply: he just kissed her.

Their kiss was longer this time, but Borna knew it was in vain.

This was the last time he ever saw Mary Bridget of the Forbes Clan of Aberdeen, who was the only child of the honourable General Malcolm Archibald Forbes of the British Army; this general had been saved once by the great Colonel Vladimir Filip Količek of the Royal Yugoslav Army—who was one of the three grandfathers of Archibald V Jones. And she did what a Forbes would always do. The voice of Vladimir Količek, when he had said 'the Scots remember', was echoing through Archibald's mind while the silhouette of Mary was disappearing in the distance.

X

1998, Cambridge, Cambridgeshire, England United Kingdom of Great Britain and Northern Ireland

James waited for Roger in *The Bath House*. It was five p.m. on a Saturday, and he was late as usual.

Alicia asked whether she should bring Roger's beer immediately or later, and James replied listlessly,

'Later as always. Or... Whatever.'

He did not seem to be in a good mood that day, and Alicia wondered why; he did not even give her any playful compliment that would always be followed by her remark that she was going to get him one day and by his teasing that she could only dream on.

It seemed that he cared only about his pint of *Guinness*, looking languorously at the place which was full of happy young people.

Roger entered the pub, said 'hi' to Alicia, spotted James and walked towards him with a big smile on his face.

'Guess what,' he spoke even before sitting down, 'Nigel has decided to come here! Apparently he's sick and tired of looking for a job in Croatia, has found none and decided to accept his old man's offer. I've already prepared a room for him and found him three job opportunities! Nothing spectacular but should do for a start.'

'Congratulations, my dear Roger. This is indeed good news,' replied James in a way which could not hide that he was not quite well for some reason.

Roger did not notice that at first, and he called Alicia,

'Alicia, dear, bring me my pint and then another round in fifteen minutes! Wait, I'm buying a round for the whole pub, in fact!'

He was loud, everyone heard that and applauded; glasses went high and the people were exclaiming,

'Thanks! Cheers!'

Alicia came with his beer and asked merrily,

'What's all of that about, Roger? Have you found a nice lady or managed to cheer up this grumpy friend of yours? Today he's not even tried to seduce me.'

'He'll try as always, don't you worry, but the important thing is that my son will be coming to live with me—and I must celebrate this!'

'What news!' exclaimed Alicia. 'This is a reason for celebrating indeed!'

Then she took a look at James and said,

'And you, arsey James, you should know that your next round will be on the house, though I'm thinking about bringing you a glass of pure water. Only Roger deserves a free beer.'

'But if you'll keep me sober, I'll not slap your wonderful ass later,' reacted James with a devilish smile on his face.

This smile, although fake (which she did not realise), was everything she needed in order to feel that everything was normal again, and she immediately stung back,

'I can hardly wait, lover boy.'

'Wait and dream on,' was James' reply, as usual. Alicia went away with a smile of relief on her face.

However, this acting could not fool Roger, who had a distinct feeling that something was not right. They spent some time drinking beer and talking casually—mostly about Nigel and Roger's wish to bring his whole family to Cambridge eventually—but James could not concentrate. Roger noticed that, and then he asked,

'James, what's wrong? I've never seen you like that.'

'Well, Roger, there's something I must tell you.'

'Something bad?'

'Quite bad.'

'If it's about your job, you know that you can always join me…'

'No, not the job. Worse than that. You can't help. The only good news is that I've already helped myself.'

Roger realised that something more serious was troubling James. The Englishman was instantly silent.

'Tell me,' he then said, grabbing his pint in expectation.

'Well, I can't tell you any detail, but it suffices that you know that I can't stay in England any longer. They checked out my papers, and they know that I'm not James Smith. I must leave before they catch me. Quite soon, in a few days in fact.'

'And do they know who you really are?'

'I don't think so. They may have linked me to a certain fake German person, that's all for now, I believe, but it's just a matter of time when they will know everything. I can't return to Croatia in any case.'

'Is there really nothing I could do? Perhaps I could pull some strings. A professor in Cambridge has a certain reputation, you know; they might listen to me.'

James started to feel somewhat better, thinking that he was not completely alone in this big world, in which he was little more than a nomad, going from one place to another not because he wished so but because he had to in order to survive. He was missing his parents, and the fatherly figure of Roger calmed him down for some time at least.

'In fact, you can help me, Roger,' he smiled unexpectedly, 'but not by pulling strings. You can buy my car, for Nigel, at a discount price—I promise.'

'Consider it done!' exclaimed Roger. 'And I'll do more than that. Alicia—another round, please!'

Alicia came with the beer and saw that James was smiling, which brought a smile to her face too and made her say,

'No more grumpiness, handsome? You see—life is good.'

'Today,' James remarked, 'it is good today.'

'And what does that mean?' she asked.

'It means that today is a good day,' interrupted Roger, sensing that the situation was in danger of becoming sullen again, too complicated for Alicia in any case, 'and we ought to have a good time for the rest of the evening.'

'That's the spirit, Roger!' laughed Alicia. Then she turned to James and said, 'I'm busy now, but I'll sit with the two of you after the last call. Be here, stallion, or I'll chase you all the way to Grantchester.'

Roger did not stay until the last call; he went home some twenty minutes earlier, and it was not clear whether he really had to go or was it just that he wanted to give Alicia and James some privacy, knowing that it was possible that they were never going to see each other again. When Roger was leaving, James told him that he was going to write, signing his letters as 'Archie'. And no, he could not explain why, not yet at least.

'Here you go, stud,' said Alicia bringing him a full pint, 'and this poor girl is going to have one with you if you don't mind.'

'Not at all, my dear charming lady. You're particularly beautiful this evening, and I'd be honoured to have a drink with you,' he said with a gentle expression on his face.

Alicia was bewildered: James said that? After years of frivolous comments and playing with words—when she would have been the hunter and he the game—he suddenly gave her a true romantic compliment, and it seemed that he truly meant it.

'James, are you well?'

'Depends on how one defines being well.'

She decided to disregard this remark and to try to bring things back to normal again,

'Well, if this could make you feel any better, we can do it right now and here under the table, lover boy, and I promise you'll never forget that. You'll finally have a proper woman!'

'I would enjoy this immensely, and I believe this would be the best experience of my life—as you're today so beautiful and attractive.'

She looked into his eyes, took a deep breath and said worryingly,

'James, you're really not well. What is the matter?'

He did not reply immediately. There was a certain sadness in his eyes; he was taking short sips of the beer, observing the empty pub soundlessly and breathing deeply. Then he suddenly touched Alicia's hand very gently, whispering,

'I'm leaving Cambridge soon. I'm leaving England for good.'

She was astounded, remaining quiet for some time and doing basically the same he had been doing previously.

'How come, James? What's wrong?'

'Well, Roger will explain to you eventually. He knows. There are things in my life, they are complicated, and I simply must leave. I can't tell you more.'

'Are you a mafia man or a spy or something? You're not going to be injured or something? Please tell me you won't.'

'No, it's much less adventurous than that. I'm simply a man who is running out of luck occasionally, and this can always be solved only if I leave a place. Please don't ask more.'

Alicia was a wise, compassionate woman—and she knew when to stop asking questions. In such moments, she would always try to make things better—mainly by using unpretentious humour—and she hence changed the topic to a happier one, stating a simple request,

'Well, if nothing could be done, I demand that we forget all of this rubbish and return to who we've always been! I'll start, you follow. James, if I grab you now and pull you under this table, you'll forget you're leaving, and you'll risk the worst kind of death only to have a woman like me all over again and every day!'

'Woman, I surely like your horniness, and I like your obsession with me even more, but this could happen only in one of the millions of parallel universes, if they exist, where James is the craziest being in the whole of that universe…'

They continued like that until they finished their beers, and then he left without saying many words, as if he was going to be back in a few days, next Saturday if not earlier. She saw tears in his eyes.

Then she had a half pint alone in the empty pub, and just before leaving the table, sighed and mumbled,

'Oh my God.'

It was a long time cycling to Grantchester. It started to rain when James was close to the *Pembroke College Sports Ground*, but he did not even notice; the rain was not heavy anyway. He knew that he was never again going to see Alicia.

XI

1998, Grantchester, Cambridgeshire, England United Kingdom of Great Britain and Northern Ireland

James was packing, and Hazel was sitting on the bed in his room.

They had already discussed the main points, and there was no need to clarify anything further. He paid what he owed, would not say why he was leaving nor where he was headed, assured her that this really had nothing to do with her, and promised to call and write from... Wherever. There were no hard feelings, as Hazel had had lost her lodgers unexpectedly several times already; she knew that she in fact had no special right to know his secrets.

'These photos,' she said, 'that you just took down from the wall. I've always been wondering who these people are. They don't look English at all, and the photos seem to be quite old. This uniform of the handsome young man, for instance, is definitely not British. And you seem to have the same eyes.'

James remained silent for a while; he did not know what to say. To reveal who he really was? Or to make up another strange story, continuing the practice of lying—which had been his lifestyle for the past six years, his recipe for surviving one way or another? He was in doubt for a moment, and then decided to tell her at least a bit of the truth. He was going to leave England in a few hours anyway, and even if Hazel had wanted to betray him, which was unlikely, she would have no time to do anything like that.

'Hazel, I've got to admit that I haven't been quite honest with you. I'm not English. I've been lying to everyone including you.'

She was dumbstruck and looked directly into his eyes remaining completely motionless, with her hands on her lap and moving only her lips when she eventually asked,

'All these years? How come?'

'This was necessary. I'm a fugitive, a refugee, a deserter running away from a violent and bloody war. And now, when the war is over, I have no home any more. I couldn't and shouldn't have involved you in that. You don't need this in your life. Everything went smoothly, and you needed a lodger. As simple as that. They may ask you a few questions about me one day, and this could be the only trouble you might have. Just imagine that I told you earlier, any sense in that?'

It did not take long before she realised which war he was talking about, since there was only one war in Europe worth remembering in the 1990s.

'Are you Bosnian?'

'No, I'm from Croatia, and these photos explain who I am. And be calm—you didn't give refuge to a war criminal, just to a simple man who was sick and tired of a bloodshed fed by brutal and primitive nationalisms. Croatia, Bosnia and Herzegovina—this was all just one war led by the worst of the locals and by fascist immigrants who originated from that part of the world.'

She had been somewhat disturbed before James started his confession, and then she became relaxed, because this short explanation revealed that the good young man James Trevor Smith—someone she still knew well despite the previous shock—was speaking again. Yes, he did not disappear in a split second after she had asked about the people on the photos, quite the contrary—his eyes were again as gentle as always, he was not showing any nervousness or irritation, and she was pretty sure that he was not lying this time. She wanted to know more, after all these years, so she asked,

'But your command of the English language, and your... And what's your real name then?'

'Borna Didić. My name is Borna Didić, and some know me also as Borna the Proud, since "the Proud" is the byname of my family from my father's side. A long story, and we have no time for that.'

'Well, Borna Didič, tell me now, who are these people on the photos, and why this explains who you really are?'

'Didić is the correct pronunciation, in fact. This "ć" should be pronounced roughly as "ch" in "cheers" while you said "č"—and this is pronounced more like "ch" in "much", you know.'

'Well, I've just learned something new,' said Hazel, ever more intrigued. 'And now back to the photos: who are these people?'

'You see these simple peasants on a meadow? These are my paternal grandparents, Roža and Ivan Didić. They were Roman Catholic Croats. And this good looking couple—he in a uniform and she looking like a Hollywood star from the 1930s—these are my maternal grandparents, Srdjan and Ljerka Jarbašić. He was an Orthodox Serb and she half-German and half-Croatian. She was Roman Catholic too, although her German side of the family had been Lutheran once—since they were Transylvanian Saxons by origin.'

'How interesting! And I know that my ancestry is Saxon too, so we might be a kind of relatives!'

'I wouldn't be sure of that,' he commented. 'I believe that English Saxons and Transylvanian Saxons were different peoples, just carrying the same name for some historical reasons.'

'Are any of your grandparents still alive?'

'No, they all died. Ivan was the last one, he died in 1995.'

'And your parents? Are they alive?'

'Alive and well, living in Croatia. I was calling them twice a week over all of these years, from the payphone. A person like me had to be extra careful, and this was why I never used your phone. You shouldn't have known, as I said.'

Hazel felt a bit displeased by being mistrusted during the six years of living together with Borna; she was, on the other hand, happy that this situation was finally disentangled. Borna stopped talking and continued to pack his things, taking little care to do it right.

'Let me help you,' she said, 'your bag needs a woman's touch. You'll leave half of your stuff behind if you continue like that.'

When everything was almost packed, the last of the photos—the only one in colour and showing an old man and a boy—was virtually the only thing left, and Borna wanted to put it directly into his pocket. Hazel spotted this and interrupted him,

'And who is this old man? Who is the boy? Is the old man your father? Is the boy your son?'

'No, my father is younger. And the boy—that's me in the early 1970s. The old man is my third grandfather. I don't carry photos of my parents with me; this might be a bit risky, as they're still alive and I'm a criminal. And such photos would anyway remind me only of my recent past, not of my ancestry. For someone of my fate, remembering who I really am is a kind of antidepressant. To remember is the only solid thing I've still got in my life.'

'Your third grandfather?' Hazel was surprised although nothing seemed to be simple in the case of Borna. 'I've thought we all have two grandfathers only.'

'Srdjan—the man in uniform and with my eyes—had not survived World War II, and Ljerka later remarried. The name of the old man was Vladimir, and he was the grandfather I grew up with. Yes, he was my grandfather no less than the other two.'

Borna was reluctant to give any further clarification on who Vladimir was and what he meant to him, so he just explained briefly.

'He was the one I grew up with, as I said, he taught me many important things, and without him I would never be here to tell you this. Now you know about these photos, may we just have a nice goodbye time from now on?'

One could for ages ponder on a possibility that Hazel actually had a crush on Borna, but it was a fact that she was unusually emotional when he was about to leave. Was it just because of the six years they had spent together under the same roof or something more—who could know?

She called him a taxi and paid for it, but this was of lesser importance. When the taxi arrived, she hugged James strongly—in the way a woman in love would do—and she simply did not want to let him go. He was sensing that, and—although he was always considering Hazel to be a desirable woman—he wanted this hug to disappear together with the nightmare he was going through. He wanted to finally become Archibald Vladimir Jones, as soon as possible, and remain that. He gave her a kiss on the cheek, and her kiss was half on the cheek and half on the mouth. And as the silhouette of the taxi was becoming blurred in the distance, finally disappearing behind the first curve at the exit from Grantchester, she muttered,

'Life isn't fair.'

Archibald Vladimir Jones was watching the smooth landscapes of Britain from an airplane which took off from Luton airport, and he realised how much he was actually fond of the country where he had lived for a bit more than six years. These had been good years.

After the terrible early affair with the Indian girl, he was not involved with any other woman there, not even for a night, but he did not feel entirely bad. Although he did not have any sex for all of these years, he met three wonderful women who were able to fill his soul with other pleasures, and these ladies were Mary, Alicia, and Hazel—all of them older than he was, too old to be called girls and too young to be considered motherly figures. However, eventually he felt frustrated by this combination of emotional satisfaction and physical torture—as he was a young man in full strength—and he decided to henceforth engage only in sexual relationships without romantic feelings. There was a new life ahead of him, and he loved that as much as he hated it.

When he had been coming to the UK in 1992, he had been expecting—according to common belief—to find a rainy place. In reality, Cambridge was not particularly rainy. Was it rainy and snowy in Basel? Was it cold? He could not know—since he knew little about this city, and as a matter a fact, about a country called Switzerland.

The life and death of
Archibald Vladimir Jones

I

2000, May

Archie was living in Basel for a bit less than two years already, and—apart from his everyday melancholy that was buried deep inside him—he felt fine. No place in the whole wide world could be enchanting enough to remove the strong feeling of resignation within this thirty-five-year-old man with no proper name, nationality or homeland, but Basel was possibly the best place for at least healing some of his wounds—not all of them but still some.

Having this on his mind, Archibald at some point realised that Basel was really the only home he had—and he decided that he was never going to leave it.

He simply did not want to search for another home, learn other languages and accents, acquire new customs, fabricate his past, cheat whenever he could, and so on, always feeling like a game animal in fear that a playful hunter was going to spot him and pull the trigger, satisfying his sick instinct for deciding on the life and death of less fortunate ones. While it was reasonable to assume that his sins were going to be forgotten and forgiven one day in the lands of everlasting war and elsewhere, he was not eager to consider this possibility as a motivation for going anywhere he had already been. Other places were not attractive either; he had found his safe hideout at last, and—just as any other hunted animal would instinctively do—he did not want to leave it. He traded the dream of the greenest fields of his childhood for a comfortable numbness.

Switzerland was a wonderful place generally, especially for someone who was a fugitive and a person unwanted beyond the Swiss borders. Everything was so logical and easy, beyond belief: as long as one was obeying the law, paying taxes and conforming to the local standards and customs, one was allowed to do whatever one wanted to do, being protected from everything that was going on outside the country.

While living in the UK was not particularly difficult, living in Switzerland was easier. The UK was rather complicated with regard to the origin of the residents—which was not unimportant for someone like Borna Didić, Helmut Meindl, and James Trevor Smith—as there was a little box for everyone: a box for the Britons (and within this one, smaller boxes—one for the English, one for the Scots, one for the Welsh, one for the Irish), a box for the people from other Commonwealth countries, a box for the Americans, a box for those from Western Europe, another one for those from Eastern Europe, a box for... And then, there were other boxes for religions: a box for the Anglicans, a Scottish Presbyterian box, a Roman Catholic box, a Hindu box, a Muslim box...

After the centuries of the imperial power of the UK, the boxes for peoples and religions were arranged orderly—they could never be the cause of a serious turmoil—and this was how this complicated society functioned to the general satisfaction of the dwellers of the boxes.

Switzerland was much simpler: there were only two boxes. Either one was Swiss or not, and the percentage of the non-Swiss residents was meticulously kept at some eighteen percent with the chance for a foreigner to become a Swiss citizen being slimmer than cycling to the Moon. In the eyes of the Swiss, an English lord, a German industrialist or a shamefully rich American rock star were the same as an immigrant from Bolivia or a refugee from Afghanistan: none of them were Swiss. Regarding religions, there were also only two boxes: one for the Protestants and the Roman Catholics—these had to pay church tax if wanting to fulfil their religious needs—and one for everyone else.

This simplicity was supplemented with the astonishing tolerance of the Swiss for any other nationality, religion or race. They knew that they needed foreigners to keep the economy going, and were therefore more than satisfied with their two-plus-two boxes which were enabling them to control their country fully.

Archie liked this reduction of lifestyle to the number two, since he still remembered the situation in the lands of everlasting war—where the number of such boxes was close to infinity, and where all of them were forming a disordered pile looking like a rubbish dump for human destinies.

Moreover, only Swiss laws were of importance in Switzerland, meaning that the Swiss were accepting international regulations if they clearly benefitting from them—and not for any other reason. Of course, they were able to take such a standpoint because of their immense economic strength and independence, but this had been developed patiently over many past centuries and not due to some lucky circumstances (as many would be inclined to believe).

Archie liked this reduction of law to only one set of clearly defined, simple regulations—and he felt safe, knowing that no one beyond the borders of this confederation could ever again question his right to die of old age outside a prison. He was obeying the law, complying with the Swiss way of life, paying taxes, and this was the only behaviour expected from him in order to benefit from the wonderful simplicity of living in Switzerland.

He had a job in the *Novartis* company in Kleinbasel.

After his skills had been checked thoroughly, he was assigned to a department responsible for relations with the partners abroad, and the logic behind that was simple: he understood the chemistry of pharmaceutics, his command of the English language was excellent, and his German was also good enough for bridging a gap between highly skilled professionals within the company and the demand for conveying their expertise to the world in which English dominated. He soon started to benefit from that financially in a way that could not be compared with the situation in Milton—he was simply earning at least three times more money than he could spend. Despite the costs of living, which were almost twice higher than in England, he was becoming richer every month. His lifestyle was still moderate—because he had lived like that before—which was in stark contrast to the swelling of his bank account.

His becoming well-off was brought to a higher level when he had a few beers with his first friend in Basel (his name was Matthias) one evening after work—when he was taught how to invest his surplus money by this man who joined him at a table in a crowded inn (in a way, similar to how it had happened with the Bavarians in Regensburg).

Matthias spoke English quite well—just as many Swiss did—and he also did not ask a single question that would make Archie feel uncomfortable; for instance, what he was doing in Basel and why. With Matthias's help, Archibald started to invest his money within a week, soon starting to understand the logic of making money without working; in a few months, he became completely independent in that.

Hence, in the May of 2000, Archibald V Jones was an established foreigner in Switzerland, like many others in the city of Basel, enjoying, as much as he could, a life free of troubles—virtually for the first time in the last ten years.

And the city of Basel was a pearl in the necklace of the most beautiful places to live in.

It numbered about 170,000 people at the time. The larger part of the city—called Grossbasel (*big Basel*)—was on the left-hand, completely Swiss bank of the Rhine, whereas its smaller part—called Kleinbasel (*small Basel*)—was on the right-hand, northern bank of the river, being surrounded by Germany completely. While comprising the same city, Grossbasel and Kleinbasel were different with regard to the inhabitants and lifestyles.

In Grossbasel, bordering France in the west, lived mainly affluent Swiss people together with accomplished foreigners who could afford the high rents, whereas Kleinbasel was, in large part, inhabited by poorer foreigners and only by some Swiss—usually young ones who still did not have enough money to cope with the high price of renting or owning accommodation on the other side of the Rhine.

Most of the historical sightseeing spots and posh places were in Grossbasel, and this was the part of the city where one would normally take a respected visitor for lunch. The impressive Basel Cathedral, the university (the oldest in Switzerland), the main city square, the main infrastructure (the railway station, the hospital, etc.), and so on, were there but still not everything that was making Basel such a good place to be. During the day, Grossbasel was to be visited; however, during the night, this was Kleinbasel. A lively suburb comprising the Red Light District among other places for having fun; generally, the entertainment and sin of the city were on the northern side of the river.

Upon arrival, Archie had started his Swiss life in Kleinbasel, in a small and inexpensive flat; and then, when he could afford it, he moved to a bigger flat in Grossbasel. However, it was difficult for him to obey the rules of a conservative Swiss neighbourhood there, and he started to think about moving back to Kleinbasel—where the situation was more appealing for a single man who was still young and thirsty for excitement and enjoyment. He had gone through a lot of trouble in his life prior to becoming stable in Basel, and having some fun was, at the time, very important to him. He simply wanted to be wild again, at least sometimes, to explore the borders of pleasure, to be completely free for the first time after his life in the lands of everlasting war had ended. Complaining neighbours could not make him free.

He asked Matthias what to do. The young Swiss—who obviously knew everything about having fun in Basel—offered him a solution after a couple of beers in a pub in Kleinbasel, where they ended up because it was well past midnight.

'Why wouldn't you live here, in Kleinbasel?' Matthias asked. 'You could find a much more luxurious place here for the same money you're paying now in Grossbasel. I'm talking about some eighty square metres or so, my friend.'

'Well... This might be a solution. I might think about it,' replied Archie, but it took him only a few minutes to make a decision and say, 'In fact—why not?'

Archie moved back to Kleinbasel. There, he rented a flat of about hundred square metres at Claraplatz—which was a square that represented the unofficial centre of that part of the city. He had too many rooms, but he simply liked the place and he could afford it—no more saving money for some threatening future events! At the time, he was not aware that the Red Light District was just some hundred metres away in the direction of the Rhine; he did not start to explore these lustful streets yet, although he was by all means not a newcomer to Basel. So far, he had concentrated only on becoming a proper immigrant.

After scanning Kleinbasel more thoroughly than before, he could not remain ignorant of the fact that there were so many beautiful young women in the neighbourhood—and these were of all possible colours and nationalities: some were black, some Asian, some East European (judging by their accent), and some clearly from South America. During the day, they would behave like everyone else—shopping, drinking coffee, sitting on benches and chatting—but they would disappear in the evening, leaving Claraplatz almost empty and without any charm; the only thing a passer-by would conclude was that this was just another tidy Swiss square with a church.

One evening, Archibald took a walk northwards, towards the 'German railway station' close to the border with Germany—and there she was: a beautiful black girl at the door of a house, calling him in bad German,

'Come, dear, come with me.'

He looked around, and there was no one else on the street. Then he spotted a police station just some thirty metres away; a policeman was standing there, being completely uninterested in the obvious solicitation by the ebony girl. It was not difficult to conclude that the house was in fact a brothel, and that prostitution was legal in Switzerland—which Archie had not known until then.

He rejected the offer and continued his evening walk. That night, however, he did not sleep well.

So many adorable girls around and so much money in his pocket? This thought continued to trouble Archibald V Jones for days, since he was a person who did not have sex for so many years. The touch of a woman was something he did not remember well—and he wanted to be touched by a woman again. The Catholic sense of right or wrong (which he had unwillingly acquired during his growing up, and which was still buried deep inside him) was melting like a snowflake in a tropical country.

II

2000, August–December

Archibald Vladimir Jones was still firm in his decision that he was never going to leave Basel. Where to go and for what reason? He was not welcome anywhere except there: this was his final home after travelling across Europe to reach the UK and eventually leave the country under pressure. Short travels abroad due to his duties at work were something he had to do, but this was just a minor thing which he did not take seriously. His connections with the lands of everlasting war were restricted to weekly phone calls to his parents—and that was it.

> 'Our birth was easy, oh my
> Like the rain, we fell from the sky
> Then a wild cat started to growl
> Our friend he was, not on the prowl.'

This was a street musician singing his song. And Archie listened. Where had the wild cat of his childhood growled? It had growled in Kletina; not in Basel, which was a wonderful place by all means but not a home of his choice. However, it had to be. Kletina was just a memory.

With these thoughts, Archie went to the Red Light District of the city of Basel for the first time.

The District was not big—comprising a few small streets only—but it was full of pubs. Most of these were brothels, in fact, having rooms upstairs where the girls would bring their clients to take care of the business. They were astonishingly beautiful—as one could actually expect in a country which excelled in everything including paid love. The Swiss wanted only attractive prostitutes, and a newcomer would often be surprised to see so many beautiful women in six or seven brothels between the Rhine and Claraplatz.

There were some streetwalkers as well, but these were not so good looking and were appearing somewhat desperate in trying to attract those customers who could not pay the full price for a delightful hour with a goddess from their dreams. They would eventually also find a Prince Charming, take him to a place less luxurious than the rooms above the pubs, and both of them would get what they were there for. Archie learned later that there were cheaper brothels and private flats, all over Kleinbasel, where the business was also carried out—all of them being registered at the police and rights offices—but the District was offering more than just plain sexual gymnastics.

In the District, a horny man would come, sit at the bar of a brothel, select a girl out of many available ones, buy her a drink and then chat with her—getting more or less a girlfriend experience as a preparation for going upstairs. This would cost the man more than on the street—and there were additional expenses for the girl as well—but this was how the Swiss quality was maintained to everyone's satisfaction. If a girl had been either insolent or not sexy enough, she could have chosen among the street, her private flat or a cheaper brothel; and if a guy had not had enough money, he could have gone there as well. The police would patrol the District occasionally but without interfering unless it was really necessary—this was all a lucrative business everyone benefitted from, after all.

Archibald came there just to have a beer and observe the pub he chose randomly. The beer was unusually expensive, but he did not care; he was there basically just to see and experience the place, and his pocket was more than full. Soon he became the target of several girls who wanted to be offered champagne at the price of fifty francs for a small bottle, and Archie refused all of them—not because he did not want to spend this money but because he was still exploring the District and hence did not want to rush.

While the men would sit at the bar, the girls would wait behind them, mainly leaning against a wall, observing the situation and waiting to be called; from time to time, a girl would approach a man at the bar at her own initiative—which would sometimes lead somewhere and sometimes not. This was all a game of lust and money, in which there were certain rules though: no sexual behaviour was allowed in the pub—as there were rooms for that upstairs. Only talking and decent touching was acceptable, and if no champagne had been ordered in ten minutes or so, the girl would have returned to her place. Archibald realised that during his first hour at the bar.

After he had refused three girls—one was African, one white, and one Asian—he left. He was extremely aroused, but he did not know how to react in such a situation, and the wisest thing to do was, he thought, to leave before doing something stupid like catching a disease or being robbed. Later, however, Matthias explained to him that the brothels were very safe and that neither of those things could have possibly happened, since the Canton of Basel-Stadt had full control of what was going on in the District.

'Just go for it,' he said, 'if you wish, there are others who are looking after your safety. The girls are clean and under control—no pimps from American films are allowed here.'

'Really?' asked Archie. 'This is, after all, prostitution, so why would anyone care?'

'Swiss prostitution—and we do care. We wouldn't want to have diseases and violence here. Just avoid streetwalkers and those with any bag on a chair—these come from France or Germany just for an evening, to lure a client and run away across the border as soon as they collect the money. Everyone knows that.'

This was enough for Archie—he trusted Matthias and decided to return to the District soon.

Her name was Marcela, and she was from Santo Domingo in the Dominican Republic. Age: early twenties. Skin: caramel. Face: perfect. Body: to die for. Personality: cheerful. After her, Archie became addicted.

By November, he slept with extremely beautiful women from Venezuela, Ivory Coast, Hungary, Martinique, Brazil, Thailand, Argentina, Morocco, Slovakia, Somalia, Russia, and the Cameroon. During these months, he became renowned all over the District for his gallantry, good spirit, and generosity—so he eventually ended up in bed with a girl from Costa Rica and one from the Philippines simultaneously; and he had to pay only half the usual price for such an arrangement, possibly because the girls were hoping that he was going to be back soon and choose them again. It was also not unimportant that he was never treating any prostitute like an object; when being with one of them, he would make love and not just have mechanical sex, so the girls—who were, somewhere deep in their hearts, still dreaming of romantic love—appreciated this conduct more than one could imagine. If they had been aware of the past of their lover, they could have understood—but they did not know, and this was helping keep things simple.

He explored every sexual technique he had not tried before—in Kletina as a young man and during his other intimate encounters—and this brought unusual calmness into his life. His lack of odour was finally irrelevant: he would compensate for the absence of his manly smell by being with a girl only for an evening and picking up another one sometime later, whenever he wanted to. Nevertheless, sometimes a girl from a few weeks ago would approach him and go with him without even asking for any money, but he would never leave without putting a generous amount onto her night drawer—usually when she would not be looking. This was adding to his reputation of a perfect gentleman.

Just as he did not have a favourite type of a girl, he did not prefer any of the brothels specifically; he would choose a girl of any race or physical attributes by simply following his lustful thoughts at that very moment—and this would occur in any of the brothels. Soon he became acquainted with many people who worked there, not only with the bartenders but also with some of those who were organising the entire business. He learned from the latter ones that all of that was not always easy, because many Canton officials were sometimes stubbornly sticking to the law, being inflexible and not willing to accept any initiative for bringing more money into everyone's pocket—including that of the Canton—and such proposals would never include any bribe but simply a more logical approach. If only there had been someone influential or persuasive enough to deal with such problems, said the owner of a brothel, things in the District would have been much easier. And all the brothels would be willing to pay a decent sum for such services on a monthly basis if necessary.

After a while, Archibald started to think about this problem. He was neither influential nor particularly persuasive, but he knew some important people in the local business circles—and he knew that many of them were visiting the District occasionally (although secretly, not hanging about in the bars). When relaxed—at a drink after work, for example—they would sometimes brag about their adventures with sexy District girls, who were so different from their conservative wives and girlfriends, and they would also sometimes complain about certain annoying things in the District.

At one of these after work drinks, Archie's boss—who respected his younger Welsh colleague for the quiet efficiency in leading his department—said,

'I'm going there at ten every Wednesday, when my wife thinks I'm playing table tennis with my cousin from Luzern, who recently came to live in Basel. Both of us, I told her, shifted our work on Wednesdays to later hours, because we could book a table only late in the evening, since it's always been terribly crowded. Of course that we go to the District on Wednesdays—and the bloody police are always there about ten. We can't hide, we can't go in—we have to wear hats and glasses to hide from them. If I got rid of them on Wednesdays at ten, my sex life would be much simpler.'

'Inconvenient, boss,' commented Archibald on the confession of his superior.

'Do you ever go there, Archibald? You should, you should. This is for people like us regardless of age,' continued the boss. 'That's why we're making all that money, apart from supporting our families. And you've got no family?'

'No, sir, I've got no family. And yes, I've been there a couple of times.'

'Good, good. And find a wife anyway, young man. If I were you, I wouldn't take a Swiss girl; I'd play table tennis and find my woman there,' the boss laughed.

In about an hour, Archie and the boss remained alone at the table, and the boss was already quite drunk. Archie saw that as his chance to ask him more about the 'troubles' in the District, so he said,

'Sir, have you ever tried to get rid of the police in the District on Wednesdays at ten?'

'My dear young man, I've been thinking about that,' replied the boss, 'but I simply can't do it myself. Everyone knows me too well. I could change my visits from Wednesdays to, say, Tuesdays, but I guess the police would be there every time I'd like to drop by. It's frustrating not to know about their schedule. I know someone who could help, but I can't approach him by myself, this would be quite embarrassing.'

'And if I went instead?'

'You could do that? Really?'

'Instruct me on where to go and what to say—and I'll go. Tell me about the offer you're willing to give, the arguments, and how to do that. I'll do it. No bribe, please, I'm a foreigner here.'

'No bribe, of course—I'm willing to offer them subtler and quite legal benefits,' said the boss, and then he started to talk.

After he had learned from his boss about the relevant structure of the administration of the Canton of Basel-Stadt (and about the names and characters of the people he was supposed to negotiate with), Archie did not rush. He first paid a visit to several brothels in the District and asked to speak with the managers. He offered them a deal with the police patrols—in a way that their schedule would be known in advance on a daily basis—so that the brothels could play their little secret games in a more relaxed way. For instance, to arrange the visits of affluent clients to a mutual satisfaction—which would lead to more money flowing into this part of the business. And everything would be completely legal: the brothel owners did not have to know how he was going to achieve that, they did not have to sign anything, and they did not have to pay him any money in advance. If they had been satisfied, all of them together would have paid him three thousand francs after three months, and this was really a small amount compared with the total money in the business.

The instructions which the boss had given him were good enough for Archibald to complete his task, although he had to improvise at certain critical moments. This was not particularly difficult for him, because he had a rich history of pretending any lying.

He benefitted from this endeavour both in the company and in the District. Being supported by his boss, he soon got a raise 'because of his excellent results', and—since he managed to build a small network of trusted people in the administration of the Canton—he continued to act as a person able to reconcile every disagreement between the Canton administration and the District. This hobby was bringing him a decent but not tremendous amount of money, and his true fee was his growing reputation in the District. He was also extremely careful never to do anything illegal; he was, after all, a foreigner who would never risk losing the only home he had.

And this was how Borna Didić, since recently known as Archibald Vladimir Jones, ended his career as a scared little man who had endured punches from just about every vicious person or force in existence. This was how he became a person who finally gained control over his life.

III

2001, March–May

Phone calls to his parents were bringing nothing new into Archie's life. Luka would frequently speak about his plans to get his son home after all these years, since the war was over, and Croatia was becoming more stable. Spending a year or so in prison, so what? This was a small price to pay for being home again—and with a good solicitor, Archie could even end up with probation only.

'I don't want to be persecuted by anyone, father, as I've never done anything wrong. This is a huge price to pay, so drop it,' would be Archibald's usual reply.

Danka would occasionally mention that the annoying woman Marta did not stop calling them, always talking mysteriously about some consequences of the encounter of her and Archie in Vienna but never wanting to explain what it was all about. She would call intermittently several times a year, and Danka—who had the natural instinct of a woman—finally asked,

'Did you make her pregnant in Vienna, son?'

'Well, this is possible, I don't know. In any case, give her my phone number and tell her to leave you alone. I'll deal with that.'

'And you're still not thinking about coming home, Borna? Maybe you should listen to your father, things here have become…'

'No, mother, I'll not listen to my father, and I'll not come home. My home is in Basel now, get used to it. If you want to see me, I'll pay for your fare, and you can come to visit me.'

Thus, they visited Basel for the first time in March; and when they saw how well their son was living, they stopped planning his return to Croatia. It was so obvious that there was nothing for him in the lands of everlasting war.

Marta called in April.

'Is this Borna? I'm Marta, the woman you slept with in Vienna in 1992. Remember? Well, I must tell you that you've got a daughter,' she said directly and without any introduction.

'Marta? Yes, I remember. And I also remember that you threw me out of your room as if I'd raped you, which I didn't, so let us make this short. Are you sure that I'm the father?' replied Archie without any drama in his voice. He was glad that this issue could be clarified, but he also did not want to be drawn into a long and possibly unpleasant conversation.

'Yes, I'm sure. I hadn't slept with anyone else for months before and later, and she was born nine months after our having sex. You can ask for a test, but she's got your eyes, I can send you a photo if you wish.'

'Srdjan's eyes,' replied Archibald without thinking.

'What?'

'Forget it.'

'Whatever. Well, what are your intentions now, Borna?' asked Marta in a trembling voice.

'My intention is to support her if she's really my daughter. Have you got an e-mail? Write down mine,' said Archie and spelled slowly and carefully one of his e-mail addresses. 'Scan her photo, mail it to me, and then we'll see. Have to go now, bye.'

Many photos arrived the next day, covering the entire childhood of a little adorable girl. And on each of them Archibald Vladimir Jones could see the eyes from the only photo he had of Ljerka and Srdjan. The girl had Srdjan's eyes beyond any doubt, and Archie needed no other proof.

He wrote back and asked Marta about the bank account for sending his support, and also explained that—due to some reasons of no importance to her—he could not reveal details of his current life. She replied that she did not care, because the girl (whose name was Andrea) had been told that her father deserted them a long time ago. The name of this evil man was not to be mentioned, and in the birth certificate, he was 'unknown'. At first, Archibald was disturbed by being erased from the world of the living once again—just as he had been losing his name several times already—but he soon realised that this was the best solution. What life would the little girl have in the prejudicial Croatia as a daughter of a traitor to this country?

Who would want to listen about the truth? Who would care? Would anyone want to hear about a man whose only crime was that he hated the nationalism and war frenzy of the 1990s, that he simply did not want to kill or to be killed only to conform to the twisted and sick ideas of that wicked time in which hell again opened its gate wide? No, Andrea's father had to remain 'unknown', and Archibald could only hope that one day he was going to be allowed to emerge from the dark and say his true name aloud. On the other hand, he had no hopes for the future, and just as he had done it many times before, he accepted his fate stoically. He was nameless already, and adding 'unknown' to this could not make things any worse.

He did not say anything to his parents, as their involvement could only make all of that more complicated or even dangerous for Andrea. He had to remain 'unknown'. At one point, Danka asked about the situation with Marta, and Archie replied that this was nothing serious, that he would take care of that.

Marta stopped calling them.

Archibald would often think about his little daughter. He wondered to what extent was she important to him. Yes, she was very important, although he knew that he was probably never going to see her. Maybe sometime in the far future, he thought, but the chances of that seemed so slim. When thinking about her growing up so far from him (and how much of that he had already missed and how much he wanted to be with her to see her becoming a woman), he would almost start to cry. A long time ago, however, he had forgotten how to cry.

Then he started to think that he could still do more than simply support Andrea financially. At least for himself, to ease the pain somewhat. It took him weeks to come up with something, and this eventually resulted in a decision to write a journal which could one day reach her regardless of whether they were ever going to meet. In May, he bought a luxurious notebook with fine leather covers, took a special, old pen, and wrote the title on the first page:

The life of Archibald Vladimir Jones
written by him for his daughter Andrea the Proud

He decided to present only facts and avoid interpreting them, since he wanted Andrea to learn about him using her own and not his standpoints. For some reason, he was writing the journal in English and not in Croatian. Maybe because he was, after so much time, remembering only the dialect of Kletina—so he was not sure whether his daughter would understand this archaic mixture of Croatian and Slovene. On the second page, he wrote a few sentences about Andrea and how one could trace her, concluding this by a request to deliver the journal to her in case of his death.

He first briefly documented the histories of the Didić, Jarbašić, and Količek families, explaining that he had three grandfathers: one who gave him the surname and personality, one whose eyes he had, and one who made him knowledgeable and persistent, all of them being equally important. This was followed by a number of pages about the extraordinary women in these families, about the whirlpool of the ethnicities, the three religions, and the wars—always these damned wars.

Although he continued to write the journal for the next eleven years, almost until his death, he wrote some one hundred pages only. However, he added maps, drawings, names and addresses of some trusted people, links to web pages, cooking recipes, guitar chords and lyrics, excerpts from the dialect of Kletina, chemical formulae of certain famous perfumes, poetry (not his), and so on. The journal eventually took the form of notes which could have been written by an explorer from the Age of Discovery; taking into account the circumstances, this was not entirely surprising.

IV

2002, April

Weizerit Sara Abel—which could be roughly translated as Miss Sara of father Abel—was from the city of Gondar in the Semien Gondar Zone of the Amhara Region in North Ethiopia. This was how she should have been addressed by a stranger properly, but she did not hear that for years. She was so far from home, forgetting it more and more, from day to day, and Basel was the only home she had.

There were occasions when someone would ask about her surname, and she was already tired of explaining that the Amhara people did not use surnames, that she should be called simply Sara or Miss Sara or weizerit Sara; in time, however, she learned that it was simply the best to say that her surname was Abel, without going into the depth of the tradition of her people. The Westerners might have been advanced in many different things, but they were generally unable to comprehend that they were not the only people on this planet, and that their rules and customs did not apply everywhere.

Weizerit Sara was not liked by other girls in the Red Light District. Not only that she was, being astonishingly beautiful, always attracting the best customers, she was also very posh and distant, neither sharing her thoughts and desires with anyone nor wanting to become part of this society that had its own life behind the curtains of the District. She was once attacked by a girl from Jamaica because of that, and this fight was short and brutal: Sara broke her nose in a split second and said that this was just a small demonstration of what she could do, since every daughter of Gondar had learned a long time ago how to deal with a Sudanese infidel or any other scum.

Sara was all alone in Basel, without any friends and hopes, and there was also nothing in Ethiopia for her to dream about. The low-intensity but everlasting clashes along the border with Sudan—which was a forgotten conflict between two ancient religions (Oriental Christianity and Islam) for centuries—had destroyed the future of her family. This was not an official war, and it was fought mainly by plain bandits who were using political and religious concepts as an excuse for their plundering raids, but the outcome was just the same if not worse—because there was no hope that this could ever end. In addition, numerous men from the region perished as conscripted soldiers in the wars on other Ethiopian borders, those with Eritrea and Somalia, and many of their widows eventually decided to flee together with their children and find another way to continue living. With the help of her mother—who was a Coptic Egyptian—Sara had reached Cairo and then managed to come to Europe. After acquiring fake documents via some of her mother's connections, she sojourned in several European countries before eventually settling down in Switzerland: this country seemed to be her final destination.

Basel, was, in her opinion, the best place she could ever find to heal her wounds.

She was not disturbed by having to be a prostitute in order to survive. Although coming from a poor country with an undeveloped schooling system, she was reasonably well educated—since her father had studied medicine in Prague, and her mother was a daughter of a solicitor who understood the power of education. In consequence of the continuation of this family tradition, Sara's knowledge of languages—of English in particular—was decent, and she also knew that signing a pact with the Devil was not always a shameful thing. Her father used to say that every contract could be broken, but he never had any chance to explain this better—since he was killed at the Eritrean border just before Sara escaped to Cairo. Her mother fled somewhere too, but Sara did not know where. After some time, Sara signed a pact with the Devil willingly and stopped thinking whether this was right or wrong.

And no, she was not waiting for her Prince Charming to rescue her from the pit of sin; there was no past, no present, no future—and hence there was no sin. Every day was bringing a totally new life: in the morning, a completely new universe would be created, lasting for the next twenty-four hours, not more than that—and everything would then start all over again the next morning. When the light of a new day would mark the birth of a brand new universe, she would enjoy lifting the window shades: the city of Basel was there, calling her to be everything she wanted to be.

Maybe Sara was just another prostitute in the District—only somewhat more reserved and calculated—but this seemed to be a very oversimplified description of her.

Archibald Vladimir Jones spotted Sara in the pub of a brothel where she worked, and the bartender told him that she was, apart from being so beautiful, cold and bitchy. No complaints from the clients though, he said. He also remarked that she could have been the best of all the prostitutes in bed, but as far as everyone else was concerned, she was an icy princess with no soul.

She would always drink coffee alone at a small table for two close to the wall opposite the bar, attract a customer in no more than an hour, go with him and then not return the same evening. How much money she would get just for an hour or so, wondered the bartender; the other girls would always come back to search for another client.

The truth was that she did not charge much more than the other girls—she was simply not greedy.

Archie became intrigued, and then he asked the brothel manager to tell him more about her. The manager told everything he knew, and Archibald decided that he was going to learn whatever he could about Ethiopia and the Amhara people before even trying to approach her (despite having counterfeit documents, Sara never tried to hide her origin). He started to read books and browse over the Internet, visiting the pub almost every evening but never going upstairs with any other girl and ignoring Sara in the manner of a schoolboy. She was very perceptive, and she spotted that, finding this game strange but amusing. Then she would forget the whole thing when a proper client would come.

Archibald requested his identity to be kept secret, which meant that she should not have been told that he was in a position to ask for her services for free; already for some time, namely, Archie did not have to pay for anything in any brothel regardless of what he would want to do there. In this case, he wanted to play a game of seduction—to remind himself of the days in Kletina perhaps—although playing such a game in a brothel was a quite different matter. His plan was to behave as an average customer but to spice up this a bit with some romantic moments, and then to return after a few days to show that he did not forget, do this again, and finally ask Sara to spend some relaxed time with him outside the District and during the day—when the ordinary people of Basel lived their nice, ordinary Swiss lives.

Archibald V Jones was seemingly in love after so many years, with a working girl he had not spoken a word with yet. He was surprised to feel the tingles of love again—and he liked that. To be in love after all the failures in the past? Why not, he thought, as there was so little to lose—nothing to lose, in fact.

It was Friday when Archie decided to finally approach Sara. For her, he was just another man who would, quite often though, come to have a drink at the bar, and he also seemed to be a bit strange—because he would never choose a girl, not even to chat with one before rejecting her offer. What was he, then, doing in a brothel where drinks were at least five times more expensive than elsewhere?

On the other hand, she still liked him somehow, maybe because he was never raising his voice or because his moves were a kind of slow and free of any nervousness; she could not say what she liked exactly, but she wanted to see him approaching her (it was not her style to lure clients at the bar—she never had to). She managed to hear that he was speaking mainly English, only occasionally German, and she also noticed that he had a favourite place at a corner far from the central point of the pub, where he would usually just sit and observe silently apart from greeting someone now and then. She could also see that he was sometimes watching her. More than once, she smiled to him, but he never reacted; in fact, maybe he did once, when raising his glass high while looking at her. She was not sure though.

That Friday evening, she was again at her small table for two; and Archie, sitting at his usual spot, sent her a small bottle of champagne—

which was usual when someone would choose a girl. She took the bottle with her and joined him at the bar.

'I'm Sara,' she said in English. 'Thank you for inviting me.'

'Thank you for joining me,' replied Archie without revealing his name. 'You speak English quite well.'

'Well, most people do nowadays.'

Archibald V Jones took a look at her before replying. She was even more beautiful than she appeared from a distance: her light brown eyes were unusually gentle under the perfectly shaped eyebrows, her full lips were smooth and looked so soft, her breasts were matching her slim stature perfectly, her bronze skin was absolutely spotless, she had the gestures of a gazelle, and she smelled... He had never smelled anything like that. Was it the smell of a special place in Africa or the smell of lust, love, desire? He could not tell. How could he, as a matter of fact, since he had never experienced the smell of weizerit Sara. Being enchanted by that smell, he did not reply immediately, and it took him some time to say,

'But most people are not as beautiful as you are, my lady.'

'What did you just say—lady?'

'Because you are one.'

'Thank you, my knight,' replied Sara and then giggled. This was the beginning of a long and relaxed conversation between two souls who had more in common than they could have even imagined.

He did not rush. At some point, she thought that this playing a game might turn into a waste of time—since she was there for money in the first place. This man was nicer than many others, but he was still just a client. Archie sensed her growing discomfort, looked at her smilingly and said,

'My dear lady, please calm down. Rest assured that your knight will take you into the castle eventually; it's just that your knight prefers to first light some candles along the way to the chambers of passion. And the name of your knight is, by the way, Archibald.'

She started to gaze into his eyes without moving at all, and this lasted for a minute or so; then she gave him a light kiss on the lips.

'My gallant knight Archibald,' she said in the manner of an innocent girl.

During the chat, she started to feel an unusual warmth inside her chest, and she suddenly found herself enjoying intensely the time she was spending with this strange man from a corner of the pub.

Who was he? Why did she feel so well in his company? Obviously being an easy-going man, like many of her past clients (some of whom had been handsomer), this mysterious knight was quite different—he was simply removing every bitterness from her heart so effortlessly, so naturally. And he was, in fact, rather good looking—masculine, strongly built but not fat, neither too tall nor too short, having gentle eyes and well-shaped hands. She started to think that she would like to be touched by these hands, with or without the money involved.

After a while, Sara leaned her head on Archie's shoulder; he then kissed her passionately and put his hand on her breast, when no one could see that. She hugged him and whispered in his ear,

'Make love to me, my knight.'

In a room upstairs, she danced for him while undressing. Then she undressed him. They were standing in the middle of the room under dim lights, kissing each other wildly and feeling their skins touching one another.

'My services are not cheap, you know. But... But give as much as you wish and stay as long as you wish,' she said.

'I'll give you the world instead, my lady,' he replied, 'but not today. You'll have to wait for that. Today I'll give you my body first, and please do not ask why.'

'Whatever,' said weizerit Sara. 'Kiss me now, my knight, take me, my knight!'

That night, she was not an African prostitute stranded in Kleinbasel—she was a woman whose body and soul were explored and adored. She did not care about the money or time, probably for the first time ever since she had lost her prostitute virginity a long time ago. She did not know that sex could be so much intertwined with pleasure. Yes, occasionally she would enjoy sex with a handsome and gentle client, but this would last just for a short time—as having sex was for her just a job, part of life, nothing much different than cooking, cleaning, watching TV or taking a walk. But it was so different with this man. She really enjoyed his touches and kisses, his hugs and the warmth of his body against hers, his hands on her breasts and his tongue all over her, the wetness, the sounds of lust, his orgasmic spasms and heavy breathing.

'Is this love?' she mumbled in the morning while watching her lover sleeping next to her. The sight of him was making her so serene and safe, which was a feeling she had not experienced for a very, very long time.

Archibald woke up suddenly, and this scared her. She slowly moved away from him and tried to make the whole situation less intimate and more official—something like 'we did it and that was it, just business'. He felt her insecurity, and knowing that talking and analysing too much could make the situation only worse, he started small talk and tried to make the morning more relaxed. Then he kissed her gently, in a way that needed no word of explanation.

He put five hundred francs onto the night drawer.

'No... That's too much. You don't have to... In fact, whatever you... I mean, that's really...' Sara tried to say something.

'That's what I should do, my dear weizerit Sara,' replied Archie with a smile.

'But how... Weizerit? How do you know?'

'My dear lady, people know when they want to know.'

She was sitting on the bed; he slowly kissed her right nipple, then the left one, and then her hand in the manner of a gentleman from past centuries. Like a proper knight.

She remained in the same position for the next ten minutes after he had left. She could not move.

After a while, she went to the window and let the sunlight in. The city of Basel was there, calling her to be everything she wanted to be.

V

2003, December

Archibald V Jones took a look at Claraplatz through a window in his living room. Sara was still asleep in the bedroom.

Being an early riser, he would often sneak out of the bed to observe how the centre of Kleinbasel was catching the first morning breath; he would enjoy watching green tramways heading in different directions, many cyclists and walkers rushing somewhere, shops preparing to open their doors, lazy goofs occupying benches to read newspapers, and pigeons flying around a Roman Catholic church like bees around a flower.

No one from the District yet, and no snow either. The District was recuperating from the night, and snow would seldom visit Basel, as the city had a mild climate influenced by the Atlantic Ocean more than by the less distant Alps in the south.

For more than ten years, he had not seen proper snow, and there was no sign of any this morning either. This was so different from Kletina, where Russian winds across the Pannonian Plain would frequently bring a white Christmas. He missed snow, proper, thick snow that would stop everything before people would clean the streets and pathways—and shy snowfall which would form only a thin, short-lived white layer meant nothing to him.

He never had to rush to work and would seldom leave before half past eight, because he needed only some fifteen minutes of cycling to *Novartis* and was also the boss in a department of about twenty people; his deputy Stefan was always coming early, and Archie would stay at work as long as it would take to finish everything for the day, usually until five or six. This worked perfectly, and no one ever complained. Contrary to widespread prejudice, the Swiss did not work long hours—

their strength was in being well educated, concentrated, and efficient. This philosophy was based on a standpoint that their economy relied on highly skilled personnel and not on overburdened robots; if one had been unable to complete a task in six to eight hours, one could not have done it in ten or twelve hours either.

Sara would usually wake up just on time to see him leaving; they would kiss and exchange a few words only, waiting keenly for the evening to come.

Having breakfast together was reserved for weekends and holidays. Sara would always take care of their morning food (because it was the duty of a woman to prepare food for her man, she would say sometimes). Archie liked that, because he was too lazy to cook ever since he had left England. She would always make a strong and spicy Ethiopian breakfast (such as *fit-fit*) that would keep them full well into the day, and this was another pleasure for Archibald—because he became very fond of Ethiopian cuisine. However, he would often search all over Basel for the meals of his childhood—such as pork greaves or blood sausages—and Sara would sometimes say that she was never going to understand how the Europeans could enjoy such things. She would, nevertheless, always take a bite or two just to please her man, since she always wanted to make him happy in every way—even if this meant eating something so awful from time to time.

Before he entered her life, she had been just a nameless, bitter and confused prostitute in a land strange to her—and then she became a lady who was welcoming every new day with a lot of joy and optimism. She finally had a home, and the name of this home was Archie and Basel.

Archibald Vladimir Jones, her lover and best friend, was still hiding his past from her stubbornly, which was in contrast to the gentleness he would show whenever she needed to feel truly loved and desired.

'I'm your Archie and I love you dearly. Don't you see and feel that? Please don't spoil this by asking too much,' he would often say. And she would then stop asking, happy that he was there with her. So what if he was mysterious? He was her Archie and that was enough for her. She was his weizerit Sara.

He would sometimes be rather quiet, and then he seemed sad, but she would never ask why. This happened mainly in the morning, when she would find him watching Claraplatz with a cup of tea in his hand; she would often undress in front of him, hug him firmly and press her naked body against his, provoking him to take her in any way he wanted to. And she would later always remain frozen for ten minutes or so after their spasms had subsided, being overwhelmed by the magic of their making love—as if the morning after the night of their first encounter was still there.

There was a drawer which he always kept locked.

'You know that I love you very much, Sara,' he would say, 'but in this drawer I keep one thing that I'm not ready to share with anyone yet. In time, be patient, dear, in time.'

And she respected that. She had checked his wallet only once, in the brothel, and she never tried to do anything similar again.

There was love and passion in the joint life of Sara and Archie—and they lived together in harmony in large part because of that—but the very foundation of their relationship was mutual respect. Secrets from their past lives had to be exposed step by step, if ever, slowly and without pushing—which both of them knew so well. For instance, he never asked her how and why she had become a prostitute; this was obviously not important to him, and she was feeling his respect for her own private reasons that had led to this part of her life. Knowing that, she felt safe and free, sensing that her life finally belonged to her only—and not to vortices of human malice or to sick games played by some strange gods. Her God was Jesus Christ, and she loved Him dearly, but she could not rule out that there were maybe other supernatural creatures who were spoiling this planet against His will.

Archie would sometimes take from his secret drawer a notebook with fine leather covers, and she would then pretend that she did not notice that. He would inevitably also take out an old-fashioned pen and start to write something into the notebook, usually sitting next to his favourite window facing Claraplatz. By what she could see, he would never write more than a few sentences; and he was doing this slowly and with a lot of effort, obviously struggling with his awful handwriting.

Once she found him at the Rhine with the notebook and the pen. She approached him and asked,

'Hi, handsome. What are you doing?'

'Just writing down some things in this notebook. Nothing important. By the way, have you ever heard of Slavoljub Penkala?'

'No, who is he?'

'He invented the modern version of the fountain pen. This is one of the originals, it cost me a lot but I wanted to have it. It still works perfectly.'

'Whatever makes you happy, my love,' she replied and then kissed him softly.

They walked to a nearby inn to have a drink and speak dirty. This was their common prelude to the night.

Sara and Archie were still going to the District often. He had to be there occasionally because of his usual duties—which were actually just a hobby—and she would hang about with some of the girls she still knew. Since she was no longer competing with them, most of the girls were nice to her, and she was also quite respected for another thing: her success in finding a life outside the District was nothing special, but she was virtually the only one who ever returned and did not pretend to be anything else than a former prostitute who managed to find something better. Most of the others who found a way out from the District would never come back, probably because they were either forbidden to do so by their husbands or simply because they were ashamed of their past.

'I'm here with my Archie,' she would have explained if someone had asked, 'and this is our neighbourhood in any case. We don't know many people elsewhere, and he also doesn't want to make new acquaintances. We are not Swiss, and I think he's inclined to keep a low profile. Why? I don't know, and I don't care. He's my man and I follow.'

Jealousy did not exist in the shared life of weizerit Sara and Archibald Vladimir Jones, in this mutual rescuing of two lovers who did not know about each other much. But this relationship without possessiveness had not come out of the blue.

Only a month after they had started to live together, he ended up upstairs with a classy Chinese woman, which made Sara very mad at first. He explained to her later that he did not stop being promiscuous and that he still wanted to have sex with every woman he would desire—and she was free to do the same. Or did she want them to break up because of that? No, she said, no breaking up.

After being angry for a while, Sara realised that both of them were of the people from the District and that their lives were everything but ordinary—hence she took some opportunities too (she would occasionally desire a black man). She enjoyed her first escape of that kind, and she never raised this question again.

Ever since this initial dispute had been resolved, they would go upstairs with their selected lovers whenever they wanted to, just winking seductively to show that another lustful story for their private moments was just about to begin. Yes, they would share their experiences afterwards, and if something had been arousing enough, they would have reconstructed the event together, the same night or sometime later. This was actually spicing up their love life tremendously, and there were also occasional orgies during which they would make eye contact while one of them would be reaching climax with someone else.

'You know, Sara,' Archie said once when she was resting her head on his shoulder after wild sex in their private bed, 'we are not common people. We suffered in the past. I don't know of your suffering, you don't know of mine, and this might remain like that for a long time—but we're definitely not common people. Things we do, I mean.'

'In what sense? I feel very common. I'm not Superwoman and you're not Superman, after all. The only thing I want is to be a regular girl, in our Basel.'

'The way we live is not conventional. Not that I complain, but sometimes I've got a feeling that you're not at peace with that.'

'You silly, silly man. Should this plain Amhara girl really tell you how conventional we are? And how much this girl likes it? Everyone does what we do, one way or another. We do what we do, and no one has ever been harmed!'

'You're at peace with that?'

'Yes, what else could a weizerit want?'

'Everyone does it?'

'If they don't, they dream of it.'

'Then we live a dream,' replied Archibald, 'and that's why I'll be all over you the whole night long.'

In their Basel, he kissed her.

'Archie, are you religious?' asked Sara on Christmas Eve. 'Should we celebrate today? Everyone does. Last year we didn't, but we were just getting to know each other, and I didn't want to ask.'

'No, I'm not religious, and I don't celebrate anything related to faith. But I'm somehow fond of this tradition. My family used to celebrate it.'

'And you don't want to talk about it…'

'No, I don't.'

'Okay, I understand. But why wouldn't we just do it? To simply feel the warmth of this day just like everyone else. We're maybe a bit strange when it comes to our lust, but in everything else we're common people, remember? I'll prepare your unhealthy food, and I can also bring some sweets from a confectionery.'

Archibald did not reply immediately. This sounded like a Kletina Christmas Eve, when his mother would have taken care of it; and while all of that was quite tempting, he was reluctant to face his memories again. Since he had left Croatia, he did not take any notice of Christmas, not even once, blaming Christian zeal for the misfortunes of his life. Catholic, Orthodox, Protestant—he had all of that flowing through his veins, and he could remember only mutual butchering due to a stupid competition about the way of worshipping the same deity. In his opinion, this stupidity made him virtually homeless and stranded in a faraway country where he did not truly belong. If the story of the man on the cross had not been told, he would have been home—and he also did not believe that the story was true.

No, he did not want to have something like that under his roof. And then again, he spotted how Sara was looking at him—she simply wanted to share this special evening with the rest of Basel, this was obvious.

'We can also go to this church here, just to feel this day like everyone else. All of my friends from South America will be there,' she continued. 'You don't have to pray or anything, just be with me.'

She wanted to blend in and forget everything from the past at least for a while. This was so clear. And Archie… He swallowed his pride and said, 'All right, dear, if this means so much to you, then we'll do it. Prepare the unhealthy food and bring the sweets.'

They had a wonderful supper under the candle lights which provided a magical atmosphere. She was in her best dress—wearing also earrings, a necklace, bracelets and rings, the best gold and silver she had—and he was in his most elegant suit, the one he had for business dinners. Sara was very meticulous in making this event special. Then they went to Claraplatz and met her friends from South America in front of the church, and Sara was extremely proud to be there with her Archibald. She seemed so happy, and this was making his sacrifice worthwhile; he did not regret a thing.

They entered the church with her South American friends to attend Midnight Mass.

This was not easy for Archie, as he despised churches—all of them but especially the Catholic ones. He still remembered how the Catholic priests in his homeland had been advocating intolerance and bloodshed; he knew that the Serbian Orthodox priests had been simultaneously doing the same, although he had never been in any of their churches. He was just standing there and waiting for everything to end; meanwhile, Sara's friends were excitingly joining the ceremony. Sara, being new in that, simply followed them.

'Did you like it, love?' asked Sara as they were leaving the church an hour later. They lived so close that he had no time to reply before they arrived home.

After opening the door, he said,

'No, I didn't like it. I was there just for you. But I don't regret a thing, because I want to please you. I did it, and that was it.'

'Do you believe in anything, Archie? I know from our bed that you're neither Muslim nor Jewish. You are a white European—so you must be connected with Christ in some way. What's on your mind?'

Archibald V Jones was reluctant to answer that at first, and he also did not want to start a long discussion, so he just remarked,

'Well, let me just end this conversation by saying that I've never seen any good coming from this man Jesus Christ.'

Sara prepared a few snacks and opened a bottle of wine. She wanted to make her man happy just as he had done for her.

'I'm an Ethiopian Christian, you know, and I believe that Jesus is my God. My faith in Him has been keeping me going through the rough times.'

'Good for you,' replied Archibald. 'But he's not been my god for a long time, and I don't believe in Him. Everything related to Him harmed me. Can you live with that?'

'Of course I can. I'm your weizerit Sara. But... How come?'

'This is really not important now if you can live with that,' replied Archie somewhat aggressively, letting her know that he did not want to go any deeper.

'Good, husband, I can live with that. But there's another thing regarding Christmas.'

'What would that be?'

'This wasn't my Christmas, I'm an Amhara girl, and our Christmas is on the seventh of January. Today I just wanted to be part of the crowd. To feel welcome here.'

Archibald grinned instinctively. He took a sip from his glass and said,

'People like us are welcome only conditionally. We've got no home of our choice, and this is why such ceremonies are useless to us. But I know what you're implying—yes, we can have another Christmas on the seventh of January.'

'Really? You wouldn't mind?'

'No, I wouldn't. My mother would always make a good lunch on that day, in memory of her true father.'

'He couldn't have been Ethiopian,' Sara laughed. 'You're too white.'

'My love, your god has made a mess beyond your comprehension. Don't ask for more explanations, just accept that I've always known that Christmas can be on the seventh of January as well. Let us go to sleep now, I'm so tired.'

Sara was pleased that her boyfriend—and she was often calling him husband—did not object to her plans for arranging another Christmas celebration in their home, the one sticking to the tradition of the

Ethiopian Orthodox Tewahedo Church, but she was still not quite happy. She was afraid for his soul, because Jesus was the only one who could save it, and Archibald was rejecting this so openly. He did not know what he was doing, she thought, but he was a good man and Christ would never reject such a soul. This was giving her some hope.

During her preparations for the Ethiopian Christmas, she built a small shrine in the flat. She knew that Archie would not mind—and he did not. She would spend at least an hour there every day praying for the soul of her Archibald, reciting all over again that he was not bad and calling Jesus to hear that.

The Christmas Eve of the sixth of January was the best evening of her life so far. Archie brought her flowers, was extremely gentle and charming, and they made love for some five hours, until dawn.

VI

2005, July

Archibald enjoyed cycling. He tried to teach Sara how to ride a bicycle—which she had never learned in Ethiopia—and she gave up after several weeks of having little success.

Stefan, who was a native of Basel, would occasionally join him and show him new cycling routes in France or Germany across the border, but Archie would mostly go alone although he was always feeling well in the company of his younger colleague. He eventually found his favourite route along the right-hand, German bank of the Rhine that was flowing northwards after leaving Basel, even though he was also fond of the mild landscapes of French Alsace more to the west.

Stefan would also often join Matthias and Archibald during their evening hours in pubs and inns, in the District or elsewhere. While it would be too much to say that they were close friends, they were still hanging about together too often to be called casual acquaintances. Stefan was never told by anyone that his boss was supposed to be Welsh according to his papers. Only the big bosses knew that (being asked by Mary Forbes never to reveal that to anyone), which was making Archie's life easier. And Matthias never asked anything; he liked this Briton and his spicy jokes, his ability to drink a lot of beer and stay articulate, as well as his explanations on how a German phrase should be said in English—which Matthias needed for his work.

Matthias saw Sara several times and was impressed by the look of Archie's girlfriend (or wife, he never found out), asking for advice on how to seduce such a girl. Archibald eventually brought him into contact with several astonishingly good looking girls from the District, but the only thing Matthias ever did was going upstairs for a short time—he never tried anything more serious than that. It was also possible that he, being a Swiss, never had any intention to go for anything else, but even this was much more than Stefan was doing—as he was a shy person who was obviously attracted very much to the District girls but would never make a move. Whenever Matthias and Archie started to talk about women, he would grab his beer and pretend that he was not there. Once a girl approached him and obviously wanted to flirt with him—ignoring Archibald and Matthias completely—but he could not say a word, holding a beer firmly in his hand as if this was going to save him from a complete disaster. His two companions asked him whether it was too much for him to be in the District, since he was a local, and he answered that it was not—he just needed some time to accommodate properly. Matthias laughed and remarked that he was also a local, not from the city centre though, and that everyone was visiting the District—so that Stefan should not have been ashamed of anything. The unspoken deal was to pretend to not know your neighbour—who would be no less embarrassed by meeting someone he knew—and everything would remain well concealed from the rest of the people in Grossbasel.

Although he had found a new and stable home in Basel more than five years ago, Archibald Vladimir Jones was still melancholic pretty often, and even the fact that he lived with perhaps the most beautiful woman in the city could not change that.

Their living together was still going well, but it became quite routine—which made him smell his armpits again. No odour whatsoever, and he began to think that Sara was with him only because he could provide her with a good life, not because of any love. He had experienced this before—having wild sexual relationships lacking true womanly emotions—and he irrationally started to search for a reason which would prove that this was happening again. The tormented mind of this man found it hard to accept that there were many kinds of love, and that people at a certain age might start to cherish things that could be very different from those which had been important in their younger days. On the other hand, sometimes he would for weeks behave like a Harlequin and make Sara laugh, and this image of him was in Sara's mind suppressing every unpleasant reminiscence of the periods of his strange silence; whenever she saw a smug smile on his face, she wanted to kiss him badly.

The first argument between Sara and Archibald came that summer, when they were celebrating three years of living together. They had never quarrelled before.

She prepared one of her Ethiopian meals while waiting for Archie to return from cycling; it was Saturday, and he was away the whole day. She had a feeling that he had been somewhat distant and too quiet for the past months, and this was making her wonder about the nature of their relationship: did he still love her, did she love him, and how and why had they ended up together in the first place? She was still an undemanding girl who appreciated very much what Archie was doing for her, the sex was great, they were laughing often, and there was nothing truly unpleasant in their living together. But something was still missing... After three years of being devoted to Archibald fully, she would accept his marriage proposal without any second thought, but this proposal had never come and she was in doubt: Was he really a man for her? Or did she want something else at the bottom of her heart?

Maybe she desired an alpha male with a strong masculine smell, which was a thing that Archibald Vladimir Jones was strangely lacking. She was not sure.

Once she saw a bitch—not a human character of that kind but a proper female dog—approaching a man that this small creature obviously did not know from before. And she was on her back immediately, showing submission. The man caressed the bitch just slightly, without thinking much, and she then started to follow him instead of a girl who was her mistress.

'Would you please leash your dog?' the man asked politely, and the girl managed to restrain the bitch only after chasing her around him.

'I apologise, sir,' she said, 'but I live with my mother only, we're just girls in the house and my dog misses a male.'

'A male? But I'm not a dog!'

'Please don't feel insulted, sir, but this is what mammals do. I'm a biology student, and I read some research about it, because I was interested. In the absence of a male of the species of a female mammal, the female will instinctively approach a male of another friendly mammal species. My dog does that all the time. Please forgive us, sir, they say that all of that is caused by smell, by testosterone or any other ingredient in the odour of a male of any mammal species.'

'You and your dog are weird, girl,' replied the man less politely.

'I'm really sorry, sir.'

This funny incident slipped through Sara's mind while she was waiting for Archibald to return and join her at their anniversary celebration. Indeed, she thought, had she ever been fully instinctive with Archie? Was the lust for him her primary instinct or was it just that she wanted to feel safe, with or without a true passion involved? Did she love him because he was really the only man she could ever dream of? She could not tell that with certainty.

It was a fact that he did not have any smell—he was completely odourless even when not taking a shower for days—but what did that mean? Then again, she was simply confused by her thoughts and did not want to spoil the evening by continuing to think too much.

Archie was not terribly late—he returned home at seven. He found Sara in a new and sexy dress, with carefully styled hair and makeup, and she wore the best jewellery she had; she looked, all in all, like a model from the catwalk of a luxurious fashion show—where millionaires would be willing to spend a fortune just too drool over the sight of such a woman. And she smelled like a garden in the most lascivious medieval Arab story from the time when religious zeal had not yet dictated games of love and lust.

Seeing her splendour, he became sentimental and forgot all of his gloomy thoughts—she was there only for him, such a goddess! Then he hugged her with a lot of emotion and kissed her on the lips gently, keeping his eyes shut. Sara suddenly felt relieved, and the evening was making sense again. She asked him to change his clothes, because this was not just another evening.

When he returned dressed properly for the occasion, they first had an aperitif, and then she brought the meal to the table. They were eating and chatting, recalling with much joy everything that had been happening over the last three years; they would laugh about their first days—when they had not fully trusted one another yet—and about other funny episodes: learning how to live together without annoying each other, compromising about sex with other people, accepting so many different types of food and teaching Sara how to cycle...

Around ten, they started to enjoy the wine, and in a bit more than an hour, two bottles were already empty. Wine was usually an aphrodisiac during their evenings—and they would often make love all over the flat after two bottles—but not this time. Sara got rather drunk quite soon, probably because of the pace of drinking and not from the amount she had drunk; after a few minutes of silence, she asked,

'Archie, how come that you've never asked me to marry you?'

'I don't know,' he replied, 'probably because I'm not that kind of a man.'

'What kind?'

'One who believes in papers. Marriage is just a piece of paper. I had many papers in my life—in several cases written without my consent—and all of that was plain rubbish. Too many things in my life were revolving around the papers that were only making me nervous.'

Sara was not pleased by this answer, as it meant nothing to her and she did not understand it. Had she been sober, she would have probably been satisfied with it, but not this time. She brought and opened another bottle, took a sip and asked with a bit of malice in her voice,

'So, you think that marrying me would be just another piece of paper? But we share our lives, for God's sake!'

Archie also took a sip of the wine and started to feel uncomfortable; he did not know where all of this was leading to, but he was definitely sure that he did not like it. He was not sure whether she was just testing him in some way or was she really serious? In any case, the evening started to take a new turn.

'I would never try to take you into a church, I know that you don't like churches, but I'll be thirty very soon and I don't want to remain a weizerit for the rest of my life. I'd like to be a weizero eventually,' Sara continued.

'What?' Archibald was confused. 'What is weizero?'

'Weizerit is an unmarried woman, and weizero is a married one, like Miss and Mrs.'

'I see,' said Archie, being sure that Sara, drunk or not, was dead serious. He immediately started to think that anything involving papers would endanger his false identity which was making his life comfortable.

'If this is so important to you, we can say our vows to each other, remain in love and know that we belong to each other for good. Without papers.'

'And our children would be bastards then...'

'Children?'

'Yes, children, Archibald Vladimir Jones. I'm a woman, and I want to have children one day. My biological clock is ticking, you know!'

She seemed rather angry, and her drinking more wine was not making this any better.

'And maybe you're not a man for me at all, maybe you don't love me at all, and maybe I don't even love you! Maybe I could have done better finding a man without any smell!'

After she had said that, Archie started to fall into a deep abyss, and there was no world around him any more: he was falling and falling and falling...

'I'm so sorry, Sara, that I've disappointed you,' he replied and immediately went to the bedroom.

'Archie... Don't... Archie...' she tried to straighten things out. But it was too late. And just as every sad drunk always wants to get more drunk and more said, she grabbed the bottle. Five minutes later, she started to hate that wine and followed him to bed.

She could not sleep, and she heard the early morning bells of the Claraplatz church for the first time since she had moved in, as she had always been sleeping so deeply early in the morning that not even a thundering sound of a war could have woken her up. Suddenly, she became fond of this nice rhythmic sound somehow, and then she took a look at Archie: he was on the other side of the bed, at some distance from her, and his breathing was everything but calm—he would often moan or change position, which was not typical of him.

They had breakfast together in silence, touched each other without saying a word and then went back to bed, where they had sex—they were again in a whirlpool of pure lust as if nothing had happened. Then they went to a restaurant to have lunch and afterwards went on a long walk along the Rhine.

Yes, they continued to live together; they were going to the District together, they did not stop to laugh together, the sex was still great—both with one another and with other people—and everything seemed to be fine. However, instead of finding a way to be more open with each other, they were sweeping their problems under the carpet (for instance, they were never again going to celebrate their anniversary). Occasional outbursts of love and passion would bring back the old days only temporarily, whereas an evil spider never stopped to weave its sticky web around them slowly but steadily.

One way or another, the very essence of the romance of weizerit Sara Abel and Archibald Vladimir Jones was seemingly lost. Why? Because one of the principal laws of the Universe is the irreversibility of things—and it does not matter if we are gods or mortals.

VII

2007, October–December

Archibald V Jones was not a person who would truly enjoy visual arts. He was a chemist interested mainly in the laws of nature. But he liked music, possibly because he could find certain intricate mathematical patterns in harmonies and rhythms—and maybe this was the reason why he had learned to play the guitar (it was easy to play it and was affordable to every Kletina boy) although he was not very talented.

However, he was still not completely indifferent to certain paintings, and these were mainly from the Renaissance and the Baroque periods, showing dreamy excerpts from the times when life had been maybe crueller but less complicated. He was also quite fond of the Croatian naive art, which was a secret link to his lost homeland. Abstract paintings were something he despised, because he considered them to be the works of amateurs who were trying to use mathematical laws of order and chaos in a fraud which had only one purpose—to fill the pockets of these untalented but intelligent individuals who felt the intellectual emptiness of their audience.

Nevertheless, Archie was a visual person, to some extent, but of a different kind—he liked the works of nature. For him, nature was the greatest painter, and its most beautiful paintings would be on display in October, which was quite the same in England, Croatia, and Switzerland. An astonishing parade of subtle shades of green and brown would then develop in the background of our lives, and every trouble would become smaller in the presence of this interplay of the two most important colours of our planet.

The October of 2007 in Basel reminded Archibald of a song by a wonderful Serbian singer and poet. The song was about love and honesty, and on how tree tops reveal their true colours only in autumn, when the green of the summer is no longer there to hide their differences and scars.

The singer and poet was a Serb who was partly Croatian, and Archie was a Croat who was partly Serbian—which raised some questions in his mind. When and how had the two of them become enemies? What was he doing there in a faraway country—and because of what? Was this the world his three grandfathers had been living and dying for? As much as Archie could remember, he and the singer and poet were seemingly sharing more or less the same view on what was right or wrong. However, the singer and poet managed to survive the madness of the 1990s comfortably, because he was renowned and therefore protected by his fame, while Archibald, a nobody, was so far from the meadows of his childhood—and there was nothing he could do about that. He was never an enemy to the singer and poet, but their fates were still so different.

The best place in Basel for enjoying October was, as far as Archie was concerned, a park called Lange Erlen in Kleinbasel, just at the border with Germany. There was a tiny zoo there—with European animals who could feel the local October naturally—and also some ponds and a creek called the Wiese; the forest was dense enough to make one forget the vicinity of the city and explore the park for an afternoon without ever feeling bored. This was a place where the colours of October would reveal themselves in their full glory, and Archibald would always go there to celebrate his favourite month of the year.

That year, however, he was melancholic when he came to Lange Erlen. The verses of the singer and poet were haunting him, and he asked himself whether the richness of the shades of green and brown was a scenery he should still like. When everything had been green in his homeland—when no one had been thinking about the nationality of his neighbour—things had been fine; but later, when the colours of tree tops became discernible, bloodshed began. And this was the main reason why he was here and not there where he truly belonged. As much as he respected and liked Basel, this city was not his true home.

In addition, he suddenly remembered—after all of these years—that Srdjan had been possibly killed in October, at an unknown place and together with some others of his kind. He unexpectedly felt so close to his unfortunate grandfather, feeling like a hunted animal deprived of home and dignity, and it slipped through his mind that his grave was never going to be visited—just as the grave of Srdjan had never been.

Archie then remembered Ljerka and her love for Srdjan. He never heard of such a real and touching story about a big and unconditional love that had ended so heartbreakingly, and he started to wonder what was behind the relationship he had with Sara. Ljerka was a true hero of a brutal era of humankind—and no analysis of a mortal could ever explain her properly—but Sara was his woman, and his destiny appeared so close to that of Srdjan in spite of lacking a true tragedy. He was seriously thinking about his departure, for some reason (maybe because he was gradually losing any interest in this world), and in these irrational contemplations, the thought that Sara was going to forget him quickly, in a week or so, was becoming more intense from day to day. He started to believe that his grave was eventually going to be deserted and forgotten, sooner or later, but he did not care—why would a dead man worry about his grave?

'Well, the Swiss are the most decent people I could ever think of, and I've got nothing to lose with them,' he mumbled. 'At least they'll not pee on my grave. I want to die here. This is my home now.'

Later events were going to show that he underestimated Sara completely. Did she love him as Ljerka had loved Srdjan—or was their love more like that of Ljerka and Vladimir? One could never know, but it was a fact that Sara was fully devoted to Archie in her own way. He could not realise that at the time, as his sanity was deteriorating, but everything after his departure was going to prove that.

I just want to go home now to Sara, he thought just before leaving Lange Erlen much earlier than any previous year. He felt lost without her as he cycled furiously through the streets of Kleinbasel.

After returning home from Lange Erlen, Archibald was very horny. Why? Quite useless to ask, since horniness could seldom be explained by any kind of logical thinking—and in Archie's case, virtually never. He took Sara without any foreplay, in the manner of a satyr (which made her climax two times), and afterwards, he told her that he would like to go to the District.

'You know that you're my weizero,' he said while they were still naked and breathing heavily, 'although we've got no paper to prove it.'

She was surprised to hear this, because she had never raised any question about their formal status ever since that awful anniversary two years ago. But she was still glad to hear it; in fact, she at first became somewhat emotional and then started to feel like a bitch in heat. She looked forward to continuing this lustful day in the District.

'And you're my *ato,*' she giggled.

'What? Ato?' Archie asked.

'Never mind,' she replied, still giggling.

'Dress up, girl, I could now bang the whole world! And I want to see you banging it with me until the morning light!'

At eleven, they were in the District, in their favourite pub (where they met for the first time).

There, everything was as usual: men at the bar and girls against the wall, waiting to be called. Archie said to Sara,

'I want to have an orgy with you and a girl and a man of your choice. Let us have a few drinks first, then you choose them, then we go upstairs. Don't rush.'

Such behaviour by Archie was not unusual, but he had not been showing it for months. She did not know that he simply wanted to get rid of his thoughts from that day, to make life nice again and see whether he could forget his past, his homeland, his parents and daughter, the singer and poet, October and everything this month was bringing, the colours of tree tops, green or brown... and to try to go on with his life the best he could.

Sara returned with a black man and an Asian girl.

'They're interested in everything,' she said, 'and she also finds you hot.'

'Then the four of us should do it,' replied Archie, again being the easiest man in the world. They went upstairs, and their body fluids drenched the room.

In the morning—which would mean for Sara and Archie eleven or twelve after spending a night in the District—Sara woke up first. Archibald was still asleep, and she was observing him with a warm feeling around her heart. She realised that she could not tell whether he was really her only and final love, but she was sure that she respected and loved him deeply. This was, she thought, quite enough for a morning with her ato in her bed—why ask for more?

Who was she, in fact, and what did he mean to her? This slipped through her mind. She was an Ethiopian refugee who had never sensed respect and love until she met him; her life before him had been an intricate game of sadness, insecurity, pain, and humiliation, a struggle to survive; and then he appeared out of the blue and gave her a new life of honour... And there he was in her bed. Her marital bed, as she felt she was a weizero although there was no paper to verify that.

Her feelings were so deep that morning, and she made a promise to herself that she was never going to let him down. No matter what. Never, even if their love was going to fade away one day.

She sneaked out of the bed and went to make breakfast. But there was nothing proper in the fridge, so she went out quickly to buy something in a local store. When she returned, Archie was already in the kitchen trying to prepare something himself.

'Stop!' she yelled.

'What?'

'Sit there and don't you ever again try to humiliate me—your weizero is here to prepare food for her ato!'

'What is that—ato?' asked Archibald, clearly oblivious of their conversation from the last evening, when lust had been the only thing on his mind. Sara just giggled and said,

'You're my man, my ato. And I'm your weizero. No papers are needed for this simple Amhara girl to know that.'

The last three months of 2007 were the best ones that weizero Sara and her ato Archibald ever had during the five years of living together. She was moving around him like a cat, seductively and softly but with much respect, and he would never miss a chance to prove that he was her man in everything that this word meant. Their love seemed to grow again, constantly and unstoppably.

VIII

2008, November

On the first of November, Archie took a day off from work.

In Basel, a traditionally Protestant city, this was not a holiday, but since a considerable number of the people were of the Roman Catholic faith, many of them would reserve this important day—called *All Saints' Day* in Catholic tradition—to visit the graves of their deceased ones, bringing flowers and lighting a few candles. Archie's boss wondered why a Welsh person would want to take a day off on the first of November, but then he quickly concluded that he knew nothing of Wales and that this was not his business anyway.

Archibald Vladimir Jones had stopped being Roman Catholic a long time ago.

His parents were always hiding from him the story of his baptism in 1966—how his soul had been meant to end up in Limbo and wait there for the Last Judgment—but not Ljerka. She once told him about the whole trouble, on a lazy Saturday when she had too much to drink. Vladimir left the room quietly as soon as he realised that this was going to happen; he was thinking that the boy should hear about that one day—but not at the age of twelve—and he simply did not want to participate in Ljerka's intention to tell the story to her grandson. The old spy knew the pros and cons, so he did not want to take part in making any decision about when and how Borna should learn about this affair.

This was, however, not the reason why Archie had become a renegade from the Holy Roman Catholic Church; the motive was much less personal.

During his life, Archibald acquired a habit of reading much and analysing the obtained information in the manner of a natural scientist—

taking into account facts only—and everything he knew from his personal experience and reading was pointing to one thing: the Roman Catholic Church was utterly hypocritical. Even if the vast number of human lives destroyed over centuries in various enterprises of this sophisticated and aggressive institution had been put aside, nothing could have explained the related betrayal of the teaching of Jesus Christ. Nothing in the Bible could justify what this movement was doing in reality. Had he ever chosen to believe in Jesus, the Holy Roman Catholic Church would have never been the framework for that.

He had tried many times to compare Catholicism with Orthodoxy and Protestantism—and he eventually concluded that the latter ones were not much better either. To become a Jew or a Muslim? He knew the Old Testament well from his learning about Christianity, and the Jews were not behaving any differently from Christians in their intolerance and exclusivity. The Quran also did not offer anything more positive. Hence, he concluded, at some point, that these beliefs were nothing more than insignificantly different versions of the same organised superstition.

Thus, it would not be an exaggeration to state that Archibald Vladimir Jones was a godless person on the first of November 2008, at least regarding the three most influential religions of Europe and the Middle East—and these were the original territories of those who had conquered the world. On the other hand, he was a man of science and therefore aware of the fact that he did not understand how and why everything around him was happening. Was this overwhelming complexity the consequence of an intricate play of natural laws or was it part of a game on the table of some unknown gods? He could not tell. However, he was sure of one thing: none of the Abrahamic religions were giving any answer to his numerous questions.

His reluctance to believe blindly in the Bible—a book that most people around him were finding indisputable—did not stop him from going to a cemetery and lighting candles in memory of his ancestors, who had given him life. It was following an ancient tradition focused on the first of November, which had nothing to do with his standpoint on religion. He simply wanted to do it on that day, because this was the date he had always been doing that without thinking much.

His parents were still alive, and he did not want to think about a day when he was going to light a candle for them. He loved his mother and father very much, and their occasional visits were the only true connection he had with his origins. They were kind of shocked when finding out that Archie was living with an African girl—so that they could have brown grandchildren one day—but they eventually accepted this fact of life without any complaint. Danka, actually, liked Sara very much—because what was good for her son was good for her too—and Luka stopped worrying once he tasted Sara's food.

Archibald brought nine candles to the cemetery. He found the place where the people were paying homage to those who were not buried there, and this was where he lit his candles.

The first candle was for all of his Catholic, Orthodox, and Lutheran ancestors who had been living and dying in the lands of everlasting war—where it was always easier to die than to live.

The second candle was for Ivan the Blacksmith, and the third for his Roža. The fourth was for their love which had shown to the world how a woman and a man could create a small paradise on Earth if being lucky to pull through the sick games of history.

The fifth candle was for Ljerka, the sixth for Srdjan, and the seventh for their love which had raised a big question to the world: *quo vadis, orbis*?

The eighth candle was for the good man Vladimir, Archie's third grandfather, and the ninth for his love for Ljerka and her devotion to him—the combination of which had brought a certain hope that good could eventually triumph over evil.

A few days after his visit to the cemetery, Archie received a phone call from his father. This was unusual, as he would always call his parents because paying for a long phone call to Switzerland was too much for their pensions. Luka was very disturbed, and he could not suppress crying.

'Borna,' he barely managed to say, 'you are now the last of our kin.'

Then he started to weep uncontrollably.

'Father? What's happening?' asked Archie, but he could not get any answer for a minute or so—his father was crying and crying and crying... Finally, Luka managed to calm down somewhat, saying,

'They died, all of your cousins. They're gone.'

He started to cry again, and Archie then heard the voice of his mother.

'Borna, there has been a tragedy here.'

'What tragedy?'

'They died in a car crash, all of your cousins from your father's side. After a wedding.'

Then she began to cry too, but she managed to regain concentration soon, continuing her explanation,

'You remember your cousin Darko? He was getting married, all of us were there, and then all five of your cousins went into a car together... Darko wanted to drive them to a hotel at five a.m. Some drinks and a slippery road... They crashed and none of them survived.'

Archibald got frozen. All of his cousins? All of them at the same time? He could not believe what he just heard. As far as he knew, none of them had any offspring—because some had not been married and some had postponed their plans until the coming of a better time for having children—and this explained why Luka said that Archie was the last of the Proud branch of the Didić clan. Before Archibald could ask more, Danka hung up, and he tried to call back several times that day but with no success. He could not reach them until the next day.

It turned out that Luka had a heart attack during the call, and this was the reason why Danka hung up. Eventually he ended up in a hospital, where they managed to stabilise his condition; the odds were, however, uncertain, and the seventy-year-old father of Archie was somewhere between life and death. Archibald wanted to catch a flight to Zagreb immediately, but his mother begged him not to do that—because he was still considered to be a traitor and scoundrel both by the law and by everyone who had once known him, which included most of the family as well. If he had been arrested or harassed otherwise, this would have certainly killed his father instantly. Of course, this also meant that he was not going to attend any of the funerals of his cousins—with whom he had played as a child—and all of that was another blow to the Archie's troubled view on the meaning of his existence in this world.

This, however, did not prevent him from paying for all of the funerals, which he did with the help of Matthias and his skills in concealing the routes of financial transactions. Before that, he had organised the transfer of his father from a state hospital to the best private medical institution in Croatia, where Luka received a treatment which probably saved his life. Matthias helped in that as well, while Archie found a way to hide from him that the money was going to Croatia (he insisted to fill in the online forms alone, to be more precise).

Weizero Sara felt that something was happening, but she did not want to ask anything. After the perfect three months at the end of 2007, things became less passionate, but their living together could have not been called tense, quite the contrary. After all, who in his right mind could expect that the months of such bliss could last forever? Until that November, they had been returning to their usual, more relaxed style of living—but this time without questions on marriage or children—and Sara was gradually putting up with a possibility that she was never going to become a mother, being eventually satisfied with her position of a beloved wife without a paper to certify that. She thought that every sacrifice was for some reason, and that the time given to all of us on this planet was way too short to cry over spilled milk; there were many reasons for happiness in her life—and she did not want to spend a single day in sorrow or discontent. Everything her ato was doing lately was giving her hope that her life was never going to be worrisome again, that she had every reason to be content and to welcome every new day with a smile on her face.

In the early November of 2008, however, their days became less idyllic. Archie became reclusive for some reason and was spending a lot of time alone—sometimes with his secret notebook, by the window facing Claraplatz, and sometimes at any place where his bicycle would take him. He would phone a lot, speaking the same strange language he was using when his parents would visit. She never asked about this language—and she actually did not care which one it was—wanting only to keep her life wonderfully simple.

Even though he inherited his eyes from Srdjan and his erudition from Vladimir, Archibald still resembled Ivan the Proud more in his social habits. Whenever something bothered him deeply, he would try to find another reality, but he was, in that, weaker than his silent grandfather. Ivan the Blacksmith would switch to another world and gather strength by avoiding unnecessary troubles. Likewise, his grandson would simply stay there and make himself unapproachable. And it would always take a long time for Archie to come back to the real world.

During his quiet days, Archibald bought a guitar, an electric one with a small home amplifier. Then he played *Stairway to Heaven* by *Led Zeppelin* flawlessly, and Sara was astonished by that.

'How come that you can play this?' she asked.

'I simply can. I can play many other tunes, although I'm not good at that,' he replied. 'But I sing terribly, so you'll never hear me singing, that would be too much.'

'Just play,' she said and took the position of a sleeping beauty, with her eyes closed.

Then he continued to play gently and with much emotion—and she listened without moving at all. Every sound coming from his fingers was making her serene and grateful for the life she had, for the warmth she was feeling in this flat and with this man, for every new day that was going to come after hugging her ato the whole night long...

He suddenly stopped playing.

'I've got to go now,' he said, 'to deal with some things at work. Will be back by supper... Or maybe a bit later. I'll not be late in any case, and perhaps we could have a drink in the District later?'

Then he made a quick phone call in that strange language, and he was gone before Sara could ask any questions. Something was happening again; this was clear.

Many other girls would be inclined to think that he was involved with another woman, but Sara knew that this was definitely not the case. They had no secrets about that, and they were still exploring the realm of passion with other people in the District—so he was definitely not searching for more excitement of that kind. She somehow felt that Archie went to the Rhine to simply be alone; this was hurting her, but she did not want to stop him. This November was, so far, a bit strange after a long period of pure happiness.

At the Rhine, Archibald started to contemplate his connections to the world outside Basel. This city was making him tranquil, the rest of the world did not—and this included Kletina, Krotko, Zagreb, Aberdeen, Grantchester, Regensburg, Cambridge, and also every other place he had reluctantly visited only because he was a respected professional who had to travel because of his work duties. He never wanted to travel outside Basel at all; he had, after all, never been anywhere as a representative of the District—and it was the District where he would be truly relaxed. This made him think that the world was really odd, but he was aware that his views on life were at least unconventional if not completely weird—so maybe he was odd, not the world.

To be the last of his kin? He, an outlaw?

He was very worried about his parents, but there was fortunately nothing bad in the latest news over the phone. Luka was recuperating well, and Danka was cooking him the healthiest and most distasteful things, trying to keep him disciplined and alive. She, a Saxon she-warrior in a tiny body, was as defiant as always and as strong as a mule, although she smoked too much.

Archibald started to think about the recent events. He was now considered to be the last of his kin from his father's side—as not only that the other grandsons of Ivan and Roža had died in the car accident, this had also happened with the granddaughters. It was virtually a rule in most of the patriarchal societies of the Balkans to disregard women in family matters, but Krotko was nonetheless accepting the continuation of a bloodline through females as well (because this was practical in the remote highland village, where the men of a family would sometimes perish because of war or disease). Although Krotko was not small, it was quite detached from the rest of the area, and any other standpoint would be unreasonable. In any case, it was a fact that Archie was the only surviving grandchild of Roža and Ivan, and the rest of the family knew only that. They were thinking poorly of him, but they could not go against the tradition.

Ivan the Blacksmith and Roža had five children, but only three of these had offspring: Archie's father and two of his sisters. Before the accident, Roža and Ivan had had six grandchildren, but Archibald was the only one to have had a child. Hence, he and his daughter were really the only ones who could carry on the legacy of the Proud branch of the Didić clan. No one in the family except him knew anything of Andrea, on the other hand. And Andrea knew nothing of him.

The Didić surname was going to survive—because of the other branches—but the infamous old family iron rod had been given to Matija and his descendants, and this meant something. Archibald had seen it only once, when his grandfather had shown it on one occasion. The current rightful owner of the rod (rusting in the cellar of the Krotko house) was Archibald's father—the oldest son of Roža and Ivan—but it was rather clear that his 'reign' could not last for more than a few years. Archie was, therefore, destined to become the next owner of the rod— and of the might of the Didić clan—but he was far from home and melancholic.

He was thinking, there at the Rhine, that this whole legend should be forgotten, just as many similar ones had become small and insignificant parts of European history.

Archibald V Jones did not forget to write down the story of the rod, there at the Rhine, in his secret notebook. He even drew a sketch of the three Didić blacksmiths—Anton, Matija, and Ivan—holding the rod together to pass it on to the next generations. At the bottom of the page, he wrote,

'Perhaps I will never hold this rod, but someone of our bloodline might come one day to take it in her hand.'

IX

2010, January

Archibald Vladimir Jones had only Sara. And he missed snow terribly.

He would sometimes appear relaxed when spending a few hours with Matthias and Stefan—or hear from Mary, Roger, and Hazel—but all of them were just good people he considered to be his friends. And friendships come and go, unlike blood relations.

Danka died in the early December of 2009. Her cigarettes killed her eventually: a massive stroke, everything was over in a few minutes. Luka could not stand the loss, and he was gone by Christmas. Andrea did not know that Archie was her father. The rest of his family—still bewitched by the power of nationalism—despised him and thought that he was a spiteful traitor who should never return. And he did not want to return.

Archie really had only Sara and only one home: the city of Basel on the Rhine.

That January, it finally started to snow properly in Basel—for the first time since Archibald had been there. He was observing from his favourite window how Claraplatz was getting whiter than ever and how children were coming to the square to play. He used to play in snow in Kletina a long time ago, and his mother would have shouted from the balcony in the evening that it was the time for supper and preparations for school tomorrow. His father would have helped him take off his wet clothes, never missing to eat with his boy afterwards.

'Is there ever any snow in Ethiopia?' Archie asked. 'It is in Africa, but there are many high mountains, especially in the Semien region where you come from.'

'I can remember that it fell only once,' replied Sara, 'but it melted in a matter of hours.'

Then he became silent again, appearing as unreachable as he had been a few minutes ago; he was observing Claraplatz with the notebook and the old pen in his hands, writing down something (obviously a sentence or two only) slowly as usual. And it had been like that for weeks already. Sara had a feeling that his new crisis was more serious than ever, that he was losing contact with the real world and that his personality was changing. Her heart was breaking.

They continued to live together pretty quietly, which meant that much of the previous passion was gone, being replaced by a profound but somewhat sad feeling of mutual respect. Strangely, their making love was still great, when it would happen—but this was not nearly as often as some time ago. They had been also having sex with people from the District until last Christmas, when Archie told her vaguely about his loss and that he was not going to be ready to do this at least for a while. Sara understood, and their presence in the District was henceforth restricted to only having a few drinks with their friends and acquaintances—which was never again going to change, in fact. Only occasionally would he emerge from his shell to again become her beloved ato, the man she cared about, but this was becoming less and less frequent as time passed by.

When Archie left the window and put the notebook into the drawer, he had a smug smile on his face, and she felt that this was perhaps going to be one of those evenings when her ato would be back from his reclusiveness—so her heart started to beat faster.

'Let us go and walk through the snow,' Archibald said suddenly. 'Would you like to?'

Then he winked and looked at her seductively.

'Now? But it's already dark,' she replied.

'And snow always looks best under street lights. Grab your boots, girl!'

This cheered up Sara very much. Was her ato really back? She had been seeing that so seldom during the last months—and of course she was willing to do it! Maybe this time he was going to be back for good!

They ran all over Claraplatz together with all the children there—who were finding these old people to be very funny and amusing. Archie taught her how to make and throw snowballs, and his jacket was soon full of white marks; she would giggle like a little girl whenever a snowball would hit him. Then she slipped and fell down onto her back; he lay over her and kissed her gently while the strings of her raven hair shone magically under the moonlight, against the virgin whiteness of the fresh snow.

He had only her.

'This snow is wet, it will not last long,' he said then, 'so we should go to the Rhine to see the banks dressed in white while we still can.'

Sara knew that he liked the Rhine more than any other person she ever met.

'I'd hated rivers before I came here, Sara, especially in winter,' he said when they came to the river bank.

'Why? But you like the Rhine so much.'

'I had to swim across a river in December once. It was more or less like now, freezing cold. I almost lost my feet due to the frostbites. It took me some time to get used to the Rhine.'

Sara realised how little she knew about her ato, but she was also wise enough not to ask much. A long time ago she had decided to simply wait until the mysteries of his life started to reveal themselves one by one, if ever.

'I learned to like it when I realised that Basel was the only home I had, and Basel without the Rhine was not Basel,' he continued. 'Now I love the Rhine more than ever, especially today because of this snow and cold.'

'You've faced some of your fears?' asked Sara shyly.

'Clever girl,' he replied.

'Archibald Vladimir Jones!'

'What now?' he said anxiously. She suddenly looked very serious.

'I've got to tell you something.'

'Tell me then. I hope it isn't too bad.'

'Basel is my only home, too. And I love the Rhine… I'm a small Amhara girl with no past, and I have only you, Basel, and the Rhine. I love all of you.'

If the great Rembrandt had been alive and in Basel, he would have asked Sara and Archie to remain in the same position until he had painted their kiss, with the Rhine and the snowfall in the background. He would have then returned home and said to his Saskia,

"My dear, I've just painted something so nice! A dreamy scenery of a mighty, slow moving river and a couple in front of it, under a lamp and dressed in snow, kissing and forgetting that there was a world around them."

Sara was overwhelmed by the evening, but when they came home, Archibald was, within a matter of minutes again in his usual mood: speaking little and being in some other universe. Her enthusiasm was gone immediately.

He could not explain the changes in his behaviour either, although he was trying hard to be more sensible. But this simply did not work—to be more logical and open with Sara, the only person he had on his side truly. His instincts were guiding him somewhere else, into dark territories, and he could not resist.

A continuation of the worsening of the relationship of Sara and Archibald came soon, because she started to feel unfairly isolated from his obvious emotional troubles. Occasional romantic episodes, like the one in the snow, would remedy the situation briefly, but this was happening too seldom and was too little. She was tired of this new coldness, so she was becoming cold too.

Quo vadis, orbis?

This was what Archibald V Jones would ask himself whenever he would feel that he was the only refugee in this world.

Of course he was not; he knew that. Sara was a refugee as well, in the first place. They were living together in a faraway country which was arguably the best in the world, their lives were good, but all of that was a bit strange so far away from the Semien Mountains and the Pannonian Plain. They would never discuss that; maybe they were thinking that disregarding the impact of the past on their lives was making everything simpler and easier.

Sara never showed any regret for being so far from the landscapes of her childhood. One could conclude that she was either tough by nature or had been too young when leaving Ethiopia to be disturbed by that. In any case, no one could ever tell what Sara was thinking about her homeland. Still, sometimes she would get rather nervous when seeing in the window of a tourist agency an advertisement for a guided tour through the Semien Mountains, and she would then comment on that angrily in her own language, waving hands and obviously using words that were not to be heard by children.

Archie would, on the other hand, always deliberately remain perfectly calm when seeing offers for having a holiday in Croatia—and these were really numerous. One could reach Croatia from Basel in some eight or nine hours of driving, it was a desirable tourist destination, and everyone was allowed to go there. Not him though. The war which had expelled him from his homeland had been over for more than ten years already, and life was there back to normal—for virtually everyone but him. He did not want Sara to know that; for her, he was just another white European—probably a native speaker of a Celtic language from Britain—who was sharing his life with her the best he could. Being aware of that, he never wanted to reveal anything about himself, as this would, he thought, result in unnecessary complications. He knew that she heard him speaking his mother tongue, and he was only hoping that she could not distinguish between Slavonic and Celtic languages—and this was indeed so. His British accent was certainly helping keep his true identity secret, not only in communication with Sara but also with everyone else.

Only Sara heard him speaking any language other than English or German, and he was very careful to keep it that way, although he had once exchanged a few sentences in Slovene with a visitor to the District—which no one had noted, fortunately. His using Swiss German shortly afterwards—when he realised that he had made a serious mistake—erased every possible memory of this carelessness; and everyone was quite drunk anyway.

The complexity of Archie's weird behaviour after the death of his parents was soon augmented with another strange habit: he started to apply perfumes a lot, although he would never do it vulgarly, and he was using only the best stuff money could buy. This was noted in the District by many—from the bartenders to the girls who wanted to be chosen by him alone or in any scenario involving Sara. But he was not willing to go upstairs at all: he would just sit at the bar and chat before going home, discussing some of his usual business activities in the District or simply having a drink for no other reason.

Sara was, of course, the first one to notice this change.

It was true that Archibald was an odourless man—which she could never understand—and it was also true that she did not like that, but his new smell was making her utterly confused.

'Why are you using these perfumes?' she asked one evening when they were walking home from the District.

'Because I can afford it and because I can smell nice this way,' he replied. 'Finally I smell nice.'

'But... Why? You're not choosing any girl, and you can always have me, with or without smelling of perfume. What's the point?'

'The point is that I want to smell of something!' he said a little angrily. 'And the point is that I've never emanated any pheromone!'

'What? Phero... What's that?'

'This is the smell of a man, which I don't have. Don't you know that already? Please don't pretend!'

'Archie, I really don't know what you're talking about, I'm your weizero and you're my ato, smell has nothing to do with that.'

He looked at her, and her eyes were wet. It seemed that she really meant it—and he realised that he should stop.

'I love you, you're my man,' she continued, 'and please don't make me sad.'

'I'm so sorry, love,' he replied and kissed her.

They did not make love that night.

While falling asleep, the new, irrational Archibald was thinking that he was going to use perfumes no matter what, since he simply liked the feeling.

Did Sara love him because of *what* he was or because of *who* he was—he could not tell. She loved him in her own way, this was beyond any doubt, but he wanted this to be due to a primordial instinct and not because he was an easy-going man and soulmate. No money was involved—he knew his proud Sara too well, and he was sure of that. However, he wanted her primitive nature to desire him without any second thought, he wanted to know that he was attracting her like no other man ever could—as this was what he had been missing for his entire life before meeting her. He wanted to feel that it was her elementary lust that was making him the love of her life, and not some unwritten contract relying on his making her life pleasurable.

It seemed that nothing could stop his eventual drowning in the sea of eternity.

Sara stayed awake long enough to see Archibald starting to breathe deeply and falling asleep. Was he really the man she always wanted to have beside her? And what was this perfume-and-smell story about, was that important? Oh yes, she loved him very much, but the nature of this love was still puzzling her. She had gone through these questions before, but she was not sure that she had done it well. The question of the smell, for example. She could no longer fool herself by declining the possibility that several of her occasional lovers from the District had in fact turned her on more than Archibald ever could—which was, when she thought it over, mainly related to the smell. Phero... Whatever. Either one was an alpha male or not.

She then thought than no alpha male could ever make her leave Archibald, because they had such a long history together, and the world did not revolve around the best orgasm a woman could have. And she had had many, many good orgasms with Archie, maybe not the best ones in her entire life—but always good ones. She was trying to find the pros and cons, and the conclusion would always be the same: Archibald Vladimir Jones was her man no matter what. Her ato.

It was a fact that she never became completely sure about her instincts, and Archie could feel the whole thing in his own way. By his own instincts or... Whatever. He continued to use perfumes, for instance, and sometimes he would ask her whether he smelled well; and Sara would mainly refuse to answer or would become angry without showing it.

To cut a long story short, all of this was bearable until he started to drink.

X

2011, July–November

Archibald signed a new contract with the *Novartis* company. He accepted a lower salary in exchange for working four hours per day, and Stefan became the head of his department.

Having a steady job was the basis of keeping his Swiss residence permit, but Archie had no financial troubles, and he did not want to spend so much time in *Novartis* any more; after going with Matthias through his finances and investments, he realised that he actually did not have to work at all—his bank account was going to continue swelling from month to month anyway. His lifestyle was still moderate—because he did not know how a well-off man should be spending money—and hence, the decision he had made was not jeopardising him in any way. After all, he remained a boy from Kletina who was a stranger to extravagance and opulence. For instance, he had not even bought a car—and he also forgot where his driving licence was.

The main thing behind his decision was very simple: he started to drink, and he did not want to stop.

Being drunk was making him serene, and this was more important to him than any health issue. He was a man of science, and he knew what alcohol was doing to his body, but he did not pay any attention to that; some time ago, he had lost any wish to remain alive for much longer. He simply did not care—and as far as he was concerned, dying at the age of fifty would not be too soon. No, he was not planning suicide, but he did not fear death either.

Sara was, of course, not happy with his obvious loss of interest in the world around him, but there was little she could do about that.

Their relationship had by then deteriorated dramatically, and only occasional sex—still being good for unknown reasons—was keeping their life under the same roof bearable. There was no romance between them any more; their living together became just a habit, and it was continuing possibly because they were too lazy to think of anything else. Only from time to time would they find themselves trying to bring back the days of happiness—but this could not change anything, because the irreversibility of nature would always defeat their every effort. Although there were many reasons for remembering the past years with joy, these could not win in a battle against the coldness which had developed in the meantime.

He continued to use perfumes, but these were hiding his smelling on alcohol more than giving him any pleasant odour, which he, due to his growing irrationality, could not realise.

Archibald was a sophisticated drunk. He would never drink anything bad and cheap, and his liquid friends were only the best wine and the most esteemed whiskey—which he could afford. He would sometimes have a beer, but this was rare. Strangely, he continued to cycle, and this was keeping him in shape—so he was not becoming a desperate, shaking drunk who would sell his soul for a glass of spirit. Instead, he was turning into a bitter man.

At some point, Archie realised that he did not have a single photo of his parents. He had no photos of Kletina or Krotko either, and his entire life in Croatia seemed to be just a mirage or a play of some childish deity. Thus, he continued to ask himself who he really was: Borna Didić (or Borna the Proud, as some would say), Helmut Meindl, James Trevor Smith or Archibald Vladimir Jones? And what he had done to deserve such a fate?

The only photos he had from his previous life were those of his grandparents: one of Vladimir and himself together, an instant camera colour photo on a thick paper, from the early 1970s; one of Ivan and Roža, who had been posing on a meadow in their simple peasant clothes; one of Ljerka and Srdjan, he in a uniform and she looking like a Hollywood star. He had only these three pictures from his life before he started to bear some false names, and it was clear that this was never going to change. Before taking another sip of whiskey, he murmured,

'Cheers, Klara Zultner, I understand you now more than ever! You don't have to explain anything!'

Whenever thinking about his life, he would observe the three photos hanging on a wall in his flat. Sara, a wise woman, never asked about the photographs he had put there recently. She wanted to ask a few times, but then she restrained herself, since Archie would always be drunk on these occasions. They had not been sharing their thoughts for quite a while, actually, and there was little sense in asking anything.

And these three photos were the only connection with the truth about the man known as Archibald Vladimir Jones. Without them, his entire life could occupy only a small painting with a few sketches from the streets of Vienna, Regensburg, Aberdeen, Grantchester, Cambridge, and Basel; and no one would ever remember this canvas, because such excerpts from everyday life could never be memorable. He had three grandfathers, this Archibald Vladimir Jones, and every answer to every question about his life was anchored to the three photos, which were the only documents that were making his existence real. Without them, he did not exist.

Mary, Hazel, and Roger would call occasionally, but Archie never wanted to pick up the phone. Sometimes he was too drunk to answer, and sometimes he was simply in another universe. He stopped caring about many things, and answering the phone belonged to this territory of his mind. Feeling comfortable in the world of reclusiveness, he lost the last friends he had. He really had only Sara, but he was too reckless to respect that.

Ever since he had started to drink heavily, Sara and Archibald were going to the District separately and would only occasionally return home together. They would share a meal as a couple infrequently, and their cuddling and kissing before going to sleep were not taking place any more. Having sex, yes, but this was everything but making love. The whole situation was very frustrating and fatiguing for Sara, because she could not find any explanation for it. Something was bothering Archie terribly, and she did not know what—because he was so unapproachable and unpredictable. And it was also rather obvious that he had no intention to stop drinking.

However, she remained quite conservative regarding their relationship, and she never again accepted an offer for wild fornication in the District—because Archie was declining such invitations constantly. This was very different from some years ago, when she would go with an attractive man so easily, only winking to Archie on her way upstairs and knowing that he was probably going to do the same later. Or vice versa, but these days were gone.

As the time was passing by, Archie was becoming even more secluded. At work, he would finish his tasks as quickly as he could and then leave without even saying goodbye to anyone, not even to Stefan; eventually he stopped communicating with his colleagues completely, apart from discussing some business issues—which he would always do as briefly as possible and without any surplus word or gesture. Not to mention that he was never smiling or joking—which he had been often doing before—and this change did not remain unnoticed.

His co-workers started to wonder what was going on, why he became stone-faced and terribly distant, and many of them asked Stefan how much he knew about that. And Stefan knew just enough from his communication with Sara to say that this had nothing to do with any of them personally and that Archibald had some private problems which were hopefully going to be resolved in due time. They just had to wait, he explained, and the good old Archie was going to be back sooner or later; he only needed some time and privacy, and all of them owed him that because he was the one who brought the department to a higher level of productivity. Indeed, Archibald remained very concentrated and efficient at work, never arriving drunk or having an obvious hangover; his results were still remarkable although he started to arrive to work later than before—but in the world of Swiss business, it was efficiency and not working hours that counted, so no one ever complained.

The same process was underway in the District as well. It had started by his silent drinking at the bar and refusing to chat even with the bartenders (who actually liked him quite a lot and would always enjoy his juicy jokes and humorous comments on the clients, the girls, and the world); this was followed by him even greeting the girls he knew—and he had known some of them for a long time, either from the pub or the bed. Soon, everyone became accustomed to his recently developed, inexplicable reluctance to engage in casual sex—which had been his trademark over a number of years.

In addition, some noted that he was drinking more than usual, but no one was quite sure, because soberness was generally not something one could count on in the pubs of the District. Of course, Sara was expected to explain that, and she said more or less the same thing she had told Stefan—that Archie needed some time to pull himself together.

The poor woman said that because she still believed in that somehow. She even went to the Claraplatz church to pray for him although she was not Catholic; after going through some prayers at a Mass—in which she had been helped by a Colombian friend of her from the District—she carried out certain Ethiopian rituals, when no one was looking, asking the same God for the same kindness.

Her deep feelings for Archibald V Jones were gone, this was clear, and she was wondering had her love ever been sincere—had all of that been just a matter of lust and comfortable living or something more—but her heart was still breaking; she was grasping at straws and was determined not to desert her man so easily.

It was heart-rending for her to see Archie decaying like that, so evidently, from day to day and for no obvious reason. Then she remembered that this was in fact not a new development—as the whole thing had been progressing for some years—which made her think about her role in that. She could recall, when thinking honestly, several occasions when she could have treated him better, but these incidents had always been short and quite innocent, just arguments which one could normally expect in a couple who had been living together for such a long time. Only the events on their 2005 anniversary could have been called a quarrel worth remembering, but this had been six years ago, and they had enjoyed lots of good times together since then. She could not find any logic in a scenario where she would be the cause of his drunkenness and other decline—but she still felt guilty for some reason.

This honourable woman did not realise that she was the only reason why he was still alive, that the whole story of Archibald Vladimir Jones would have ended some time ago if she had not been there for him.

At dusk in early September, Sara was returning from the Claraplatz church after she had tried to convince Jesus to show some mercy. She did not know if there was any sense in doing that, but she had to try, as she knew that Jesus was her God. Maybe he was just laughing, from somewhere above, at his silly children who were only temporarily occupying the physical world? He could help, Sara thought. In this situation, a Catholic church was as good as any other for her to pray for Archie's soul.

While leaving the church, she saw Archibald in front of it: he was standing there, observing a large window above the church door and speaking a monologue in his native language, waving his hands and trying to explain something to the deity who owned the large building; he was, of course, rather drunk. This was not a nice sight, and people started to assemble.

Sara approached him slowly and carefully, trying not to scare him; then she touched his arm gently and said,

'It's your Sara, dear. Let us go home now. You can tell your story from the window.'

'Sara... My dear Sara. My weizero! You see, I've got something to say to this gentleman who lives behind these walls,' he replied joyfully, being obviously happy to see her. He suddenly became calmer and quieter.

'I know, love, but you can really do this from our window. It's right there, see?'

'Will he hear me from there?'

'Of course he will, but the police won't. And they might hear you here. Do it for me, Archie, you know who I am,' she played her best card, knowing that he was always very protective.

'Of course I know! You're my weizero Sara, the best woman in the world!' he said. 'Police? Yes, we should go home now, they might take you away from me. And I can't allow that to happen.'

The show ended abruptly, the people continued to go wherever they were going to, and the drunk and his girl vanished from everyone's sight in a matter of seconds, disappearing somewhere behind the walls of one of the houses surrounding the square. Claraplatz returned to normal, and the short incident was forgotten in no time.

After a few days, Sara met Matthias and told him what had happened. She then learned from him that Archie had had a similar performance in front of the Basel Minster (a Protestant cathedral in Grossbasel, close to the Rhine) about two weeks ago; and it had been Matthias who had saved him from troubles there. He had first taken Sara's ato to an Irish pub, where they had a few beers together, and then he escorted Archie home, because walking straight was proving difficult for the man who apparently had some unresolved issues with the supreme divinity of Western civilisation.

The behaviour of Archibald V Jones was becoming more bearable as October was approaching. This, on the other hand, did not mean that the good old Archie had returned. He was drinking much less and was also not repeating the conversations with Jesus in front of churches all over Basel, which was at least a kind of relief for the people around him. They did not know that he had actually caught a disease that was eventually going to kill him—and this disease was incurable sadness.

He gave up.

Eventually he resigned his job in *Novartis* without telling anyone, apparently thinking little about his legal status in Switzerland. Perhaps he thought that his connections in the offices of the Canton would help find another solution for his papers, but it was equally possible that he did not think at all about any consequence of his decision. Once he realised that Sara and Matthias did not know, Stefan told them what Archie had done. Matthias tried to calm Sara down a bit by reassuring her that Archie's investments were going to be more than sufficient for keeping them going financially for quite some time, if not indefinitely, provided that Archie was not going to do something stupid. However, she was not worried about the money at all; she could always go back to the District as a prostitute if necessary, she was still young and desirable enough for that. It was only that her heart was breaking although she did not have romantic feelings for her ato any more.

It would require a great psychologist or psychiatrist to explain how, and when exactly, the sadness of Archibald Vladimir Jones became an incurable illness. On the other hand, it seemed that this somewhat coincided with the sixteenth of October, when he wrote the last entry in his notebook with fine leather covers, mumbling something in his mother tongue by the window facing Claraplatz. He was obviously discussing something with Jesus while struggling with his handwriting. Sara was there and she saw it.

After that day, he almost stopped drinking. He would have a beer or two in the District but was not bringing any alcoholic beverage home. Sara was relieved by seeing her ato sober again, but this did not mean that things became easier—as he stopped communicating with everyone, including her, almost completely. The best she could do was to get a few words from him about very plain issues—on what to cook, for instance—but he was generally not showing any interest in what was happening around him. All in all, he was spending most of the time in bed, sleeping intermittently as much as fourteen hours a day, regardless of whether it was daylight or dark. There was no pattern. He did not even notice that Sara had got rid of every empty bottle in the flat.

He was still cycling a lot, and in spite of his otherwise unhealthy style of living, had no obvious problem with the functioning of his body; he was still looking like a very fit man, and one could easily conclude that he was in his late thirties rather than mid-forties. This was in contrast to his general appearance, as he stopped caring about his looks: he would shave once a week at best, wear dirty clothes, and take a shower only when his skin would start to itch. Sara was at first trying to warn him on that, but this brought no change; then she started to replace dirty clothes with something clean; he would pay no attention, and the whole ritual would just repeat from day to day. Then she finally gave up. He also stopped using perfumes, but this had no effect on his odour—he still had none, no matter how much he would sweat and avoid water. Hence, besides emanating no pheromone, Archie was seemingly a walking antibiotic—as even bacteria was running away from him.

On the thirty-first of October, he cycled to Lange Erlen for the first time that month, which was unusual—since he had been going there for years almost every weekend in October. He stayed at Lange Erlen the whole day, spending most of the time reading what he had written into his notebook. There were numerous grammatical errors in his notes, the handwriting was barely readable, and the sketches were at the level of a fourth-grade boy from the Kletina elementary school. But he did not want to make any corrections: the notes were completed, his life was completed.

The next day, he went to Hörnli cemetery. He had with him the only photos that were making him a real person: one of Vladimir and himself together, an instant camera colour photo on thick paper, from the early 1970s; one of Ivan and Roža, who had been posing on a meadow in their simple peasant clothes; one of Ljerka and Srdjan, he in a uniform and she looking like a Hollywood star. His notebook was also with him. The cemetery was full of the Roman Catholic inhabitants of Basel, and perhaps some of other religions were also using this day to pay their respects to their deceased ones.

He knew the place where one could light candles for those who were not buried there—and this was his destination. Before going there, he had taken a long walk through the beautiful cemetery, observing impressive tombstones and spotting that a number of them contained names and words which were not German.

Archie lit his candles. He then sat down on a nearby bench and started to read the history of his family from the notebook, whispering the stories of the Didić, Jarbašić, and Količek families. And of the three grandfathers he had: of the one who gave him the surname and personality, of the one whose eyes he had, and of the one who made him knowledgeable and persistent. And of the extraordinary women in these families. And of the whirlpool of ethnicities, religions, and wars—always these damned wars. He then shed some tears for his good parents. This was not spotted by anyone, as there were many other people crying on the benches nearby.

After he had stopped crying, he remained on the bench for a while, completely still and silent. Then he took from a pocket the only three photos he had about his life outside Basel, glued together with sticky tape.

'I really don't need these any more,' he mumbled, 'everything is in the notebook which is never going to be read by anyone. A nobody remains a nobody.'

He leaned the photos against a small wall close to the candles, and then he left without looking back. A wind during the night of the first to the second of November had caught the burning candles and set the photos alight.

XI

2012, March

Archie had not written anything in his notebook since last October, and then he opened it to make the only correction ever to this text. He added two words to the title, changing it into

> and death
> The life of Archibald Vladimir Jones
> written by him for his daughter Andrea the Proud

Only he knew what was written in the notebook, and Sara was going to be the first one to read this sometime later.

He closed the notebook and sealed it with red wax and a piece of black ribbon, following an old method of securing important documents. His thoughts were finally at least protected from the world in which he never managed to find shelter. Archibald Vladimir Jones was sad, only that, being at peace with his sadness and reluctance to continue living.

Ever since he had left Croatia, he had to hide not only his identity but also his thoughts which had to remain concealed during his intricate games of survival. There were so many occasions when he wanted to give his opinion, but he knew that he would have been in danger of being exposed if he had ever tried. Hence, he was always reserved when speaking about serious things, even with the people he knew well.

It was too late to ponder on that—his life was going to end soon, he felt that, and the notebook contained his thoughts as they truly were. Therein, he was free. He did not plan to commit suicide, but he sensed that one of these days his heart was going to stop by itself. While he was not very interested in knowing when and how, he was confident that this was going to happen before long.

Some people believe that dreams can tell us something about the future, and some do not. Archie, for his entire life, belonged to the latter, but he was not sure any more that dreams were so innocent.

Is it possible that there is another dimension of the Universe, in which soul and flesh are intertwined more than we can understand? A dimension which is by human fear interpreted as proof of the existence of gods, and by scientific curiosity as a territory where we may search for solutions that could bring an end to our lack of wisdom and knowledge. Is this dimension penetrating our dimension in an incomprehensible way, causing all of these strange things which we see either as divine acts or as challenges to set up new models and equations that could explain the mysteries of nature?

Archibald V Jones was not bothered by such questions; the only thing he knew was that he was dreaming about the Black Queen for quite some time already, from night to night.

In the tradition of Kletina and the surrounding areas, Black Queen was a personification of evil, a medieval cruel witch who lured travellers and merchants returning from a marketplace; she would usually rob and kill them, but sometimes she would take into her chambers those who would catch her eye. These young men would serve her until she would become bored, and then she would release her raven who would dig their eyes out and eventually murder them. According to the legend, she ruled the country, and maybe because of that, it was thought that she was actually Barbara of Cilli, who had in Kletina in 1405 married Sigismund of Luxemburg (a distinguished German nobleman, Prince-elector of Brandenburg, King of Hungary and Croatia, King of Germany, King of Bohemia, King of Italy, and Holy Roman Emperor).

The first Količek who had settled in Kletina documented this wedding. For this reason, it came to Archie's mind that his dreams about Black Queen were maybe not only a consequence of his unbearable sadness but also of some old debts to be paid. Could it have been, for instance, that the first Količek of Kletina had been desired by the evil sorceress and that he had resisted her successfully—making her mad and irritated—so that her unfulfilled lust continued over many centuries, until she saw a chance for revenge against another Količek? There was only one person who could pay this debt, and this man was constantly dreaming that he was on a road leading to his hometown.

In his dreams, Black Queen was an extremely beautiful and seductive woman, travelling in a black chariot pulled by four big black horses. When spotting him on the road, she would slow down and ask him to join her; he would refuse by saying that he was heading home, to Kletina and his people. Without saying another word, she would frown and make her horses gallop, leaving a big cloud of dust behind.

The eighth of March during Archibald's life in Yugoslavia, prior to 1991 and the breakup of the country, was called Women's Day. This tradition was highly esteemed in the world of socialism but was seldom even noted in countries of Western democracy, which applied to Switzerland as well. It was the least political of all socialist anniversaries—and in many of these countries, including Yugoslavia, it was not even a holiday. Memories in the head of Archibald Vladimir Jones—which were, for good reason, free of any ideological prejudice—were telling him that this was the sweetest anniversary ever set up by humankind. This was a date when a part of the world would remember the whole ordeal of women from the beginning of our species, recognising the fact that wives and mothers were those who were supporting all but one corner of the house of a family—and only the remaining corner relied on the strength of husbands and fathers.

Ever since his early childhood, Archie would always on that day buy a red carnation bouquet for his mother, and Danka would be very proud of that. She knew that he had to spend his own pocket money to buy the bouquet, but she would never try to offer him any compensation, in the hope that this was building his character and showing him that there were more important things in life than shiny metallic discs and colourful paper. If he had had a girlfriend at the time, Archie would have bought her flowers too, mainly because all of his friends were doing the same. In his early twenties—when the problems with his lack of odour became discernible—he stopped doing that.

Being from a family of intellectuals, Sara was not ignorant of Women's Day, since many people in Ethiopia knew about it. However, her ato was, as far as she could conclude, British, and she did not expect him to know anything about it. Thus, every eighth of March would be uneventful in their home.

It was Thursday on that date in 2012, and Sara was not home—she had gone to Bern with some of her friends from the District, just leaving a note for Archibald that she was going to be back on Friday evening. Leaving notes on this or that was the main channel for their communication, and Archie found the note when he woke up at noon. She had, apparently, left sometime in the morning. As always, she had prepared food for him, and he did not have to take care of anything apart from taking the rubbish bag out. Despite the weird routine of their living together, Sara remained conservative regarding the role of a woman in the house; since Archie was covering their expenses, she was a proper weizero who was taking care of the rest. He was the one who was bringing money into the house—though not by working but by his investments—and she was not willing to change her role as long as it was like that. Although she could return to the District as a prostitute, she hated this thought and was also still hoping for a miraculous change in Archibald's behaviour.

He first went to the cemetery and put four red carnations bouquets there where he had lit candles about four months ago: one for his dear mother Danka, because he had been buying her one for almost twenty years; one for Ljerka, since she would have received such a present from him too seldom although living so close; one for Roža, who had been living too far away to ever receive any; and one for Klara, who became the closest soulmate he had. On the way home, he stopped at a flower shop and bought another, really big bouquet of the same kind. This one was for Sara.

After returning to the flat, he took the rubbish bag out and then cleaned the place to perfection. When everything was spotless, he put the flowers into a vase which he placed on a table in the living room, where Sara would always put things of importance. He did not eat anything.

Then he took a piece of paper, grabbed his old pen—which was so far reserved for his journal only—and wrote a note for Sara. And the note read:

My weizero, Sara, believe me that you have been the love of my life. Your ato, Archibald Vladimir Jones

He left the note and the pen close to the vase and then went to the bedroom, taking two things with him: the notebook and an envelope containing his will. He lay down on the bed, put the two documents next to him, closed his eyes and waited for his last dream to come.

Black Queen was not done with this young Količek yet. Just as his ancestor had been doing it, he had been rejecting her for weeks; and no seductive outfit, outstanding hairstyle or makeup—chosen carefully to accentuate her magnificent body and beautiful face—could make any difference. In her anger and frustration, the wicked enchantress became obsessed with taking command over the soul and body of the only remaining Količek of Kletina who possessed the traditional erudition and wit of this annoying family. She had to have him! And she knew where to find him; there were not many roads leading to his home.

Archibald Vladimir Jones was on a road to Kletina. He could already spot the ruins of the castle in the distance, and he knew that his hometown was there, hidden behind the hills that were blocking his view. Then he saw a big cloud of dust approaching him from this direction.

As the cloud was coming closer, Archie started to recognise the shapes—four big black horses were pulling a chariot in which there was a beautiful woman dressed in black and with a black bird resting on her shoulder. He knew who she was. This time, she did not only slow down—the chariot stopped in front of him.

'I greet you, young Količek,' said the woman. 'We meet again. What's your first name?'

'My first name? Perhaps Archibald, I don't remember well,' he replied.

'Or James, Vladimir, Trevor, Helmut, perhaps even Borna?' she provoked him to confuse him. It was always easier with confused men.

She stepped down from the chariot and started to walk towards him as seductively as she could, swaying her hips, keeping her head high and looking directly into his eyes.

'Well... Well, it could be. My name? I don't remember many things. I only know that I have to go home and be with my people. And my home is there,' replied Archie insecurely while pointing with his hand in the direction of Kletina.

She came very close to him, and he could not avoid noticing how beautiful this woman was. Her alluring eyes were looking deep into his mind, attracting him more than anything he could remember. She said,

'But my home is also there, don't you know? I'll take you home, come with me and I'll ease your pain. You've suffered enough.'

She caressed his face with her soft hands, kissed him on the cheek, then on the lips, and pressed her body against his. Then she took him by the hand and started to guide him towards the chariot while her raven was flying above them. Archie followed her, having only one thought on his mind: he was going home.

'You can't have him!' someone shouted from behind them.

The witch looked back and saw three angry and determined women there: Mary, Hazel, and Alicia were approaching them with flaming swords in their hands. Black Queen sent the raven to deal with them, and they disappeared in a split second.

When they were halfway to the chariot, an army materialised before them; this multitude of warriors consisted of a light cavalry of Vlachs and Croats, armoured Teutonic knights on heavy horses, and foot soldiers in the French and Austrian uniforms from the time of Napoleon. They were led by Jarul, legendary Juraj Didić, and the first Zultner who had settled in Transylvania. A horseman in Norman armour drew his sword from the scabbard—it was Roger, and he shouted,

'You can't have him!'

Black Queen summoned thunders elegantly, effortlessly, and the army was gone in a split second.

She and Archie were soon in the chariot, heading to her residence which had in the meantime changed from a ruin into a shiny place. Then they saw an Ethiopian knight from the ancient Order of St Anthony, standing on the road and blocking their way to the castle; under a glistening helmet, Sara said to herself that every daughter of Gondar had learned a long time ago how to protect what was worth protecting; then she drew her sword and shouted,

'You can't have him!'

Black Queen produced a strong wind, and the Ethiopian knight was blown away in a split second.

When the chariot reached the outskirts of Kletina, Archibald noticed that the streets were empty and the windows and doors firmly shut, hiding behind them the deepest fear known to humankind. The horses slowed down, because there were three women on the street: Roža, Ljerka, and Klara were blocking their way. They did not have any weapons, but Black Queen became worried—since the women were reciting spells and prayers known only to witches.

'You can't have him!' shouted Klara, the oldest of the women.

Black Queen was a powerful sorceress, and she asked the demons from her dimension to help her. In a split second, the three women vanished.

The streets in the centre of Kletina were also empty when the chariot reached them. Black Queen was caressing Archie's head that was resting on her shoulder. She would occasionally kiss him passionately, being more and more aroused by the presence of her newest victim, who was there not only to satisfy her morbid lust but also to pay some debts. As they were getting closer to a narrow road leading uphill to the castle, she was becoming hornier than ever in the expectation of a final game with her prey. And when the chariot took a turn to the narrow road, she saw two silhouettes before them. Danka shouted,

'You can't have him!'

Luka and Danka then started to run madly towards the chariot, having no weapons or powers but only instinct to save their boy. Black Queen simply ordered her horses to gallop over them; in a split second, the sacrifice of Archie's parents was in vain.

The evil seductress was fully concentrated on her plans for having her way with her quarry, finally after so many centuries, as her castle was only minutes away—and no one else was there to try to stop her. Then she saw three men in front of the castle gate. She recognised one of them—it was Vladimir Filip Količek—but the other two were not known to her.

For the first time in the history of her raids, her black horses first stopped in fear and then started to neigh and move back from the three men.

None of the men exclaimed that she could not have him. Instead, Ivan the Blacksmith came closer and calmed down the horses just as he had done it many times before in Krotko. Then he said in his typical serene voice,

'We are the three grandfathers of this boy, and he's coming with us.'

Then Srdjan approached the chariot and added,

'Come, dear Borna, I want to kiss you. I never could.'

Vladimir did not say anything. He was observing the sky and looking for the raven; and when he spotted the bird, he just pointed in the direction of Black Queen. The raven attacked the witch, dug out her eyes and feasted on her heart.

Borna stepped down from the chariot. Then he went away with his three grandparents and found peace at last.

'Yes, he's dead. No doubt about that,' said a doctor.

Sara was standing stone-faced and speechless in a corner of the room, keeping her arms crossed in order to hide the shaking of her hands—which would start whenever she tried to change position. She had found him a few hours earlier. In spite of her hopes that Archie's crisis could end for no obvious reason—just as it had started—deep in her heart she had been sensing that finding him like that was a more probable outcome.

'Hmm... I can't find any reason,' continued the doctor. 'He was, as far as I can tell at the moment, an athletic middle-aged man in good shape, with no obvious signs of an illness. I must carry out an autopsy.'

'Do you... Really you must? Can't I just bury him?' asked Sara in a low voice.

'Yes, I must. A relatively young man with no record of any illness dies for no apparent reason? We must rule out every possibility of foul play.'

Then the medics took Archie's body to the morgue, and Sara remained alone with two police officers. They asked her a number of questions, being rather polite and understanding, but they did not stay long. Other matters, they said, were going to be discussed later.

Upon her arrival some hours earlier, Sara spotted the notebook and an envelope next to Archibald. She was surprised to see the notebook again and wondered about the envelope. He was looking like a sleeping Harlequin, lying on his back with a smug smile on his face, and she suddenly wanted badly to give him a kiss—as he was there with an expression on his face so familiar to her from the time of their happiness. In the hope that her kiss was maybe going to wake up the old Archie— once her knight in shining armour—from a bad dream, she pressed her moist lips against his...
After calming down from a hysterical attack, Sara sat down on the floor and started to think what to do. She hid the notebook and the envelope (and the note for her, she found it in the living room), because whatever was written therein, it did not belong to anyone but her ato— he certainly did not leave it there to be found by some Canton officials. She read the note for her, and this assured her that she was right. Then she called the medics, who called the police.

Two days later, she was asked to come to a hospital where Archibald's body had been brought for an autopsy. Still being in shock, she had not read anything from the notebook and the envelope, and it also seemed to her that this was not of any importance for the visit to the doctors. She also did not understand the reason for being summoned to the hospital. For the first time in many years, she felt so unprotected, and then she realised how much Archie had been keeping troubles away from her— which she had always taken for granted. And not only that she felt unprotected, she was also terribly alone again, lost and broken.
'Mrs Jones,' said a doctor who was normally assuming that Sara was Archibald's wife, 'we are rather confused here. The autopsy couldn't reveal any reason for your husband's death. We did all the tests we could, but there was apparently nothing wrong with him. Could you tell us

something about his lifestyle or anything else that might clarify this situation?'

'Well... He behaved strangely for several months or even for a year or so,' Sara said, 'but nothing was pointing to his death.'

And she then explained what had been happening during the time of his madness—that he had been drinking excessively, had resigned from his job, had become reclusive, and so on.

'Could it be that he was drinking too much and that this killed him?' Sara finally asked.

'No, not at all,' replied the doctor. 'But I've got another question. He was working in *Novartis* for many years, right? And he was an expert in the chemistry of pharmaceutics, as I've been told.'

'Yes, he was working there. But I've got no idea what his work was about. He was obviously well read, but this meant little to me.'

'Was he bringing any chemicals home? And do you have any working knowledge of chemistry, by the way?' the doctor continued.

'Was he bringing something home? I really don't know. And about me—I am a former prostitute from the Red Light District, and my only working knowledge of chemistry is from there. That kind of chemistry, you know...' replied Sara.

The doctor was silent, looking at a certain point on the wall behind Sara. What happened? Either the death of this man had been caused by something supernatural or he had invented a perfect, untraceable poison, what else? The latter possibility would make a great topic for a PhD thesis he craved for, but this African girl was obviously not the one who could help. And he had some great plans for the evening anyway, so why would he bother himself with the mystery of the death of an insignificant foreigner? He woke up from his contemplation and then said,

'It seems that all of that will remain a mystery, this happens occasionally. There's no sign of a foul play, at least not of any which modern science could detect, and I've got no other choice than to bring this matter to a close by concluding that the cause of his death is unknown.'

'And what will happen now? What should I do now?' asked Sara, feeling uncomfortable and as if being accused of something.

'You?' grinned the doctor. 'The same as what I'll do—both of us can go home.'

After leaving the hospital, Sara felt somewhat relieved, because she was afraid that a twisted mind could have blamed her for killing Archibald or something like that. She could barely breathe from the immense pain in her chest, she felt so fragile, and she really needed no more stress. Then she went northwards, in the direction of the Rhine. Kleinbasel was on the other side of the river, she had a bottle of whiskey at home, and the only thing she wanted to do was to get drunk.

After almost emptying the bottle, she first called Matthias and then Stefan. The three of them had to somehow organise the funeral of one Archibald V Jones—who died in Basel at the age of forty-seven.

XII

2013, January–April

Sara's life turned upside down after the departure of Archibald Vladimir Jones.

First of all, there were some legal matters that needed to be taken care of. The basis of her Swiss papers was a job she officially had for years as a waitress in a pub in the District, which was an arrangement that Archie had with one of his business partners there. Of course, this job did not exist—she was neither doing that nor receiving any salary. Maybe the pub owner would have been willing to continue with this deception, cherishing the memory of Archibald, but Sara did not want to visit the District ever again after the funeral of her ato in spite of possible consequences of her stubbornness. Fortunately, Stefan managed to find her a job in *Novartis*; the salary was low, but the only purpose of this job was to secure her residence permit. She still had enough money, and it was also possible that more was waiting for her after the execution of Archie's will.

Sara moved out from the flat at Claraplatz. The rent was high, but this was not the primary reason for her leaving the place. She could afford it at least for some time with all the cash left by Archibald—and she generally cared little about money—but the flat was spooky without her ato, too big and too empty, full of memories and some blunt pain that would accumulate in her chest whenever she would be spending too much time there. After realising that she started to virtually live on the street rather than home, Sara knew that it was a time to go. She stayed in Kleinbasel but as far from the District and the Rhine as possible.

The issue of Archie's testament was a bit complicated, and she had to discuss this with Matthias—who advised her to see a solicitor.

She opened the envelope sometime after her Christmas in January, read it and found nothing illegal, illogical or suspicious in it: Archibald left two thirds of his assets to some Andrea Velich from Auckland in New Zealand, and one third to Sara. No one else was mentioned, and Sara wondered why would she need a solicitor, especially because all the data were precise and complete to the finest detail. The sum was mindboggling: she was about to inherit a bit more than two million francs in money, bonds, and shares. She presented the will to Matthias to show him how well it was written, although she had no idea who the woman from New Zealand was.

'That's my point,' said Matthias. 'See a solicitor, it appears that you'll not have any problem paying for his services. This will just make it easier for you.'

'And it also seems that we now know whence Archie had come from—he was obviously a New Zealander. Although the language he would have spoken occasionally still confuses me—I thought it was some Celtic language from Britain,' remarked Sara.

'Confusing? No, not at all,' laughed Matthias, 'many Scots live in New Zealand.'

The execution of the will went smoothly. Sara's solicitor turned out to be very professional: she got what she was meant to get, and the rest went to New Zealand. Did Matthias ever speak with the solicitor about taking care of some legal ambiguities relating to the games that Archie had been playing regarding his and Sara's legal statuses in Switzerland? Maybe, but Matthias never said anything about it.

There was a widespread prejudice that the Swiss were cold and egoistic people, always polite but never empathic or devoted to anything but their own gains; and this was usually thought to be the reason for their tremendous success in the world where every passion would lead to a conflict. However, Stefan and Matthias showed that this was not always the case, at least because they remained supportive of Sara while she was trying to recuperate from the shock and find some future for herself. And they never asked for anything in return. Moreover, they never tried to hit on the attractive woman, who was all alone and possibly available. There was nothing for them in helping Sara—they simply behaved as true gentlemen.

After everything about Archibald's financial legacy had been settled during February and March—and this meant that life was kind of back to normal—Sara opened his notebook in April for the first time. It was her choice to delay this until her soul would be ready, and it took her more than a year to reach this state of mind.

The first thing she noted was that the title contained a prophecy, an inserted word: death. He was also mentioning a daughter he obviously had—called by him Andrea the Proud for some reason. Was it possible that this was actually Andrea Velich from Auckland in New Zealand? Sara could not tell, as 'the Proud' did not seem to be a proper surname, although she had to admit that she did not know much about surnames in different cultures. First of all, she had no proper European-style surname. Then she started to read, struggling with the terrible handwriting of her ato just as she had to in the past when trying to decipher his notes.

The first twenty or so pages astonished her: her ato had been neither from New Zealand nor from Britain but from another country. Did she ever hear of this country? No, she did not, and she had to consult a map to see where it was. It turned out that this was a small European country not far from Switzerland. And his name was not Archibald Vladimir Jones. This was just the last of the names he was using over the years, as he had many before: James, Trevor, Helmut, and finally, Borna—his true name. Sara also spotted that the information on Andrea the Proud was changing as his text (supplemented with some drawings) was progressing: there were new addresses, new bank accounts, and so on. She finally learned why the middle name of Archibald Jones was Vladimir. The story of his family was completed on page thirty-two, and Sara also noted that Archie appreciated the ordeal of the women around his three grandfathers very much. She then understood why he had always treated her with so much respect—which to some extent continued even throughout the time of his decay.

The story of Ivan the Blacksmith and his Roža was simple—this was a happy love in spite of everything they had to go through to deserve to die of old age and sleep in the same grave. The same applied to Danka and Luka. The loves of Ljerka were more complex, and Sara could not resist wondering about the nature of her love for Archibald. Did she love him in the same way as Ljerka had loved Srdjan or was her devotion to her ato more like that of Ljerka to Vladimir?

By reading pages thirty-three to fifty-nine, Sara found out what Archibald V Jones had had to go through to eventually settle in Basel. The phone numbers and addresses of Roger, Mary, Hazel, and Alicia were also there, together with a comment which read 'call them if you ever need help'. Sara did not know if this was a message for her, Andrea the Proud or both of them.

Pages sixty to eighty-one were dedicated to his love for Sara. After seeing this, the weizero of Archibald Vladimir Jones was crying for days, returning to these gentle and respectful words all over again and being unable to continue the reading until the last day of April. That day, she decided to go on no matter what, because she was sure: Archibald was her Srdjan and Vladimir in one person.

Pages eighty-two to ninety-six were bringing stories for Andrea the Proud, mainly excerpts from Archie's growing up and similar plain things, and it seemed that Archibald Vladimir Jones had loved his country much more than his country had loved him. On page ninety-five, it became completely clear: Andrea the Proud was indeed Andrea Velich from New Zealand.

The last pages, numbered ninety-seven to one hundred and two, were explaining why Archie wanted to die. And why he was sure that he needed no poison, rope or gun to end his life—because nature was there to help him.

'Oh my God,' mumbled Sara, 'my Archie died of sadness. Just like that—of pure sadness.'

That evening, Sara went to the Rhine for the first time in more than a year. So far, she was avoiding, as much as she could, to come close to this water which Archie had liked so strangely. She knew how much he had struggled to fight his fears and learn to like a river again—and to teach her how to like it together with him. The daughter of Gondar then became determined that she would never betray her ato. No, not her! She knew what she had to do.

She was standing there and looking at Grossbasel on the other side of the river. For a while, her mind was completely empty—she was just enjoying the view and the smell of the water. She could not even think about the happy days she had had at the Rhine with Archibald. At some point, she became aware of the fact that she was the only one who knew the whole story of Borna the Proud, Helmut Meindl, James Trevor Smith, and Archibald Vladimir Jones. There was no one else in the whole wide world who could tell it!

The daughter of Gondar decided that she was going to find Andrea Velich, one way or another, and bring her to the grave of a distinguished Scotsman Archibald V Jones, as this man was definitely not the greatest ever but did not deserve to be forgotten just like that. The last coherent thought on her mind was that she had to instruct her solicitor what to do.

Sara Jones then started to cry, and the Rhine was there to embrace her tears like a comforting mother.

XIII

2014, July

Andrea Velich was visiting Europe for the first time after she had left for New Zealand with her mother twelve years ago.

She arrived in Switzerland first (her destination was Croatia), because in Basel she had an appointment with a solicitor who had taken care of a mysterious inheritance she had received last year. Not only that she wanted to hear some explanation for why she came into the possession of such a huge number of Swiss francs, she also needed advice on what to do with a number of bonds and shares that she inherited together with the money.

She could not tell whether her mother knew something about this whole strange situation. However, Andrea could spot her uneasiness whenever a question on that would be raised. Feeling uncomfortable quite obviously, the only thing Marta would say was,

'I don't know what this might be about. You're a grown-up now, and I'm quite sure you can find an answer by yourself.'

Marta was a bitter, nervous woman who never got married, and the only insight into her intimacy was a photo of her late fiancé on a wall in their small but comfortable house. While Marta was a very devoted and caring parent, her daughter sometimes missed knowing more about her mother's past. It seemed to Andrea that Marta's love life had ended irredeemably that day when her fiancé had been killed, but there was no way of knowing that for sure. Andrea could even not remember any man in her mother's life, although she could not rule out that Marta would spend some time with one when not seen. However, this never happened publicly, neither in Croatia nor in New Zealand.

They moved to New Zealand at the time of Marta's worst despair, when she realised that her struggle to make a proper living for her and her daughter in Croatia was futile. Despite holding a university degree, every job she could find would be underpaid or full of the worst capitalist harassment; good jobs were reserved for those who had either some connections or the money for a bribe. Then she remembered that she had numerous relatives in Auckland. She wrote them a letter, and they responded immediately, with a lot of joy and by making all necessary preparations for her easy start down under. Ever since, the lives of Marta and Andrea were free of the frustrations for being underestimated or even humiliated by those who were clearly either dishonest and corrupt people or champions of the post-socialist plundering of the country.

'And that's all you know?' asked Andrea. 'A person named Archibald Vladimir Jones, whom I've never heard of, left me all of that money just like that? No explanation, no reason, nothing?'

The solicitor changed the position in his chair, and playing a game he was expected to play by the one who was paying him, replied,

'Unfortunately, that's all I know, yes. I'm just a solicitor, and my job was to make all of that legitimate. And it was legitimate—you inherited two thirds of his valuables beyond any doubt. He was a British citizen from Wales, his papers were spotless, he had no criminal record, all of his incomes were completely legal, and all the taxes were paid. I made a copy of the whole file for you, everything is here in this folder.'

'And the data about me are also there, I suppose. How did you know they were genuine?'

'Take a look. Your Croatian citizen personal number is there. I contacted the Croatian embassy, there was no mistake. I also acquired a certificate from Auckland about you changing the surname from Velić to Velich. Everything matches.'

'So strange… But why me from Croatia and New Zealand? This Jones was Welsh…' said Andrea while looking at the papers. 'Can you tell me who was the person who inherited the remaining third?'

'Dear Miss Velich, I'm afraid I can't do that right now. You'll also find no information on him or her in the folder. I must ask whether I'm allowed to reveal the identity of this person. But call me tomorrow and I might be able to answer your question.'

'Dear sir, I'd be very grateful, money is not an issue, you know.'

'No, it isn't, as I've been paid quite handsomely already. Let us go now through your bonds and shares... Free of any charge, of course.'

Sara could not sleep that night. She even wanted to go to the District and tell everyone that Archie's daughter was in Basel, but there were at least three reasons for not doing that. First, she was done with the District; second, Archie was gone, and she was not sure of how many people could still remember him well; third, she was rather confident that this would have never been a wish of her ato. Everything Andrea was supposed to know was in the notebook, Sara believed, and it was up to Archie's daughter to decide who was going to be faced with the story about his life and death. The story belonged to Andrea Velich, and Sara had no problem in passing on the notebook to her although she had no copy of it: she had memorised it to the last detail.

Sara decided to meet Andrea at the entrance to the Hörnli cemetery. She could not think of a better place.

Andrea saw a bronze-skinned woman waiting for someone, and she was pretty sure that this was the one she had spoken with over the phone; there was no one else there, in the first place. The woman was petite but nicely built, in an elegant black dress, wearing decent jewellery and having a hairstyle that suited her face perfectly. When Andrea came closer, she could also see that this lady was even more beautiful than from a distance, as her light brown eyes were giving her a gentle look that could not be recognised from far away.

The first thing Sara spotted were the eyes of the approaching girl: these were Archie's eyes beyond any doubt. This was Andrea Velich, she knew it. Just as every girl of her age, she was dressed casually, but the movements of the young woman were catlike—and Sara was sure that she was going to make men crazy at some point in the future. Andrea's truly elegant and feminine moves could not remind Sara of Archibald, for obvious reasons, but the way this girl started to smile brought back some memories... Of Archie from the moments when they would have enjoyed the time between making love and falling asleep. Her heart started to beat faster, and she asked,

'Andrea Velich?'

'Yes, I'm Andrea,' replied the girl, 'and you must be Sara. Nice to meet you.'

'Nice to meet you too. I'm glad you've come; I've been waiting for a long time to meet you.'

'For a long time?' Andrea was surprised. 'How could you know anything about me? The solicitor didn't want to tell me who was the second beneficiary of the will—so how could you know?'

'Because the solicitor didn't know everything. He knew about the money, and I've known about other things. By the way, I'm the second beneficiary,' clarified Sara as much as she could at the moment. 'Everything will become clear soon, would you please just follow me now?'

'Well, that's what I really want to do, because all of that has become rather strange,' replied Andrea rather confusedly. They walked for a while without speaking, and then Sara decided that it was time to take a risk and say what had to be said eventually; she spoke in a low voice,

'This is the Basel cemetery. And this is where I buried your father. I was his wife.'

'What? Who? What? My father?' shouted Andrea and started to shake, searching for a place to sit down; then she simply grabbed the nearest tree fearing that her legs might stop supporting her.

'What the hell are you talking about, woman?' continued Andrea with a hostile expression. 'Shut up! Just shut up!'

Sara just stood there and did not try to approach Andrea, giving her some time to calm down; and when Andrea stopped breathing heavily, the Ethiopian woman continued,

'It's a shock, I know. But I'm on your side, can't you recognise that? I'm just trying to tell you what no one else ever will. We all have a father, mine is dead too, and it's your right to know who your father was. I know who my father was, and this makes my life easier.'

Andrea then spotted a bench, ran there and sat down, still shaking but shedding no more tears. There was nothing in her head but a big swarm of bees that were not letting her think straight. She even forgot that Sara was there with her. After coming closer, the Amhara woman sat down next to Andrea, touched the girl's shoulder and kept her hand there until some connection between them was re-established. Then she asked,

'From where do you think your mother was receiving extra money? I didn't know of you until quite recently, and he also didn't know for a long time.'

'He didn't?' asked Andrea, and Sara then spotted tears running down the smooth cheeks of the girl again. 'How come?'

'Because life isn't fair.'

'I want to stay here for a while,' said Andrea, 'but please don't speak about him until we reach his grave. Speak about something else. Maybe about you and your life, and I'll tell you about mine.'

The two women remained there for two hours, on that same bench. They became a kind of friends, perhaps for life—but life has never been fair, and we cannot know that for sure.

'I'm ready to see his grave now,' said Andrea after realising that her life was never again going to be the same, 'but I'm not sure whether I want to hear more about him there or anywhere else. Perhaps sometime and somewhere, and perhaps never.'

Respecting her wish, Sara took her by the hand silently and guided her towards Archibald's grave. The grave was humble, but Sara made it look decent over the last two years. On the tombstone, it was engraved

Archibald V. Jones
a distinguished Scotsman
1965–2012

'Here he is,' she said, 'and I'm not sure, but I might join him in this grave one day. Who knows, things in life change, but maybe my place is here with my ato, when the time for that comes.'

Andrea already knew about the meaning of weizerit, weizero, and ato, from her previous conversation with Sara. Knowing how her father had been treating her woman, she felt proud at least for a while.

'Scottish?' Andrea was surprised. 'But the solicitor said he was Welsh. What am I, then?'

'He was neither—he wasn't British at all. He just spoke English perfectly, but this was nothing but a disguise.'

'But who am I then? Does anyone know that?' asked Andrea in a trembling voice.

'Here is a journal which explains everything,' replied Sara. 'He wrote it for you, and I was keeping it safe. Read it, everything is there.'

Andrea took a look at the notebook with fine leather covers but did not want to open it.

'But tell me now, I want to know now!' shouted Andrea, and her tears started to flow again.

Sara took Andrea's hands into hers, looked deep into her eyes, waited until both of them became still, and then she said,

'You're Andrea the Proud, the last of your kin.'

Andrea did not understand a word. Who was proud? And why? What was all of that supposed to mean to her? What was going to happen, what was she expected to feel? She could not remain calm.

'And what to do now, Sara? What should I do now? Everything was so easy when I didn't know anything!'

'Go there where you should go, child. And take the old family iron rod of your clan into your hand, as you're its rightful owner now!'